Dear Readers,

Many years ago, when I was a kid, my father said to me, "Bill, it doesn't really matter what you do in life. What's important is to be the *best* William Johnstone you can be."

I've never forgotten ater, I like to think that I am still trying to be the best William Johnstone I can be. Whether it's Ben Raines in the Ashes series, or Frank Morgan, the last gunfighter, or Smoke Jensen, our intrepid mountain man, or John Barrone and his hard-working crew keeping America safe from terrorist lowlifes in the Code Name series, I want to make each new book better than the last and deliver powerful storytelling.

Equally important, I try to create the kinds of believable characters that we can all identify with, real people who face tough challenges. When one of my creations blasts an enemy into the middle of next week, you can be damn sure he had a good reason.

As a storyteller, my job is to entertain you, my readers, and to make sure that you get plenty of enjoyment from my books for your hard-earned money. This is not a job I take lightly. And I greatly appreciate your feedback—you are my gold, and your opinions *do* count. So please keep the letters and e-mails coming.

Respectfully yours,

WILLIAM W. JOHNSTONE

VALOR OF THE MOUNTAIN MAN

WARPATH OF THE MOUNTAIN MAN

PINNACLE BOOKS
Kensington Publishing Corp.
http://www.kensingtonbooks.com

PINNACLE BOOKS are published by

Kensington Publishing Corp.
850 Third Avenue
New York, NY 10022

First Pinnacle Books Printing: July 2006

10 9 8 7 6 5 4 3 2 1

Printed in the United States of America

VALOR OF THE MOUNTAIN MAN

1

The territorial prison was an adobe brick building that stood in the middle of 180 acres between 14th East and 21st South in the town of Sugar House in the Utah Territory. Though built to house less than two hundred men, it was already crammed to the breaking point with some of the meanest men west of the Mississippi—from footpads to rapists to bank robbers to murderers, sooner or later they all ended up here.

In Cellhouse No. 1, over thirty men slept on cots in corridors between the cells, eating their meals in three shifts and using buckets for privies since the toilet facilities were so primitive.

The place was barely tolerable in the heat of summer, but now that the fall was upon the region and the nighttime temperatures often fell into the twenties, the situation was almost unbearable.

One of the hardest men in the group of very hard men indeed, Ozark Jack Berlin, leaned over the bucket full of piss and shit and spat out his food. He was a big man, standing three inches over six feet, with muscular shoulders as broad as an ax handle. His face was rough-featured, set under a full head of unruly black hair, with a nose that'd been broken more than once and lips that were thin and cruel.

"This stuff ain't fit for man nor beast!" he groused to the half-breed Modoc Indian sitting on a cot next to his. The Indian had long black hair hanging down over his ears to his collar, and his reddish-bronze skin framed a hooked nose over full lips that he was constantly licking.

Blue Owl looked up from his plate, which was empty except for a small piece of biscuit he was using to sop up the gravy from the maggot-riddled horse meat. "If you no want yours, shove it over here," he growled. "It's better'n buffalo meat any day."

Berlin handed Blue Owl his plate. "I tell ya', Blue Owl, I think it's 'bout time to bust outta this joint."

Blue Owl didn't answer, being busy shoving Berlin's food into his mouth, but he cut his eyes to the side and nodded his agreement.

"I got me an idea how we can do it," said Berlin.

Blue Owl grunted, his eyebrows raised.

"Today's payday for the guards. I figger they'll all head for town soon's they get their money to spend it on whores an' whiskey."

Blue Owl nodded again, his Adam's apple bobbing as he swallowed.

"That'll only leave one man in Cellhouse No. 1, an' a couple more in the other parts of the building. If'n we can get our hands on the guard's gun, we can break into the armory an' steal us some more weapons an' take over the rest of the prison."

Blue Owl burped loudly, wiping his lips with the back of his hand. "Then what, Jack?" he asked. "We gonna walk all the way to Salt Lake City?"

Berlin smiled, shaking his head. "Naw. We'll take the guards' hosses an' the supply wagons they keep around back, and head toward Colorado. They's plenty of sod-busters an' farmers 'tween here an there. We'll just take what we need along the way."

Blue Owl shrugged, flipping his hair out of his face with a thick, meaty finger. "Sounds all right to me. Anyway, it'll beat sittin' here an' waitin' to be hung."

* * *

After the evening meal, prison guard Joe Johnson moved through the cell block, picking up plates and tin cups from the inmates. Following protocol set up by the warden, he wore no weapon while in the company of the criminals he was working with. He was watched by guard Billy Thornton, who was standing outside the bars of the cell block, a .44 Colt in a holster on his hip and an American Arms 12-gauge shotgun cradled in his arms.

It was a ritual they'd played out countless times, and Thornton was bored. He leaned against a wall and covered his mouth with a hand as he yawned. He'd been up most of the night playing poker after his shift the night before, and hadn't slept well when he'd finally crawled into his bed in the morning. As Joe Johnson leaned down to take Berlin's plate from him, Berlin glanced over his shoulder and saw Thornton leaning back against the wall with his eyes closed.

Quick as a flash, Berlin grabbed the back of Johnson's head and hit him in the throat with his closed fist.

Johnson's eyes bulged and his mouth opened as he gulped for air like a fish out of water. As the skin of his face turned blue and he dropped to his knees, his hands at his throat, Berlin turned and called to Thornton.

"Hey, Billy. Somethin's wrong with Joe. He's choking!"

Thornton came to attention, looked into the cell block, and saw his friend Joe on his knees, his face blue and his mouth open and gasping as he jerked wide eyes back and forth.

Thornton quickly grabbed the keys to the cell door off his belt and shoved the bars open. He ran to Joe's side and went down on one knee to see if he could help.

Blue Owl stepped up behind Thornton, put his hands together, and swung them like a club into the back of Thornton's neck.

The guard dropped as if he'd been poleaxed.

Berlin grabbed the shotgun before it could hit the dirt

floor of the cell, and Blue Owl slipped the .44 Colt from Thornton's holster as he fell facedown on the ground.

Berlin ran toward the cell door, shouting over his shoulder to one of the men standing there as Johnson finally gasped his last breath, "Grab them keys, boys. We're gettin' outta here!"

Sam Cook, in prison for raping and killing two women, took the keys off the unconscious Thornton's belt and followed Berlin and Blue Owl through the door. Behind him, the other thirty men in the cell block scrambled to their feet and rushed after them.

Berlin slowed to a walk as he rounded the corner in the corridor leading from Cellhouse No. 1. He eared back the hammers on the shotgun and pointed it ahead of him as he walked toward a desk at the end of the corridor.

Bob Colton, head guard, was sitting behind the desk, finishing his supper of fried chicken and mashed potatoes. He looked up, and almost choked on his chicken leg when he saw Ozark Jack Berlin stalking toward him with the double-barreled shotgun aimed at his gullet.

"Howdy, Bob," Berlin said amiably. "How 'bout you take that hogleg outta your holster and put it on the desk there?"

Colton swallowed, and gingerly pulled his pistol out of his holster and placed it on the desk in front of him.

"Don't do nothing stupid, Ozark," he croaked through a suddenly dry throat.

"Stupid would be stayin' here to be hanged, Bob. Now, get to your feet and walk on back into the cell back there, or I'll spread your guts all over the wall."

As Colton walked down the corridor, Berlin called, "Sam, put him in the cell with the others and lock the doors."

Less than thirty minutes later, Berlin, Blue Owl, and the other thirty men were in the prison armory, where they had armed themselves with pistols, shotguns, and rifles, and were stuffing their pockets with boxes of ammunition.

Two other guards who happened upon the group were stripped of their weapons and placed in the cell house with the others.

The prisoners then made their way to the stables, saddled up ten horses, hitched up a couple of teams to two supply wagons, and raced out of the prison gates. The day-shift guards continued to sleep in their barracks, unaware of the prison break.

As the escapees rode down the trail away from the town of Sugar House toward the mountains in the distance, Blue Owl inclined his head toward the men riding in the wagons. "We ain't gonna make much time with them wagons, Ozark. What're we gonna do?"

Berlin shrugged. "There's plenty of farms 'tween here and the high country. We'll just stop along the way and take what horses and supplies we need." He grinned, exposing blackened teeth. "After all, who's gonna stop us?"

2

Warden Joshua M. Stevens came out of a sound sleep with his heart hammering as someone pounded on his door.

His wife, Sofie, blinked her eyes and stared at him in fear at the harsh sound.

"Josh, what's that noise?" she asked sleepily, rubbing her eyes.

"Go back to bed, dear," he said, climbing out of bed and pulling on a robe. "It's just someone at the door. I'll take care of it."

On the way to answer the door, Stevens paused to pick up a Colt off a dining room sideboard. Being the warden of a prison that housed hundreds of desperados made a man cautious—especially when awakened in the middle of the night.

"Who is it?" Stevens called from behind the closed and locked door, earing back the hammer on his pistol. Over the years, he'd made plenty of enemies, some of whom had vowed revenge when they got released.

"It's Brock Jackson, Warden," the answer came.

Brock was the assistant warden, Stevens's second in command at the prison.

Stevens eased the hammer down on the Colt and opened the door.

"What the hell are you doing here at this ungodly hour?" Stevens asked irritably as he showed the man in.

Jackson twirled his hat in his hand nervously as he entered the warden's drawing room.

"There's been a prison break, Josh," he said without preamble.

Stevens's heart began to pound again at the news. "Anyone injured?" he asked.

Jackson nodded, his eyes grim. "One of the guards, Joe Johnson, was killed. Another, Billy Thornton, was knocked unconscious, but he's recovering."

"Tell me what happened while I boil some coffee," Stevens said curtly, walking toward the kitchen.

After a fire was lit in the stove, Stevens took a cigar out of a box and lit it, sitting at the kitchen table.

"Ozark Jack Berlin and that breed Blue Owl killed Johnson, and when Thornton went in to help, they knocked him out and took his weapons." Jackson shrugged. "After that, they got the drop on the other night-shift guards, broke into the armory, and stole some weapons and ammunition, then took horses and wagons out of the stables and hightailed it toward the mountains."

"How many got out?"

"Over thirty . . . all from Cellhouse No. 1," Jackson answered.

"Damn! Those are the worst men we've got," Stevens said, a worried look on his face.

"You're right about that, Josh. There ain't a one of 'em that wouldn't cut the throat of a baby if it meant they'd go free."

Stevens sighed. "Anybody told Mrs. Johnson about Joe yet?" he asked.

"I sent one of the guards who's a good friend over to break the news to her."

As the coffee began to boil, Stevens got to his feet and poured them each a cup.

"Well, I'll get dressed and head on over to the telegraph

office. I've got to notify the governor as soon as it's light."

"What do you want me to do?"

"We don't have enough men to go chasing them, not and still guard the prison. You'd better get on over to the Army post and see if they'll send a patrol out after them."

"Yes, sir."

"And Brock . . ."

"Yes?"

"Tell the captain over there to send plenty of good men. Let him know what kind of galoots they'll be going up against."

"Yes, sir."

Ten miles east of Salt Lake City, Ozark Jack Berlin held up his hand as his men crested a small ridge looking down on a valley below. The sun was just peeking over the horizon, sending bright orange and red rays over the farm below.

There was a main house, a large barn, and off to one side a bunkhouse. In a corral next to the barn, about fifteen horses could be seen.

Berlin nodded. "Looks like just what we need, boys," he growled.

His men pulled out their weapons and leaned over their horses as Berlin led the charge down the side of the hill.

As they galloped down the slope, a man and a woman appeared on the porch of the house. The man gave a yell and the woman disappeared back inside. Men began to boil out of the bunkhouse, some still in their long underwear and pulling their boots on.

The battle was over quickly, the seven hands and the ranch owner no match for thirty hardened gunmen. Within minutes, eight men lay dead on the ground, along with one of Berlin's men.

Berlin, breathing heavily, pointed to the corral and

barn. "Get them hosses saddled an' see what else you can find in the barn and bunkhouse," he called. "We need some clothes an' supplies, an' don't forget to get their guns and ammunition 'fore we leave."

Blue Owl cut his eyes toward the house, where the woman had disappeared. "You go ahead, Boss. I got me some business in the house."

Berlin grinned. "Save a little for the rest of us, Blue Owl. Don't cut her up till we get our turn."

Blue Owl stared at him. "But Ozark, that's half the fun."

"You can cut her when the rest of us are done, but it's been a long time since most of us have had a woman, so take it easy."

Blue Owl nodded as he turned his horse's head toward the house.

Later, Berlin took stock of what they'd found. Most of the men were able to get out of their prison coveralls and into jeans and shirts, though some were too big to fit into the clothes of the farmer and his hands. They also found enough horses in the corral and barn to get all of the men on horseback and off the wagons, along with more guns, rifles, shotguns, and even some dynamite the farmer used to bust up tree stumps.

All of the food was taken from the house. Then, with the farmer's wife's body still lying on the bed in their bedroom, Berlin put a torch to the house.

As they walked their horses toward the distant mountains, Berlin said, "A couple'a more farms like this, an' we should have enough supplies and horses to get us through the mountains an' into Colorado."

Blue Owl glanced at the snow-covered peaks. "It'll be hard goin' if the snows come early," he observed.

Berlin laughed. "Not as hard as goin' the other way. I suspect the Army'll be on our trail by now."

Blue Owl smiled. "If they try to follow us up into the high country, it will be easy to ambush them."

"That's what I figured. If we can kill enough of 'em, they'll soon tire of chasin' us," Berlin said, spurring his horse into a canter toward the mountains ahead.

Army Captain Wallace Bickford looked across his desk at Brock Jackson. "Are you telling me thirty of the worst criminals in your prison just walked out last night?"

Jackson nodded grimly. "Yeah, Captain. Only, they didn't just walk out. They killed one guard and smashed another's head in. Like I told you, these men are all killers—about as bad as men can be. If we don't do something soon, they're gonna leave a trail of blood behind them that'll make newspapers all over the country."

Captain Bickford looked out the window for a moment. "Mr. Jackson, I want to be honest with you. I just got a batch of fresh recruits here. Not only have these boys not seen any action yet, I'm just not sure they're up to a job like this."

Jackson leaned forward, his hands on the desk. "Captain, ready or not, the Army took them in and made them soldiers. Now, they got a job to do and I'm afraid there isn't anyone else available to do it."

Bickford pursed his lips. "Maybe it'll be all right if I send them out with a couple of sergeants who've been around for a while."

Jackson stood up, a tight smile on his face. "Good. But Captain, be sure and send plenty of men. If I'm right, there are gonna be quite a few who don't come back."

"That's what I'm afraid of, Mr. Jackson," Bickford said.

Jackson put his hat on. "I'll be sure and tell the governor how cooperative you've been."

Bickford smiled ruefully. "Yeah. Maybe he'll be so grateful he'll write the letters to the families of the boys who don't come back."

3

Smoke Jensen pushed the batwings to Louis Longmont's Saloon open and stepped inside. Out of long habit, he stood to the side of the door, his back to the wall, until his eyes had adjusted to the relative gloom of the establishment.

Cal and Pearlie followed him inside and did the same on the other side of the door, hands near their Colts until they were sure there was no danger waiting inside. Such were the actions that years of standing by the side of one of the most famous gunfighters in the West had taught them.

Louis Longmont, owner of the saloon, looked up from his usual table in a far corner and smiled over his coffee, smoke from the long black cigar in his hand swirling around his head, stirred by a gentle breeze from the open windows in the walls.

"Smoke, boys, come on in," he called, waving them to his table.

As they approached, Longmont's eyes drifted to Smoke's waist. Then his eyebrows raised in surprise. He'd noted Smoke wasn't wearing his usual brace of pistols on his belt.

He looked up at his friend walking toward him, noticing again his imposing stature. Standing a couple of inches over six feet, with wide, muscular shoulders and a narrow waist, wearing his trademark buckskins, Smoke still looked dangerous, even though he was unarmed.

Louis, an ex-gunfighter himself, couldn't imagine what had made Smoke leave his ranch at the Sugarloaf, a few miles north of the town of Big Rock, without wearing his pistols.

Louis was a lean, hawk-faced man, with strong, slender hands and long fingers, nails carefully manicured, hands clean. He had jet-black hair and a black pencil-thin mustache. He was, as usual, dressed in a black suit, with white shirt and dark ascot—something he'd picked up on a trip to England some years back. He wore low-heeled boots, and a pistol hung in tied-down leather on his right side. It was not for show, for Louis was snake-quick with a short gun and was a feared, deadly gunhand when pushed.

Louis was not an evil man. He had never hired his gun out for money. And while he could make a deck of cards do almost anything, he did not cheat at poker. He did not have to cheat. He was possessed of a phenomenal memory and could tell you the odds of filling any type of poker hand, and was one of the first to use the new method of card counting.

He was just past forty years of age. He had come to the West as a very small boy, with his parents, arriving from Louisiana. His parents had died in a shantytown fire, leaving the boy to cope as best he could.

He had coped quite well, plying his innate intelligence and willingness to take a chance into a fortune. In addition to the saloon in Big Rock, he owned a large ranch up in Wyoming Territory, several businesses in San Francisco, and a hefty chunk of a railroad.

Though it was a mystery to many why Longmont stayed with the hard life he had chosen, Smoke thought he understood. Once, Louis had said to him, "Smoke, I would miss my life every bit as much as you would miss the dry-mouthed moment before the draw, the challenge of facing and besting those miscreants who would kill you or others, and the so-called loneliness of the owl-hoot trail."

Sometimes Louis joked that he would like to draw against Smoke someday, just to see who was faster. Smoke allowed as how it would be close, but that he would win. "You see, Louis, you're just too civilized," he had told him on many occasions. "Your mind is distracted by visions of operas, fine foods and wines, and the odds of your winning the match. Also, your fatal flaw is that you can almost always see the good in the lowest creatures God ever made, and you refuse to believe that anyone is pure evil and without hope of redemption."

When Louis laughed at this description of himself, Smoke would continue. "Me, on the other hand, when some snake-scum draws down on me and wants to dance, the only thing I have on my mind is teaching him that when you dance, someone has to pay the band. My mind is clear and focused on only one problem, how to put that stump-sucker across his horse toes-down."

As Smoke and Cal and Pearlie took their seats at his table, Louis asked, "You gents want some breakfast?"

Pearlie, who never turned down food, grinned and said, "I thought you'd never ask. Eggs, bacon, pancakes, and some of those fried potatoes Andre is famous for."

Cal just shook his head. "Dang, Pearlie, we ate once this mornin' already."

Pearlie assumed a hurt expression. "But that was hours ago, Cal, an' it was a long ride in from the Sugarloaf."

Smoke smiled. "All right, boys." He glanced at Louis. "Would you ask Andre to bring us all some eggs and bacon and coffee?"

Louis called out toward a window in a back wall leading to the kitchen. "Andre, we got some hungry cowboys out here. Fix them something special."

Andre, Louis's French chef and friend of many years, stuck his head out the small window, saw Smoke and the boys, grinned, and nodded. He loved cooking for them, especially Pearlie, who was lavish in his praise of the chef's cuisine.

The waiter brought cups and a fresh pot of coffee, and poured it all around. Once the men were drinking, Louis stared at Smoke and inclined his head toward his friend. "I notice you are only half-dressed this morning. Any particular reason?"

Smoke looked down at his naked waist, grinning ruefully. "Well, after that last little fracas, when Sally had to dig two bullets out of my hide, she sat me down for a long talk."

"And?" Louis asked, knowing Smoke loved Sally enough to do almost anything she asked.

"The upshot of it was, I'm not getting any younger. She thinks I'm too old to go traipsing around fighting every saddle tramp and would-be famous gunslinger who wants to make a name for himself by shooting Smoke Jensen."

Louis, who was a couple of years older than Smoke, frowned. "And her solution for this deplorable situation?"

Smoke shrugged. "She said if I quit wearing my guns, there would be less chance of my getting shot."

Louis shook his head. "Typical woman's thinking. And what if by chance some gunny braces you anyway?"

Smoke glanced at Cal and Pearlie sitting next to him. "I'm supposed to let Cal and Pearlie . . . show them the error of their ways while I stay out of it."

Louis leaned forward, his eyes earnest. "Smoke, old friend, you know I respect Sally more than any other woman I've ever met, but she's dead wrong this time. Taking your guns away from you is like taking the fangs off a rattlesnake and thinking he'll lie down with the rabbits."

Smoke laughed. "I agree with you, Louis. In fact, I'm gonna take you out to the Sugarloaf and have you tell that to Sally."

Louis leaned back, a look of terror on his face. He held up his hands in front of him. "Oh, no, Smoke. I'd facedown a gang of cutthroats for you, stand with you against a band of bloodthirsty Indians, but I wouldn't have the nerve to face up to Sally when she's in her 'protect my man' stance. She'd tear me apart."

Cal and Pearlie laughed at Louis's description, remembering the times Sally had saddled up her horse, packed her Winchester and snub-nosed .36-caliber handgun, and gone riding to protect Smoke's back. They knew Louis was right.

The conversation was halted when Andre and the waiter appeared bearing platters heaped with scrambled eggs, layers of steaming bacon, fresh-cut tomatoes, and fried potatoes.

Smoke looked at the red, ripe tomatoes on the platter. "Andre, where did you get fresh tomatoes at this time of the year?"

Andre grinned, puffing up a little at the compliment. "Monsieur Smoke, I have constructed myself a greenhouse out behind the saloon. There I can grow the tomatoes, and other vegetables, almost year-round."

"You'd better not tell Sally," Smoke said, spearing a few slices off the platter. "Otherwise, she'll be down here raiding your crop. She hates the taste of the tinned ones we eat in the winter."

"Madame Sally may have all she wants," Andre said, "and be sure to tell her I have a new recipe she asked about, the one with the duck à l'orange."

Pearlie glanced up from the prodigious pile of food on his plate. "Duck? I ain't never ate duck fit to swallow."

"That is because you have never eaten duck prepared by Andre," Andre said haughtily as he turned on his heel and went back into the kitchen.

"I hope I didn't hurt his feelin's," Pearlie said, a worried look on his face.

"Don't worry, Pearlie," Louis said. "Andre's ego is impervious to insult."

"Whatever that means," Pearlie muttered, lowering his head and resuming the stuffing of food into his mouth.

The men had finished their meal and were enjoying after-breakfast coffee and cigarettes when the batwings swung open and four men walked in.

They stood in the doorway, brushing trail dust off their clothes for a moment before proceeding toward the bar.

Smoke's eyes took in their garb. Two of the men were dressed mostly in black, with shiny boots, vests adorned with silver conchos, and pistols worn low on their right hips. They appeared to be related, bearing a strong resemblance to each other, and both looked to be in their early twenties. The men with them were more nondescript, wearing flannel shirts, trail coats, and chaps, but they also wore their pistols in the manner of gunmen rather than trail hands.

When the men bellied up to the bar and ordered whiskey, Louis whispered, "Uh-oh, looks like trouble."

Smoke glanced at the Regulator clock on the wall, which showed it to be ten o'clock in the morning. "Yeah, it's awfully early to be drinking liquor."

As the men downed their shots, one glanced over and noticed Louis and Smoke looking at them. He frowned, put his glass down, and sauntered over toward them.

He stopped a few feet from the table and stared at Smoke. "Hey, mister," he said belligerently, "you look familiar, like I seen you someplace before."

Smoke shrugged, his face flat. "I've been someplace before."

The man's face looked puzzled as he tried to figure out if Smoke was making fun of him for a moment. Then he scowled.

"I got it, you're Smoke Jensen."

"Congratulations," Smoke said evenly.

The man glanced over his shoulder, as if to see if his friends were watching.

"My friends an' me traveled a long way to find you."

"And just who might you be?" Smoke asked.

Louis slid his chair back a little and straightened his

right leg, letting his hand rest on his thigh next to his pistol, ready for trouble.

"My name's Tucson," the man said.

"You must be from Arizona," Louis said.

Tucson's eyes flitted to Louis. "How'd you know that?" he asked.

Louis shook his head, grinning. "A lucky guess."

Smoke turned his back. "I'm afraid you're out of luck, Tucson. I'm not hiring anyone at the ranch just now."

Tucson scowled again. "I didn't come lookin' for work, Jensen."

Smoke looked back at him. "Then why did you come?"

"I came to kill you."

Smoke's expression didn't change. "Any particular reason?"

"Yeah. A few years back, you killed my cousin."

"What was your cousin's name?"

"Billy Walker."

"And where did this happen?"

"He came up here from Texas. Billy rode with a man named Lazarus Cain."

"Now I remember," Smoke said, smiling. "Cain was a crazy Bible-thumper who thought God was protecting him. Turned out he was wrong."*

"Billy weren't crazy," Tucson said angrily. "You gut-shot him an' left him to die."

"If he rode with Cain, he deserved to die," Smoke said simply, and turned back to his coffee.

Tucson let his hand drop next to his pistol. "Stand up and face me like a man, Jensen!"

Pearlie and Cal got to their feet. Pearlie took the rawhide hammer-thong off his Colt and stood off to the side, as did Cal.

* *Guns of the Mountain Man*

"Settle down, mister," Pearlie said slowly. "As you can see, Mr. Jensen ain't wearin' no guns."

Tucson glanced at Smoke's waist. "Why ain't he heeled? He afraid to die?"

Pearlie shook his head. "Nope. It's just that Smoke's a mite tired of killin' scum like you, fellow. You see, he's done killed a couple of hundred or more an' he's gettin' sick of it. Now me, I ain't killed near that many, so it don't bother me none if you want to try your hand."

As Pearlie spoke, Tucson's friends edged away from the bar to stand next to him, their hands near their weapons.

Cal grinned cockily. "Four to two, Pearlie. That ought'a make it about fair."

Louis stood up, sweeping his black coat behind his back, exposing his pistol. "Four to three, Cal," he said, smiling around the cigar stuck in his mouth.

"Hold on just a minute," Smoke said, standing up. "I'm not used to letting other people fight my battles for me."

He stepped over to stand just inches from Tucson. "You think you're pretty fast with that hogleg, son?"

"Fast enough to beat you, old man," Tucson said.

Smoke squared around. "Then go for it! If you can get it out and fire before I take it away from you and stick it up your ass, then you'll have your revenge."

"But . . . but you ain't got no gun," Tucson said.

"I don't need a gun to beat a pup like you, Tucson. Grab leather!"

Tucson's hand went for his gun. Before he had it half out of his holster, Smoke's left hand moved quicker than the eye could follow.

He grabbed Tucson's right hand where it was holding the handle of his pistol, and squeezed.

The sound of Tucson's fingers breaking was like dry twigs snapping, and he yelled in pain and let go of his gun, doubling over and holding his broken, mangled hand against his chest.

At the sound of their friend's screams, the men behind him went for their guns.

Three shots rang out almost simultaneously and the three men were blown backward to land spread-eagled on their backs.

Tucson stopped moaning long enough to glance in horror over his shoulder. "Goddamn!" he muttered at the speed with which his friends had been killed.

Smoke shook his head. "That could be you lying there, spilling your guts all over the floor, boy. Now get on your horse and ride off, while you still can."

Without another word, Tucson ran out of the door, and a few moments later they could hear his horse's hoofbeats as he hightailed it out of town.

Smoke looked at the dead bodies lying on the floor. "What a waste," he said, shaking his head.

Meanwhile, Louis stared at Cal and Pearlie. "I'd never have believed it," he said.

"Believed what?" Cal asked, holstering his pistol.

"Yeah, what?" Pearlie asked, sitting back down and calmly finishing his coffee.

"You boys almost beat me to the draw," Louis said.

"What do you mean, almost?" Cal said with a grin.

4

Ozark Jack Berlin and his men slowed their horses as they approached the outskirts of the small mining town named Lode in the mountains east of Salt Lake City.

Berlin glanced at Blue Owl, riding next to him. "Tell the men to ride with their guns loose," he said.

Blue Owl smiled grimly. "You expecting trouble from these desert-rat miners?" he asked scornfully.

Berlin stared at him for a moment. "You never know, Blue Owl. These men have been workin' for years to pull silver outta those mountains, an' they're liable to not take kindly to anybody who tries to take it away from 'em."

Blue Owl nodded and jerked the head of his horse around to pass the word among the men riding behind them.

As they rode down the muddy center of the town, the men looked around. The town consisted mainly of tent-buildings, some with wooden storefronts and tents on the rear. The businesses consisted mostly of brothels and saloons, with a couple of small general stores selling food and mining equipment. There didn't seem to be a jail or sheriff's office, which caused Berlin to feel a little better about the town.

Several of the men whistled and yelled at some of the prostitutes, many of whom were standing at the doors to their brothels, waving and showing lots of leg and chest to the men as they rode by.

When they came abreast of what appeared to be the largest saloon, Berlin pulled his horse to a stop. He dismounted and tied the animal to a rail. As his men gathered around, he said, "We're gonna go in here and have a few drinks to clear the trail dust outta our throats."

The men grinned and laughed, until Berlin held up a hand. "But," he warned, "I'll shoot the first man who causes any trouble or brings attention to us. Understand?"

The men sobered and nodded and followed Berlin into the saloon. The room was a very large tent with what appeared to be handmade tables and chairs scattered around a dirt floor. The bar consisted of two twelve-inch-wide boards placed across a couple of sawhorses in front of a wooden wall holding hundreds of bottles of whiskey, most without labels on them.

It being early in the day, about ten in the morning, the place was largely unoccupied, with only ten or twelve men sitting at various tables.

Berlin walked to the bar, took a couple of boiled eggs out of a large jar, and slid the jar down the wooden planks toward the men with him.

The bartender glanced around at the thirty men crowding into the space near the bar, smiling in anticipation of a very profitable morning trade.

"What'll it be, gents?" he asked.

Berlin pointed to several bottles of amber-colored liquid on the wall. "Give us four bottles of your best whiskey an' some glasses," he said.

The barman raised his eyebrows. "But them bottles are twenty dollars apiece," he said, his eyes looking at Berlin's not-too-prosperous-appearing clothing.

Berlin reached in his pocket and pulled out a handful of gold coins, tossing them negligently on the bar.

"Yes, sir!" the barman said, and put the bottles and a tray of small shot glasses on the bar.

"Let's find some tables," Berlin said, taking one of the

bottles and a glass and walking to a table at the rear of the saloon.

Once he was seated, at a table with Blue Owl and Sam Cook, Berlin leaned forward, speaking in a low tone of voice.

"Have you thought about what we're gonna do next?" he asked.

Cook upended his glass and swallowed the whiskey in one long draught, coughed, and shook his head.

Blue Owl let his eyes roam over their men sitting at nearby tables. "We got to make a choice, Ozark," he said.

"Yeah?"

"Once word gets out about the jailbreak, there are gonna be lawmen all over the state looking for us. Traveling with thirty men makes us stand out like a sore thumb."

"And just what do you think we ought'a do about it?" Berlin asked, sipping his whiskey.

Blue Owl stared back at him. "If we want to disappear, get away clean, it'd be better if we took off on our own."

Berlin leaned back in his chair, shaking his head. "And then what, Blue Owl? Get us a job punchin' cattle, or digging holes in the ground lookin' for ore?"

Blue Owl let his eyes drop. "We could rob us some banks, or hold up some stages," he said in a low voice.

"Penny-ante stuff," Berlin said. "Look at what we got here, Blue Owl." He looked around at the men sitting nearby, slowly getting drunk on the whiskey he'd bought.

"We got us a ready-made gang here. Thirty of the meanest, most bloodthirsty men in Utah. Ain't nobody can stand against us. We can ride into towns, take what we want, an' nobody can do nothin' about it."

"You're forgetting about the Army, Ozark. I figure it won't be long before they're on our trail."

Berlin grinned. "That's where we got the real advantage, Blue Owl. The Army has to wait for orders 'fore they do anything. If we keep movin', crossin' state an' territorial lines, the Army ain't never gonna catch up to us."

"What if they do?" Blue Owl asked.

Berlin shrugged. "Then we blow 'em outta their saddles, just like we do anybody else who tries to cross us."

"If we're gonna go up against the bluecoats, Ozark, we're going to need more guns."

Berlin leaned forward again. "That brings us to my next plan. . . ."

After they finished off the whiskey, Berlin and his men got on their horses and rode down the street until they came to the livery stable.

Berlin and Blue Owl went inside. An old man with a gray beard was using a pitchfork to throw hay into stalls for the animals inside.

"You the owner?" Berlin called.

The man stopped, leaned on the handle of the pitchfork, and nodded. "Yep."

"Got any mules?"

"I got four, but they ain't for sale. I can rent 'em to you for a day or two though."

"That ain't good enough, old-timer," Berlin said, stepping forward. He pulled a long-bladed knife from a scabbard on his belt and in a quick motion, slashed the blade across the man's throat.

As the owner groaned and fell to the ground, Berlin motioned for Blue Owl to gather up the mules and lead them outside.

They took the mules and rode back down the street toward a large general store in the middle of town.

Berlin and Blue Owl, followed by the rest of the men, went inside. They began to pile up supplies, beans, bacon, flour, sugar, and jerked meat on the counter, waiting until the other customers had finished and left the building.

Berlin nodded at Blue Owl, who walked to the door, pulled the shade, and turned the sign on the door around until it said CLOSED.

"Hey, what the hell do you think you're doing?" the owner asked, coming around from behind his counter.

Sam Cook, without saying a word, drew his pistol and slammed the barrel down on the man's head, knocking him out cold.

As Cook dragged him by his boots back behind the counter, the rest of the men proceeded to load all the supplies on the mules, taking additional clothing and stuffing it in their saddlebags.

Berlin and Blue Owl walked to the back wall of the store. There were over twenty rifles, assorted handguns, and boxes of ammunition stacked there. Berlin began to hand the guns out to the men, along with the ammunition.

"Blue Owl," he said, "take some of those boxes of dynamite and fuses along too. We might need 'em if the Army gets too close."

In less than half an hour, the mules were loaded down with boxes and canvas bags of supplies, including several boxes of dynamite and two cans of gunpowder. Meanwhile, Berlin had gone to have a talk with the local assayer. Then he returned to the store.

He was the last to leave. He shut the door, leaving the sign on it saying the store was closed for the day.

He mounted up and waved his hand. "Let's ride, men," he called. "We're burnin' daylight."

"What about the whores?" an eighteen-year-old boy named Billy Bartlett asked.

"There'll be other towns, Billy," Berlin said.

Lieutenant Jonathan Pike held up his hand to the forty troops riding behind him. They were in the main street of Lode, and he could see a crowd of miners and prostitutes gathered around the general store.

Sergeant Bob Guthrie leaned to the side and spat a stream of brown tobacco juice onto the mud of the street. "What do you make of it, Lieutenant?" he asked.

"I don't know," Pike answered. "Keep the men here and I'll ride up and see what all the commotion is about."

Guthrie wiped his mouth with the back of his hand.

"Do you think we could let the men get a drink or two in that saloon over there, sir?" he asked. "It's been a long, dusty ride."

Pike grinned. "Yeah, Sarge, but beer only. No whiskey. If we happen to run into those escaped prisoners, I don't want any drunk men doing my fighting for me."

"Yes, sir!" Guthrie said with enthusiasm.

While Guthrie got the men organized and into the saloon, Pike walked his horse toward the crowd up ahead.

He dismounted and approached a man who seemed to be in control.

"Excuse me, sir," he said. "I'm Lieutenant Pike with the Army. May I ask what's going on here?"

The man turned, frowning. "Howdy, Lieutenant. My name's Wilson Smith, an' I guess you could say I'm the mayor of this here town." He paused and glanced at the door to the general store they were standing in front of. " 'Bout four hours ago we had a group of twenty or thirty men ride through here. They killed the livery owner . . . slit his throat clear through, an' they knocked out the owner of this general store. Doc's in there stitching up his head now."

"Why'd they kill the livery owner?" Pike asked.

"To get his mules, I guess. That's 'bout the only thing we can find that's missin' down there."

"Mules? Why would they need mules?"

"Why, to haul off the stuff they took from the store, I guess."

"Excuse me, Mayor. I'm gonna go inside and talk to the owner."

"Best be careful, Lieutenant. He ain't in too good a mood."

Pike nodded and stepped through the door.

He found an elderly man in a black coat and white shirt leaning over the counter, upon which lay another man with blood on his face and shirt.

Pike walked up and introduced himself, then said, "Could you tell me what they took?"

The owner of the store glanced at him, an angry look on his face. "Damned near everything that wasn't nailed down, Lieutenant, that's what. Clothes, food, rifles and pistols, ammunition, and even some dynamite and gunpowder."

"Damn!" Pike exclaimed. He knew having the escaped prisoners thus armed was going to make his job that much harder.

"About how long ago did they leave?"

"How the hell do I know?" the man asked angrily. "I was stretched out dead to the world."

The doctor glanced over his shoulder at Pike. "Best we can tell, it was about four hours ago."

Pike glanced at his watch. It was now almost three-thirty in the afternoon. It would be dark long before they could catch up to the escapees, and he didn't relish coming upon them in the dark.

"Is there anyplace in town I can billet my men until tomorrow?" he asked.

"You going after those bastards?" the store owner asked.

"Yes, sir," Pike answered. "But I want to track them in daylight, not at night."

As the doctor leaned back, finished with his sewing, the owner sat up. "I'm Josh Collins. I own one of the houses down the street. It's got a sign on the front that reads Pleasure Palace. Now, it ain't really no palace, but it's got enough beds and couches in it so's your men can get outta the weather."

Pike nodded. "Thank you, Mr. Collins. I'll give you a voucher so you can send your bill to the Army."

"Don't need no voucher," Collins said. "Long as you get the sons of bitches that did this to me, I'll call it square."

"That's what the Army's paying us to do, Mr. Collins," Pike said, though he knew it wasn't going to be easy, not now when the men were as heavily armed as his own troops.

5

Cal glanced at Pearlie as they rode back with Smoke toward the Sugarloaf. He raised his eyebrows, wondering if he should say anything. Smoke had been uncharacteristically quiet on the return trip, not laughing and joking as he usually did on these excursions to town.

Pearlie returned Cal's look, shrugging. He too was unused to Smoke's quiet mood.

Cal considered his options. He'd been more than an employee of Smoke's for several years—in fact, both Smoke and his wife Sally looked upon Cal as more a son than a hired hand. Cal had come to work at the Sugarloaf while just a boy in his teens. He'd been on his own, penniless and starving, and had actually tried to hold up Sally one morning while she was on her way into town to buy supplies.

After he drew down on Sally and asked her for some food, she got the drop on him with the snub-nosed .36-caliber pistol she carried in her purse. Cal laughed and showed her that the ancient pistol he was pointing at her was unloaded anyway.

Realizing the boy was starving, Sally took him to the Sugarloaf and offered him a job. He'd been part of the family ever since.

"Smoke," Cal said hesitantly.

"Yeah?" Smoke answered, his eyes fixed on the trail ahead and his jaw clenched.

"You been awfully quiet this trip. Anything wrong?"

Smoke glanced at Cal, and his eyes softened. "So, you noticed?"

Both Cal and Pearlie laughed. "Hell, yes," Cal said.

Smoke took a deep breath. "It's just that I'm not used to relying on someone else to pull my fat outta the fire."

"What do you mean?" Pearlie asked.

Smoke patted his hip where his pistols usually lay. "I feel naked without my Colts. After more years than I care to remember with them at my sides, it just doesn't feel right not to be wearing them."

Cal nodded. "Why don't you try talkin' to Sally about it, Smoke? She's usually reasonable about these things."

Smoke looked at Cal, a small grin on his face. "You ever try talking a woman outta something when she's got her mind set on it, Cal?"

Cal shook his head. "No. Matter of fact, I ain't had a whole lot of experience with women at all, Smoke."

"Keep it that way, Cal, and you'll have a whole lot less gray hair when you get to be my age," Smoke observed.

"You could just put the guns back on and tell Sally that's the way it's gonna be," Pearlie observed.

Smoke nodded. "I could, but the problem with that is it would make Sally very unhappy. And since I love her, her unhappiness would make me unhappy too."

Pearlie shook his head. "Love is a bitch, ain't it?" he said to no one in particular.

"It sure can be sometimes," Smoke said. "Other times, it's the greatest feeling in the world."

Sally Jensen walked out on the porch of their cabin when she heard Smoke's and the boys' horses arrive.

As he dismounted, Smoke said in a low tone, "Not a word about what happened in town."

"Are you men hungry?" Sally asked, wiping flour off her hands onto her apron.

Pearlie grinned. "Now, Miss Sally, what kind of a question is that?" he asked.

"You ever know Pearlie to admit he wasn't hungry?" asked Cal. "The man's stomach is a bottomless pit."

"We had breakfast at Louis's," Smoke said as he stepped up on the porch and gave her a hug and a kiss.

"Then I guess you didn't leave room for any bear sign," Sally said, smiling.

"Bear sign?" Pearlie asked, licking his lips.

Bear sign, the sugary doughnuts that men were known to ride dozens of miles to sample, were one of his favorite foods.

"I made a couple of dozen, but since you've already eaten . . ." Sally began.

Pearlie took a few quick steps toward the porch. "Outta my way, Smoke. I can hear them bear sign callin' my name," he said as he pushed by Smoke and Sally.

Cal, slightly more deliberate, tipped his hat at Sally. "If you don't mind, Miss Sally, I'd kind'a like a few of them too. That is, if Pearlie ain't already eaten 'em all 'fore I get through the door."

"I might have room for one or two also," Smoke said, walking into the kitchen with his arm around Sally.

As the boys sat down to eat, Sally poured them all mugs of rich, dark coffee. When she leaned down to put the mugs on the table, she sniffed loudly.

"You boys smell like gunpowder," she observed, standing back from the table with her hands on her hips. "Anything happen in town I ought to know about?" she asked.

Cal and Pearlie glanced at each other, then at Smoke, waiting for him to answer.

Smoke paused, a bear sign halfway to his mouth. He pursed his lips, as if considering how he should respond.

Sally nodded, looking in turn at each of the men sitting at her table. "Uh-huh, I know when all of you get lockjaw at the same time that something must have happened while you were in town."

Smoke laid the bear sign down, took a sip of his coffee, and leaned back in his chair, staring at Sally. "You're right, as usual, dear."

"Come on," she said impatiently, "give."

"While we were eating breakfast at Louis's, we were braced by three young gunnies looking to make a reputation for themselves," Smoke said evenly.

"Didn't they see you weren't wearing any weapons?" Sally asked, a look of alarm on her face.

"Didn't make no difference to that kind'a men, Miss Sally," Pearlie said. "Once they knew who Smoke was, they was bound and determined to egg him into a gunfight."

Sally arched an eyebrow. "And what did you do, Smoke?" she asked.

Smoke shrugged. "What could I do, Sally? I wasn't wearing any guns, at your request."

"So why do I smell gunpowder on you all?"

Smoke's face got dark. "Because, when those gunslicks drew on me, Cal and Pearlie saved my bacon by drawing and shooting them before they could kill me."

Sally sighed and stepped over to the table, putting her hands on Cal and Pearlie's shoulders. "Thanks, boys," she said.

Smoke threw his napkin down on the table and stood up, his face angry. "And I'll tell you something else, Sally," he said. "It's gonna happen again, sooner or later, long as you insist on me not wearing any guns."

He turned and walked rapidly out of the room, calling over his shoulder, "I'm gonna ride out and take a look at the herd."

Cal and Pearlie, embarrassed to be present at this scene of domestic disturbance, kept their heads down as they ate bear sign and tried to pretend they hadn't heard anything.

Sally walked around the table and sat down at Smoke's

seat. She stared at Cal and Pearlie. "You boys think I'm wrong in asking Smoke not to wear his Colts?"

Pearlie, his face flaming red, shrugged. "We know it's 'cause you love Smoke and don't want him to get shot no more, Miss Sally." He paused, glanced at Cal, then continued. "But you been out here in the West long enough to know that don't make no difference to the kind'a men who come lookin' to make a reputation by killin' the famous Smoke Jensen."

Cal looked over at Sally. "Pearlie's right, Miss Sally. Makin' Smoke go without his guns ain't gonna keep him safe . . . it's more than likely gonna get him killed."

Sally looked out the window, tears in her eyes, as she thought over what they'd said. After a few moments, she nodded to herself and got up.

"You boys finish the bear sign," she said as she walked to the door and took Smoke's gunbelt off the peg in the wall where it had hung since she'd asked him not to wear it anymore.

She hung it over her shoulder and walked out the door toward her horse, reined in at the hitching post in front of the cabin.

As she stepped into the saddle, Cal and Pearlie looked at each other. "Finally," Pearlie said, "she's showin' some sense."

Smoke was sitting on his horse, hands crossed over the pommel, looking out over the herd of cattle in the valley below, when Sally rode up, reining in beside him.

When he glanced over at her, she took the gunbelt off her shoulder and handed it to him. "Here," she said simply.

"What's this?" he asked.

"Take it, please, Smoke," she said. "The only reason I asked you not to wear it anymore was I was getting tired of either taking bullets out of you myself, or standing around while Doc Morrow did it."

Smoke took the belt and slipped it around his waist, buckling it up. "You sure this is what you want?" he asked.

She leaned over and put her hand on his where it lay on his thigh. "Smoke, the only thing I want is for the man I love to stay alive. I don't look good in widow's black."

Smoke leaned to the side and kissed her gently on the lips. "I promise you, I'll be extra careful, Sally," he said, his voice growing husky.

She looked around at the lush green grass and the maple and birch trees that were just beginning to come alive with the colors of fall. "You suppose we might get down off these horses and sit under that maple tree over there and talk about it for a while?" she asked, a mischievous look in her eyes.

Smoke grinned. "If we get down off these horses, I have a feeling we're gonna be doing a whole lot more than talking."

Sally swung down out of the saddle, unhitched the belly-strap and let her saddle fall to the ground. She took the saddle blanket off the horse, hung it over her arm, and walked toward the nearest tree, looking back over her shoulder with an unmistakable invitation in her eyes.

6

As the dawn sun peeked over mountain tops to the east, Lieutenant Jonathan Pike knocked on Sergeant Bob Guthrie's room at the Pleasure Palace.

Guthrie, his hair disheveled and his eyes still full of sleep, cracked the door. "Yes, sir?" he asked.

Pike glanced over Guthrie's shoulder, seeing a large thatch of red hair sticking out from under the covers and an empty bottle of whiskey lying on its side on his bedside table.

"Sun's up, Sergeant," Pike said, trying to hide a smile. "We're burning daylight."

"Yes, sir!" Guthrie said, covering a wide yawn with the back of his hand. "I'll get myself presentable and muster the men soon's I can."

"I'll wait for you in the dining room, Sergeant," Pike said. "And," he added as Guthrie started to close the door, "I'll have breakfast waiting for you, so no . . . further delays."

Guthrie grinned. "Yes, sir. I'll get right on it."

After he closed the door, the woman in the bed stuck her head out, rubbing eyes that were red from a late night. "That mean you don't have time for a mornin' pick-me-up?" she asked.

Guthrie shook his head. "I said I'd get right on it,

Mary Belle," he said as he dropped his trousers to the floor. "An' that's just what I intend to do."

He laughed as he dove beneath the covers, his cold hands making Mary Belle yelp as he grabbed her.

Guthrie's breakfast was cold by the time he arrived at Lieutenant Pike's table, and his cheeks showed patches of whiskers he'd missed in his hasty attempt to shave.

"I'm afraid your eggs are cold, Sergeant," Pike said, frowning.

Guthrie bent his head and dug right in. "I been in the Army nigh on twenty years, Lieutenant," he said with his mouth full. "I'm used to bad food, long days, an' cold nights."

Pike's face relaxed in a slight smile. "I trust last night wasn't too cold for you, Bob?"

Guthrie grinned without looking up. "No, sir. Last night the temperature was right tolerable."

"Good," Pike said. "'Cause it's liable to be the last warm night we spend for quite some time. The outlaws headed up into the high country, and I intend to follow 'em till we catch every last one of the scoundrels."

Guthrie looked up from his eggs, a frown on his face. "You think that's wise, sir?" he asked. "It's not gonna be an easy campaign, followin' those galoots up into the mountains."

"What do you mean?" Pike asked, sipping his coffee and staring at the sergeant.

"Well, number one, they're gonna know we're comin' after 'em, an' if they're at all smart, they're gonna have someone watchin' their back trail. Once they find out we're on their trail, it'll be an easy matter for 'em to set an ambush along the trail where they'll have the high ground."

Pike leaned back in his chair, his gaze stern. "So, you think we should just let them go on their way after all they've done?"

Guthrie shrugged. "Not exactly, sir. But they ain't gonna do no one any harm up in those mountains, especially with winter just around the corner. It's my guess they'll soon get tired of wanderin' around up to their asses in snow and freezin' their butts off an' come down to civilization. If we check the map, we can find out where they're liable to come down and have someone waitin' for 'em when they do."

Pike looked out the window, his lips pursed as he considered what Guthrie had said. After a moment, he shook his head. "No, Sergeant, I don't relish just giving up the hunt. Captain Bickford assigned me to track these criminals down and bring them to justice, and I intend to follow my orders."

"Even if it means gettin' half our men killed?" Guthrie asked, his eggs ignored on the plate in front of him.

Pike nodded. "My men didn't sign up in the Army for easy duty, Sergeant, and I think you overestimate the fighting ability of our foes. After all," Pike said, spreading his arms, "these men we're tracking are ordinary killers, not military geniuses. I think when they see the number of men after them, they'll more than likely give up without a fight."

Guthrie clenched his jaw and went back to his breakfast, knowing it was no use arguing with an officer who had his head up his butt. He knew the men from the prison wouldn't just give up, and he also knew that before this campaign was over, there was going to be blood on the snow of the high lonesome. . . .

Ozark Jack Berlin crawled out of his sleeping bag and stood up, checking the weather. The wind was blowing out of the north, carrying with it small particles of ice and snow and chilling him to the bone.

The night before, he'd made camp for his men in the shelter of a group of boulders piled against the steep side of a mountain ledge. The fire they'd built was nothing but coals now, and was giving off little heat to combat the frigid cold of the north wind.

Berlin stepped over to Blue Owl's sleeping bag and nudged the sleeping figure of the Indian with his foot.

"Blue Owl," he growled, "get your ass outta bed an' get the men movin'. We need a fire an' some coffee 'fore we freeze to death."

As Blue Owl stirred, trying to come awake, Berlin made the rounds of the other men, kicking them awake and telling them to get up and get ready to travel. By the time he'd finished, Blue Owl had the fire going and several pots of coffee cooking on the coals.

Billy Bartlett and Moses Johnson, a black man who'd killed a farmer and his family when they'd refused him work, were filling skillets with eggs and slabs of fatback bacon, while kettles of pinto beans bubbled and boiled on iron trestles over the flames.

Soon, thirty men were gathered as close to the warmth of the fire as they could get, drinking steaming coffee from tin mugs and wolfing down eggs, bacon, and beans as if they hadn't eaten in weeks.

Blue Owl, his shoulders hunched inside a buffalo robe he'd taken from town, held his coffee mug in both hands to keep them warm and glanced up at Berlin, who was standing next to him smoking a cigarette and staring at the mountains to the east.

"Yo, Boss," he said, "what are your plans for today?"

Several of the gunmen who were sitting nearby looked up, waiting for what Berlin had to say.

"We ain't got no choice but to head eastward," Berlin said. "We got a town full of angry miners and half the goddamned Army behind us, so I guess we'll just keep on movin' east."

Blue Owl shook his head, staring at the flames of the campfire. "If we keep goin' east, that means we gotta climb higher up in those mountains, an' it's gonna get colder'n a well-digger's asshole up there."

He looked up at the clouds overhead. "We got us a big

norther blowin' in, an' this is just the beginnin' of the bad weather we're gonna face if we go any higher up into the mountains."

Berlin took a last drag off his cigarette and flipped the butt into the fire. "I'm open to suggestions, Blue Owl. If'n you got any better ideas, now's the time to give 'em."

"I think we ought'a head on back down the mountain. We got more'n enough men an' guns to fight off the Army."

Berlin nodded. "And then what?"

"Then we could head south, skirtin' the mountains, till we come to a pass somewhere's where we don't have to go up into snow country."

"Uh-huh," Berlin said, a sneer on his face.

"Well?" Blue Owl asked. "What's wrong with that plan?"

Berlin shook his head. "Just about everything. First off, you want to engage the Army in a fight on level ground with these men." He indicated the group of murderers and rapists and robbers sitting around the fire listening to them with a wave of his hand. "Men who might be brave enough, but they aren't exactly trained in fightin' on horseback against men who are."

He paused to bend down, grab the coffeepot, and pour himself another cup of coffee. After he took a drink, he continued. "Secondly, assuming we could win against the Army, and the miners from the town we just passed through, by the time we'd traveled fifty miles, someone would have telegraphed ahead an' there'd be another group of Army men, or lawmen, or bounty hunters waitin' for us."

"So, what's different about your plan?" Blue Owl asked.

Berlin put his coffee cup down and built himself a cigarette, turning his back to the wind so he could get it lit.

"First off, while we make our way up into the mountains, we're gonna station some men on our back trail to warn us if the Army tries to come after us. If they do, then we'll fix up a nice little surprise for 'em that'll take them out without gettin' half our men killed."

"What about the telegraph you're so worried about?" Blue Owl asked. "The miners in the town back yonder can still telegraph ahead an' have people waitin' for us."

Berlin shook his head. "No, they can't," he said. "By the time they figure out the Army's failed, they won't know which way we're headed. Once we reach the pass at the top of the mountains, we can go north, east, or south, an' nobody's gonna know which way we've gone."

"What about the weather?" Billy Bartlett asked, holding his arms around himself and shivering in the cold.

Berlin nodded. "I'll admit it's gonna get a mite cold, but we got plenty of supplies, an' we'll be able to get more from the soldiers we kill if'n they come after us. With any luck, we'll only be up here for a week or so. Then we can head back down the other side of the mountains to warmer weather."

A large, barrel-chested man with a thick beard stood up from the other side of the fire.

"You got a question, Mack?" Berlin asked.

"Yeah," Mack replied, squaring his shoulders and letting his hand hover near the pistol on his belt. "I want to know who made you the boss. I don't recall no election."

Berlin's eyes narrowed. "You got an objection to me callin' the shots, Mack?" Berlin asked, shifting his coffee mug from his right hand to his left as he talked.

"Yeah, you ain't got no right to—"

Before Mack could finish, Berlin drew in a lightning-fast movement and fired through the flames. His slug took Mack in the chest, knocking him backward to land spread-eagled on his back in the gathering snow on the ground. Blood pumped out of his chest to mix with the ice and snow in a scarlet pool, steam rising from the liquid as it cooled.

Berlin looked around at the men gathered around him, his smoking pistol still in his hand. "Now, you men got to make a choice. This ain't the Army, an' it ain't prison. Any of you who wants to can go your own way, an' there'll be no hard feelin's."

Blue Owl glanced over at the body of Mack on the ground and laughed. "Yeah, Boss, I can see that," he said as other men in the group joined in with nervous laughter.

"No, I mean it," Berlin said. "Any of you who want to can leave, but those of you who stay have got to know who's runnin' things around here. If you stay, you're gonna do things my way, or you can do like Mack and take your chances that you're faster with a gun than I am. Any questions?"

The men all shook their heads and went back to eating their breakfast and drinking their coffee, some glancing nervously at Mack's body lying nearby.

7

Lieutenant Jonathan Pike sat on his horse at the head of his column of men as they prepared to ride out of Lode, Utah, on the trail of the escaped prisoners.

Mayor Wilson Smith stood nearby, watching as the men readied their mounts.

"Mayor," Pike said.

"Yes, sir, Lieutenant?"

"I need you to do me a favor," Pike said.

"Whatever you need, Lieutenant."

"Would you send some telegraphs for me?"

"Sure, where to?" the mayor asked.

"I'd like you to notify Fort Collins and Denver in Colorado, and the sheriff's office in Cheyenne, Wyoming, of what's happened here the past couple of days. If for some reason those criminals get by us in the mountains, they've got to either turn north to Wyoming, or south toward Colorado. I'd like the authorities to be aware that they may have to take action, if we fail to stop them."

Mayor Smith nodded. "I'll take care of it, Lieutenant, you got my word."

Sergeant Guthrie walked his horse up next to Pike's. "There's one other thing, Mayor," he said, cutting a corner off a square of chewing tobacco and sticking it in his mouth.

"What's that, Sergeant?" Smith asked.

"If worse comes to worst an' we lose this battle, there's a small chance those men may head back down this way. If I were you, I'd make sure the town was ready for 'em if they decide to backtrack down here."

Smith smiled grimly. "Oh, we'll be ready for 'em, Sergeant. They won't get another chance to raid this town."

Guthrie nodded, glanced at Pike, and waved his hand to the men in the column behind him. "Forward, ho!" he growled, and began walking his horse toward the mountain peaks in the distance.

Jesus Santiago squatted next to a small fire on a bluff overlooking a winding trail up the mountainside. The fire was set back from the edge of the cliff among stunted pines, its smoke whipped into nothingness by the strong winds coming from the north.

Santiago slapped his hands on his arms, then held his hands in front of the flames, trying to get some warmth from the fire. "God almighty!" he exclaimed. "I'm freezing my ass off up here."

Wiley Gottlieb walked from the ledge, where he'd been looking along the path through binoculars, and took a small bottle of whiskey from his saddlebags. He pulled the cork and took a long drink, wiping his mouth with the back of his hand. "Ozark Jack Berlin is crazy if he thinks the Army is gonna be fool enough to follow us up here in this blizzard," he growled.

Santiago glanced up at heavy, dark clouds through swirls of snow and particles of ice slanting with the wind. "You think this is a blizzard, Wiley?" he asked. "Hell, this is nothing but a little fall storm. Just wait till we get to the high country; then you'll see what a real blizzard looks like."

"It gets any colder'n this an' I may just take Ozark up on his offer to hightail my ass back down the mountain," Gottlieb said, putting his whiskey bottle back in his saddlebag and walking back over to the edge of the overlook.

He put the glasses to his eyes and pointed them back down the trail.

Santiago had begun to stir the coals, trying to coax more heat from the fire, when Gottlieb yelled, "Jesus, I'll be goddamned!"

Santiago jumped up and ran to stand next to Gottlieb, staring in the direction of his binoculars. He could see, through the mist and snow and sleet, a line of shadowy figures on horseback winding their way up the trail in the distance, their blue and gold uniforms clearly visible through the gloom.

"How many you make it?" he asked Gottlieb, who was still staring through the binoculars.

Gottlieb shook his head, "I can't tell for sure, but it looks to be fifty or more."

"Damn, Ozark was right," Santiago said, rushing back to the fire and scattering the wood, kicking snow and ice over it to put out the fire. "We got to get going and warn the others."

They caught up with Ozark Jack Berlin and the rest of the escapees an hour later. It was only midafternoon, but the storm made the light low and gloomy and cut visibility to less than two hundred yards.

Berlin nodded when they told him of what they'd seen. "I figured the Army wouldn't give up," he said, looking around at the land surrounding them.

Up ahead, the trail they were riding could be seen passing between two walls of stone as it traversed through a small valley.

Berlin began to point at different men as he gave his orders. "Billy, you and Moses and Wiley and Jesus take another ten men and head off to the right. Get your horses up that hillock and out of sight, then get the dynamite and gunpowder and plant some charges along the top of that cliff, under boulders and such." He reached into his saddlebags and handed Billy Bartlett a handful of cigars. "Get these goin' so you won't have to worry 'bout gettin' the fuses lit when the time comes. On my signal, light the fuses and get under cover. After the charges blow, step up to the ledge and use your rifles to pick off any survivors."

As Billy and the other men spurred their horses up the hill, Ozark Jack told the remaining men to do the same on the other side of the trail. "We'll box the bastards in and then pick 'em off one at a time," he said, grinning around his cigar as he followed his men up the trail.

Sergeant Guthrie was riding point, hunched over his saddle, trying to keep his mustache from icing over. It was no use. Even the bandanna he had over his face was becoming coated with a layer of ice and slush from the frigid wind in his face.

"I knowed I should'a quit when I had my twenty in," he muttered to himself, grabbing his saddle horn with both hands as his mount's hooves slipped on icy rock on the trail.

He glanced back over his shoulder. His men were riding two by two along the winding trail, all hunched over as *he* was. He knew they were in dangerous territory, riding without being able to scout out the area ahead of the troops, but Lieutenant Pike was adamant that they make good time. He'd refused Guthrie's request to send a small party of men ahead to make sure it was safe to proceed.

"Damned fool's gonna get us all killed," Guthrie muttered to himself, watching the fog of his breath torn away by gusty winds.

When the trail turned around a corner and seemed to disappear into a valley between two rock walls ahead, Guthrie reined his horse's head around and trotted back down the line of troops to where Pike was riding.

"Sir," Guthrie said, "I don't like the looks of that valley up ahead. It's a natural place for an ambush."

Pike raised his head and stood up in his stirrups to get a better look. He stared at the valley, then at the cliffs overlooking the trail.

"I don't see anything, Sergeant," he said after a moment.

You damn fool, Guthrie thought, you expect 'em to stand up and wave at us if they're waiting to bushwhack us?

"That's the point, Lieutenant," Guthrie persisted. "We can't see nothin' in this weather. Let me stop the men an' send a patrol ahead to check it out."

"You want me to stop the men out here in the open and let them freeze while you go traipsing up ahead to see if anyone's waiting to fire on us?" the lieutenant asked sarcastically.

"But sir," Guthrie began.

"No, carry on, Sergeant," Pike said. "I think it'd be better to get the men into that valley where we have some cover and let them take a break there. We can build some fires and warm up the horses and men and have some coffee before we move on."

Guthrie shook his head as he jerked his horse around. He hoped the outlaws were as dumb as his leader, or there was going to be hell to pay.

Guthrie was well into the valley when he heard the first explosion. He looked up in time to see sheets of flame explode from both sides of the cliffs on either side of the men, sending boulders, dirt, debris, and tons of snow cascading down toward them.

Without thinking, Guthrie dove sideways off his horse to land sprawled on his face in ankle-deep snow. He scrambled on hands and knees to get as close to the side of the cliff as he could, hunkering down between two large stone formations there.

Seconds later he was buried under an avalanche of dirt and snow as blackness opened up and swallowed him.

* * *

As soon as their dynamite and gunpowder exploded, Berlin's men moved to the edges of the cliffs ringing the small valley below.

Putting rifles to shoulders, they waited for the dust to clear. Below them was a scene of unbelievable carnage . . . men and horses were half-buried under tons of rocks, dirt, and snow. Horses and men were screaming in pain and terror, trying to escape the falling boulders.

As the dust settled, blown away by rushing north winds, Berlin's men began to fire their weapons into the milling mass of humanity below.

One after another, both men and horses were felled by hundreds of bullets raining down upon them. A few gallant soldiers managed to draw weapons, and fired blindly into the night sky, unable to even see their targets.

Within moments all movement in the valley had ceased, though eerie sounds of moans and muted cries for help still came from some of the men who were wounded but still somehow alive.

Berlin and his allies climbed on their mounts and descended to the valley of death below, holding their guns at the ready. They lit torches and held them aloft as they walked their broncs among the dead horses and men scattered along the valley floor. Occasionally, they would come upon someone still alive, moving slightly or raising a hand pleading for mercy.

The outlaws were relentless, stopping momentarily to gaze down upon helpless soldiers before slowly taking aim and putting them out of their misery with a single gunshot to the head or chest. . . .

Guthrie came awake, choking and gagging as he tried to breathe dirt. He managed to get his hands up to his face and clear a small opening so he could breathe.

He shook his head, trying to remember where he was and what had happened to him. It felt like his horse was lying on top of him, and he could barely move his arms.

When he realized what had happened, he slowly began to dig his way out of the dirt and snow covering him. He managed to get his face clear and wipe his eyes after about ten minutes. It was full dark now, with no sign of any light from stars or moon.

He was lying between two boulders under a pile of small boulders and dirt, hidden from view in the darkness. His body was still covered, and he couldn't get his hand down to his pistol when he saw several men riding around with torches in their hands. He put his facedown on the dirt so they wouldn't see the whites of his eyes, and listened.

He could hear men moaning and screaming in pain, some crying out for help or begging for mercy. Then he heard several shots ring out as other men laughed and yelled curses at the wounded men.

"Sons of bitches are slaughtering my men," he said to himself as he struggled to free his lower body and get to his weapon.

Still unable to reach his gun, he lay still when two horses rode within six feet of him. He could hear the men talking as they walked their mounts up the trail.

"We got all the guns and ammunition we can carry, Ozark," one of the dark figures on horseback said.

"Good. Hurry up and kill anyone left alive and let's make tracks. Colorado's waitin' for us, Blue Owl."

They rode on out of sight, swallowed by the night, as Guthrie struggled to free himself from a half ton of dirt and rocks.

By the time he was able to scramble out from between the rocks, all of the outlaws were gone, leaving behind forty-five men lying dead in the snow, some still on horseback, their dead mounts beneath them.

Guthrie walked among his men, tears stinging his eyes and freezing on his cheeks as he looked up the trail after the outlaws.

"I swear to God, I'm gonna come after you and see

every one of you bastards in the ground for what you done here tonight," he vowed, shaking his fist in the air.

Finally, he turned to the grisly task of searching each and every body lying on the ground to see if anyone had survived the ambush.

He found Lieutenant Pike sitting with his back to a boulder, over fifteen gunshot wounds in his body, his right leg twisted at an unnatural angle beneath him.

Guthrie stood over him, shaking his head. "You were a damn fool, Lieutenant, but nobody deserves to die like that, not even you."

After he made sure there were no survivors, having to shoot several horses that were too badly injured to survive, Guthrie hunted down a horse among the few that had managed to survive and were scattered in the surrounding area, got in the saddle, and headed up the trail.

Before he left, he made the rounds again of his fallen comrades, taking several extra rifles, a couple of extra pistols, and as much ammunition as he could stuff in his saddlebags. He also took as much food as he could carry, knowing it was going to be a long, hard ride through the high country and food was going to be scarce.

He loaded the extra rations and weapons on the back of another horse, and tied a dally rope to its saddle, using it as a packhorse.

He intended to go after the outlaws until he had a chance to avenge his men. Sergeant Bob Guthrie was going to war, and he didn't intend to stop until he had killed every one of the men who'd slaughtered his friends.

He'd heard the leader of the band mention Colorado as their final destination, and he was going to ride hard and fast and see if he could be there waiting for them when they arrived.

8

Smoke and Sally Jensen were sitting on the porch of their cabin, enjoying the first cup of coffee in the morning, when a rider approached.

"Yo, the cabin!" called the voice of Monte Carson, sheriff of Big Rock.

Smoke stood up. "Howdy, Monte. Come on in."

Monte dismounted, tied his horse to the hitching rail near the porch, and ambled up the steps.

He tipped his hat. "Mornin', Sally," he said.

"Good morning, Monte," she answered, getting to her feet. "Would you like some breakfast, or coffee? Smoke and I were just fixing to have some eggs and bacon."

He nodded, a grin appearing on his face. Sally's cooking was known far and wide as the best in the area. "That'd sure hit the spot, Sally."

After she'd gotten him a mug of coffee, Sally went back into the kitchen to fix breakfast while Monte and Smoke stayed on the porch.

Monte built himself a cigarette and leaned back, crossing his legs with the mug on his knee.

"What brings you way out here to the Sugarloaf so early in the day, Monte?" Smoke asked.

Monte took a drag on his cigarette and let the smoke trickle from his nostrils as he answered. "I got a wire from the mayor of a little town in Utah called Lode yesterday."

"Lode? I don't think I know it," Smoke said.

"It's a small mining camp a few hundred miles from Salt Lake City. It's just up in the mountains there."

Smoke nodded. "And what did this wire say that was so important you had to ride out here?"

Monte took a sip of his coffee. "It seems there was a prison break at the Utah Territorial Prison a few days ago. Evidently more than thirty of the most dangerous felons in the place managed to break out and make their getaway."

"Uh-huh."

"They proceeded to steal some horses and guns and made their way up to this little town. When they got there, they stole more guns and horses, and lots of supplies, and headed up into the mountains after killing the livery owner."

Smoke frowned. "What's that got to do with us here in Colorado?"

"The Army sent men after them, and the man in charge asked the mayor of Lode to wire all the towns near the border in Wyoming and Colorado that the escapees might just head on down our way if they made it through the mountains."

Smoke smiled, shaking his head. "That won't be an easy task, with the winter storms starting in the high country."

Monte nodded. "I know it's a long shot, an' we'll probably never see hide nor hair of 'em, but I thought I'd use the wire as an excuse to ride around the area and warn all the outlying ranchers to be on the lookout."

"Well, I'm glad you did, Monte. It's been far too long since you've paid us a visit out here. Sally was just asking the other day about how you and Mary were doing."

"My wife's fine, Smoke, though her cookin' don't compare to Sally's."

"I heard that, Monte," Sally said from the doorway, "and I intend to tell Mary what you said next time I see her."

Monte assumed a look of horror and held up his hands. "Don't you dare, Sally. She'd have my hide if she heard that."

Sally laughed. "Come on in, you two. Breakfast is on the table and it's getting cold."

While they ate, Smoke told Sally what Monte had said about the escaped criminals.

"Do you really believe there's any chance they'll come all the way down here before they're caught?" she asked.

Monte shook his head and spoke around a mouthful of scrambled hens' eggs and bacon. "No, I don't really think so, Sally. I imagine the Army will catch up with them before they get too far. In my experience, men in prison aren't smart enough to escape the Army for long."

"I hope you're right, Monte," Smoke said. "There are lots of folk living up in the high lonesome that wouldn't stand a chance against those kind of odds."

Monte grinned. "Don't tell me you're worried about all your old mountain-men friends who still winter up in the mountains."

Smoke shook his head. "No, not at all. If they try to bother any of those old beavers, they'll find out they've bitten off more than they can chew," Smoke said. "But, since gold has been discovered up in the Rockies, a lot of miners have moved up there with their families, and most of them are pilgrims that don't know how to take care of themselves against a crew like these prisoners."

Monte finished off his eggs and bacon and took a final drink of his coffee before standing up. "Well, it most probably won't come to that anyhow. Thanks again for the food, Sally. It was wonderful, as usual."

As he walked out the door, Sally called, "Give my regards to Mary."

"I'll do it," Monte answered, climbing on his horse.

"And let us know if you hear any more news about those men," Smoke added.

"Will do. Adios," Monte called as he waved good-bye and spurred his horse down the road toward the next ranch.

Smoke reached inside the door and got his hat and gunbelt off the peg next to the door.

"What are you doing?" Sally asked.

"I'm gonna ride on up to the north pasture where Cal and Pearlie and some of the boys are mending fences. Might as well let them know to be on the lookout for any strangers."

"Just a minute," Sally said, walking into the kitchen. She took a platter of fresh biscuits, put them in a paper sack, and handed it to Smoke.

"Take these with you. It's been a couple of hours since Pearlie has eaten, so I know he'll be hungry."

Smoke laughed. "Pearlie's always hungry, but I'll take the sinkers. It'll give him an excuse to quit working for a while and eat."

9

The early winter storm was clearing, and a bright sun filled azure skies without giving out much heat as Ozark Jack Berlin and his men rode a trail down Blue Mountain toward the banks of the White River.

Berlin held up his hand to stop his men as he pulled a map taken from the general store in Lode out of his saddlebag.

He lit a cigar and puffed as he used his finger to follow the line on the map that was labeled "White River." He glanced up, peering into the distance to where he could see a scattering of buildings near the riverbank where a smaller creek branched off.

Blue Owl walked his horse up next to Berlin. "You figure out where the hell we are yet, Boss?" he asked.

Berlin nodded. "That looks like the White River, an' that there smaller branch seems to be Douglas Creek. If that's so, then that town must be Rangely, Colorado."

"Don't look like much of a town to me," Blue Owl said.

"It ain't. Probably just a bunch of miners an' such tryin' to scrape a livin' outta the rocks up here."

Blue Owl pulled a pair of binoculars out of his saddlebag and put them to his eyes. They were marked U.S. ARMY, and he'd taken them off a soldier just after he put a bullet through his head.

"I don't see no telegraph lines nor poles," he said, grinning. "That means they ain't heard about us yet."

Berlin returned the smile. "Yeah, an' this time of the mornin', most of the men are gonna be up in the mountains diggin' in their mines. Won't hardly be anyone left in town to give us any trouble."

Blue Owl nodded. "I hope they's some womenfolk in town. It's been too long since I had me a woman."

"Well," Berlin said, putting his map away and drawing his pistol, "ain't but one way to find out, is there?"

He spurred his horse and took off at a gallop, his men riding hard behind him.

They raced across the wooden bridge over the White River, their hoofbeats beating a hollow tattoo of sound as they entered the town's limits.

The town consisted primarily of faded clapboard buildings and wooden cabins arrayed in a straight line on either side of the main street. There was an assay office, a general store, three saloons, a two-story hotel and boardinghouse, a livery stable, and fifteen or twenty smaller houses on the outskirts of the town.

As the thirty outlaws raced down the main street, several older men and a few women ran for doorways, ducking into buildings to get out of the way of the running horses.

Two middle-aged men stayed in the street, both reaching for pistols, to be gunned down before they could clear leather.

Berlin jerked his horse to a stop in the center of town. "Fan out!" he hollered to his men, waving his arm in a circle. "Make sure there ain't nobody left armed until we can see the lay of the land."

In less than an hour, every living soul in the town was rounded up and gathered together in the largest saloon, called the Nugget. There were twenty-two men, ranging in age from thirteen years old to more than seventy.

There were also fifteen women, ten of whom were obviously prostitutes or saloon girls. The other five were elderly women whose husbands were out at their mines working.

Berlin stood at the bar, a bottle of whiskey next to him, as he looked over the prisoners, who were huddled on one side of the large room.

The bartender was hurriedly pouring whiskey all around for the outlaws, while Moses Johnson and Billy Bartlett held shotguns on the prisoners.

"Jesus," Berlin said to Jesus Santiago, "you and Sam Cook get on over to the assay office and see if there's any gold there we can take."

"Yes, sir, Boss," Jesus said, gulping his whiskey down and heading for the door, followed by Sam Cook.

"Now, you people, just take it easy an' nobody has to get hurt," Berlin drawled to the townspeople. "We're gonna take some supplies an' be on our way soon, so no need gettin' all riled up and doin' somethin' stupid."

"You bastards will never get away with this," an elderly man off to one side said, drawing himself up and staring at Berlin.

"And just who's gonna stop us?" Berlin asked in a low voice.

"When the men get back from the mines they'll track you down and kill every one of you sons of bitches!" the man answered.

"Billy," Berlin said gently, "teach this man some manners."

Billy Bartlett grinned and let go with one of the barrels of his shotgun. The gun exploded, sending a charge of buckshot into the man's midsection, almost cutting him in half and spraying the people around him with blood and guts.

"Now," Berlin said loudly over the screams of the women in the room, "are there any other complaints I need to deal with?"

Several of the men managed to quiet the women while

looking over their shoulders at the gunmen who were covering them.

When no one spoke up, Berlin nodded. "Good. Then that settles it." He glanced out the window at the boardinghouse and hotel across the street, then walked over to the crowd and grabbed one of the women by the arm.

"Get your friends and come with me," he said gruffly.

"Where are we going?" the woman asked, terror in her eyes.

"My men an' me been on the trail for a while now an' we're in need of some feminine companionship," Berlin answered.

As the younger women followed him out of the door, he called over his shoulder to his men, "Ten of you come on with us. The others can stay here and keep them covered. We can take turns till everybody's had their fill."

Blue Owl grabbed his bottle and started toward the door. "Not you, Blue Owl," Berlin said. "You got to go last."

"Why's that?" Blue Owl said angrily.

"'Cause I don't want you an' that pigsticker of yours spoilin' the goods till everybody else has had a chance at 'em," Berlin answered.

Blue Owl grinned. "Oh," he said, smiling and returning to the bar.

"Moses," Berlin said, "send a couple of men to stand guard at the town limits in case some of the miners come back before dark."

"Yes, sir, Boss."

In two hours, all of the men with Berlin had their turns with the prostitutes, including Blue Owl. Only one of the girls was damaged beyond repair. Blue Owl had left his woman in pieces on a bloodstained bed in the hotel.

Berlin gathered his men, along with twelve pounds of gold dust from the assay office, assorted food and supplies from the general store, and enough ammunition to replace what they'd used on the soldiers, and they prepared to take their leave from Rangely.

"You people stay here in the saloon until after we're gone, an' nobody'll be any the worse for wear," Berlin said, walking back and forth in front of the townsfolk.

"If you stick your heads out before then, we'll blow 'em off," he warned.

He led his men out the door and they all mounted up. "Sam, you and Moses open up the livery and scatter the hosses so they can't follow us later," he ordered.

After that was done, he trotted out of town, heading south by southeast toward the next town.

Sergeant Bob Guthrie arrived in town three hours later, just before dark. He was met by a group of men holding rifles and shotguns.

"Who the hell are you?" a tall, thin man with a full beard asked angrily.

Guthrie held his hands out where the men could see them. "I'm Sergeant Bob Guthrie, United States Army."

"What do you want here?" the man asked, lowering his rifle, but keeping his hand on the trigger.

"I'm followin' a band of outlaws that killed my men up in the mountains. There's about thirty of 'em, an' they're mean as snakes."

"Get down off your horse, Sergeant," the man said. "Your outlaws have already paid us a visit."

He stuck his hand out. "I'm Jacob Walker, sort'a the mayor of Rangely."

Guthrie took his hand. "Howdy. How long ago did they leave?"

"'Bout three hours or so," Walker said, leading Guthrie into the saloon where the people had been held prisoner.

Guthrie sank into a chair, exhaustion evident on his face. "I been in the saddle over twenty hours now, tryin' to catch up to those bastards," he said.

"Emmett," Walker said to the bartender, "get Sergeant Guthrie some grub an' some coffee. He looks like he could use it."

While he ate, Guthrie told the townspeople the story of the prison break, the trouble in Lode, and the subsequent slaughter of his command.

Walker looked around at his fellow citizens. "I guess we got off lucky then," he said. "They only killed four here, along with stealing all our gold and some supplies."

"You folks have a telegraph here?" Guthrie asked.

Walker shook his head. "Nope. Nearest one's over at Meeker, sixty miles to the east."

"Which way did they head?" Guthrie asked.

"Southeast. That means they're either heading to Rifle or Grand Junction."

"How big are the towns?"

"Rifle's just 'bout the same size we are," Walker said. "Grand Junction has a railroad line and is quite a bit bigger."

"You say Grand Junction has a railroad?" Guthrie asked.

"Yeah. It goes over toward Crested Butte and then on down to Pueblo." He walked over to the bar, reached behind it, and pulled out an assayer's map of the territory. He unfolded it on the table and showed it to Guthrie.

Guthrie thought for a moment as he studied the map. "I'd figure they're gonna head for Rifle first, being's it's the smallest town an' probably don't have much law."

"You're probably right," Walker said.

Guthrie looked up. "If I can trade for a couple of horses, I'm gonna hightail it to Grand Junction, notify the Army by telegraph there, then take the railroad down to Crested Butte. With any luck, I'll be waitin' for 'em when they finally get there."

"If you don't mind my saying so, Mr. Guthrie," Walker said, "you don't look in any shape to make that journey tonight."

Guthrie leaned back in his chair. "You're probably

right, Walker. I'm liable to fall off my horse and break my neck if I don't get some sleep."

Walker poured him another cup of coffee. "From the looks of the sky, we got another winter storm coming in soon. Those outlaws won't be able to make much time over the mountains between here and Rifle if it snows. Why don't you get some sleep and start off first thing in the morning? That'll still give you plenty of time to get to Grand Junction and get the train to Crested Butte ahead of those outlaws."

Guthrie drained his coffee and stood up. "I think I will, Mayor. I'm much obliged to you."

"You get the men who raided this town and we'll call it even, Sergeant."

Guthrie turned eyes cold and black as stone on Walker. "Oh, I intend to do that, Mr. Walker. You can count on it!"

10

Sergeant Bob Guthrie awoke at noon the next day, to weather that was cold but with no traces of the storm of the previous week. The mayor of Rangely provided him with two fresh horses and he took off toward Grand Junction, a trip of approximately fifty miles. He planned to use the horses in tandem and hoped, if the weather held, to make the trip in three days or less.

Ozark Jack Berlin and his gang of outlaws didn't fare so well. A blue norther, sweeping down out of Canada, hit them with the force of a freight train, dumping two feet of snow and dropping temperatures below zero on their trip toward Rifle, Colorado.

They arrived at Rifle more than ten days after they left Rangely, a journey that would usually only take four days. They were cold, saddle-weary, and dead tired when they rode into sight of the small mining town.

While on the outskirts of the town, Berlin gathered his men around him, their faces crusted with ice and snow.

"All right, men, we been through hell on the way here," he said. "We're gonna need a place to rest up and recuperate from the trip, so I want you all to be on your best behavior while we're here. No shootin' an' no killin' till we're ready to leave town. You got that?"

The men nodded wearily, all anxious to get in front of a fire somewhere and warm up. Their blood lust was for the moment dampened by their misery in the frigid air surrounding them.

As they rode slowly into Rifle, Blue Owl looked around at the clapboard buildings and tents of the town. "Hell, Boss," he said, "it don't look like there's much here for the taking anyway."

"That's true, Blue Owl, but I want you to keep a tight rein on the men while we're here. Ain't no need of gettin' the town all riled up till we've rested a mite an' got our strength back."

"You think they might've heard anything 'bout us yet?" Blue Owl asked, peering through the falling snow at the few townspeople who were foolish enough to be outside in such weather.

"Naw. I don't see no telegraph wires, so there ain't no way they know anything 'bout us so far."

The men reined in their mounts in front of the largest saloon in town, called the Mother Lode, and hurried through the batwings, standing inside the door and stamping snow and ice off their boots before taking tables in the almost empty room.

Berlin went over to the bar. "Bring my men whiskey, an' plenty of it," he growled. "We're 'bout frozen to death."

The barman raised his eyebrows. "You men been out traveling in this weather?" he asked incredulously.

"We were on our way here from up north," Berlin said, "when the storm hit. For a while, we didn't know if we were gonna make it or not."

"You're plenty lucky to have made it through the passes 'fore the snow accumulated," the barman said, bringing several bottles of whiskey out from under the bar. "Another day, an' you would've been trapped up in the mountains till the snow melted."

Billy Bartlett and Moses Johnson walked over, picked

up the whiskey bottles and some glasses, and took them to the nearby tables.

Berlin inclined his head toward the large Franklin stove in the corner. "You think you could stoke that stove a mite?" he asked, shivering. "We'd sure appreciate a little extra heat in here."

"Sure thing," the barman said. "An' if you and your men want some grub and a place to bunk down, the boardinghouse up the street sets a fine table."

Berlin nodded, pouring himself a large glass of whiskey and drinking it down. "Much obliged, mister," he said. "Soon's we get a little firewater in our gullets, we'll head on over there."

"Livery's right next door too," the man added. "With this storm, it'd be best to get your animals under cover soon's you can."

"We'll do that," Berlin said, taking his bottle and heading over to the table where Bartlett, Blue Owl, and Sam Cook were sitting.

"What's the plan, Boss?" Cook asked.

"I figure we'll hold up here a couple'a days, till the storm passes. We can use the time to get our mounts rested an' our bellies full." He looked around at his men, some of whom were still shivering from the cold. "After all, we ain't in no hurry to get anywhere since we took care of the Army."

Guthrie rode into Grand Junction three and a half days after he left Rangely. He pushed his horses, both of which were on their last legs, and rode directly to the train station on the eastern edge of town.

He dismounted and rushed to the ticket window. "I need to get to Crested Butte as soon as possible," he said.

The ticket master shook his head. "That might be a bit of a problem, mister," he said. "Had a big storm go through the area south of here last couple'a days. Some of the passes might be blocked with snow."

"When will you know?"

"We're gonna send an engine with a snowplow on the front through this afternoon. If it makes it, the engineer will telegraph us from Crested Butte and we'll send the next train on ahead."

Guthrie bit his lip, thinking for a moment. "Any chance of me hitchin' a ride on that snowplow?"

The ticket master frowned. "What's so all-fired important about getting to Crested Butte in such a hurry?" he asked.

"There's a group of thirty outlaws headed that way," Guthrie answered. "If I don't get there first and warn the town, there's liable to be dead people lyin' all over the streets of Crested Butte by tomorrow."

"Well, since it's a kind'a emergency, I'll check with the engineer and see if he'll let you ride along." The man paused, then continued. "I gotta warn you, though. It won't be an easy ride, what with the cold and snow and everything."

"I'll take my chances," Guthrie said. "A lot of lives depend on me getting through."

The ticket man nodded, and Guthrie asked, "Where's the telegraph office?"

The man pointed toward the center of town. "Right up the street there, you can't miss it."

Guthrie walked to the telegraph office and entered. He grabbed a sheet of yellow foolscap off the table and began writing a message to the Army post at Glenwood Springs, fifteen miles east of Rifle. He hopped they could send men to the small town in time to avoid a massacre if Berlin and his men headed there. Fort Collins, a much larger post, was too far away to do anything in time. Guthrie had been stationed for a short time at Glenwood Springs and he knew it was a small post, but at least they might be able to warn the town of Rifle that Berlin was on his way.

* * *

It was a measure of the smallness of the post at Glenwood Springs that the commanding officer was a shavetail lieutenant. He was fresh from officers' training and Glenwood was his first command. His name was Riley Woodcock. He was twenty-two years old, with a lack of experience to match his young age.

Sergeant Mark Goodson was the real leader of the small command, and Goodson prayed nightly that nothing untoward would happen that would test his young commanding officer's mettle.

It was Sergeant Goodson who got the wire from Sergeant Guthrie, and he was shaking his head as he carried it into Lieutenant Woodcock's office.

Woodcock looked up from his morning coffee. "Yes, what is it, Sergeant?" he asked, not liking the worried look on Goodson's face when he'd entered the office without knocking.

"Just got this wire from Grand Junction, sir," he said, handing the paper to Woodcock.

Woodcock read the wire, then laid it on the desk, a look of anticipation on his face. As much as Goodson prayed for nothing to happen, Woodcock had waited eagerly for some trouble in which he could act heroically and make a name, and perhaps gain a promotion, for himself.

"What's the status of the men, Sergeant?" Woodcock asked, standing and striding to the corner coatrack and buckling on his sword.

Goodson sighed. He'd been afraid of something like this ever since he'd read the wire. "Ready, sir," he said fatalistically.

Deciding to try to salvage the situation, Goodson added, "It seems a small matter to occupy you, sir. Perhaps I could take a squad of men and ride over to Rifle and warn the civilian authorities there of what may be coming."

Woodcock glanced over his shoulder. "There are no civilian authorities in Rifle, Sergeant. You know that." As he settled his hat on his head, he continued. "If anyone is to save the good people of Rifle from these desperados, it's got to be the Army."

"Yes, sir," Goodson said unhappily.

"Gather the men together in front of my office, geared up and ready to ride. Full arms."

"Yes, sir," Goodson said, snapping off a salute. As he walked out the door, he hoped the outlaws had headed someplace other than Rifle. He had no desire to go up against thirty armed and dangerous men with this kid leading the way. It was a sure recipe for disaster, he thought as he rounded up his men.

Thirty minutes later, Goodson had fifteen men sitting on their horses in formation in front of Woodcock's office.

Woodcock strolled out the door, set his hat firmly on his head, and climbed into the saddle.

"Sergeant, you may lead the men by columns of two off the post."

"Yes, sir," Goodson said. "Forward, ride!" he called, waving his hand and leading the way south by southwest toward the town of Rifle.

Lieutenant Woodcock rode alongside halfway down the column, sitting straight in the saddle, sure he was on his way to finding his destiny.

11

Ozark Jack Berlin was enjoying the first real rest he'd had since escaping from prison a couple of weeks before. He and his men had been constantly on the run, sleeping and eating mostly on the trail, through some of the worst weather he'd ever seen.

This was the first time he'd been able to sit back and take it easy since he'd been caught after robbing that train up at Moab, Utah, and sentenced to ten years hard labor at the territorial prison. If he could only manage to keep his men in line and out of trouble, they might just stay here until the weather warmed up a bit. He didn't relish any more mad dashes through the mountains with winter storms beating them in the face.

Still, there was always the possibility someone would be on their trail. With this thought beginning to worry him, Berlin got out of his bed at the boardinghouse and walked down the hall to the room being shared by Jack McGraw and Tony Cassidy, two of the men who'd helped him rob the train that'd gotten him prison time.

He banged on the door until a hungover and sleepy-looking Jack McGraw opened the door.

"What the hell do you . . . oh, it's you, Boss," McGraw said, opening the door all the way and stepping to the side.

"I been thinkin', Jack," Berlin said.

"Yeah?"

"We might just be gettin' a mite careless lately. There's an outside possibility somebody may be on our back trail."

McGraw nodded, rubbing his eyes and trying to staunch the massive headache a fifth of whiskey from the night before was causing.

"I think we ought'a post a couple'a men on the north side of town, just in case trouble comes lookin' for us."

"Yeah?" McGraw said again, still not following what his boss was saying.

"You and Tony are gonna take the first watch. I want you to station yourselves in that little saloon right inside the town limits to the north. If you see anybody that don't look right, you hightail it on over to the boardin'house here and give us a warnin'."

"But Boss," McGraw whined, "it's might near freezin' outside."

Berlin's face got hard. "I don't aim to make the same mistake got us caught the last time, Jack. Now you and Tony get your asses over to that saloon . . . an' go easy on the whiskey while you're on watch. Beer only, you hear me?"

McGraw rubbed his temples. "Beer's about all I can handle right now anyway, Ozark," he answered.

"Get Tony outta bed and haul your butts over there. I'll send somebody to relieve you in time for lunch."

"Yes, sir," McGraw said with poor grace as he turned to wake his friend up.

Sergeant Bob Guthrie was standing in the cab of the snowplow engine, sweating from the heat coming from the furnace as the engine slowly plowed through three feet of snow on the railway line between Grand Junction and Crested Butte. It had been slow going through the previous day and last night, with the mountain passes having accumulated snowdrifts four and five feet high, but they were getting close to breaking through to lower elevations where the snow wouldn't be so bad.

"You think we'll make it by noon?" Guthrie yelled to the engineer, trying to be heard over the roar of the steam engine as it struggled to push the plow through the snow.

The engineer leaned his head out of the window and spat a brown stream of tobacco juice into the snow alongside the tracks before he answered.

He glanced ahead of the engine, shielding his eyes from the glare of sun off the snow, then leaned back into the engine compartment. "I reckon so. This ought'a be 'bout the last of the heavy snow. From here on in, it's gonna get flatter, an' that means we can go faster."

"Good," Guthrie said.

"You never did tell me why you're in such an all-fired hurry to get to Crested Butte," the engineer said. "There ain't much there to get all excited about."

"I got a date with some outlaws," Guthrie said shortly.

The engineer laughed. "Hell, if that's all you're lookin' for, you can find them just 'bout ever'where you look in these parts. 'Bout the only kind'a men who come to the high lonesome in the winter are either miners crazy with gold fever or men on the run from someplace else."

"Well, these men are the worst of the lot," Guthrie said, his lips tight. "They need killin' in the worst way, an' I intend to oblige 'em."

When the squad of Army men crested a hill overlooking the town of Rifle, Sergeant Mark Goodson reined his horse to a stop and waited for Lieutenant Riley Woodcock to ride up next to him.

"Why are you stopping, Sergeant?" Woodcock asked.

"I was thinkin', Lieutenant," Goodson said. "If those outlaws are already in Rifle, maybe we'd better split up the men and sneak into town one or two at a time. No need to warn 'em we're comin' after 'em."

Woodcock thought for a moment, then shook his head. "I don't intend to split up my command, Sergeant.

That's a mistake General Custer made against the Sioux, and it cost him the lives of all his men."

"But Lieutenant," Goodson started to protest.

"You heard me, Sergeant. Let's ride in showing the colors at full force. If those outlaws have any sense, when they see the United States Army arrive, they'll give themselves up without a fight."

Goodson started to remind the lieutenant they hadn't given themselves up the last time they faced the Army, but then figured it wouldn't make any difference. The lieutenant had his mind made up, and didn't appear ready to listen to reason.

"Yes, sir," Goodson said. He stood up in his stirrups and addressed the men. "Make ready your arms," he called. "I want every one of you ready for trouble the minute we hit the town limits."

"I'll take the point from here on in, Sergeant," Woodcock said, spurring his horse to lead his men into the town.

"Damn fool!" Goodson whispered to himself as he followed the lieutenant down the hill toward Rifle.

Tony Cassidy was sitting next to a window overlooking the main street of Rifle, nursing a beer and eating boiled eggs, when he saw the squad of Army men riding into town.

He almost choked on his eggs as he punched Jack McGraw in the shoulder. "Look at that, Jack," he whispered urgently.

McGraw turned his attention from the prostitute he'd been talking to and glanced out the window.

"Goddamn!" he uttered, pushing her off his lap and putting his beer down.

"How many you make it?" he asked.

"Looks like seventeen," Cassidy answered. "And they're loaded for bear. They all got their rifles at the ready."

"You ease out the front door and keep an eye on 'em,"

McGraw said. "I'll sneak out the back door and let Ozark know what's goin' on."

"You think they're comin' here after us?" Cassidy asked.

"They didn't ride through this weather to pick flowers, Tony," McGraw answered as he walked rapidly toward the back door of the saloon.

He ran as fast as he could, stumbling through the two feet of snow on the ground, until he came to the back door of the boardinghouse, where the rest of the men were staying.

He pounded up the stairs and burst into Berlin's room without knocking.

"What the . . . ?" Berlin said, jumping out of bed, his pistol in his hand.

"Soldiers, Ozark, 'bout seventeen of 'em an' they're headin' up Main Street as big as you please."

Berlin began pulling his trousers on over his longhandles. "Get the rest of the men up and ready," he ordered.

Within several minutes, the entire gang was gathered in the sitting room of the boardinghouse. Berlin began to give orders rapidly. He assigned six men to upstairs windows with rifles, and told the rest to sneak out the door and spread out in the alleys fronting Main Street.

"We'll catch the dumb bastards in a crossfire," he said, checking the loads in his pistol as he spoke.

As they walked their horses down the middle of Main Street, Goodson tried to reason with Woodcock one last time. "Let me get the men to dismount an' spread out, Lieutenant," he pleaded. "We're easy targets out in the middle of the street like this."

Lieutenant Woodcock glanced around at the town. There were only a couple of miners visible on the boardwalks, and no horses were seen reined in front of the various saloons at this early hour.

"I think we're wasting our time, Sergeant. I see no

evidence of thirty men gathered in this town. Perhaps the outlaws were caught in that storm and haven't made it down out of the mountains yet."

"Just the same, sir," Goodson began, but he never got to finish his sentence.

Explosions of gunfire erupted from the upper stories of a boardinghouse to their right, knocking four soldiers out of their saddles without warning.

The soldiers' horses began to crow-hop and jump under the onslaught of the fire from above, making the soldiers unable to return fire.

Just as Goodson got his mount under control, men began to pour out of alleys and doorways on either side of them, firing and shooting as fast as they could.

Lieutenant Woodcock was hit in the left arm and stomach and blown off his horse, along with seven more of his men, in the first volley of gunfire.

Goodson leaned over the neck of his horse, pulling his Colt from its holster, as he spurred his mount forward toward the men in the street.

He got off three shots, killing two of the outlaws before a bullet hit him square in the forehead, blowing brains and hair out of the back of his skull. Goodson was dead before his body hit the ground.

The last four soldiers managed to wound only two more of the outlaws before they were killed in the assault. Main Street of Rifle, Colorado, was immersed in a heavy cloud of cordite and gun smoke when the battle ended, just three minutes after it began.

The townspeople, showing good sense, remained indoors, not wanting any part of whatever was going on in their town.

Berlin reloaded his pistol as he walked among the dead and dying soldiers, some of whom were moaning and crying for help as they lay in the bloodstained snow of Main Street.

"Hey, Ozark," Blue Owl called. "There's an officer here who's still alive."

Berlin strolled over to where Blue Owl was standing over a man with lieutenant's bars on his uniform.

Berlin squatted in front of Woodcock, who was holding his stomach and groaning in pain.

Berlin slapped him in the face to get his attention. "Lieutenant, how'd you know we was here?" he asked.

"Go to hell," Woodcock grunted, staring at Berlin with hatred.

Berlin cocked his pistol and put it against Woodcock's right knee. "I'm gonna ask you one more time, Lieutenant. Who told you we was here?"

"You wouldn't dare!" Woodcock said, his eyes wide with fear and pain.

Berlin pulled the trigger, blowing Woodcock's right kneecap off and shattering the bones of his leg.

"Aiyeee!" screamed Woodcock, rolling to the side and retching in the snow next to where he lay.

Berlin rolled him back over and put the pistol against his left knee. "You gonna answer me?" he growled.

"All right . . . we got a wire from an Army Sergeant in Grand Junction," Woodcock rasped, barely able to speak. "He said you'd killed all his men and were headed this way."

"Son of a bitch," Blue Owl said. "We must've let one of those soldiers live back in the mountains."

Berlin stood up and holstered his pistol. "Well, this changes our plans a mite. We gotta get movin', 'fore somebody else gets on our trail."

"You gonna finish this one off?" Blue Owl asked.

Berlin looked down at Woodcock, who was watching blood pump from his shattered leg.

"Naw, the bastard'll be dead in five minutes the way he's leakin' blood all over the ground. Let him suffer as long as he lasts."

"What are we gonna do now?" Blue Owl asked.

"Round up the men. We're headin' south."

12

As soon as the snowplow engine made it to the train station at Crested Butte, Colorado, Sergeant Bob Guthrie thanked the engineer for his help and jumped to the ground. He ran as fast as he could through the several feet of accumulated snow to the office, and asked for directions to the sheriff's office in town.

"You can't hardly miss it, stranger," the laconic stationmaster drawled. He walked to the door and pointed down the main street. "Ain't but one street in Crested Butte, an' the sheriff's office is smack dab in the middle, on the left 'bout halfway down the street."

"Thanks," Guthrie said, already moving in the direction the man had pointed.

When he got to the sheriff's office, he entered, to find a long, tall man, thin as a string bean, sitting leaned back in his desk chair with his boots on the desk and a steaming mug of coffee wrapped in his hands on his chest.

"Howdy, mister," the sheriff said. He inclined his head toward a potbellied stove in a corner with a pot of coffee warming on the top. "Grab yourself some coffee to ward off the chill and have a seat."

Guthrie slapped his arms against his chest, kicked snow off his boots, and made his way toward the coffeepot.

"If you call this a chill, I'd hate to see what it's like when you say it's cold," he said.

The sheriff smiled. "Oh, this is just a little fall storm. We won't get the real cold weather for another month or so."

Guthrie poured the coffee, which was so dark and thick he thought it could float a horseshoe, and walked over to take a chair in front of the sheriff's desk.

"I'm Wally Pepper," the sheriff said, "and if you're looking for the law in this town, I guess I'm it."

"I'm Sergeant Bob Guthrie," Guthrie said, holding his mug with both hands as he sipped, trying to stop shaking from the cold.

"Well, we're a mite far from any Army posts, Sergeant," Pepper said, putting his feet on the ground and leaning forward with his elbows on the desk.

"That's what I'm here about," Guthrie said. "About two weeks ago, thirty of the worst killers in Utah escaped from the territorial prison."

Pepper's eyes narrowed and his expression became more serious.

"Since then, the desperados have been making their way in this direction," Guthrie said. "Along the way, they've slaughtered over forty men in my command, along with an unknown number of civilians in Lode, Utah, and Rangely, Colorado."

Pepper pursed his lips as he ran a hand over a two-day growth of beard. "You say there's thirty of these killers?"

"Thereabouts," Guthrie answered. "Before I came down here, I wired the Army post at Glenwood Springs in hopes they'd send some men to Rifle to see if they could stop the bastards before they killed anyone else."

"Ain't no telegraph in Rifle," Pepper said, as if to himself, "so I guess we won't know for a while if they managed to do any good or not."

"That's what I wanted to talk to you about, Sheriff. If the Army failed to stop them, an' they keep on their same track, they'll be headed here to Crested Butte in the next few days."

"And you think we ought'a arrange a little welcome for these killers?" the sheriff asked, a slow grin curling his lips up over blackened stubs of teeth.

Guthrie leaned back in his chair, glad to see the sheriff was getting his drift. "Yes, sir. They are all hardened criminals with nothing to lose, so they kill at the drop of a hat."

"And I guess I can assume they're well armed?"

"They've stolen all the rifles and ammunition, along with considerable amounts of dynamite and gunpowder, they need to go through this town like grain through a goose," Guthrie said.

"Well," the sheriff said, "we'll see about that. The miners in this town work hard for their money, and they ain't exactly gonna be thrilled at the idea of a bunch of prison rats trying to steal it."

"I don't mean to push, Sheriff, but we may not have much time."

Pepper held up his hand. "Hold onto your water, Sergeant. We got us a fire bell at the end of town. Come on with me and I'll ring the damned thing and before you know it, the town'll be full of men armed to the teeth, ready and willing to fight for what's theirs."

True to his word, in less than an hour, Sheriff Pepper had over a hundred men gathered in front of his office, and about thirty women who looked every bit as hard.

"Folks," the sheriff said, standing on the boardwalk in front of the crowd. "The sergeant here tells us we got us a gang of cutthroats and killers headed this way. They've managed to make a mess of a couple of towns on the way here, and the sergeant is worried they might do the same to Crested Butte."

One of the men, heavyset, with arms as big around as barrels and a full beard, held up a short-barreled shotgun. "You tell the sergeant to step back outta the way, Sheriff, an' watch us teach those bastards a lesson they won't soon forget!" the man shouted, to resounding cheers and yells from the rest of the crowd.

"Jacob, I'm glad to hear you say that," Sheriff Pepper said. "Why don't you and Billy Bob and Sammy head on up north of town and stake out the trail coming from Rifle. If you see those sons of bitches headed this way, you scamper on back here and let us know."

As the men in the crowd nodded agreement with this plan, the sheriff rubbed his hands together. "Meanwhile, I'd suggest most of you stay here in town for the next couple of days in case we need you." He hesitated, then grinned. "I'm sure Sadie and the rest of her girls can use the extra income."

"You're right about that, Sheriff," a woman with a large feather hat and painted face hollered. "And to make sure everybody has a good time, drinks are gonna be half price till the outlaws are killed."

A young man who looked to be no more than eighteen years old hollered back, "How about the rest of your merchandise, Sadie? That half price too?"

Sadie threw back her head and laughed. "I'll tell you what, Joe. You last longer'n ten minutes, an' you can have it for free!"

The crowd yelled their approval as the young man's face turned beet red, until finally he began to laugh too.

The sheriff took Guthrie to a nearby boardinghouse, and offered to buy him supper for him taking the trouble to travel through the mountain passes to bring them a warning.

Guthrie shook his head. "That's not necessary, Sheriff. Those bastards killed my men, an' my commanding officer. I intend to track 'em until either they're all dead an' buried, or I am."

Sheriff Pepper nodded. "Vengeance is a powerful motivator, Sergeant. Just be sure it don't cloud your mind enough to cause you to make fatal mistakes."

"Those *bandidos* made the mistake, Sheriff, when they killed my friends. I ain't gonna rest till they're made to pay for what they done."

As they headed out of Rifle, Ozark Jack Berlin sent a half-breed Indian named Spotted Dog ahead to check out the trail. Spotted Dog had been a scout for the Army, until the day he'd raped and killed a ten-year-old girl who'd wandered off the Army base.

Luckily for Spotted Dog, he'd managed to get away from the post before he was caught. Otherwise, he'd never have lived long enough to be sentenced to hang. The escape from the territorial prison had come one month to the day before he was due to be executed.

Spotted Dog was an excellent tracker, and headed out ahead of the gang, staying off the trail so he wouldn't be seen by anyone who might be waiting for them.

The gang was just rounding a turn in the trail when Spotted Dog came galloping toward them.

Berlin held up his hand, halting his men, and sat waiting for Spotted Dog to arrive.

"Ozark," he yelled as he reined his sweating horse to a halt in front of Berlin.

"Yeah, what'd you see, Dog?" Berlin asked, bending into the wind to light a cigar.

"There are several men ahead, waiting in ambush in rocks that look down on the trail."

"How many you talkin' 'bout?"

"I see four, but may be more in bushes," Spotted Dog answered, accepting a small bottle of whiskey Blue Owl offered and taking a long drink.

"They must've gotten word we was comin' somehow," Berlin said, almost as if to himself.

"You think it could'a been that sergeant that officer told us about in Rifle?" Blue Owl asked.

Berlin shrugged. "Don't really matter who or how; fact is, we got to change our plans now," he said. "If they got men on the trail out here, then the town's bound to be ready for us too."

Berlin sat there in his saddle, thinking and smoking for a few minutes. Finally, his gaze lit on the railroad tracks off to the left of the trail, and he nodded.

"I know what we're gonna do."

He jerked his horse's head around and began to ride out cross-country, having to go slow through the snow.

Blue Owl rode next to him, the gang following along behind.

"Where the hell you goin', Boss?" Blue Owl hollered, trying to be heard over the wind.

"We're goin' to catch a train, Blue Owl," Berlin answered.

13

Ozark Jack Berlin led his gang cross-country, keeping the small buildings of Crested Butte, Colorado, in view off to their left. He stopped occasionally to consult the map he'd taken from the general store in Lode, checking to make sure they were headed in the general direction the train tracks took when they left the town.

A little over four hours after leaving the trail, they crossed the tracks several miles from the southern limits of Crested Butte.

Berlin followed the tracks until they made a wide turn around a small hillock. He reined his horse to a stop.

"Blue Owl, take a couple of sticks of dynamite and blow that big maple tree down over there," he said, pointing to a large tree next to the tracks.

"All right," Blue Owl said, reaching into his saddlebags.

After the tree had been felled and was lying across the tracks, Berlin led his men back into a strand of trees and out of sight.

"When is the train due?" Wiley Gottlieb asked.

"How the hell should I know?" Berlin answered.

"Well, should we make a fire and cook some coffee?" Gottlieb asked. "I'm 'bout near frozen through."

"Sure," Berlin answered, "but try an' use old wood so

it won't smoke so much. We don't want them to see the smoke over in Crested Butte."

The men managed to get their fill of hot coffee, laced with whiskey, before the mournful whistle of the oncoming train sounded about an hour later.

"Mount up, men," Berlin shouted. "We got us a train to catch."

When the train rounded the bend in the tracks, the engineer saw the tree blocking the rails and hit the brakes, causing the wheels to lock and send up bright red and orange sparks as the train slowed.

Berlin shouted, "Let's ride!" and led the way out of the trees and down the slight slope toward the train before it had stopped completely.

The engineer held up his hands and stepped to the doorway of the engine when he saw the gang of outlaws riding toward him with guns drawn.

He stood there until Berlin reined to a halt next to the engine.

"You gents are outta luck," the engineer said, a worried frown on his face. "We ain't carryin' no money nor gold on this trip."

Berlin grinned. "You got us wrong, mister," he said. "We ain't gonna rob you . . . we just want a ride."

While some of the gang tied ropes to the tree and pulled it off the tracks, others went car to car, confiscating weapons and what small amounts of money and jewelry the passengers had.

Once they had everyone covered, they went to the baggage cars, threw the suitcases and valises out onto the ground, placed ramps up to the cars, and led their horses onto the train.

While they were loading the horses, Berlin had Spotted Dog climb up the telegraph pole near the track and cut the wires to keep anyone in Crested Butte from warning the towns down the line that they were on their way.

While Spotted Dog was cutting the wires, Berlin took four sticks of dynamite and stuffed them under the tracks behind the train. When the dynamite exploded, the rails were left bent and curled, with twenty feet of track destroyed.

"Now, won't have to worry 'bout nobody comin' after us on this track," Berlin muttered to himself as he surveyed the damage.

When they had everything loaded, Berlin sent Billy Bartlett up to the engine to tell the engineer to start the train.

As it began to slowly move forward, Berlin put all the passengers into one car with a couple of men left to keep them covered, and told the rest of his men to spread out and get some sleep.

"Where we goin'?" Jack McGraw asked.

"I'd like to put a few hundred miles 'tween us an' the Army," Berlin said, glancing again at his map. "I figure we can ride this train down near Pueblo an' get off there. That ought'a be far enough to throw 'em off our trail."

Sergeant Bob Guthrie was having breakfast the next morning with Sheriff Waldo Pepper at the boarding-house where he was staying while in Crested Butte.

Pepper finished his eggs and bacon, sopped up some gravy on his biscuit, and stuffed it in his mouth. As he chewed, he pulled out his pocket watch.

"It looks like your bandits ain't gonna be coming this way after all, Sergeant," he said in his husky voice. "Maybe the Army men you sent after 'em from Glenwood Springs got 'em after all."

Guthrie shook his head. "Maybe, Sheriff, but it just don't figure."

"Well, they've had plenty of time to get here by now if they was coming," the sheriff said, leaning back in his chair and sipping his coffee.

"You're right about that," Guthrie said. "Maybe we

oughta take a ride out to the men you've got stationed north of town and see if they've seen or heard anything."

Pepper shrugged. "If you say so, Sergeant, but I'm beginning to think this is a waste of time."

They saddled up their horses and rode northward out of town, toward the sentries Pepper had placed there.

They hadn't traveled more than a few miles before Guthrie slowed his horse and shaded his eyes against bright sunlight.

"What's that you see?" Pepper asked, following the sergeant's gaze.

"Smoke," Guthrie answered shortly. "The damn fools you've got on sentry duty have a fire goin'."

Pepper shrugged. "So what? It's damn cold out here."

Guthrie gave him a look, his eyes flat. "If we can see the smoke, Sheriff, the outlaws can too. You think they're dumb enough to ride into an ambush?"

"I didn't think of that," the sheriff replied.

"Come on," Guthrie said, spurring his horse forward.

When they got to the small rise where the sentries were keeping watch, they found them sitting around a large fire, holding their hands out to keep them warm.

"Howdy, Sheriff," one of the men called. "We ain't seen hide nor hair of anybody all morning."

Guthrie just shook his head, muttering to himself as he turned his horse's head northward and rode up the trail toward Rifle, followed by Sheriff Pepper.

Two miles from the sentry post, they came upon a collection of horse tracks still evident in the snow on the trail. The tracks showed where the gang had stopped and milled around for a while. Then the tracks led off the trail cross-country to the southwest.

Guthrie leaned over his horse's head, his arms crossed on his saddle horn. "Looks like the outlaws saw your sentries an' decided to take out cross-country, Sheriff."

"Damn!" Sheriff Pepper growled. "There ain't nothing

out there for a hundred miles, 'cept mountains. If they try and cross those on horseback in this weather, they're gonna freeze to death 'fore too long."

Guthrie shook his head. It just didn't make sense. The outlaws weren't that stupid, he thought to himself.

He walked his horse off the trail, following the outlaws' tracks. After twenty yards, he came to the railroad tracks.

"Son of a bitch," he said, slapping his thigh.

"What is it?" Pepper asked, coming up next to him.

"Which way does the railroad go when it leaves Crested Butte?" he asked.

"Why, it curves off to the southwest 'bout a mile or two out of town," Pepper answered.

Guthrie jerked his horse's head around. "Come on, Sheriff. I think the outlaws plan to stop the train after it leaves town and use it to get out of the area."

"Damn!" Pepper said. "I hope we're not too late. We had a train go through town yesterday."

When they got back to Crested Butte, a man ran out into the street, waving his arms at them.

"Who's that?" Guthrie asked as they slowed their horses.

"It's Sam Wright, the telegraph operator."

"Sheriff," Wright said when they stopped in front of him. "The telegraph line is down south of town. I ain't gettin' no signal at all."

Pepper looked over at Guthrie. "Looks like you was right, Sergeant."

"You better get some men together an' let's go see if we can fix the wire," Guthrie said. "And tell the station-master to hold the next train when it gets to town. He's gonna have another passenger."

"I'll be goddamned," Pepper said two hours later when they came upon the destroyed track.

Guthrie sighed. "How long will it take you to get the track repaired?" he asked.

Pepper shrugged. "At least a couple of days in this weather."

"Maybe we can fix the wire an' send a message on down the tracks," Wright said hopefully.

Guthrie shook his head. "The outlaws are too smart for that," he said. "They'll probably stop the train every few hours an' cut the wire in a different place. I think our only chance is to work fast to get this track repaired and go after them by train, at least until I can get to a town that has a workin' telegraph."

Pepper nodded. "I'll get every man in town working on fixing the rails. Maybe we can cut the time down to one day."

Guthrie nodded. "I'll contact the stationmaster in town and see if we can get an engine down here that might be able to catch them 'fore they get too far. If we cut all the cars loose, I can make faster time than they can."

Pepper's gaze followed the tracks as they disappeared in the distance. "I wonder what they're gonna do with all the passengers on that train they stopped."

Guthrie stared at him, his eyes haunted. "You probably don't want to know, Sheriff."

14

The train carrying the outlaws sped through mountain passes, stopping only to take on water when the boiler got low. There was plenty of food, so on the few occasions when they came to small towns, Berlin had the engineer keep the train at full speed through the stations.

Once his men were rested up from their long journey on horseback from Rifle to Crested Butte, Berlin decided to do something about the passengers.

He had the engineer stop the train on one of the mountain passes, high among the peaks of the Rockies.

He pulled his pistol from its holster and walked back to the passenger car where the civilian prisoners were being kept under watch by his men.

"All right," he called from the front of the car. "All you men, get your belongings together and get off the train."

One of the men, a drummer selling the latest in mining tools, stood up, terror in his eyes. "You aren't going to shoot us, are you, mister?" he asked, his hands trembling as they held his bowler hat in front of him.

Berlin grinned. "Nope, I'm just gonna put you off the train so's my men won't have to spend all their time watchin' you."

Another man, dressed in dungarees and a heavy buckskin coat, leaned over to glance out the window. "They won't have to shoot us, drummer," he said, pulling his coat tight around him as he straightened up. "Chances are, we're gonna freeze to death soon as the sun goes down."

"You can't do this to us," a woman traveling with a daughter in her teens cried. "We'll all die out here in the wilderness without food or water."

Berlin shook his head. "Oh, don't worry, miss," he said, his voice husky. "I ain't throwin' you women off the train, just the men."

The cowboy in the buckskin coat shook his head, took a leather valise down from the rack over the seats, and walked toward the door to the car, mumbling, "You'd be better off with us, lady."

Once the male passengers were all off the car, standing in a group next to the tracks, Berlin told one of his men to have the engineer start the train.

As the whistle blew and steam poured from the engine and the wheels began to roll slowly down the track, he put his pistol back in his holster and walked over to stand before the girl in her teens sitting next to her mother.

"You," he said, grabbing the girl by her wrist, "come with me. I got something to show you up in my car."

"Let her go!" the mother screamed, reaching for his arm.

Wiley Gottlieb stepped over and pulled her back. "Take it easy, Mama. You're gonna be busy enough back here with us so's you won't have to worry none 'bout your little girl."

The rest of the men laughed and moved forward, grabbing the other women on the train, even the seventy-year-old grandmother in the front seat.

The work crew from Crested Butte, working well into the night, managed to get the tracks repaired in sixteen hours.

After Sheriff Pepper stopped the next train through the

town, Guthrie had the conductor disconnect all the passenger cars, leaving only the engine and coal car attached.

Guthrie stepped onto the engine platform, leaned down, and shook Sheriff Pepper's hand. "Thanks, Sheriff, for all you and your men done."

"You sure you don't want some of us to ride along with you?" the sheriff asked.

Guthrie shook his head. "It ain't your problem now, Sheriff, but you could do something else for me."

"What's that?"

"Have your telegraph operator wire some of the towns to the north, where the wires ain't been cut. Then, they can try to wire other towns in a circle around us until they get word to Pueblo to be on the lookout for the stolen train."

"Damn, that's a good idea," Sheriff Pepper said.

Guthrie shrugged. "It's worth a try, though with these winter storms, some of the other lines might be down too. If they manage to get through, tell the sheriff in Pueblo to try an' get the Army to send some men to help. It's too big a job for one or two men to handle alone."

"You got it, Sergeant."

"Adios, Sheriff Pepper. Try not to freeze your balls off this winter."

Pepper grinned and tipped his hat as the train pulled out of the station. "I'll sure do my best, Sergeant," he called.

The next morning, after twelve straight hours riding the engine through the mountains, Guthrie came upon the group of men Berlin had kicked off his train.

He had the engineer stop the train when he saw the group huddled around a fire next to the tracks. Two bodies lay nearby, covered with pine tree branches.

"Thank God!" the drummer hollered, running for the engine.

Soon, the men had filled Guthrie in on what Berlin had done, and how he'd kept the women on board.

"Come on up," Guthrie said. "It's gonna be crowded with all of you in the engine, so leave the dead ones where they are. We'll send someone back for 'em from the next town."

As the cowboy in the buckskin coat swung on board, he looked at Guthrie. "You goin' after those bastards all by yourself?"

Guthrie nodded.

The cowboy grinned. "If you don't mind, I might just ride along with you for a spell."

"This ain't your fight, cowboy," Guthrie said, his eyes narrow.

"It is now!" the cowboy growled. "Back in Texas, where I hail from, we don't let men treat womenfolk that way and get away with it."

"These are pretty dangerous men, Texas," Guthrie said evenly, letting his eyes fall to the empty holster on the cowboy's belt, noting it was tied down low on his hip.

"So am I, Army," the cowboy replied. "So am I."

15

Smoke Jensen and Pearlie were riding in the back of a buckboard, throwing bales of summer hay off for the cattle to eat, while Cal drove the wagon.

"I can't hardly believe we got snow coverin' the ground so early in the season," Pearlie complained, straightening up and sleeving sweat off his brow.

Smoke glanced at heavy dark clouds covering the sky. "Yeah, looks like it's gonna be a cold winter this year."

Cal laughed from the front of the wagon. "Hell, I ain't never seen a warm one up here in the high lonesome, Smoke," he said.

"I told you when I saw how fat the squirrels were getting from eating all those acorns, it was going to be a particularly bad one this year," Smoke said.

"Hold on a minute, Cal," Pearlie said. "I want to build me a smoke 'fore you take off again."

Cal stood up and climbed over the seat to join Smoke and Pearlie in the back of the buckboard. "I think I'll have one with you," he said.

"Be careful you don't set this hay to burning," Smoke said.

"Hell," Pearlie replied as he put a lucifer to his butt, "least it'd keep us warm."

Smoke had started to reply when he noticed a trio of riders coming toward them across his ranch.

"Looks like we got company coming," he observed, sitting on a bale and pulling a long, black cigar out of his pocket.

He'd just gotten it lit when Sheriff Monte Carson and two other men reined in next to the wagon.

"Howdy, Monte," Smoke called. "What brings you out here on such a cold morning?"

"Smoke, I got some bad news. This here is Sergeant Bob Guthrie, from Utah, and Jed McCulloch, from Texas."

Smoke looked at the two men Monte introduced. He liked what he saw. Guthrie was of medium height, broad-shouldered, with a square body and a face wrinkled from years under the sun. McCulloch was tall and lanky, with a wiry build, sky-blue eyes, dark, unruly hair under a large, Texas-style Stetson hat, and a grin that made him look like a kid in his teens.

Smoke smiled. "You any relation to Big Jake McCulloch down in Texas?" he asked the Texan.

Jed's lips curled in an answering grin and he nodded. "He's my uncle."

"I met Big Jake a couple of years ago when I was down at the King Ranch getting some breeding stock. Jake's ranch is only slightly smaller than King's," Smoke said.

Jed nodded. "That's right, but Jake's has got better grass, and better stock."

Smoke laughed. "So I hear."

He turned his attention back to Monte Carson. "What's the bad news, Monte?"

"You remember those escaped outlaws I told you about last week? The ones escaped from the territorial prison in Utah?"

"Uh-huh," Smoke said.

"Well, Bob and Jed here have been on their trail. Seems they stole a train up in Crested Butte a couple of days ago headed toward Pueblo."

"Stole a train?" Smoke asked. "Don't you mean robbed a train?"

"No," Guthrie replied. "They stopped the train and

got on board, including their horses. After they rode it for about a hundred miles, they put the male passengers off, but kept the women."

Smoke's eyes hardened and his jaw muscles tightened. He knew what that meant. While most men of the West adhered to a code of conduct that kept women and children safe, he knew there were some so depraved they would prey on anyone that crossed their paths.

"How'd you two come to be on their trail?" Smoke asked.

Guthrie's face got somber. "It was my command sent after 'em in Utah. They ambushed us up in the mountains an' killed all my men, including the lieutenant in charge. I been doggin' their trail ever since."

Smoke's eyes drifted to Jed.

"I was one of the passengers on the train they highjacked," he said. "When Bob here picked us up after the outlaws put us off the train, I decided to ride along. I don't much care for men who abuse women and children."

"The train carrying the outlaws roared through Big Rock without stoppin' early yesterday morning," Monte added. "Late last night, Bob and Jed came followin' 'em in their own train."

"We were dead tired after riding for almost thirty-six hours straight," Guthrie said. "We decided to take a short break for some food and much needed sleep. When we started out this morning, we found they'd dynamited the tracks behind them, evidently to keep anyone from following 'em. The sheriff here said if we wanted to track 'em on horseback, there wasn't anybody knew the country better'n you, Mr. Jensen."

Smoke looked at Monte. "You wire Pueblo to be on the lookout for the outlaws?" he asked.

Monte nodded. "I told 'em to put up a barrier on the tracks to keep 'em from blasting through town. If those bastards stay on the train till it gets to Pueblo, they're gonna be in for a surprise."

Smoke stroked his chin, thinking. "It's about thirty

miles cross-country to Pueblo, more like fifty the way the tracks go."

"I don't figure they'll stay on the train all the way to Pueblo," Guthrie said. "So far, the man who's been leadin' 'em has been pretty smart. He's bound to know they'll be waitin' for him somewhere's down the road."

"Who's the man in charge of the gang?" Pearlie asked.

Guthrie looked at him. "Ozark Jack Berlin," he answered shortly, frowning as if the name left a bad taste in his mouth.

"Ozark Jack Berlin the famous train robber?" Cal asked, his eyes wide. Cal was addicted to dime novels, and followed closely the exploits of famous men of the West, both good and bad.

"Yeah," Guthrie replied. "He's hard an' mean as they come, an' he knows trains."

Smoke climbed up onto the seat of the buckboard. "Come on back to the house," he said. "We'll get some food and provisions and then we'll see what we can do about Mr. Berlin and his men."

As they started off toward Smoke's cabin, Jed said, "We might ought'a take some extra provisions along, just in case we find the women alive."

Smoke nodded. "I'll ask my wife Sally to come along. She's pretty handy at fixing people up who've been hurt."

Guthrie protested, "This ain't no job to take a woman along on, Mr. Jensen."

Monte Carson laughed. "Wait until you meet Sally," he said. "She ain't a woman to take no for an answer if she thinks somebody needs her help."

"Still . . ." Guthrie started.

"Don't worry about it being too tough a job for Sally," Smoke said. "She came up here to teach school when there wasn't hardly nothing but Indians and mountain men and a few settlers in these parts. She can handle anything thrown at her, and then some."

* * *

Sally came out on the cabin's porch when she heard the men ride up.

"Hello, Monte," she called, wiping her hands on an apron tied around her waist.

"Mornin' Sally," Monte replied, tipping his hat as he climbed down off his horse.

"Sally, this here is Jed McCulloch and Sergeant Bob Guthrie," Smoke said, introducing the two visitors.

"Pleased to meet ya, ma'am," Jed said, while Guthrie touched his hat and nodded.

"Come in, gentlemen," Sally said. "It's a little late for breakfast, but I've got a batch of bear sign hot out of the oven and a fresh pot of coffee."

Pearlie jumped down off the wagon and walked straight past Sally toward the door to the cabin.

Cal, climbing down more slowly, said, "You boys better make tracks toward the kitchen if you want any of Miss Sally's bear sign. If we leave Pearlie alone in there, he's liable to eat 'em all 'fore we can get through the door."

"Bear sign?" Jed asked, a puzzled smile on his face.

"I think you call them *pan dulce* down in Texas," Smoke said. "They're sweet as molasses and light as a cloud the way Sally makes them."

After the men were all seated around the kitchen table, with a platter of bear sign and mugs of steaming coffee in front of them, Smoke filled Sally in on what Monte and the two men had told him about the outlaws.

Sally's face became serious when she heard about the women being kept as hostages. "Oh, dear," she said, a hand to her mouth. "Those poor women."

"I'm going to lead Monte and the boys cross-country to see if we can intercept the train, Sally," Smoke explained. "I think you might ought to come with us, bringing your medical kit, so's you can help take care of the womenfolk if they're still alive."

She nodded. "You're right, Smoke. I'll go get my things together while you men finish your food."

She got up from the table. "Pearlie, if you and Cal can

tear yourself away from the bear sign, would you get a couple of horses out of the remuda?" she asked. "I'll need them as pack animals for the supplies we're going to need to go cross-country."

"Yes, ma'am," Pearlie grunted around a mouthful of doughnuts and coffee.

"How about that buckboard?" Jed asked. "Wouldn't it be better?"

Smoke wagged his head. "The country we're gonna be traveling over won't be suitable for a wagon," he said. "It's gonna be hard enough to get the horses through the snow in some of the passes."

"You mean, we're going up over the mountains?" Guthrie asked, a look of surprise on his face.

"If you want to make up for lost time, it's the only way to go and have any chance of catching those men."

Guthrie fingered his Army overcoat. "I'm afraid I didn't come dressed for that kind of trip."

Cal grinned. "Don't worry, Sergeant. We got plenty of cold-weather duds in the bunkhouse. Pearlie and me'll fix you up where you'll be warm as toast."

An hour later, with extra canteens filled with hot coffee and a sack of fried chicken Sally had left over from dinner the night before tied to the packhorses, the group took off toward mountain peaks in the distance.

The weather was cold, but sunny, with the temperature hovering in the midforties.

"Leastways, there don't appear to be any snow on the way," Guthrie said.

Smoke inclined his head toward the mountains, where the white, snow-covered peaks were partially obscured by roiling, black clouds.

"Not for another six or seven hours," he said, "but I expect along about nightfall, we're gonna get a storm that'll drop a couple of feet of snow by morning."

"How can you tell?" Jed asked.

Sally laughed. "Smoke spent his formative years living up in the high lonesome with an old mountain man named Preacher," she said. "He learned to read the clouds and wind like some men learn to read books."

Smoke nodded. "Living up in the mountains, if you don't learn to foretell the weather, you don't live through your first winter."

16

Ozark Jack Berlin made his way through the passenger cars until he climbed into the engine compartment. He nodded hello to Jack McGraw, who was busy shoveling small logs from the tender into the furnace of the steam engine, and stepped up next to the man at the controls of the big engine. He leaned over and yelled into the engineer's ear, "Yo, I want you to stop the train when we get about ten miles north of Pueblo."

The engineer looked over his shoulder at Berlin, fear evident in his eyes. "What you want'a stop out here for? There ain't nothin' out here but snow an' mountains."

Berlin sighed. He knew the man thought he was going to be killed when the train stopped.

He patted him on the shoulder and forced a good-humored grin on his face. "Don't worry, old-timer. Me an' my men are just gonna get off the train. You don't have nothin' to worry about."

The engineer nodded, clearly not convinced, and reached up to pull the throttle lever back a few notches, causing the train to begin to slow down.

Berlin turned his back to the engineer and said in a low voice to McGraw, "Soon's the train comes to a stop, put a bullet in him."

McGraw winked and stood up, dusting wood dust and

bark off his hands as he leaned back against the wall of the compartment.

Berlin left through the rear door and made his way back toward the passenger cars.

As the train slowed more and more, he made his way from car to car, telling his men to get their gear together. They were going to make tracks as soon as the train came to a halt.

While he walked among his men, even Berlin, who was no stranger to violence or cruelty, was surprised by the condition of the women his men had been occupying their time with. Two were dead, their bodies covered with ugly black and blue marks showing they had been sorely tested before they died.

The remainder were either unconscious, or crying and moaning pitiably, most not in much better shape than those who'd been raped to death.

Just before the train came to a complete stop, Berlin heard several gunshots from the direction of the engine.

"Damn!" he muttered, drawing his pistol and running toward the front of the train. "It shouldn't've taken McGraw that many shots to kill the engineer," he said to himself as he busted through doors on his way.

When he got there, the train groaned to a stop, the engine idling loudly in the quiet mountain air.

"What the hell happened?" Berlin hollered when he found McGraw leaning out of the compartment window, his still-smoking pistol in his hand.

McGraw glanced back over his shoulder. "When I turned my head for a minute to look out the window, the engineer dove out the door and hit the ground running," he said.

Berlin shook his head. "He must've figured you was gonna shoot him," he mused.

"Yeah, I guess so," McGraw answered.

"Did you get him?"

"Nah. By the time I got my gun out and fired, he was

too far away." McGraw grinned. "He run pretty fast for an old fart, though."

"Well, it can't be helped."

"Why'd you want him shot anyway?" McGraw asked. "He ain't given us no trouble nor nothin'."

"'Cause I didn't want him taking the train into Pueblo an' tellin' the authorities 'bout us gettin' out here," Berlin said.

"Oh," McGraw said. "Well, if that's all that's bothering you, I can fix the engine where he won't be able to get it started any time soon."

"How?"

McGraw shrugged. "I'll just shut it down and drain all the water out of it. He won't be able to make any steam until another train comes along and transfers some water into the boiler."

Berlin nodded. "That's a good idea, Jack. The way we fixed those tracks back at Big Rock, another train won't be along for several days anyway."

McGraw grinned. "And without no food nor water, the engineer and the girls will probably be frozen to death by then. Won't nobody be left alive to tell 'em which way we went or when we left."

Berlin slapped McGraw on the back. "Come on, Jack," he said, "get your gear together an' let's get the hell outta here 'fore it starts to snow again."

McGraw began turning switches on the engine. "I'll be there soon's I turn this thing off and drain the water."

In less than an hour, the men had their horses off the train and saddled up and ready to go.

Blue Owl came up to Berlin, an evil glint in his eyes. "You want me to get back on the train and kill the women?" he asked.

Berlin shook his head. "No, let the bitches freeze to death," he said. "It'll be a lot slower for them that way."

Blue Owl, who had a deep and abiding hatred for all

women, nodded, his lips curling up in a smile. "Yeah. Why let them off easy with a bullet or a knife when we can let them die slow and painful?"

"Exactly my thoughts," Berlin said. He jerked his mount's head around and waved his arm in the air. "Come on, men. Let's ride!"

It was heavy going for Berlin and his gang. The trails that ran between the mountain passes were clogged with snow that reached almost to their mounts' chests, and they'd only managed to travel six miles by the time the sun began to set.

Just when he thought they were going to have to make camp in the open, an unappetizing thought with temperatures plunging to well below freezing, Blue Owl called out, "Hey, Boss, look over there!"

In the distance, barely visible through the ground fog that was beginning to form as the temperature dropped, was a log cabin nestled among a grove of pine trees. The roof had several holes in it, and the mud caked between the logs was absent in places, but at least they'd be able to get out of the worst of the weather.

When Berlin kicked open the door, the smell of the animals who'd made the place a temporary home was strong and musty.

"We're in luck," Berlin said when he spied an old potbellied stove in a corner. "Blue Owl, send some of the men out to gather wood and bring in some of our provisions. At least we'll be able to keep warm an' fix up some coffee an' grub."

Before long, with all the men crammed into a space meant for four or five, and with the stove glowing a dull red, the cabin began to heat up to a comfortable level.

While some of the men patched the worst of the holes in the walls with pine needles and branches to keep the wind out, others used shovels they'd brought along to dig down in the snow and uncover enough grass for the horses to eat. Leaving the animals covered with blankets to keep out the worst of the cold, the men gathered inside to drink hot coffee and eat jerked beef and beans cooked on the stove.

After they'd eaten their fill, most of the men got their sleeping blankets and spread out on the floor to grab some shut-eye, lying almost shoulder to shoulder in the small cabin.

Berlin took a final mug of coffee, lit a cigar, and motioned for Blue Owl and Sam Cook to follow him outside where they could talk.

He turned an old barrel upside down and placed it against the south wall of the cabin, out of the frigid wind blowing from the north.

He pulled his coat tighter around him and sipped the coffee, letting cigar smoke trail from his nostrils as he talked.

"We got to make us some plans, men," he began. "We're gonna be goin' into areas where there's more people, an' that means more law. It's time to take stock of who we got ridin' with us to make the best use of 'em."

Blue Owl upended the small flask of whiskey and took a deep drink. "You're right, Boss. We got some good men with us, but some of 'em ain't exactly cut out for what we got in mind."

Berlin nodded. "That's why we're gonna do like the Army. We're gonna divide up into squads, with good men leadin', an' mix up the weaker ones among 'em so's each squad will be more effective. When we raid, we got to hit hard an' fast an' not give anybody a chance to get organized against us. In and out 'fore they know what hit 'em."

As Cook and Blue Owl agreed, Berlin said, "So, I need you two to let me know what you think of each of our men. I don't know all of 'em as well as you two do since I ain't been inside with 'em as long as you have."

"How many squads you want?" Cook asked, thinking.

"I figure five to begin with, with six men in each group. As time goes on an' we lose men, which we're bound to do sooner or later, we'll mix 'em together, trying to keep at least six or so men in each group."

"So, you're figuring for each of us to lead a squad, so we're gonna need two more leaders?" Blue Owl asked.

Berlin nodded.

"I think Jack McGraw an' Billy Bartlett ought'a be leaders," Cook said.

Blue Owl shook his head. "Naw, Billy's too young. He's pretty good, but I think we need somebody a mite older . . . like Wiley Gottlieb."

"I agree," Berlin said. "We'll let the men know the plan in the morning, and we'll let each squad leader pick one man at a time until everybody's been picked."

Cook looked skeptical. "That's gonna piss the ones off who're picked last," he said.

"I know," Berlin agreed. "That's why we're gonna do the picking in private, just the five squad leaders. Once the men are all chosen, the leaders will tell the men who's gonna ride with who."

Blue Owl smiled. "That'll make planning the attacks easier too, not having to discuss it with all thirty men."

"So, we're in agreement then?" Berlin asked.

When they nodded, he said, "Good. Then let's get inside where it's warm an' get some shut-eye. I have a feeling tomorrow's gonna be a busy day."

17

By four o'clock in the afternoon, Smoke and his party were well up into the mountains in an area between Big Rock and Pueblo, Colorado. They hadn't yet made it to the railroad tracks running between the towns, but Smoke figured they only had a couple of more miles until they crossed the tracks.

Jed McCulloch, riding along next to Sergeant Bob Guthrie, kept sneaking glances at Sally, who was riding just behind Smoke. She was dressed in jeans and a flannel shirt, and was wearing a leather coat made from deerskins with a fur lining. She had her .32 Smith and Wesson short-barreled pistol in a holster around her waist, tied down low on her leg in the manner of a gunfighter.

Jed, though he hailed from Texas, had never seen a woman who looked so at home wearing a pistol and riding a horse, as if she were born in the saddle, and yet who still managed to be remarkably attractive and feminine at the same time.

He leaned sideways in his saddle to speak in a low tone to Bob. "That Sally Jensen is some kind of woman."

Guthrie nodded. "At first, I didn't believe the stories Sheriff Carson told us about her, but now that I see her in the saddle, ridin' along just as good as the men, I realize he wasn't exaggeratin' a bit when he said she wouldn't have any trouble keepin' up with us."

"What do you think of Smoke?" Jed asked.

"I think he looks every bit as hard an' tough as the stories I've heard about him make him out to be."

Jed nodded. "My uncle Jake told me about some of his exploits when he was down Texas way visiting the King Ranch. I thought he was pulling my leg at first, but now that I met him in person, I'm not so sure."

"Some of the more famous gunfighters out here in the West tend to make up stories to make 'em seem bigger than life," Guthrie observed, "but this Jensen feller seems just the opposite. He don't seem to want to brag about his past like most of the gunnies I've been around."

"Well, if we ever catch up to those bandits, I guess we'll have a chance to see just how good with a gun he is."

"If he's half as good as people say, Ozark Jack Berlin won't stand a chance."

Up ahead, Smoke held up his hand and reined his horse around. He glanced up at the sky, where dark clouds were gathering and moving toward them over mountain peaks to the north.

"Looks like we got a storm brewing," he said to the group. "We don't have more'n a couple of hours of daylight left, so I guess we better get to building us a camp for the night."

Everyone nodded their agreement. The temperature had been falling steadily for the past two hours, and they were tired and chilled to the bone from being in the saddle most of the day. They were all ready to take a break and have some hot food.

"Pearlie, you and Cal remember what I taught you that time we spent up in the high lonesome?" he asked.

Cal and Pearlie nodded. "Sure, Smoke," Pearlie said.

Smoke pointed to a flat area just ahead. It was a small clearing among a stand of pine trees, with a collection of boulders on one side.

"Get your axes off the packhorse and see if you can cut

us some branches off those trees to make a lean-to up against those rocks. That'll keep the worst of the wind and snow off us when the storm hits."

As the boys got down off their horses and began to unpack the tools they'd need, Smoke looked at Jed and Bob. "If you two will search around for some fallen wood for the fire, Sally can unload the provisions for supper and I'll hobble the horses over in those rocks so they'll be out of the weather."

"Why not just cut some wood off'n those trees," Jed asked, "rather than digging around in the snow for fallen wood?"

"The wood on the trees is too green to make a good fire, and it'll also give off a lot more smoke," Smoke answered. "We don't know where the outlaws may be, but it wouldn't be a good idea to send up a lot of smoke to tell 'em where we are."

"Oh," Jed said shortly, chagrined that he hadn't thought of that.

By the time Cal and Pearlie had cut enough branches to form a lean-to that would keep the wind and snow off, Sally had a large fire going and was cooking supper while water boiled for coffee.

Smoke laid out some grain for the horses, then stood in front of the fire, holding his hands palm out to get them warm.

Sally glanced up from where she squatted next to a large iron skillet full of frying meat. As she stirred a kettle full of beans, she said, "Coffee should be about ready now, dear."

The men gathered around the fire and filled their mugs with the steaming brew, glad to get something warm inside them as the air got colder and colder and snowflakes began to drift lazily down through the trees.

After they'd eaten, the men leaned back against their saddles, pulled blankets up to their necks, and either built cigarettes or lit cigars to enjoy with after-supper coffee. Sally lay down next to Smoke and pulled a blanket over the both of them as the men talked.

Jed looked around at the group and smiled. "You look like you got you a good crew here, Smoke," he said, inclining his head toward Cal and Pearlie. Cal was lying with his blanket over his head, already snoring softly, while Pearlie had a plate with his third helping of food on it, still shoveling it in as if he hadn't eaten in weeks.

Smoke looked at the boys and nodded. "They'll do to ride the river with, I suspect."

Guthrie blew on his coffee to cool it a mite, and asked, "How long they been with you?"

Smoke laughed shortly. "Seems like forever, doesn't it, Sally?"

She smiled, only her face visible above the blanket. "Yes. I can hardly remember a time when we didn't have them with us."

"Cal there looks a mite young," Jed observed. "He must've joined up with your outfit when he was just a tyke."

"That's a funny story," Smoke said, looking at Sally and grinning.

"Well, we ain't got nothin' else to do. Let's hear it," Guthrie said.

"Cal showed up on the Sugarloaf one day, wearing nothin' but rags, and tried to hold up Sally," Smoke began, then stopped. "You were there, Sally, why don't you tell it?"

"Cal was only fourteen years old that year," Sally said, sitting up a little so she could talk better as she told the story. . . .

It was during the spring branding, and Sally was on her way back from Big Rock to the Sugarloaf. The buckboard was piled high with supplies, because branding hundreds of calves made for hungry punchers.

As Sally slowed the team to make a bend in the trail,

a rail-thin young man stepped from the bushes at the side of the road with a pistol in his hand.

"Hold it right there, miss."

Applying the brake with her right foot, Sally slipped her hand under a pile of gingham cloth on the seat. She grasped the handle of her short-barreled Colt .44 and eared back the hammer, letting the sound of the horses' hooves and the squealing of the brake pad on the wheels mask the sound. "What can I do for you, young man?" she asked, her voice firm and without fear. She knew she could draw and drill the young highwayman before he could raise his pistol to fire.

"Well, uh, you can throw some of those beans and a cut of that fatback over here, and maybe a portion of that Arbuckle's coffee too."

Sally's eyebrows raised. "Don't you want my money?"

The boy frowned and shook his head. "Why, no, ma'am. I ain't no thief, I'm just hungry."

"And if I don't give you my food, are you going to shoot me with that big Navy Colt?"

He hesitated a moment, then grinned ruefully. "No, ma'am, I guess not." He twirled the pistol around his finger and slipped it into his belt, turned, and began to walk down the road toward Big Rock.

Sally watched the youngster amble off, noting his tattered shirt, dirty pants with holes in the knees and torn pockets, and boots that looked as if they had been salvaged from a garbage dump. "Young man," she called, "come back here, please."

He turned, a smirk on his face, spreading his hands, "Look lady, you don't have to worry. I don't even have any bullets." With a lightning-fast move he drew the gun from his pants, aimed away from Sally, and pulled the trigger. There was a click but no explosion as the hammer fell on an empty cylinder.

Sally smiled. "Oh, I'm not worried." In a movement every bit as fast as his, she whipped her .44 out and fired, clipping a pine cone from a branch, causing it to fall and bounce off his head.

The boy's knees buckled and he ducked, saying, "Jimminy Christmas!"

Mimicking him, Sally twirled her Colt and stuck it in the waistband of her britches. "What's your name, boy?"

The boy blushed and looked down at his feet, "Calvin, ma'am, Calvin Woods."

She leaned forward, elbows on knees, and stared into the boy's eyes. "Calvin, no one has to go hungry in this country, not if they're willing to work."

He looked up at her through narrowed eyes, as if he found life a little different than she'd described it.

"If you're willing to put in an honest day's work," she added, "I'll see that you get an honest day's pay, and all the food you can eat."

Calvin stood a little straighter, shoulders back and head held high. "Ma'am, I've got to be straight with you. I ain't no experienced cowhand. I come from a hardscrabble farm, and we only had us one milk cow and a couple of goats and chickens, and lots of dirt that weren't worth nothin' for growin' things. My ma and pa and me never had nothin', but we never begged and we never stooped to takin' handouts."

Sally thought, *I like this boy. Proud, and not willing to take charity if he can help it.* "Calvin, if you're willing to work, and don't mind getting your hands dirty and your muscles sore, I've got some hands that'll have you punching beeves like you were born to it in no time at all."

A smile lit up his face, making him seem even younger than his years. "Even if I don't have no saddle, nor a horse to put it on?"

She laughed out loud. "Yes. We've got plenty of ponies and saddles." She glanced down at his raggedy boots. "We can probably even round up some boots and spurs that'll fit you."

He walked over and jumped in the back of the buckboard. "Ma'am, I don't know who you are, but you just hired you the hardest-workin' hand you've ever seen."

Back at the Sugarloaf, she sent him in to Cookie and told him to eat his fill. When Smoke and the other punchers rode into the cabin yard at the end of the day, she introduced Calvin around. As Cal was shaking hands with the men, Smoke looked over at her and winked. He knew she could never resist a stray dog or cat, and her heart was as large as the Big Lonesome itself.

Smoke walked up to Cal and cleared his throat. "Son, I hear you drew down on my wife."

Cal gulped. "Yessir, Mr. Jensen. I did." He squared his shoulders and looked Smoke in the eye, not flinching, though he was obviously frightened of the tall man with the incredibly wide shoulders standing before him.

Smoke smiled and clapped the boy on the back. "Just wanted you to know you stared death in the eye, boy. Not many galoots are still walking upright who ever pulled a gun on Sally. She's a better shot than any man I've ever seen except me, and sometimes I wonder about me."

The boy laughed with relief as Smoke turned and called out, "Pearlie, get your lazy butt over here."

A tall, lanky cowboy ambled over to Smoke and Cal, munching on a biscuit stuffed with roast beef. His face was lined with wrinkles and tanned a dark brown from hours under the sun, but his eyes were sky-blue and twinkled with good-natured humor.

"Yessir, Boss," he mumbled around a mouthful of food.

Smoke put his hand on Pearlie's shoulder. "Cal, this here is Pearlie. He eats more'n any two hands, and he's never been known to do a lick of work he could get out of, but he knows beeves and horses as well as any puncher I have. I want you to follow him around and let him teach you what you need to know."

Cal nodded. "Yes, sir, Mr. Smoke."

"Now let me see that iron you have in your pants."

Cal pulled the ancient Navy Colt and handed it to Smoke. When Smoke opened the loading gate, the rusted cylinder fell to the ground, causing Pearlie and Smoke to laugh and Cal's face to flame red. "This is the piece you pulled on Sally?"

The boy nodded, looking at the ground.

Pearlie shook his head. "Cal, you're one lucky pup. Hell, if'n you'd tried to fire that thing, it'd of blown your hand clean off."

Smoke inclined his head toward the bunkhouse. "Pearlie, take Cal over to the tack house and get him fixed up with what he needs, including a gunbelt and a Colt that won't fall apart the first time he pulls it. You might also help pick him out a shavetail to ride. I'll expect him to start earning his keep tomorrow."

"Yes, sir, Smoke." Pearlie put his arm around Cal's shoulders and led him off toward the bunkhouse. "Now, the first thing you gotta learn, Cal, is how to get on Cookie's good side. A puncher rides on his belly, and it 'pears to me that you need some fattin' up 'fore you can begin to punch cows."

Both Jed and Bob chuckled at the tale. "That's a hell of a way to hire on hands," Jed said. "My Uncle Jake would've just shot the boy and let him lay where he fell."

"Sally's not like that," Smoke said, putting his arm around her and hugging her closer to him. "She can almost always see the good in others, even when most of us men can't."

Pearlie glanced up as he finished the last of his food. "That don't stop her from blowin' hell outta anybody that tries to do harm to Smoke or one of her hands, though," Pearlie said.

"I can see she's wearing a pistol, though I admit I didn't think she'd had much cause to use it," Jed said, eyeing Sally with a speculative look in his eye.

"Oh, she's saddled up and gone to war with me and for me on more than one occasion," Smoke said. "Don't ever underestimate the fury of a woman who's protecting one of her own."

Jed nodded solemnly. "I won't, I promise."

"How about you, Pearlie?" Guthrie asked, flicking his cigarette butt into the dying fire.

Pearlie looked up from building his own cigarette. "I was on my way to makin' my reputation as a gunslick," he said. "I'd hired out my gun to a galoot named Tilden Franklin, who was intent on takin' over the territory, includin' Smoke's ranch."

"Oh, so you also came to work for Smoke after taking up guns against him?"

"Yeah, only when the man I hired out to began to rape and kill innocent farm folks, I found I didn't have no stomach for the gunslick work, so I changed sides . . . an' I been with Smoke ever since."

Guthrie turned to look at Monte Carson, who was lying a little off to one side, quietly smoking his pipe and drinking his coffee.

"Sheriff Carson," Guthrie began, "I been meanin' to ask you where you hail from. I know I seen your face sometime in the past, but I just can't remember where."

Monte nodded slowly. "I thought that 'bout you too, Bob, an' it came to me a while back. I was in the Army 'bout a hundred years ago when I was knee-high to a toad. If my memory serves me correctly, you were a corporal when I was a private."

Guthrie snapped his fingers. "Now I remember. You was a lot thinner then, no bigger around than a stick, and had a lot more hair."

Monte laughed, patting his ample stomach. "Well, a lot of years with a woman who is almost as good a cook as Sally has added a few pounds."

Cal snorted, coming awake and raising his head. "You folks gonna jaw all night?" he asked, rubbing his eyes sleepily.

"Cal's right, men," Smoke said. "We need to make an early start and it figures to be a long day tomorrow. Let's call it a night."

18

The next day, Smoke's band had their breakfast eaten and the horses fed and were on their way by dawn. The air was bitterly cold and snow was still falling, though lightly. The new snow that fell during the night was making rough going for their mounts, and it took them almost two hours to find where the railroad tracks crossed their path.

As they approached the tracks, Guthrie rode ahead and got down off his horse to look at the rails.

"Which way should we go?" Cal asked. "What if they stopped the train 'fore it got this far?"

Guthrie straightened up from where he was squatted next to the rails. "Looky here, men," he said. "The snow on the tracks is only half as deep as on the bank next to 'em. The train must've come through here late yesterday or early last night. That means we ought'a head south, toward Pueblo."

Smoke stood up in his stirrups and looked to the south. "Your reasoning is impeccable, Sergeant," he said. "And from the looks of that smoke on the horizon, someone's got a large fire going down that way."

The group followed his gaze, and could see distant plumes of smoke rising in the air.

"You think it's the outlaws?" Jed asked, unconsciously fingering the butt of his pistol.

Guthrie shook his head. "I doubt they'd be that stupid, but if they was smart, they'd wouldn't've been in prison."

"Only one way to find out," Smoke said. "Let's ride."

Their going was faster since they were keeping their mounts on the railroad tracks, so it only took them three hours to come within sight of the fire they'd seen.

Smoke held up his hand when they crested a ridge overlooking the scene below. They could see the train engine and its cars sitting still, covered with a layer of snow. Off to one side was a large fire, with stacks of wood from the tender behind the engine piled high next to the flames. Figures could be seen lying on the ground close to the fire, covered with blankets, trying to keep warm.

"That don't look like the outlaws," Guthrie said, peering through his Army binoculars.

"No," Smoke agreed, shielding his eyes from the sun overhead with his palm. "I think it's the passengers."

"Let's hope they're still alive," Sally said, spurring her horse into a gallop down the hill.

The men hurriedly followed, not wanting her to get there first in case there was going to be gunplay.

When they arrived, they found the engineer of the train going from blanket to blanket, encouraging the women lying there to drink water he'd warmed in buckets next to the fire.

"Oh, thank God you've come," he called when he saw the riders. "I got some sick womenfolk here that need tending to."

Sally jumped down from her horse and ran to assist him. "Smoke, get some coffee going and see if you can make some beef soup with that steak we had left over from breakfast."

The engineer stood up, stretching his back. "That'd be right nice. We ain't had no food nor coffee for mite near twenty-four hours. I been trying to keep 'em alive with hot water, but they need something more'n that in their stomachs."

The women looked pitiful. Most had ugly black bruises and cuts on their faces, and some were missing teeth; all of them looked as though they'd been badly mistreated.

"Those bastards!" Sally muttered when she saw what had been done to the women.

The engineer walked over to Smoke and said in a low voice, "There's three of 'em that didn't make it. I got their bodies in one of the cars, covered with blankets."

"Why'd they let you live?" Guthrie asked. "That ain't like them to leave witnesses."

The engineer gave a lopsided grin. "They didn't intend to, that's for sure. One of 'em had me covered, and was just waitin' to plug me, when I surprised him and jumped off the train whilst it was still moving."

Jed glanced around at the women. "I guess they figured the women wouldn't survive the night as cold as it was, and didn't want to waste ammunition on them."

"You're probably right," the engineer agreed. "When I saw them take off, I snuck back along the tracks until I got to the train. After I did what I could for the women, I took some wood outta the tender and made us a fire to keep us warm and to melt some snow to heat up some water to drink."

"Why didn't you just start the engine and head on into Pueblo?" Guthrie asked.

"The bastards shut down the engine and drained all the water out so's it wouldn't run no more. Can't make steam for the engine without water."

Smoke turned to Cal and Pearlie. "Boys, get the shovels off the packhorse. If we can shovel enough snow into the boiler we should be able to get the engine running again."

"That's gonna take a heap of snow," the engineer said, cratching his head.

"Well, we can't leave you out here in this weather," moke said, "and those women look like they're going o need medical care as soon as possible."

While Sally and the engineer spooned beef soup and offee into the women, Smoke and the rest of the men ook turns shoveling snow as fast as they could into the oiler of the engine. It took until almost nightfall before he engineer said they had enough to get him to Pueblo.

While he started a fire in the engine to melt the snow nd make steam, Smoke pulled Sally aside. "Sally, I want ou to ride to Pueblo with the train. The doctor in town s going to need your help fixing up these poor women."

Sally nodded, her face grave. "Yes. Some of them are n pretty bad shape."

Then she turned back to Smoke, put her arms around is neck, and kissed him hard on the mouth. "Smoke, ou ride with your guns loose and be careful."

He nodded, squeezing her tight. "I will."

She leaned back and stared into his eyes. "But whatever you do, plant the men who did this. They don't eserve to live another day!"

"You can bet on that," Smoke said with feeling.

Just before the train took off, Smoke asked the engieer if he saw which way the outlaws went when they ode off.

He nodded. "Yep. They took off to the southwest. hat's about the only way they could go, since the passes o the north are gonna be plugged with snow until the pring melt."

Smoke glanced over his shoulder in the direction the en had taken. It was toward Big Rock and the Sugaroaf, and a lot of ranches owned by friends of his lay in he outlaws' path.

"Would you do me a favor when you get to Pueblo?" he asked.

"Sure thing, mister. Whatever you want."

"Send a telegraph to the U.S. marshal's office in Denver. Tell them to get as many men down here as fast as they can. I have a feeling there's gonna be blood all over the mountains before we're though with these sons of bitches."

The engineer nodded. "You're right about that," he said. "I've been out here a long time, and I've never seen men as hard as them."

19

Ozark Jack Berlin and his men were tired, and becom-
ng increasingly irritable from the constant cold they
vere enduring in the mountains. Most of the men were
ised to sleeping in hotels and eating at cafés and board-
nghouses. None were accustomed to living outdoors,
ind certainly not under conditions such as they'd en-
lured the last couple of weeks.

When the horse of one of the members of Jack
McGraw's squad bumped the flank of Dan Gilbert's
nount, Gilbert drew his pistol, and was on the verge of
hooting the man when Berlin drew his gun and fired in
he air.

"Goddamnit!" Berlin shouted, lowering the pistol
intil it pointed at Gilbert's face. "I'm the leader of this
iere gang, an' nobody draws a gun unless I tell 'em to!"
ie shouted, earing the hammer on his Colt back.

Gilbert, his face ashen, slowly raised his hands. "I'm
orry, Boss. I didn't mean nothin' by it."

Berlin shook his head. "Put that thing away 'fore I cram
t up your ass, Dan," he said, holstering his own weapon.

After Gilbert complied, Berlin addressed his men. "I
now we're all tired an' saddle-sore. We need fresh mounts
in' fresh grub, an' soon as we come to a ranch, we'll get

both. But until then, keep your tempers in check or I'll give you something to be mad about."

The men all nodded agreement, some pulling their coats tighter around them against the chill in the air from the north wind blowing down out of the mountains. Luckily, they were riding southward, so the wind was against their backs and not in their faces, which made it only marginally more bearable.

Berlin jerked his horse's head around and rode on down the trail, satisfied he'd kept his men in line for the present. But he knew he'd better find them fresh horses and a place to get out of the weather soon, or he was going to have a revolt on his hands, one a few harsh words and the threat of his pistol wouldn't keep quiet.

Just before noon, when Berlin was thinking about stopping for a fire and some lunch, he noticed a trail of smoke rising over the next hill.

He signaled his men to keep the noise down, and he rode ahead to scout out the situation. Just before he got to the edge of the hill, he got down off his horse and walked until he could see below.

There was a ranch house, with smoke coming from a chimney. There were no horses visible, and the corral near the house was empty, but there was a large barn fifty yards from the house, and he figured the livestock would be in there due to the recent snow. What looked to be a bunkhouse was next to the barn, with the snow undisturbed around it.

He got back up on his horse and rode back to his men. "We're in luck, boys. There's a ranch down there an' it looks ripe for the pickin'."

"How many you think we're going up against?" Blue Owl asked.

Berlin shook his head. "I don't know. The bunkhouse looks empty, an' there ain't no smoke comin' from its chimney, so I suspect the rancher has let most of his hands go for the winter."

"If that's so, shouldn't be too many to worry about," Jack McGraw growled, pulling his pistol from its holster and checking the loads.

"Well, we're gonna be careful anyway," Berlin said. "Jack, you and Wiley take your squads around to the east an' come at 'em from that direction. I'll take my men an' Blue Owl's and Sam's an' head straight down the hill. Wait for my signal, then we'll go in with guns blazin'."

"Yessir, Boss," Jack McGraw said as he turned his mount to lead his men off to the left along the ridge overlooking the cabin below.

Berlin built himself a cigarette, lit it with a lucifer he struck on his saddle horn, and settled down to wait for McGraw and Gottlieb to get their men in position.

By the time he'd finished his smoke, he reckoned the men were ready. He drew his pistol and eared back the hammer. "Let's go!"

He spurred his horse into as fast a gallop as the deepening snow would allow, and led his men down the hill toward the house below.

The people in the house must have heard or sensed something, because while Berlin and his men were still a hundred yards from the house, the door opened and a man with a rifle stepped out on the porch. When he saw the gang of men riding hard toward him with pistols and rifles drawn, he drew a bead and fired.

George Goodwin, a heavyset man whose particular specialty was robbing stages, was hit dead center in the chest and blown backward over his horse's rump.

Before the man could fire again, a fusillade of bullets from the gang spun him in a circle and dropped him on the porch in front of the door to the house.

Seconds later, a woman wearing an apron and a long dress crawled out onto the porch, took a quick look at the man, then picked up his rifle.

She jacked a shell into the chamber and began to fire as fast as she could work the lever. Two more of Berlin's men went down with shoulder and leg wounds before McGraw's men came riding around the corner of the house. McGraw, who carried a double-barreled twelve-gauge shotgun, let the woman have it with both barrels, catching her in the chest and somersaulting her backward to lie half inside the doorway, her guts spread all over the porch.

"Check out the house," Berlin called to McGraw, then turned to Blue Owl. "Take your men and make sure the bunkhouse is empty."

While they were doing that, Berlin took his men and rode over to the barn. He carefully pulled open the big double doors, and found fifteen horses in stalls in the enclosure, along with two mules.

"All right," he said to himself, "fresh horses."

When he got to the house, he was met by McGraw. "The house is empty, ain't nobody else around."

Berlin turned just as Blue Owl entered the door. "Same thing with the bunkhouse. Don't look like it's been used for a few weeks or more."

Berlin nodded. "We're in luck. This must be a small operation an' the rancher just hires hands for brandin' and calvin' when he needs 'em."

Blue Owl glanced at the bodies on the porch. "It's a cinch he ain't going to need them no more."

"Throw those bodies out into the snow so's we can close that door," Berlin said. "An' send a couple of men out there to see if our wounded are still kickin'."

He went over to the fireplace and put another couple of logs on the fire. "Gottlieb, you an' your men get in the kitchen an' see 'bout fixin' us up some grub while I warm this place up a little."

* * *

Later, after the wounded had been taken care of and the men had all eaten, Berlin sat in front of the fireplace and stretched his legs out on an ottoman close to the fire.

"Blue Owl, figure out a schedule an' send some men out to keep watch. We don't want any surprise guests while we rest up."

"The men ain't going to like going back out in that cold, Boss," Blue Owl said.

Berlin turned hard eyes on the half-breed. "They'll like it even less if they don't do what I say. The people of Pueblo must know the train's overdue by now. If they send out search parties, or somehow manage to get in touch with one of the towns we went through, they're gonna be sending men out after us. You want'a be asleep when they come callin'?"

"No, I guess not."

"Keep the watches short so's they don't get too cold. I noticed a case of whiskey in the kitchen. That ought'a keep 'em warm enough till they can get back here under cover."

"Jack, you really think they're that close on our trail?" Blue Owl asked.

Berlin shook his head. "No. I figure we got five or six days 'fore we really have to worry about anyone on our back trail. But my momma didn't raise no fools. I don't intend to be caught nappin' if they're closer than I think."

"You're right. It don't never hurt to be careful," Blue Owl said as he turned to give the orders.

"Especially if somebody else is freezin' their butts off watchin' out for me," Berlin mumbled to himself as he took another sip of his coffee.

20

Sam Cook shivered and slapped his hands against his sides while standing guard over the ranch house. He took a couple of quick sips of the whiskey he'd been given, but other than burning all the way down to his stomach, it didn't seem to help much.

This escape ain't exactly going the way I thought it would when we busted outta that prison, he thought to himself. He was more than a little pissed off that Ozark Jack Berlin had assumed he was the leader of the gang, without so much as a vote among the members, or even discussing it with anyone.

What gives that son of a bitch the right to boss me around? he asked himself for the fiftieth time. Hell, I'm just as tough as he is, maybe even more so, and I'm a damn sight smarter, thought the man who'd been arrested and sentenced to prison for beating a bartender almost to death for giving him watered-down whiskey.

He was also angry because of the squad members he'd been allotted. They were a motley crew at best, and there wasn't a one of them he'd trust to watch his back in a fight. Johnny "Four Fingers" Watson, a common footpad and burglar, had no expertise with a gun at all; Murphy Givens, in prison for shooting a man in the back, was certainly no prize when it came to courage or willingness to fight face-to-face; Josiah Breckenridge, a half-black son of a bitch, was big enough, standing over six feet tall and weighing in at over two hundred pounds, but he had the intellect of a six-year-old, hence his conviction for soliciting the services of a white woman on her way to church one Sunday morning when he was already drunker'n a skunk; Sylvester "Sly" Malone was perhaps the only man who knew which end of a gun the bullets came out of, but he had a real problem with whiskey, preferring it to water at all times, and never without one or two bottles in his saddlebags, usually more than half empty. Not exactly a man to inspire confidence in a leader, Cook thought as he tried to figure out what he should do. The other member of his squad, Phil Blackman, was laid up in the cabin with a hole in his leg from the assault on the ranch.

That damned Berlin is bringing too much attention to us, he thought as he sipped his whiskey and walked around in circles trying to stay warm. Pretty soon, we're gonna have half the lawmen in the territory on our trail, and it's just a matter of time before we're all dead or back in that rattrap of a prison, he told himself.

Finally, he made a decision. He had to break with Berlin before the fool got them all killed. His squad had been given the watch from midnight until dawn, what he'd heard cowboys call the dog watch because you had to be dumber'n a dog to take it.

He climbed on his horse and rode slowly over to round up the rest of his men to see what they thought of his idea.

Once they were all gathered together, he put it to them straight. "Men, sooner or later, Ozark's gonna get us all killed, running around shooting up the countryside like this."

"You figger on goin' up again' him?" Breckenridge asked, a doubtful look on his face. "He's meaner'n a snake, an' twice as fast with that six-killer of his," he added as he cut a chunk of tobacco off a plug and stuck it in the corner of his mouth.

Cook shook his head. "No, that wouldn't solve the problem. Riding with so many men just brings too much attention to us. I think we'd do better to go off on our own. Nobody's looking for five men . . . they're all looking for a gang of thirty."

"Berlin ain't gonna take kindly to no suggestion we split up," Four Fingers Watson said. "Matter of fact, he's liable to get downright testy about it."

"That's why we're not going to ask his permission," Cook said. He nodded at Watson. "You're an experienced burglar, so I want you to sneak down to the barn where Berlin put all the horses."

Watson looked unsure. "What if they see me?"

Cook shook his head. "They won't. By now, they're all whiskeyed up and sleeping like babies."

"What do you want me to do once I'm there?" Watson asked.

"Take one of the packhorses and load it up with as much food and ammunition as you can, then come on back up here. If we take off on our own, we're gonna need some grub to tide us over until we can get to a town."

"Where you figuring on heading to?" Malone asked.

"The closest town is Pueblo, off to the northeast. I figure if we go in one or two at a time, they won't place us as members of Berlin's gang."

"Then what're we gonna do?" Breckenridge asked.

"Stay there a day or so until things calm down, then head on off to some smaller towns, where we can rob a bank or two to get traveling money."

"What if Ozark Jack comes after us?" Givens asked, a look of fear on his face.

"He won't dare come near Pueblo. He knows they're gonna be on the lookout for his gang there, so he's bound to steer clear of that town for sure."

"I don't know," Breckenridge said. "It all sounds pretty risky to me."

"Not half as risky as riding with Berlin until every U.S. marshal and Army man in the country is after us."

After some more discussion, the men agreed with Cook's plan, and Watson got on his horse and walked it down toward the ranch, staying on the side of the barn where he couldn't be seen by the men in the ranch house.

Less than an hour later, the five men, along with their packhorse, were headed northeast, back along the way they'd come, toward Pueblo.

"We'll ride back along our back trail so as not to leave Berlin any tracks to follow," Cook explained. "We'll stay in the tracks we made coming here until we get a few miles up in the mountains, then cut over toward Pueblo."

He laughed. "By the time they realize we're gone, it'll be too late for them to take out after us."

Smoke and his party were about a day and a half behind Berlin's men. They'd been delayed by the necessity of taking care of the women the gang had left behind, but Smoke was pushing the horses as fast as he could to make up for lost time.

Luckily, the snow was helping, for the gang had left a trail that even a blind man could follow. Thirty horses riding through snow made quite a mess, one not easily missed, and the outlaws were in too much of a hurry to try to disguise their trail. Berlin had not been smart enough to have his men ride off in different directions and join up later to confuse anyone on his trail.

Smoke suddenly held up his hand.

"What is it, Smoke?" Monte Carson asked, riding up next to him.

Smoke leaned over his saddle horn and pointed at the ground. "Look there, Monte. There's some tracks coming back in this direction along the back trail of the gang. See where they cut off and head off to the north?"

"How many you figure, Smoke?" Jed McCulloch asked from behind Monte.

"Looks like five or six, near as I can make it," Smoke answered.

"What'a you think's goin' on?" Pearlie asked. "You think they're splittin' up or somethin'?"

Smoke wagged his head. "No. This looks like a party of men came back along this way six or eight hours after the main party went south. See how the snow's covered some of the older tracks, but not the newer ones?"

"If you say so, Smoke," Jed said. "I never was much good at tracking."

"Smoke could track a field mouse in a blizzard," Cal said.

"What do you think we should do, Smoke?" Bob Guthrie asked. "Should we split up an' some of us follow these new tracks?"

Smoke shook his head. "No. There's too many of them for us to divide our forces. Since these are the most recent, we'll probably stand a better chance of catching them before the larger party, so let's see where they take us."

Two hours later, Smoke once again held up his hand. A couple of hundred yards ahead he could see a group of five men seated around a small fire under some pine trees.

"You think they're part of the bandits?" Jed asked, letting his hand fall to his pistol.

"Don't know," Smoke said. "But, there's only one way to find out," he muttered as he spurred his horse forward at a slow walk toward the group ahead.

As they got closer, Guthrie said in a low voice, "Be careful, Smoke. I think I recognize that big black man sittin' off to the side."

"You sure?" Smoke said.

Guthrie nodded. "Yeah. You don't forget somebody that big, especially when he's killin' your friends."

Smoke released the rawhide hammer-thong on his Colt and kept moving forward.

One of the men looked up and saw them coming. He

rolled to the side and grabbed for a rifle lying next to the fire.

Quicker than it takes to tell it, Smoke drew and fired in one lightning-fast movement. His slug took Johnny Four Fingers Watson in the side of his neck, blowing out his Adam's apple and almost taking his head off.

As the other four men drew pistols and began to return fire, Smoke leaned over his saddle horn and took his reins in his teeth while he steered his mount with his knees and spurred him forward at a full gallop.

Cal and Pearlie drew and followed, catching Monte Carson, Jed McCulloch, and Bob Guthrie by surprise.

Pearlie's first two shots hit Sly Malone in the stomach and chest, doubling him over to fall into the fire, sending sparks and flames scattering in all directions.

Cal and Murphy Givens fired at the same time. Givens's bullet creased Cal's neck at the shoulder muscle, spinning him sideways in the saddle just as Cal's slug hit Givens low in the stomach, in the groin area. Givens screamed, dropped his pistol, and doubled over, holding what was left of his manhood with both hands.

Smoke snapped off two quick shots at Sam Cook as he dived behind a nearby tree, pocking bark off the tree but missing the outlaw by inches.

As Cook leaned around the tree and took aim at Smoke, both Jed and Guthrie fired simultaneously, followed seconds later by Monte Carson. One shot missed, the other two did not. Twin holes appeared in Cook's forehead, snapping it back and breaking his neck as his brains exploded out of the back of his head.

The big black man, Breckenridge, jumped behind his horse and pulled a short-barreled shotgun from his rifle boot. As he leaned over the horse to fire, Monte Carson shot, knocking the horse to its knees just as Smoke put a bullet in the middle of the big man's chest.

Breckenridge stumbled backward, still on his feet, and brought the shotgun up again, blood pouring from the hole in his chest.

Pearlie, Jed, and Guthrie all snapped off shots, riddling the man's body with holes and blowing him backward to land spread-eagled in the snow, blood from seven wounds staining the snow bright scarlet.

While Jed and Monte rushed to kick Breckenridge's pistol out of his reach, Smoke jerked his horse's head around and rode over to Cal, who was sitting leaned over his saddle horn, his hand to his neck with blood running from between his fingers.

"Are you all right, Cal?" Smoke asked as he jumped out of the saddle and ran to his side.

"Hell, no, Smoke!" Cal replied, a lopsided grin on his face. "I been shot."

"Damn, Cal," Pearlie yelled as he raced over to help. "If I told you once, I told you a thousand times, duck when you hear gunshots."

Cal gave Pearlie a look, his eyes filled with pain though his lips were still curled in a smile. "If I'd ducked, Pearlie, the bullet would've hit me in the head 'stead of the neck, you dumb cowboy."

Once Pearlie saw Cal wasn't hit too bad, he grinned back. "That's what I mean, Cal. Yore head's harder'n any other part of your body. Wouldn't've hurt near as much had you taken one in the pumpkin."

"Let me see that," Smoke said, prying Cal's hand away from his wound.

There was a shallow groove, half an inch deep, running from the front of Cal's neck to the rear. Though it was bleeding fairly heavily, as neck wounds do, it wasn't life-threatening.

"Pearlie, get some fatback out of my saddlebags," Smoke said. "We'll put it on the wound and wrap it tight with a bandanna. That ought to stop the bleeding."

As Pearlie brought over a slab of pork fatback from Smoke's saddlebags and unwrapped it, he shook his head. "It's a waste of good bacon to use it like that," he said.

"Well, Pearlie, I'll be sure an' save it for you when I'm done with it," Cal said sarcastically.

"Hey, Smoke," Monte called. "This one's still alive," he said, standing over Murphy Givens, who was rolling and writhing on the ground, moaning in pain.

Smoke, once he saw Pearlie was taking care of Cal's wound, walked over to the fire. As he passed, he used his boot to kick Sly Malone's body out of the flames. He rolled it in the snow a couple of times to put out the fire in the outlaw's shirt, but he was already dead.

Then Smoke squatted next to Givens and peeled the man's hands back from his wound. There was a large hole in his lower abdomen. Cal's bullet had torn through the man's bladder and coursed downward to take his penis and balls off. He was bleeding rapidly, and there appeared no way to staunch the flow of blood. The wound was too severe.

"How bad am I hit?" Givens moaned through clenched teeth, staring up at Smoke through terror-filled eyes, afraid to look for himself.

"You're hit about as bad as can be," Smoke said. "You better make your peace with whoever you believe in, 'cause you're sure as hell going to meet your Maker soon."

"Goddamn!" Givens cursed. "I knowed I shouldn't've listened to Cook."

"Where is the rest of the gang?" Guthrie asked, leaning over the dying man.

"Go to hell, Army," Givens said, noticing Guthrie's uniform. "I ain't no rat."

Guthrie straightened up. He took Givens's pistol and emptied out all the shells but one. Then he squatted again and put his face next to Givens's. "Tell us where they are, an' I'll let you have this pistol to put yourself outta your misery," he said calmly.

"Uh-uh," Givens said, shaking his head.

"All right then," Guthrie said. He turned his attention

to Smoke. "Smoke, you're a mountain man. What do you think will get him first, the buzzards or the wolves?"

Smoke scratched his chin. "With that much blood around, I'd bet on the wolves. Course," he added, "the buzzards'll finish up what the wolves leave."

"Damn you!" Givens said, holding out his hand. "Give me that pistol."

"Not until you talk," Guthrie said, his voice hard.

"All right, damn you. They're holed up at a ranch 'bout ten miles south of here," the man said, his voice harsh and clotted with pain.

Smoke looked up, judging the distance and direction. "That must be the Sanders ranch," he said to himself.

He leaned over and stared into Givens's eyes. "What happened to Mr. and Mrs. Sanders?" he asked.

"What'a you think?" Givens said. "Now, I played square with you. Give me that pistol."

As Guthrie started to hand the gun to the man, Smoke reached out and took it from him. He squatted next to Givens, holding the gun just out of his reach. "Joel and Bertha Sanders were sixty years old, you scum. They were worth more than all of you bastards put together."

Givens's voice took on a whining quality. "But they fired on us first," he croaked through dry lips.

Smoke pitched the pistol off to the side, where Givens couldn't get to it.

"When you get to hell, mister, tell the devil to keep the door open, 'cause your friends are gonna be coming soon."

Givens's eyes opened wide when he saw Smoke throw the gun away. "But you promised. . . ."

"So, sue me," Smoke said, and stood up. "Come on, I know a shortcut to the Sanders place. Maybe we can catch them while they're still there."

"What about these bodies?" Jed asked, looking around at the dead men scattered everywhere. "Shouldn't we bury them or something?"

"To hell with them," Smoke said. "Wolves got to eat, ame as worms."

As they climbed on their horses, Guthrie said in a low oice, "They didn't bother to bury my dead, so let 'em lie ere till something hungry enough to eat shit takes 'em."

21

Blue Owl leaned over the bed where Ozark Jack Berlin was sleeping and shook his shoulder.

Berlin came instantly awake, jerking a Colt from under the covers where he was holding it.

Blue Owl held out his hands, "Whoa, Boss," he said, stepping back a step. "It's just me."

"What is it? What do you want?" Berlin asked sleepily, rubbing his eyes with the back of his hand.

"We got trouble, Boss. Sam Cook and his men took off during the night."

"What?" Berlin asked, sitting up in the bed and swinging his legs over the side.

"Yeah. They snuck into the barn and took one of the packhorses, and some of the grub and ammunition too."

"That dumb son of a bitch," Berlin growled, grabbing his hat from the table next to the bed and striding out of the room.

He found the rest of the gang crowded into the parlor of the ranch house, waiting for him.

"Any sign of anybody on our trail?" he asked.

Blue Owl shook his head. "Not yet anyway. I got a couple of men up on the hill keeping watch."

"Anything else?" he asked, walking into the kitchen

and pouring himself a mug of coffee from the pot on the stove.

"Yeah. Billy Bartlett thought he heard some gunfire a little while back."

"From which direction?" Berlin asked as he blew on the coffee to cool it before taking a drink.

"Off to the northeast, he thought, though it's kind'a hard to tell with all the echoes from the mountains."

Berlin shook his head. "That idiot must've headed back toward Pueblo, right into the hands of whoever's on our back trail."

Blue Owl nodded. "That's the way I figure it," he said.

"How long ago did Billy hear the shots?"

"About half an hour."

"That means we don't have much time. Get the men saddled up an' let's make tracks outta here, 'fore they get here."

"You think they'll be coming here?" Blue Owl asked.

"Of course. Whoever fired those shots ain't ridin' around in the mountains this time of year for their health. They're on our trail, an' I don't suspect they'll give up just 'cause they killed a few of us."

"You think they got Sam and his men?"

Berlin grinned. "Yeah, an' it serves him right too. He always was dumber'n a snake. Now, let's get movin'. We're burnin' daylight."

U.S. Marshal Ace Wilkins was having lunch at the Lucky Lady Saloon in Pueblo when a young boy came running up to his table.

"Marshal," the boy cried, breathless from his run, "Jake over at the ticket office told me to tell you the train's finally coming in."

"The one that was due three days ago?" Wilkins asked around a mouthful of steak.

"Yes, sir."

"Tell him I'll be right over," the marshal said, flipping the boy a shiny coin for his trouble.

"Thank you!" the boy said, stuffing the coin in his back pocket and running out the door.

By the time Marshal Wilkins finished his lunch and walked the two blocks to the train station, the train was already in. He noticed there was quite a crowd around the passenger car, and some men were loading what looked like people into several buckboards standing nearby.

He pulled his hat down tight on his forehead against strong north winds and walked up to one of the buckboards. A pretty woman with long dark hair and hazel eyes seemed to be in charge, giving orders for the men to be gentle with the women they were hauling out of the passenger car and loading onto the buckboards.

"Miss," Wilkins said, tipping his hat.

Sally Jensen turned around, pushed a stray lock of hair out of her eyes, and said, "Yes?"

"I'm U.S. Marshal Ace Wilkins," he said. "Would you mind telling me what's going on here?"

"Not at all, Marshal. My name is Sally Jensen, and these women were taken captive by a band of escaped prisoners from the Utah Territorial Prison while on the way here. During their trip, they were repeatedly raped and beaten within an inch of their lives, and three women were killed by the outlaws."

Wilkins's expression grew hard. "How many men we talking about, Miss Jensen?" he asked, glancing at the women in the buckboards, then turning quickly away at the sight of their bruised and battered faces.

"It's Mrs. Jensen, Marshal, and I'm told there were about thirty or so."

"That many?" Wilkins said, as if to himself. He focused his attention back on Sally. "How is it you escaped similar treatment, Mrs. Jensen?"

"I wasn't on the train, Marshal. I was with my husband

and some others in a party that was tracking the criminals. I left the party to accompany the women here for medical care, while the others went on."

"And just who is in this tracking party?"

"My husband, Smoke Jensen; two of our ranch hands; the sheriff of Big Rock, Monte Carson; a Sergeant Bob Guthrie from the Army; and another man named Jed McCulloch from Texas."

"Smoke Jensen? *The* Smoke Jensen?" he asked, eyes wide.

Sally smiled. "I'm only aware of the one, Marshal. Now if you'll excuse me, I need to get these women to the doctor's office where they can be properly cared for."

"Before you go, Mrs. Jensen, do you know which way the outlaws headed when they left the train?"

"South, I believe," she said over her shoulder as she tucked a blanket tighter around one of the injured women. "Oh, Marshal," she added, turning back around. "Smoke asked if once I got here I could notify the U.S. marshal's office and the Army about the outlaws."

Wilkins tipped his hat again. "Consider us notified, ma'am," he said.

After Sally and the buckboards headed toward the doctor's office, Wilkins walked as fast as he could toward the telegraph office. With only two deputies in town, he was badly outnumbered, and he intended to telegraph the nearest Army post to ask for help. He knew he would have little chance of getting any men from Pueblo to join a posse, as they were too intent on digging in the ground for gold to go traipsing off on a chase for outlaws.

Once the telegraph was sent, Wilkins rushed back to his office to round up his deputies. Being a U.S. marshal often meant going up against impossible odds, and Wilkins didn't intend to let the number of outlaws he was chasing keep him from doing his duty. But just to be sure, he would hold off telling his deputies just how many men they were going to be up against until they were well out of town. No need to give them the bad news until it was absolutely necessary.

22

Smoke and his men cut cross-country toward the Sanders ranch. He paced the horses, knowing there was no need to hurry. The Sanderses were beyond help, and he didn't want to arrive at the ranch with worn-out mounts in case the outlaws were still there.

As they rode, Jed leaned over in the saddle to talk in a low voice to Sergeant Bob Guthrie. "Bob," he said, glancing forward at Smoke's back as he talked, "did you see how fast Smoke was on the draw back there?"

Bob nodded. "Yep. I blinked an' he already had his gun out an' was ridin' hell-bent for leather at the outlaws."

"Not only that, but he fired at full gallop and hit that first man in the neck at more'n twenty yards." Jed shook his head. "I ain't never seen shooting like that before, and I've ridden with some pretty bad hombres with a six-shooter."

Smoke, who had heard every word of the conversation, twisted in his saddle, a grin on his face. "Now, don't put too high a mark on it, boys," he said. "You're right, I hit my target in the neck, but I was aiming at his chest."

"Oh," Jed said, his face burning red at being overheard. "I guess it was a lousy shot then, Smoke. You were only off twelve inches while firing from the back of a running horse at better'n twenty yards."

"And as far as the speed of my draw is concerned,"

Smoke continued, ignoring Jed's sarcastic compliment, "I've always found it's more important to be accurate than fast. It doesn't do much good to be first on the draw if you miss and your opponent doesn't. It's the end result that counts in a gunfight."

Cal laughed at the exchange. "That's right. Smoke always says the man who ends up forked-end-up loses, no matter who cleared leather first."

Bob glanced at Cal and Pearlie, riding behind Smoke. "Speakin' of that, that was some pretty fancy shootin' by you boys too," he said with admiration.

Pearlie blushed. "Well, Smoke's a pretty good teacher. He's worked with us a lot over the years to make sure we hit what we aim at."

Pearlie hesitated, then grinned. "Course, with Cal bein' such a magnet for lead, he usually gets nicked a place or two in most every gunfight we been in."

"That's not true, Pearlie," Cal protested. "Why, only last year we had a shootout an' I wasn't touched."

"What's that, one out of five or six?" Pearlie asked. "Why, Cal, you got more scars from bullets on you than that old target we got out behind the bunkhouse at the Sugarloaf."

"That's just 'cause you miss the target more'n you hit it when we're practicin'," Cal retorted, smiling.

"I been shot a few times myself, Cal," Bob said, enjoying the easy camaraderie of the group. "It's no shame to be hit, 'specially if you live to fight another day."

Jed shook his head. "I ain't never been shot," he said. "Does it hurt much?"

Smoke looked over at him. "Not much, at least at first. Early on, the shock of the bullet hitting you deadens the pain. Often, you don't know how bad it is until later. Then it begins to burn like you've been branded."

Bob glanced at Jed. "Let's hope you never find out what it's like. For me, if I never get shot again, it'll be too soon."

Smoke raised up in his stirrups. "There's the ranch house up ahead."

Bob pulled his Army binoculars out of his saddlebags and rode up next to Smoke to get a look.

After peering through them for a few minutes, he said, "I don't see no horses in the corral, but the barn door's shut an' they could be in there."

Smoke pointed to the south end of the house. "Look over there. It looks like plenty of horses took off that way."

"You're right, Smoke," Bob said, lowering the glasses. "How can you see that without binoculars?"

"Smoke can tell the sex of an ant at fifty paces," Pearlie observed proudly. "He don't hardly ever need them glasses you use."

"It comes from lots of years living with mountain men in the high lonesome," Smoke said. "You get used to looking at things from far off. I guess the talent stays with you."

"How do you want to approach the ranch?" Jed asked.

"Let's separate and come at it from different directions," Smoke said. "That way, if it's a trap, they won't be able to get more than one of us in their sights at a time."

The men agreed and rode off in four different directions, to approach the ranch house from all sides.

Cal broke off and rode to the barn, keeping the building between him and the ranch house. He drew his pistol, eased the big double doors open, and slipped inside. In a few moments he was back outside, waving to Smoke that the barn was empty.

Smoke realized there was probably no one inside the house, so he rode up to the front, guns drawn, and kicked the door open.

Quickly searching the premises, he soon found the cabin to be completely empty. He stepped out on the porch and waved the others in from their positions on all sides of the house.

Monte Carson climbed the steps. "Any sign of the Sanders couple?" he asked.

Smoke shook his head. "No, but look there," he said, pointing to the porch.

Dried bloodstains could be seen on the wooden planks of the porch, along with blood and pieces of dried meat on the wall next to the door.

"That don't look good, Smoke," Cal said, glancing around.

"No, it doesn't."

"Uh-oh," Pearlie said in a low voice from the front of the porch.

"What is it?" Smoke asked, walking over to him.

Pearlie didn't say anything, but pointed off to one side of the house, where two lumps could be seen under the snow that had accumulated in the front yard of the house.

Smoke jumped down off the porch and went to the two forms under the snow. He squatted and gently brushed the snow aside, to find Mr. Sanders's face staring up at him through dead eyes.

"Damn!" Smoke muttered. "They didn't even have the decency to cover them up or bury them."

"What'd you expect, Smoke?" Guthrie asked from behind him. "They killed dozens of my men an' left 'em for the buzzards and wolves. I've told you before, these men are little better than animals."

Smoke turned angry eyes up at Guthrie. "Then that's how we'll treat them. We'll hunt them and kill them like the animals they are."

"When do you want to start?" Guthrie asked, a half-crazy gleam in his eyes.

Smoke stood up and brushed snow off his trousers. "First, we have to bury Mr. and Mrs. Sanders. Then we need to get some rest for us and the horses."

"And some hot food wouldn't hurt none neither," Pearlie said, glancing toward the cabin, as if anxious to see what was left in the kitchen.

Smoke smiled. "Yeah, you're right, Pearlie. Like they say, an army travels on its stomach."

"If the soldiers were all like Pearlie, they'd never get anywhere 'cause they'd be stoppin' to eat every thirty minutes," Cal said derisively.

"Well, Mr. Smart Mouth, since you're not hungry, I'll just eat your share of the grub," Pearlie said, striding up the stairs and into the cabin.

"Like hell you will!" Cal said, following close behind him.

23

U.S. Marshal Ace Wilkins rode slowly down a mountain trail that led south from Pueblo, keeping his eyes peeled for any sign of a campfire or other evidence of the presence of the outlaw band he was hunting.

Behind him rode his two deputies, Louis McCarthy and Samuel Bogart, men who were barely out of their teens but who felt it was exciting to be deputy marshals, a thought that Marshal Wilkins knew would soon sour as they found that the job usually meant long hours on a lonesome trail doing work that was ninety percent boring and ten percent terrifying.

The three lawmen had with them five privates in the U.S. Army, all that the commanding officer of the post nearest Pueblo had said he could spare. He gave as a reason continuing troubles with renegade Pawnee Indians, who'd been raiding some mining camps in the mountains north of Pueblo.

From the looks of the men sent to ride with him, Wilkins was fairly certain the captain in charge had sent his most useless troops, men who would probably be more trouble than they were worth if push came to shove.

After hearing the report from Sally Jensen, Wilkins had decided to make a wide sweep to the south, in hopes of getting ahead of the outlaws and catching up to them before they had time to get to any nearby ranches or mines and cause more deaths.

He'd twice had to twist in his saddle to warn the soldiers against making so much noise. They were talking and laughing about their good luck in going on a hunting expedition with the marshal and his deputies, instead of the boring assignments of searching frozen mountain passes for whiskeyed-up redskins.

Just as he was getting ready to call a halt to the search for the day and make camp, Wilkins's nose twitched. He thought he'd caught a whiff of smoke on the air.

It didn't smell like campfire smoke, more like a cigarette burning. The sun was almost down, and the air was gloomy with presundown semidarkness and the persistent ground fog that rose every evening as temperatures fell.

Off to their right, Wilkins saw the rosy glow of a lit cigarette among bushes next to the trail. With a start, he realized they were riding into an ambush.

He simultaneously drew his pistol and jerked his horse's head around while yelling, "Look out! It's a trap!"

Men stepped out of the forest and underbrush on either side of the trail and opened fire as Wilkins spurred his horse off the trail and over a ledge to a steep, precipitous incline.

The deputies managed to get their pistols out and fire a few shots before they were hit.

Louis McCarthy took a slug in his right shoulder, twisting him half around in the saddle so that the next bullet hit him dead center in the middle of his back, between his shoulder blades, pitching him over his horse's rump to land facedown in the snow.

Samuel Bogart wasn't so lucky. He was hit twice in the stomach, doubling him over his saddle horn and making his horse rear up and charge straight into the outlaws' guns. Bogart was hit four more times before he fell off his horse almost at the feet of the outlaws who were standing in the trail drawing down on the men.

Two of the soldiers, who were riding in front, were both wounded by multiple gunshots before they could clear leather. Both died in their saddles before they hit the ground.

The three soldiers riding in the rear never hesitated. As one, they whirled their mounts around and skedaddled back up the trail, leaning over their horses' heads and whipping them with their reins as fast as they could. The last man in line took a slug in his left buttock, but he kept riding, never even feeling the blow in his terror.

Marshal Wilkins's horse ran and jumped, trying to keep its balance as it half-stumbled down the steep hill next to the trail. Bullets whined around Wilkins's head, buzzing like a swarm of angry bees, as he did all he could to stay in the saddle. He knew if he was thrown off, he was a dead man.

Fifty yards down the hill, his mount's left hoof hit a hole, covered by deep snow, and snapped his leg like a stick.

The horse swallowed his head and sent Wilkins flying ass over elbows out of the saddle. A small Norfolk pine broke his fall, and he landed in a snowbank covering some bushes.

He lay still behind the bush as bullets pocked the snow around him, two of which hit and killed his horse. Wilkins ducked his head and cursed silently when the bronc screamed in pain in its death agony.

Two of the outlaws started down the hill to see if the marshal was dead, but stopped when one of the men sprained his ankle badly on the steep slope.

"Come on, men," that outlaw said as he clambered painfully back up the hill, limping on his injured foot. "If he's not dead, he'll freeze to death up here without no horse."

As they disappeared out of sight over the edge of the slope, Wilkins moved on hands and knees off to one side to get behind a large pine tree. He'd lost his pistol in his mad rush down the hill, and was trying to decide if he should make a run for his horse to get his long gun out of his rifle boot when he heard a scream from above that chilled his blood.

A voice drifted down out of the darkness. "Well, looky here, boys. One of those star-packers is still alive."

A raspy, hoarse voice cried, "No!" followed shortly by the single report of a gunshot.

"Damn!" Wilkins whispered to himself. He shook his head, knowing both his deputies must've been killed in the attack. So much for the glory and excitement of being a marshal, he thought bitterly as he eased over to his horse and slipped his rifle out of its scabbard. He grabbed his saddlebags, threw them over one shoulder, put the rifle over the other one, and started walking away from the trail.

If it was the last thing he ever did, he was going to make those outlaws pay for what they'd done today, he vowed as he trudged through knee-deep snow down the mountain.

Smoke was taking his watch, sitting on the porch of the Sanders cabin, smoking a cigarette and drinking a cup of coffee to keep awake while the other men slept.

The moon was almost full and cast a ghostly glow over the snow and trees of the mountainside. On any other occasion, Smoke would've been thinking about how beautiful the high lonesome is in winter. But this night, his heart was outraged at the fate of the Sanders couple, two people who'd never done any harm to anyone and who'd just wanted to live out their lives together in the beauty of the mountains around their ranch.

His jaw muscles were bunched and tight as he sipped his coffee and smoked, thinking of how sweet it would be when he finally caught up with the bandits.

Suddenly, his eyes caught movement in the trees above the cabin. He was on his feet in an instant, his Henry rifle in his hands as he stared at the trail leading down to the cabin from the mountain.

He saw three figures on horseback riding as rapidly as the scant light would allow, all leaning forward as if their lives depended on getting wherever they were going in a helluva hurry.

Smoke reached behind him and banged once on the door to alert the others they had company coming, then knelt down behind the rail running around the porch and placed his rifle on it for steady aim. He eared back the hammer and waited to see what would happen.

When the men got within a hundred yards, the one in front yelled, "Yo! The cabin!"

Smoke stood up, holding his rifle in plain sight, letting the moonlight sparkle off the barrel.

"Hold it right there, gents!" he hollered back.

"Don't shoot, mister," one of the men on horseback screamed as they all jerked their mounts to a halt in front of the house. "We're soldiers!"

"Get down off your horses and approach the cabin with your hands held high," Smoke commanded just as Monte and the others came out of the front door of the house with guns in their hands.

The three men, one of them limping badly, walked slowly toward the house with their hands up.

"Monte," Smoke said, "get some lights on, would you?"

"Sure, Smoke," Monte said, and turned back into the house to light some lanterns in the parlor.

When the men got to the porch, the leader said, "We were ambushed a couple of hours ago by some escaped convicts." He inclined his head at the man standing next to him. "My friend here took a bullet in the ass an' he needs some help."

Smoke took in their Army uniforms and saw that their saddles also had Army insignia on them, so he lowered his rifle and said, "Come on in, boys. We'll get you some hot coffee and food and see what we can do about your friend's wound."

* * *

The men were given hot coffee and some reheated biscuits and beans, and while they ate, Pearlie worked on the wound in the injured man's butt. The bullet had gone through the fleshy part of his hip muscle and posed no real problem.

"What's your name?" Smoke asked the one who seemed to be the leader of the men, though all were privates.

"I'm Marcus Giles," the heavyset man growled around a mouthful of beans and biscuit. "That there is Johnny Wyatt an' Carlos Balboa," he added, inclining his head toward his compatriots across the room.

"Tell us what happened," Smoke said.

"Well, our capt'n sent us out to ride the mountain with this U.S. marshal named Wilkins. Seems Wilkins had been in Pueblo when this woman came in on the southbound train with a load of other women who'd been beaten up an' raped by these men who escaped from the territorial prison over in Utah."

When he mentioned Sally, Smoke breathed a silent sigh of relief. Evidently she'd made it to Pueblo without any trouble.

"Go on," he said when the man paused to drink more coffee and take in another spoonful of beans.

"Marshal Wilkins an' his two deputies an' us began to move south along the trails from Pueblo. He said he was hopin' to flank around the outlaws an' catch 'em 'fore they could do any more harm."

"And you did catch up to them?" Monte Carson asked.

"More like they caught us," the man named Balboa interjected.

Giles gave him a look that shut him up, then continued his story.

"Yeah. We was goin' down this trail just 'fore dark, an' all of a sudden, from outta nowhere, these men jumped outta the bushes an' commenced to fire on us."

"The marshal led you into a trap?" Guthrie asked, a look of disbelief on his face.

"It weren't his fault exactly," Giles said defensively. "The outlaws gave us no warnin' at all, just sorta appeared."

"What happened to the marshal and the two deputies?" Smoke asked.

Giles shrugged his shoulders. "I don't know 'bout the marshal. He yelled to look out just before the outlaws opened fire, an' jumped his horse off'n the trail into the brush." Giles hesitated, a look of sadness on his face. "The two deputies an' two soldier friends of ours were blown outta their saddles 'fore you could spit."

"So, at least four men are dead, but you don't know if the marshal survived or not?" Smoke asked.

"That's right."

"And you didn't bother to go back and check on him to see if he was wounded or lying out in the snow somewhere?" Sergeant Guthrie asked, a look of extreme distaste on his face.

"No," Giles replied belligerently. "They was a whole lot of men out there takin' potshots at us. We weren't about to go back just to see if anybody was left alive. There weren't hardly no way a man could'a survived that shootin.'"

"Where did this shooting take place?" Smoke asked.

"'Bout five or six miles northeast of here."

"Isn't your post up near Pueblo? To the north?" Guthrie asked, an edge in his voice.

Giles's eyes glanced at the sergeant's stripes on Guthrie's uniform and he sullenly nodded his head.

"Then why were you traveling south?" Guthrie continued.

Giles's face burned red. "Uh, we didn't rightly know which way to go to get away from the outlaws. We was plannin' on turnin' back toward the post in the mornin' "

Guthrie nodded, but it was clear from his face he didn't believe a word the man was saying. He stood up and walked out the front door onto the porch, where he slowly built himself a cigarette and stood there smoking, looking at the stars.

Smoke said, "Finish your food, Private Giles."

He walked out onto the porch to join Guthrie.

"You think they were planning on deserting, don't you?" he asked Guthrie.

Guthrie nodded. "It's plain to see they're the bottom of the barrel. That's probably why their captain sent them with the marshal. He was probably glad to get rid of them."

"You think there's any chance this Marshal Wilkins is still alive?" Smoke asked.

Guthrie shrugged. "Most likely not, but I've known a lot of marshals in my day, an' most of 'em are damned hard to kill."

Smoke nodded his agreement. "We'd better ride on out to where the attack took place and see what we find. If nothing else, we can bury the deputies and soldiers who were killed and see which way the outlaws headed after the attack."

Guthrie looked at Smoke. "You think we should wait until daylight? I don't rightly relish the idea of ridin' into an ambush like the marshal did."

Smoke shook his head. "No, we can't afford to wait. If by some chance the marshal, or one of the other men, is still alive, they'll freeze before morning if we leave them out there. Besides, as cold as it is, the outlaws are going to be sitting around a fire somewhere, not hiding in the bushes waiting to see if anyone returns to the scene of the ambush."

"I hope you know what you're talkin' about, Smoke," Guthrie said, pitching his cigarette butt over the porch rail into the snow in the front yard.

"Well, if I'm wrong and the outlaws ambush and kill us all, I'll apologize, Bob," Smoke said with a grin.

Guthrie returned the smile as he walked into the house. "I'm gonna hold you to that, Smoke."

24

After the ambush, Ozark Jack Berlin led his men away from the area in case someone else was following the men he'd killed.

As they rode, Blue Owl pulled up next to him. "Say, Boss. You notice two of them men were wearing Army uniforms."

Berlin nodded. "I noticed."

"I thought by going south we'd get away from the Army," Blue Owl said, scowling.

"Me too," Berlin said. "At least they didn't send a whole company after us. I'm not too concerned 'bout five or six men."

"Yeah, but the Army's got telegraphs," Blue Owl observed. "They're bound to notify their posts farther south to be on the lookout for us, 'specially after all the bluecoats we've killed lately."

"I know," Berlin said. "That's why I've decided not to go any farther south just yet."

"No?"

"No. I think we'll turn an' head back up into the mountains. Long as these winter storms keep comin', it's gonna keep the Army from comin' after us in force."

"It's gonna be slim pickin's up in the mountains, Boss," Blue Owl observed, frowning. "The men are expecting to get rich robbing banks and trains and such. They aren't gonna take kindly to being told we're going back up into the high country."

Berlin glanced at him. "Don't be too sure 'bout there bein' slim pickin's in the mountains. Remember, there're more mines than you can shake a stick at, there's ranchers with no banks to keep their money in, and best of all, there ain't a whole lot of law up here to bother us."

"I hadn't thought of it that way."

Berlin nodded. "That's why I'm leadin' this here gang an' not anybody else, Blue Owl. You tell the men it won't do no good to rob a bunch of banks an' get a bunch of money an' then not be able to spend it 'cause the Army's got us danglin' from the end of a rope."

"You're right, Boss. It won't do no harm to winter over in the mountains, pick off a few mines and ranches, and then head down south next year when the heat's off and everybody's forgotten all about us."

"My thoughts exactly, Blue Owl. I'm gonna leave it up to you to convince the men to stick with us through this. The more of us there are, the less chance anybody'll be able to stand against us when we come calling."

"You leave the men to me, Boss," Blue Owl said, a hard look on his face. "Anybody don't like the way things are being handled can argue about it with my pistol," he said, patting the handle of his Colt.

"That's what I like about you, Blue Owl," Berlin said with a grin. "You have such a way with words."

Once the three soldiers had eaten and gotten their fill of coffee, and Carlos Balboa's butt wound was properly bandaged, Smoke's group saddled up their mounts and had the men lead them back toward where the ambush had taken place.

The soldiers were understandably reluctant to return to the area, but Smoke finally convinced them it would be safe, that the outlaws had undoubtedly left by now.

When they rounded a turn in the trail, Private Giles reined his horse to a halt, pointing down the path. "I think it was just up there, Smoke," he said.

Smoke got down off his horse. "You men stay here," he said. "I'll go on ahead on foot and see what I can tell from the tracks."

Smoke walked down the trail, his head down, reading tracks as easily as if they'd been a book telling him what had happened earlier that night. The moon was still up, so he had sufficient light to make out the marks in the snow.

He found where the outlaws had been camped, and saw how they'd spread out into the brush alongside the trail. Something must have alerted them to the arrival of the marshal and his men, he thought. Evidently the marshal's party had made enough noise so that the gang knew they were coming and had time to arrange an ambush. Either that, or the outlaw leader was smart enough to have men stationed along his back trail to warn him of anyone tracking them.

Smoke walked around the scene, seeing just how it'd come down. He found the dead bodies sprawled just where they'd fallen. One of the men had a bullet wound to the head surrounded by powder burns, indicating he'd been still alive after the assault and someone had put a bullet in his head at close range.

Twenty yards farther up the trail, he found disturbed snow alongside the road where the marshal had jumped his horse down the slope. There was no blood alongside the marshal's horse's tracks, so perhaps he hadn't been hit.

Smoke pursed his lips and gave a shrill whistle, indicating for his men to come on up.

When they arrived, he pointed down the slope. "Here's where Marshal Wilkins took off," he said.

Pearlie leaned over his saddle horn. "That's a mighty steep slope, Smoke. I don't see how his horse could'a stayed on his feet, 'specially in the dark."

"Speaking of horses," Smoke said. "Why don't you and

Cal ride around and see if you can round up the dead men's mounts. We're going to need them to carry the bodies when we're done."

Pearlie nodded, and motioned for Cal to follow as he rode off up the trail.

"What're you gonna do, Smoke?" Guthrie asked.

"I'm going down that slope and see if the marshal is still alive," Smoke answered.

"That's a helluva drop-off," Jed said, shaking his head doubtfully at the idea of riding a horse down the slope.

Smoke swung up into the saddle. "Don't worry, boys," he said. "This is a mountain pony I'm riding. He's used to much worse."

With that, Smoke spurred the horse forward over the hill and down the slope, taking it slow and easy and letting his mount pick the best way down.

At the bottom of the hill, Smoke found the marshal's horse, lying dead, its legs twisted under it and several bullet holes in it.

Smoke eyed the tracks around the horse, and noted the saddlebags were missing and the rifle boot was empty.

"Well, well, well," he said to himself. "It looks like the marshal survived the trip down. Now let's see if he's survived the cold."

Smoke got down off his horse and led it by its reins as he followed the marshal's tracks in the snow. He saw no other tracks, so he knew the outlaws hadn't bothered to track the marshal, which meant he had a good chance of still being alive.

After he'd gone two hundred yards, Smoke saw the tracks heading out of the clear and into the brush. The marshal was looking for cover to hole up until dawn, Smoke thought.

He didn't want to walk up on the man and perhaps get shot for an outlaw, so Smoke cupped his hands around his mouth and hollered, "Marshal Wilkins!" several times as loud as he could.

From twenty yards off to the right, Smoke heard the unmistakable sound of the lever action of a rifle.

"Marshal, we've come to help you," Smoke called. "We're friends . . . don't shoot."

A weak voice called back from the darkness of the undergrowth, "How do I know you're friends?"

"How else would I know your name, Marshal?" Smoke called back. "Some of your men escaped and brought us back here. Come on out and I'll keep my hands in the air."

"I can't," the voice said, becoming weaker by the moment. "My damn feet are near frozen."

"I'm coming in," Smoke said, and walked into the bushes.

He found the marshal burrowed down in the snow, pine boughs and limbs pulled over him to keep the cold out, his rifle barrel pointing out through the cover at Smoke.

"If you'll point that rifle somewhere else, I'll help you outta there," Smoke said.

"Come on, mister," the marshal replied, lowering the rifle. "I'm in no shape to fight back if you're not who you say you are anyway."

Thirty minutes later, Smoke had the marshal back up the slope, having put him on his horse and led the horse back the way they'd come.

"Pearlie, Cal, build a fire, quick," Smoke said as he clambered over the crest of the hill.

While Cal and Pearlie got a fire going, the other men helped the marshal off the horse and laid him on a ground blanket next to the flames.

"Thank God you came," he rasped through swollen, chapped lips. "I managed to get my saddlebags off my horse, but my matches were wet and I didn't have no way to start a fire."

"Another couple of hours an' you'd've froze to death,"

Guthrie said as he pulled the marshal's boots off and began to rub his feet.

"Oh, shit! That hurts," the marshal cried.

"You got the beginnings of frostbite here, Marshal. You're gonna be lucky if you don't lose some toes."

"Better my toes than the whole foot," the marshal grunted through gritted teeth.

Smoke grinned. He liked this man. Not one to whine and complain about his hard luck.

"What about the other bodies?" Smoke asked Jed, who was busy fixing a pot of coffee to boil on the fire.

"They looked like they'd been stripped. Their boots and most of their belongings were gone, including their guns and ammunition."

Smoke looked around and noted three new horses tied up next to his men's. "I see you found some mounts," he said to Pearlie.

"Only three, Smoke. The other one either ran off or was taken by the outlaws."

"Would you see about getting the dead men on two of them? We're gonna need one for the marshal here."

"You mean we're not going to bury them here?" Jed asked.

Smoke shook his head. "No. Seeing as how we're going to have to take the marshal back to Pueblo, might as well save time by sending the bodies back too."

"But I thought we were going after the outlaws," Guthrie protested.

Smoke glanced at the outlaws' tracks. "They've turned and headed back up into the mountains," Smoke said. "There's no hurry."

"But Smoke, what if we lose their tracks under new snow?" Guthrie said.

"We won't. Cal and Pearlie and I will go on tracking them. You and Jed can take the marshal and bodies and other soldiers back to Pueblo," Smoke said, accepting a cup of coffee from Jed.

"No! I want to go with you," Guthrie said, anger in his voice. "Those bastards killed my men!"

"Bob, be reasonable," Smoke said in a low voice. "I don't trust those other soldiers to go back to Pueblo. The marshal is in no shape to travel by himself, and Jed would only be one against three if the soldiers decided to hightail it south instead of north." Smoke put his hand on Guthrie's shoulder. "I think it'd be safer all around if you went back with them and explained things to the Army captain up there."

"But . . ."

"With any luck, you'll be able to convince him of the need to send another squad up into the mountains to go after the outlaws. Remember, there are lots of miners and ranchers up there who are going to need our protection."

"Damn it, Smoke," Guthrie argued with feeling, "I want revenge for what they did to my men."

"You'll get it, Bob. Just be mighty convincing when you talk to that Army captain."

Monte Carson stepped forward. "You want me to help you track these bastards, Smoke?"

Smoke shook his head. "No, Monte. This figures to be a long campaign . . . hell, it might take weeks before we manage to catch up to them. Your place is back at Big Rock."

"But, hellfire, Smoke," the sheriff protested. "It'll just be the three of you goin' up against more'n thirty of those outlaws."

"Like I said, Monte, that's liable to be weeks from now. The people of Big Rock elected you to take care of the town, not traipse all over the mountains looking for escaped convicts. Besides, what if the outlaws turn south again and decide to hit Big Rock? You need to be there to make sure the town's ready . . . just in case."

Monte ducked his head, turning his hat over in his hands. "I guess you're right, Smoke, but that don't mean I like it."

"I don't particularly like it either, Monte, but sometimes, we have to do things we don't want to do."

Monte turned to his horse and climbed in the saddle. "Remember, Smoke. I'll be in Big Rock if you need me."

Smoke nodded. "I know, Monte. You take care on the ride back to town, you hear?"

Monte grinned fiercely. "I just hope those sons of bitches do try to tree Big Rock. They'll be in for the surprise of their lives."

25

Ozark Jack Berlin led his men in a wide circle back to the west, edging upward into the mountain range just above Big Rock, Colorado.

"Why're we going this way?" Blue Owl asked. "Aren't we heading back toward the men who're trailing us?"

"Yeah," Berlin replied, grinning. "It's something they'll never suspect."

"There someplace special you're heading to?" Blue Owl asked as he unfolded the map Berlin had been following and laid it across his saddle horn. "I don't see nothing but mountains on this here map. No towns or nothing."

"That's just it, Blue Owl. There's nothin' up here to make them suspect we'd head this way, so they're not likely to look for us up here."

"But they'll know we're here soon's we hit some ranches or mines," Blue Owl protested.

"Who's gonna tell anybody?" Berlin asked, looking sideways at the Indian. "I don't plan to leave nobody alive to tell anybody what we done."

"But we gotta have someplace to hide out," Blue Owl said, glancing at the sky as snow began to fall again. "The men are getting kind'a tired of camping out in this weather, and it figures to be a mite colder the higher we go up into the mountains."

"Look on the map, where I made an X," Berlin said.

Blue Owl held the map closer to his eyes. "I see the X, but I don't see nothing near it 'cept the words 'Hot Springs.'"

"When we were in Lode, I asked the assayer if there were any caves up here. He said there were some old Indian caves near the hot springs area. I figure we can hole up there and make our raids from that place. It'll get us outta the weather, an' there'll be hot water to use if we need it."

Blue Owl looked at him. "Hot water? You think any of these men are planning on taking a bath?"

"You never know, Blue Owl. A few weeks stuck in a cave together may make them want to get some of the stink of the trail off."

Blue Owl laughed. "That'll be the day."

"One good thing," Berlin said.

"What's that?"

Berlin held out his hand, and it was quickly covered with snow. "This snow's gonna make trackin' us almost impossible."

"Yeah, but if it keeps falling like this, it's also gonna make it rough going for our mounts."

Berlin shrugged. "From the looks of the map, we don't have that much farther to go anyhow."

Smoke, along with Cal and Pearlie, followed the tracks left by Berlin's gang. As the snow continued to fall and the wind picked up out of the north, the tracks were becoming increasingly more difficult to see.

"Smoke," Pearlie said, pulling his hat down tight on his head and tying a bandanna around his face, "if this keeps up, we ain't gonna be able to track squat by afternoon."

Smoke, who had the collar of his buckskin coat pulled up over his ears, nodded. "I know."

He reined in, fished a compass out of his pocket, and held it out, glancing from it to the tracks for several minutes.

"What're you doin'?" Cal asked from Smoke's other side. He was hunched over with his hands in the pockets of his coat, steering his horse with his knees.

"Since we aren't going to be able to see the tracks much longer, I'm trying to get a fix on the direction they're taking right now. Once the tracks are covered up, we'll just keep going in that direction until we catch up with them."

"What if'n they change course?" Pearlie asked.

"Then we're out of luck," Smoke said, "and we'll just have to wait until we hear some news of where they hit next. One thing's for sure. They're not going to stay under cover for long without causing some trouble somewhere."

"What's that compass tell you?" Cal asked, shaking snow off the brim of his hat.

Smoke's eyes grew thoughtful. "Looks like they're making a wide circle back to the northwest."

"The northwest?" Pearlie said. "But that's back toward Big Rock, ain't it?"

"Yes," Smoke replied shortly. "It looks to me like they're headed up into the mountains north of town."

"But, there ain't nothin' up there but some mines an' ranches," Cal said.

"Yeah," Smoke replied, "mines and ranches run by friends of ours."

Two hours later, with all evidence of the outlaws' tracks completely covered, and the snow falling so thick they couldn't see the trail in front of them, Smoke decided to make camp.

"We've got to get these mounts under cover, before we get stranded out in the open," he said, almost having to yell to be heard over the howling of the wind.

"I don't see no cover handy," Pearlie yelled back.

"Let's head straight up the mountain," Smoke replied.

Within twenty minutes, they came to a thick grove of pine trees nestled up against a cliff.

"Perfect," Smoke said, getting down off his horse.

"You and Cal get some branches and tree limbs for a lean-to. I'll hobble the horses and get them some grain out of the packs."

"How about getting a fire started first?" Cal asked.

Smoke shook his head. "Nope. You're forgetting what I taught you, Cal. The horses get taken care of first, 'cause without them, we're as good as dead."

Within half an hour, the lean-to shelter was keeping the worst of the wind and snow off the men and horses, and Smoke had a roaring fire going up against the side of the cliff.

"Why'd you build the fire next to the cliff?" Pearlie asked. "Looks like it'd be better out in the open so's we could get around it on all sides."

"No, it's just the opposite," Smoke said. "Building it up against the stone cliff keeps the flames out of the wind and heats up the rock. Once we go to sleep and the fire dies down, the rock wall will continue to put off heat for several hours. That way, no one has to stay awake to tend the fire and the wind won't scatter our coals all over the place."

Pearlie reached down, picked up the pot of coffee, and poured mugs for everyone. "It's shore nice campin' with an old mountain man," he said, grinning. "You learn all sorts of things."

Smoke stared at him through narrowed eyes. "The first thing you gotta learn, Pearlie, is not to call the mountain man who's teaching you things *old*."

"Yeah," said Cal from the other side of the fire. "If you make Smoke mad, Pearlie, he's liable not to let you have seconds on the grub."

"Old? Did I say old?" Pearlie asked, smiling over his mug of steaming coffee. "I meant to say *experienced* mountain man."

Smoke laughed. "That's better, Pearlie. Now, why don't you take that skillet of bacon and eggs off the fire before all we have to eat is charcoal."

* * *

The next morning, Smoke awoke to find two feet of snow covering the ground as far as they could see. Though snow was still falling, the wind had died down and the temperatures had moderated to tolerable levels.

Smoke climbed out of his sleeping blankets, stirred the coals into life, and added some wood from the pile they'd gathered the night before. While coffee and biscuits were heating, he stepped out of the lean-to and surveyed the mountain range around them.

Soon, Cal and Pearlie stirred and squatted next to the fire, holding their hands out to the flames to warm them as they drank coffee and munched on warm biscuits with pieces of jerked beef in them.

"What's the plan, Smoke?" Pearlie asked.

"Well, it's obvious we're not going to be able to track the outlaws through this layer of snow," Smoke said, holding his mug with both hands and sipping the steaming brew.

He built himself a cigarette and lit it off a twig from the fire. "I think it's time to head for home."

"You mean the Sugarloaf?" Cal asked, a hopeful look in his eyes.

"Yeah," Smoke replied. "We need to let the horses get some rest, and if we're going to go up into the mountains and take this gang on by ourselves, I want to get some extra provisions and equipment."

"You plannin' on gettin' some of the hands to go up there with us an' help us out?" Pearlie asked.

"No. Tracking these men in the high lonesome is a job for as few men as possible. We're going to need to travel light and fast, and be able to hit and run." He shook his head. "Can't do that with a whole passel of flatlanders along to slow us down."

"That why you got Jed and Bob to head back to Pueblo?" Cal asked.

Smoke nodded. "Yes, in part. They're both good men, but neither are experienced in high-mountain tracking.

I'd hate to see them get killed because they didn't know what to expect."

"Speakin' of knowin' the high-mountain country, Smoke," Cal said, "you think we'll run into any of your mountain-man friends up there?"

Smoke nodded. "I hope so," he said, glancing up the mountainside as if he could see them in his mind's eye. "The mountain men know just about everything that's going on in their neighborhoods. If the outlaws are hiding out up there, some of the old beavers will know where."

"You think we'll see Bear Tooth, or Long John Dupree, or Bull Durham?" Cal asked.

Smoke smiled. "I take it you remember ol' Bear Tooth, huh?"

Both Cal and Pearlie nodded, smiling. They'd met Bear Tooth a couple of years back when Monte Carson's wife, Mary, had been kidnapped by Big Jim Slaughter and they had gone with Smoke to help rescue her.*

"Well, if he's still alive and kicking, which I suspect he is, we'll certainly try to find him. Nobody in the high lonesome knows more about what's going on up there than Bear Tooth. He's a natural-born gossip and likes to keep track of who's coming and going in his neck of the woods."

"He'd be a big help if we go up against them outlaws too," Pearlie said. "He's right handy with that Sharps Big Fifty he carries."

Smoke grinned. "There is that to consider too. The way I figure it, there's way too many of them for us to try and attack them head-on."

"That mean we're gonna do like them *ninjas* you an' Sally are always tellin' us about?"

Smoke laughed. "Yeah, sort'a like we did up in Jackson Hole against Big Jim Slaughter with Muskrat."

**Heart of the Mountain Man*

Cal laughed. The old mountain man named Muskrat Calhoon, because he smelled like a muskrat, had been an instant friend of both Cal and Pearlie.

"You mean, hit and run, terrorize them so they don't know who or what is after 'em, and keep doggin' 'em till they go crazy with fear?" Pearlie asked.

"That's about the size of it," Smoke replied.

"Ol' Bear Tooth would love that," Cal said. "I think he was kind'a miffed to miss out on the excitement we had up in Jackson Hole."

"If we manage to find him, and he agrees to help us," Smoke said, "I have a feeling he'll get his fill of excitement this go-around."

26

After some roaming back and forth, and checking the map again and again, Ozark Jack Berlin finally managed to find the area marked as hot springs in the mountains.

He crested a small rise in the trail and looked down into a shallow valley to find a seven-foot-wide stream winding through it with steam rising from the pool in the middle of the valley like ground fog on a humid morning. In the walls of the cliffs surrounding the valley could be seen dark openings of caves scattered around the periphery of the area. Out in the middle of the valley floor, near the steaming pools of hot mineral water, there were three clapboard and log cabins that looked to be in moderately good repair.

"Well, men," Berlin said, sitting back against the cantle of his saddle, "here's our new home for the next few months."

"I didn't know there was cabins here," Blue Owl said. "I thought you said we'd be living in caves."

Berlin shrugged. "The assayer I talked to didn't mention nothin' 'bout no cabins. Guess they been built since he was up here."

He glanced at Blue Owl. "'Course, if you want, you can stay in the caves instead."

Blue Owl shook his head. "No. I had my fill of caves back in California."

Berlin raised his eyebrows. "I didn't know the Modoc lived in caves."

Blue Owl gave a sly smile. "We didn't, usually. But once, after the Battle of Lost River, the Army chased us across some lava fields near Thule Lake. We hid in some caves and they decided not to try and get us out."

He showed his teeth. "It was a smart decision on their part. They would've lost a lot of men trying."

Berlin looked thoughtful. "You know, Blue Owl, you make a good point. Those caves would be a whole lot easier to defend if by chance somebody comes callin' on us here."

"Yeah. Those cabins are kind'a out in the open. It'd be too easy to surround them if we came under attack."

"Well, I guess what we'll do is fix up the caves with supplies an' provisions an' ammunition in case that happens. We can stay in the cabins, with guards posted on all sides to warn of any upcomin' attack, an' at the first sign of it, we'll get on into those caves, where we can stand off an army if we need to."

"Sounds good to me," Blue Owl agreed. He pointed. "See the way the caves are backed right up against the cliffs overhanging them? If we put men in caves on both sides of the valley, there ain't no way anybody could get at us without getting in a cross fire between the two sides. It's a natural fort that'd be hard to attack."

"That's what we'll do then," Berlin said, spurring his horse down the trail to the valley below.

By the end of the day, his men had the caves on either side of the valley fitted out with enough supplies and ammunition to last them several weeks in the event of a siege by the Army or anyone else. The men then spread out with minimal belongings in the cabins, which were easier to heat and keep warm, where they would stay unless they were attacked.

While several men began to cook supper and heat coffee, the other men used the time to wash out stinking, soiled clothing in the hot water of the springs. A few of the more fastidious even waded out and applied soap to bathe, to the hoots and hollers of those less concerned with personal hygiene.

Berlin and Blue Owl strolled around the camp, checking out the preparations the men had made in the caves.

"You notice the temperature down here near the water?" Berlin asked.

Blue Owl nodded. "Yeah. It's about twenty degrees warmer than up on the ridge."

Berlin grinned. "So, if we do get attacked, we'll be warm down here while our attackers will be freezin' their asses off up on the ridge."

Blue Owl walked into one of the caves, lighting a torch he'd made by twisting a pine bough around a stick of wood. As he got toward the back of the cave, the ground began to rise and the ceiling got lower. Soon, he was crawling on hands and knees.

"What the hell are you doin'?" Berlin asked, following the Indian.

"See how the smoke from the torch blows toward the entrance to the cave?"

"Yeah. So what?"

"That means there's an opening back here somewhere. I want to see if it's big enough for a man to get out of."

"Why would you want'a do that?" Berlin asked.

Blue Owl stopped his crawling and turned around. "Just suppose we get trapped down here in this valley, Boss. Wouldn't you like a back door to use to escape, just in case?"

Berlin pursed his lips, then grinned. "You got a point, Blue Owl. Lead on."

After another fifty yards, and having to get almost

down on their stomachs, they came to a hole in the roof wide enough for a man to squeeze through, if he sucked in his gut.

They exited the hole to find themselves in a small area between two tall cliff walls, no more than fifteen feet across and narrowed at both ends by bushes and small trees so that it was invisible from more than fifty yards away.

"This is perfect," Blue Owl said, looking around.

Berlin nodded thoughtfully. "Yeah. The only problem is, once we get out of the cave, we'd be on foot up here in this godforsaken wilderness. I'd almost rather be shot than escape only to starve to death on foot."

Blue Owl thought for a minute, then snapped his fingers. "I'll tell you what, Boss. Later on, when nobody's looking, I'll take a couple of the extra horses and bring them here, with enough grain and water to keep them happy. Ever so often, I'll bring more so's they don't starve to death. That way, if push comes to shove, you and I'll have a way out if need be."

"That's a good idea," Berlin said. "Why don't you pack enough grub for a couple of days and leave it here too?"

Blue Owl nodded. "It never hurts to have a backup plan, does it?"

Berlin smiled. "And enough men to keep our enemies busy while we make our getaway."

It took Smoke and Cal and Pearlie a day and a half to get back down to the Sugarloaf from where they'd left the outlaws' tracks.

By the time they arrived, having ridden all through the last night, they were cold, hungry, and almost asleep in their saddles.

As they approached the cabin, Smoke called out, "Yo, the cabin!" to let Sally know they were coming so as not to surprise her.

She burst out of the cabin door and ran to his horse,

taking him in her arms as soon as he stepped out of the saddle.

"Oh, Smoke! I'm so happy to see you."

"Me too, darling," he replied, stifling a huge yawn with the back of his hand.

She leaned back, looking from him to Cal and Pearlie. "You men look exhausted," she said.

"Cold, tired, an' most of all, hungry!" Pearlie said.

"Come on in the house," Sally said. "The fire's going and I've got a roast I can heat up and some leftover biscuits from breakfast that are probably hard as a rock."

"I could eat a rock," Pearlie said, starting toward the house.

While the men thawed out by the fire and ate roast, boiled carrots, and biscuits, Smoke told Sally of their exploits on the trail of the bandits.

After he finished, he asked her what had happened to her.

"Once we got the women seen by the doctor and taken care of, I got on the next train headed for Big Rock. By then, the tracks had been repaired and it was an uneventful trip."

"How'd you get out to the Sugarloaf?" Smoke asked.

"Louis Longmont loaned me a wagon," she answered. "He offered to ride with me, but since it was the middle of the day, I told him I'd be all right. Before I left, I wired Pueblo and told the man there to let me know of any news about the men hunting the outlaws. I knew you'd wire me if you got to a town with a telegraph, but I wanted to make sure I heard anything as soon as it happened."

She stopped talking when she noticed Cal and Pearlie were almost asleep in their chairs.

"Cal, you and Pearlie go on over to the bunkhouse and get some rest," she ordered, standing up.

"Yes, ma'am," they both said sleepily, and filed out of the door.

Sally turned to the pump at the sink and began to fill a large bucket with water.

Smoke glanced over at her. "What are you doing?" he asked.

She put the bucket on the stove and began to fill another.

"In case you don't realize it, Smoke Jensen, you smell like you've been holed up for the winter with a bear. I'm fixing you a hot bath to take before you go to bed."

"Aw, Sally," Smoke protested. "I'm dead tired. We've been in the saddle for two days straight."

She put her hands on her hips. "And you smell like you've been in those clothes for a month. You're not getting in my bed smelling like that, mister." She gave a shy smile. "Now, if you want to sleep out in the bunkhouse with Cal and Pearlie, you go right ahead."

Smoke let his eyes roam up and down her supple body. Then he grinned. "No, I think I can stay awake long enough for a bath," he said.

She grinned back. "Only long enough for a bath?" she asked, her voice husky.

"Oh, maybe a little longer than that, if I have a good enough reason to stay awake."

"We'll just have to see if I can come up with a good reason then," Sally said, a blush creeping up her neck to light up her cheeks.

When Sally went into the bathroom with her fourth bucket of hot water to pour into the bathtub, Smoke was leaning back with his eyes closed, asleep in the tub.

She added the water, then got down on her knees next to the tub. She leaned him gently forward, took a washcloth, and began to scrub his back.

As he moaned in pleasure, she lightly ran her fingers over the many scars from old gunshot and knife wounds that crisscrossed his back like a road map.

"Smoke," she said quietly.

"Yes, dear?"

"You know when I asked you to hang up your guns and not go on any more . . . hunting trips?"

"Yes."

"Well, after seeing what those . . . men did to those women, I've changed my mind."

"Oh?"

"Yes. Monsters like that need to be stopped before they kill again. If you want to go back up into the mountains and make sure they never hurt anyone again, I'm all for it."

Smoke looked over his shoulder at her. "I'm glad to hear you say that, Sally," he said. "'Cause the outlaws are up in the mountains north of Big Rock, and it figures that they don't intend to just sit up there enjoying the winter in the high lonesome. If no one stops them, some of our friends and neighbors are bound to get killed sooner or later."

"Are you planning to go up there after them?"

"If it's all right with you, Sally. I figure if Cal and Pearlie and I go up there alone, we'll have a much better chance to take them out than if the Army goes up there with a lot of men who don't know how to survive in the mountains, especially in the winter. I could never live with myself if those bastards aren't stopped before they kill again."

"Well, Smoke, I'm sure you and the boys will have something to say about that, won't you?"

"Yes, dear," Smoke said sleepily, leaning back so she could do his chest and stomach.

When she was done, she handed him a towel. "Now you're clean as a newborn baby. Go get into bed and I'll join you in a few minutes."

Smoke climbed out of the bath and dried off, then walked slowly into the bedroom.

Sally changed out of her dress into a nightgown she wore for special occasions, brushed her hair, and cleaned her teeth. Then she sprayed on some perfume she'd bought while on a trip to the East to see her parents a few years back.

She went into the bedroom and stood in the doorway. Smoke was lying on his back, dead asleep, snoring softly.

Sally shook her head, smiled, and crawled into the bed, cradling Smoke in her arms while she too fell asleep.

27

The next morning, Smoke awoke to find Sally in his arms. He inhaled deeply. She smelled like lilacs in June. Good enough to eat, he thought.

He leaned over and kissed her awake.

"Good morning, darling," she mumbled, coming awake. "Are you ready for breakfast?"

He shook his head, pulling her to him.

"Me neither," she said with a moan as he kissed her.

Later, after Smoke was dressed, Sally stood at the stove in the kitchen. "Go wake up Cal and Pearlie, would you, dear?" she said. "I wouldn't want them to sleep through breakfast."

"Fat chance," Smoke said with a laugh. "Pearlie's never slept through a meal in his life. I'll bet he's already smelled that bacon cooking and is on his way here right now."

A knock came at the door, and Cal and Pearlie walked in. "Did I hear my name?" Pearlie asked, not waiting for an answer, but heading for the counter where a platter of bear sign was cooling.

As he reached for one, Sally tapped his hand with her

spatula. "Uh-uh, Pearlie," she said, "not until after you have some real food first."

"But Miss Sally," the cowboy protested, looking pained. "Bear sign is real food."

"Come on and sit down, Pearlie," Smoke said from the table. "You know you've never won an argument with Sally."

He shook his head and walked to the table. "That's right, Smoke, an' if she wasn't the best cook in the territory, I wouldn't put up with it neither."

Cal laughed. "You ought not talk like that, Pearlie," he said. "Ever'body knows you think Miss Sally hung the moon."

"Yeah," Pearlie whispered back, "but don't tell her, it'll just go to her head."

Sally brought heaping plates of scrambled hens' eggs, bacon, sliced tomatoes, and fried potatoes to the table. "Cal, if you'll pour the coffee, I'll get the biscuits out of the oven."

"Yes, ma'am."

While they ate, Smoke discussed his plans for the hunt for the outlaws, with Sally every now and then offering suggestions.

"The real problem is going to be figuring out where they've holed up," Smoke said.

"They could be almost anywheres up there," Pearlie said.

Cal shook his head. "That's not true, Pearlie. With all the snow that's fallen, we can eliminate some of the places where they'd have to go through deep passes to get to."

"That's a right smart idea, Cal," Smoke said, pointing a fork at him. "I'll get one of the maps out that Preacher and I worked on in our years up there, and see if I can figure out which areas are still accessible to flatlanders. They are for sure not going too high this time of year, not without ponies that are experienced mountain climbers."

"I'll bet they don't have none of those special shoes

you and Preacher used to go through heavy snow neither," Pearlie said. "That means they're gonna have to stick pretty much to the trails up there. They won't be able to go cross-country at all."

Sally nodded. "That does narrow it down some, Smoke. And since they are, as you say, flatlanders, they won't be comfortable camping out. That means they'll probably try and find some old line shacks or miners' cabins to stay in. There can't be too many of those suitable for thirty men."

"You're right, Sally. They're gonna need at least three or four cabins to get out of the weather in. Most of the mining camps like that are marked on my map. It'll just be a matter of going to the ones easiest to get to. Sooner or later, we're bound to run across them."

She looked at him, her eyes serious. "Just make sure you see them before they see you, Smoke. I told you before, I'm getting tired of patching up bullet holes in your hide."

Smoke gave her a look, then smiled. "Sally, if I can't sneak up on a bunch of men who've never been up in the high lonesome before, I wouldn't be much of a mountain man, would I?"

"But don't forget, dear," she replied, "these men have all been on the run before, and anyone who's been riding the owlhoot trail for any length of time soon learns how to watch their back trail. I'm afraid they won't be as easy to surprise as you think they will."

"You're right again as usual, Sally. Any animal that's been hunted does develop an instinct for survival sooner or later." He looked at Cal and Pearlie. "We'd do well to keep that in mind, boys."

After they'd finished eating, Smoke told Sally he was going to take a ride into Big Rock. He wanted to see if Monte had gotten back all right and he wanted to pick up some supplies from town they were going to need for their expedition into the mountains.

"You want us to go with you, Smoke?" Cal asked.

Smoke shook his head. "No, not this time. I want you boys to curry the horses and give them plenty of grain. They're gonna need all their strength for the trip." He smiled. "Then I want you boys to get some extra shut-eye. We've been pushing it pretty hard the last week or two, and I want you fit as fiddles when we take off tomorrow."

Pearlie yawned. "I can go for that, Smoke."

Cal laughed. "You don't have to tell Pearlie to hit the hay twice, Smoke," he said. "The only thing I know of Pearlie likes almost as much as eatin' is sleepin'."

"I'll go with you, Smoke," Sally said. "I need to pick up some supplies for the ranch. The hands have been complaining they're getting short of nails and wire for the fence repairs they've been doing."

"Good. I'll enjoy the company," Smoke said, putting his arm around her shoulders. "It'll be a nice quiet trip before I head for the mountains."

Ozark Jack Berlin stood in the cabin where the outlaws had stored their provisions, his hands on his hips. He shook his head.

Blue Owl, standing at his side as usual, glanced at his leader. "What are you thinking, Boss?" he asked.

"We're gettin' kind'a low on provisions, Blue Owl." He turned and walked to the door to the cabin and stood there, looking out over the mountains that surrounded them. "Maybe it's time we made a little foray into a nearby town to resupply ourselves."

"The nearest town is Big Rock, Jack," Blue Owl said.

Berlin looked at him. "How big is this Big Rock?" he asked, stroking his chin.

"Not much bigger than a gnat's ass. Why?"

"I'm just wonderin' how much risk we'd run by goin' in there an' buyin' some supplies with the gold we stole."

"Buying? You mean taking, don't you?"

Berlin shook his head. "No. Since it's the closest town to us, I'd rather not bring any attention to ourselves by stirrin' up any trouble. I think it'd be better if you took just a few men in there, not too many so as not to cause any talk, an' just bought what we need."

Blue Owl grinned. "That's a right good idea, Boss. I've been hankering for some female companionship ever since we left those women on the train."

Berlin glared at him. "No, you don't! I said I don't want any attention to be drawn to you. Leavin' a woman all cut up ain't exactly the way to sneak in and out of town, Blue Owl."

Blue Owl looked pained. "Aw, Boss. It just won't seem right to go all the way to town and not get close to any womenfolk."

"That's the way it has to be, Blue Owl," Berlin said sternly. "Otherwise, I'll send somebody else."

Blue Owl nodded, a resigned look on his face. "All right. You're the boss."

"And make sure while you're in Big Rock, you don't forget it neither."

Fat chance of that, Blue Owl thought as he left the cabin to find some men to go to town with him. He was getting tired of the way Ozark Jack Berlin was ordering him around, but he wasn't quite ready to call him on it . . . yet.

After picking up Monte Carson at his office, Smoke and Sally went to Louis Longmont's saloon to have an early lunch.

As they waited for Louis's French chef Andre to prepare their food, Monte told them about his trip down from the mountains.

He shook his head, letting smoke from his pipe trickle from his nostrils as he talked. "I'll tell you the truth,

Smoke. A couple of times I thought I wasn't gonna make it. Snow up to my mount's withers, the air blowin' cold as a well-digger's . . . uh"—he hesitated and glanced at Sally, his face turning red—"well, you know."

Sally grinned, not at all offended by the earthy language men in the West often used. "I know what you mean, Monte," she said. "Why, last week when I tried to cook some of the hens' eggs from the chicken coop, they were frozen solid. It's been a really cold winter, and it's just begun."

Monte nodded, glancing at Smoke. "Like I said, I'm lucky I didn't get frostbite on that trip. I was sure glad to see Big Rock when I finally got here." He laughed. "Hell, first thing I did was go to my house and hug the big Franklin stove Mary uses to keep the house warm."

Smoke smiled. "This has been just about the coldest winter I can remember for a long time, all right."

Louis Longmont, sitting at the table with them, leaned forward. "How do you think that's affecting those hombres you're looking for, Smoke?"

"For one thing," Smoke said, finishing his coffee, "they've got to be mighty uncomfortable up in the high lonesome as cold as it is. From what I can gather, most of them are flatlanders, not used to the weather we're having up here in the high country."

"What about supplies?" Sally asked. "How are they getting them?"

"The marshal over in Pueblo said he had reports they'd been stealin' them," said Smoke, "along with extra guns, ammunition, and even dynamite and blastin' powder.

"Course, with the weather so cold, and thirty or so men to feed, they're gonna be going through lots of grub and supplies," Smoke added, thoughtfully. "That means it won't be long before they have to hit another ranch or town to resupply themselves."

Conversation ceased when Andre and a young black waiter brought platters of food to the table, and the four friends set to eating the best food west of the Mississippi.

Sally glanced up from her plate of roast duck à l'orange, served with mint jelly and freshly steamed vegetables from Andre's private garden.

"I swear, Andre," she told the beaming chef, "if Louis wasn't such a good friend, I'd try to hire you away from him to cook for us at the Sugarloaf."

Smoke shook his head. "Can't do that, Sally," he said. "Because before long, we'd all be so fat we'd have to ride a buckboard instead of horses."

Sally took a bite of duck, licked her lips, and sighed. "Yes, dear, but it would be worth it."

28

Blue Owl and six other men from the outlaw gang reined in their mounts in front of the general store in Big Rock. They had two extra horses to be used to pack the supplies they came for.

As they dismounted, he reminded the men, "The boss don't want no trouble, so keep your mouths shut and behave yourselves just like ordinary citizens."

Moses Johnson, the huge black man, grinned and rubbed his stomach. "If'n it means we get some more food to eat, I'll be quiet as a mouse in church. I been 'bout to starve to death on those meager rations Ozark Jack's been handin' out at the camp."

Blake Whitney, a skinny, rail-thin man with pale skin pockmarked with old smallpox scars, laughed. "Yeah, Moses," he said, looking up at the man who towered almost a foot taller than he, "you look like you're just wastin' away."

The seven men entered the general store, laughing as if they had nothing to worry about.

Ed Jackson, who owned the store along with his wife, Peg, looked up from behind the counter where he was arranging some tinned peaches and canned milk.

"Howdy, gents," he called, smiling. "Welcome to my store."

Blue Owl nodded and didn't reply as he and his men

spread out and began to fill flour sacks with groceries and staples.

The small bell over the door rang as a gangly boy of about eleven years old entered.

"Hello, Jerry," Ed said, opening a jar of peppermint sticks on the counter.

The boy said hi, and dug deep in his pockets and brought out a shiny new penny. He placed it on the counter and then reached into the jar and pulled out a stick of candy.

Ed winked at him. "Go on, Jerry, take another."

"But I only gots the one penny, Mr. Jackson," the boy said.

"That's all right. You need two to ward off the chill outside," Ed said, tilting the jar so he could get another stick.

"Gee, thanks, Mr. Jackson," Jerry said. He took the extra stick of peppermint and put it in his pants pocket. The other one he stuck in his mouth, and ran out the door.

As the men piled their goods on the counter, Moses Johnson reached into the jar and took out a handful of the sticks. "That candy sure do smell good," he said.

Ed glanced at the large pile of goods the men were stacking up. "You gents look like you're getting enough food to feed an army," he said as he began to total up the bill on a scrap of paper.

"We figure on doing a little mining up in the high country during the winter," Blue Owl said, scowling. "Don't want to have to stop to come back for supplies any more than we have to."

Ed grinned, shaking his head. "Well, boys, this ought'a last you at least till next spring."

Jerry sucked contentedly on his peppermint as he skipped and ran down the boardwalk toward the center of town. When he got to Sheriff Carson's office, he stopped, seeing a new poster tacked to the wall. As he read what was on it, his eyes got wide and the peppermint dropped out of his mouth.

He pushed the door to the office open and ran inside. Monte's deputy, Jim, was sitting at Monte's desk, his feet up on the desk, snoring softly.

"Mr. Jim," Jerry said, excitement in his voice. "Where's the sheriff?"

Jim started awake, dropping his feet off the desk guiltily.

"Why do you need him, Jerry?" Jim asked, rubbing his eyes and laughing. "Somebody robbin' the bank?"

"No, sir!" Jerry replied. He pointed out the door. "But I think I seen some of the men on that poster outside."

Jim got suddenly serious. He jumped up and grabbed a shotgun off the rack on the wall. "Where'd you see 'em, Jerry?" he asked, filling his pockets with shotgun shells.

"Down at Mr. Jackson's store. They was buyin' all kinds of things."

Jim knelt down, his hands on Jerry's shoulders. "How many of 'em were there, boy?"

Jerry shrugged. "I don't know. Five or six, I guess."

"You run on home now, and stay off the street. You hear me?" Jim said sternly.

"There gonna be gunplay, Deputy?" the boy asked, his eyes wide.

"If you're right about this, there damn sure will be!"

Smoke and the others were just finishing their lunch when Deputy Jim rushed into Longmont's.

"Uh-oh," Monte said when he saw the look on his deputy's face and noticed he was carrying two shotguns cradled in his arms.

Jim stopped inside the batwings, looked around until he saw where Monte was sitting, then rushed over.

Monte held up his hands. "Catch your breath, Jim, then tell me what's got you all riled up."

"There's some men over to the general store, Sheriff," Jim gasped between breaths.

"There generally is, Jim," Monte said calmly.

"Yeah, but Sheriff, little Jerry says the men fit the description of that poster you put up 'bout them outlaws you been lookin' for."

"What?" Monte said, jumping to his feet.

Smoke stood up too. "Sally, you stay here while we check it out," he said, unfastening the rawhide hammer thongs on his Colts.

Louis did the same, and got to his feet along with Smoke and Monte. "Andre," he called.

When the chef stuck his head out of the kitchen, Louis said, "I'm going to be down the street. Shut and lock the front door, just in case there's trouble."

"Oui, monsieur," Andre said, wiping his hands on his apron and following them to the door.

Sally reached in her handbag, pulled out her snub-nosed .38-caliber Smith and Wesson revolver, and started walking out with the men.

"Sally, I don't want you involved in this," Smoke said.

Her face got that look on it that told him not to push it. "I don't particularly want you involved either, Smoke Jensen, but I don't have any more choice in the matter than you do."

With that, the four men and Sally walked out of the door. Monte and Jim ran across the street and began to walk up the boardwalk toward the general store, while Louis and Smoke did the same on their side of the street. Sally positioned herself in a doorway next to Longmont's Saloon, and eared back the hammer of her .38 while she waited to see what was going to happen.

Blue Owl and Moses Johnson were out in the street in front of the store, tying down the supplies on their packhorses while the five men with them stood next to their horses.

Marcus Weatherby and Slim Bartholomew were building

cigarettes when Marcus glanced up and saw the men headed down the boardwalks toward them.

He dropped his paper and tobacco and grabbed for his gun. "Uh-oh, looks like trouble comin', Blue Owl," he said in a low voice, moving around to get behind his horse.

Blue Owl glanced over the back of the packhorse and cursed. "Goddamnit!" he said, knowing they'd been recognized.

"Get on your mounts and shag tail, boys!" he yelled, whirling around and jumping for his horse.

Moses Johnson grabbed the short-barreled shotgun out of his saddle boot and aimed over the back of the packhorse.

"They're goin' for their guns!" Monte yelled, pushing Jim to the side out of the line of fire just as Moses let go with both barrels.

Monte dove behind a water trough in the street just as several of the shotgun pellets tore into his right arm just below the shoulder.

The outlaws swung into their saddles and jerked their mounts' heads around, trying to get out of town.

Smoke and Louis, in one coordinated movement, crouched, drew, and began to fire their pistols.

As they shot, Marcus Weatherby and Blake Whitney were blown out of their saddles, bullets in their chests.

Blue Owl and Moses Johnson spurred their horses down the street, leaning over their saddle horns and firing as they rode.

Jim stepped back out of the doorway Monte had pushed him into and let go with his shotgun, knocking Slim Bartholomew backward off his horse, a load of buckshot in his gut.

Blue Owl fired across his saddle, his bullet hitting Jim in the thigh and knocking him to the ground, his shotgun empty on the ground next to him.

George Carver and John Ashby fired at Smoke and Louis, their bullets pocking the buildings next to where they crouched, making them dive to the ground.

Smoke rolled to the side, aimed, and fired, hitting Carver between the shoulder blades. He flopped forward, but somehow managed to stay in the saddle as his horse galloped down the street.

Louis lay on his back, firing between his boots, but his shots went wide as the men jigged their mounts back and forth as they rode.

Sally stepped out of her doorway, spread her legs, and starting firing her .38, unmindful of the bullets whizzing past her head.

Her first two shots missed; her third hit Carver for the second time. As the bullet entered his right temple, his head jerked to the side and he catapulted out of the saddle, to be trampled by John Ashby's horse as it thundered past.

Her gun empty, she stood helpless as Blue Owl aimed his pistol at her as he rode past.

With a grunt, Monte Carson scrambled to his knees and raised his shotgun with his left hand, his right arm hanging useless at his side.

He pulled both triggers, and his load tore into Blue Owl's hand, knocking his pistol to the ground before he could fire at Sally.

Blue Owl, John Ashby, and Moses Johnson continued their mad dash out of town as Smoke and Louis ran to Monte's and Jim's aid.

"You all right?" Smoke asked Monte, while Louis checked on Jim's leg, taking a bandanna from around the deputy's neck and tying it around the leg to slow the bleeding.

"Yeah, damn it!" Monte exclaimed, cradling his wounded arm in his left hand. "But three of the bastards got away."

Satisfied his friend was going to live, Smoke glanced over his shoulder at Sally, relieved to see she was unharmed.

"Sally," he yelled, "go get Doc Spalding!"

Sally nodded once, quickly, and ran up the street toward the doctor's office.

Monte turned to look at Jim. "Is he going to be all right?" he asked Louis.

"Yes. It appears you saved his life by knocking him out of the way when that big black let go with his shotgun."

"Thanks, Sheriff," Jim groaned from where he lay on the boardwalk.

"Damn fool," Monte replied, a smile on his face. "You should'a stayed there an' you wouldn't be bleedin' all over the street."

Jim nodded, returning the smile. "Yeah, but then there'd be four of 'em ridin' off 'stead of three."

Louis, satisfied Jim's bleeding was under control, pulled his pistol and stood up. "I'd better see if any of them are still alive," he said, walking toward the bodies lying in the street in front of the store.

"I'll help you," Smoke said, standing. "Maybe we can get one of them to tell us where their camp is."

As it turned out, all of the men were dead, so no information could be gotten as to the whereabouts of their camp.

After Monte and Jim were taken to Doc Spalding's office, Louis and Smoke and Sally went back to Louis's place for some coffee and dessert.

Over a magnificent flan, Louis asked Smoke, "What are you going to do now?"

Smoke finished his flan, built a cigarette, and leaned back with a cup of coffee in his hand. "Well, they didn't get the supplies they came to town for, so that means they're going to have to hit a ranch or mining camp soon."

"Uh-huh," Louis agreed, tilting smoke from his nostrils toward the ceiling.

"I'm going to get the supplies I came for, then take Cal and Pearlie up into the high lonesome to see if we can get to them before they hurt anyone else."

Louis's eyes lit up and he leaned forward. "You want some company?"

Smoke slowly shook his head. "No, old friend. As much as I'd like that, with Monte and his deputy both injured, the town's going to need someone who knows how to use a gun to be on guard in case those outlaws make another try here."

"They wouldn't dare," Louis said.

"Don't be too sure, Louis. If they're as short of food as I think, you never know what they're liable to do."

29

Smoke and Sally drove their buckboard down the street from Longmont's to Ed Jackson's general store.

Once inside, after Sally had inquired about Ed's and Peg's health, and had caught up on all the recent gossip, and after Sally and Smoke had filled Ed in on the happenings after the outlaws left his store, Smoke went about getting the supplies he would need for his upcoming campaign against the outlaw gang.

He bought a large supply of dynamite, gunpowder, extra ammunition for his Sharps fifty-caliber rifle, three black Stetson hats, three sets of black shirts and trousers, and three black duster-type overcoats, along with two tins of bootblack. He also grabbed a stack of old burlap bags to take along.

When Ed asked about the burlap, Smoke explained it was to put over their horses' legs so standing for long periods of time in snow up to their chests wouldn't cause their legs to get frostbite.

While Smoke was getting his supplies, Sally busied herself picking out food staples that would last the three men for several weeks up in the mountains, along with some of the extra supplies of nails and fencing the hands at the Sugarloaf had requested.

Soon, they were on their way home.

Smoke looked at Sally out of the corner of his eye. "You did pretty good back there in the gunfight," he said. "It's not easy hitting a man at full gallop with a handgun."

She glanced at him, a small smile on her face. "I had a good teacher."

"I want you to know, when I saw you step out on that boardwalk right in front of those outlaws riding past, my heart almost stopped," he said, a serious look on his face.

She placed her hand on his arm. "That's how I feel every time you go out wearing your pistols. I never know if you're going to come back to me in one piece or not."

He patted her hand. "I'll always come back to you, Sally."

"You'd better, Smoke Jensen. If you don't, my life wouldn't be worth living."

When they pulled the buckboard up to their ranch house, Cal and Pearlie were waiting, looking rested after their shut-eye.

"Everything go all right?" Pearlie asked as he helped Cal unload the buckboard.

"Yes," Smoke said shortly as he lifted a couple of boxes of dynamite onto his shoulders.

Sally grinned and shook her head. "One good thing from the trip to town," she said. "You boys will have a few less outlaws to contend with."

"What?" Pearlie asked.

Smoke laughed. "Sally here shot a couple of them right out of their saddles in front of Longmont's."

"You got to tell us 'bout that," Cal said, his eyes wide.

"Come on into the house and I'll fix us some dinner and Smoke can tell you all about it," Sally said over her shoulder as she entered the house.

While they ate, Smoke told them about the outlaws' trip into town, and how only three of them managed to get away.

"Jimminy," Cal said, shaking his head. "I knowed we should'a gone to Big Rock with you."

Pearlie nodded gravely. "See, you were right, Miss Sally. Ever time Smoke goes anywhere without Cal an' me to cover his back, he gets into trouble."

She laughed. "Well, we won't let that happen again, boys. I'm counting on you to make sure nothing happens to him up in the mountains."

"You can bet on that, Miss Sally," Cal said. "Pearlie and me'll make sure he don't take no chances with them galoots."

Sally shook her head. "Cal, what are we going to do about your language? When you get back, we need to spend some serious time with one of my English grammar books."

Cal dipped his head and concentrated on his food. "I'd rather go up against an outlaw any day than fight them schoolbooks," he mumbled.

Pearlie, trying to change the subject, interjected, "Smoke, why'd you buy all them new clothes?"

"We're going to be going up against a group of men with superior numbers, Pearlie. That means we're going to have to use stealth instead of brute force. Since we'll be doing a lot of our work at night, I wanted us to wear dark clothing so as not to be able to be seen in the dark."

"What about those tins of bootblack?" Cal asked. "You think the outlaws are gonna care if our boots are shiny?"

Smoke laughed. "The bootblack is for our faces, Cal. It's about time for a full moon, and nothing shows up in moonlight like a white face."

"You mean we got to put that stuff on our faces?" Pearlie asked.

"Not only our faces, but on our hands and arms as well," Smoke said.

Ozark Jack Berlin stepped out of the cabin when he heard hoofbeats approaching the camp.

His eyebrows raised when only three men rode in, with no packhorses.

Blue Owl, his right hand wrapped in a blood-soaked bandanna, reined to a stop in front of Berlin.

"What the hell happened?" Berlin asked, grabbing Blue Owl's reins.

He swung down out of the saddle. "We were ambushed before we could get out of town with the supplies," Blue Owl replied, shaking his head.

"What about the other men?"

"Whitney, Weatherby, Bartholomew, and Carver all got hit. They didn't make it."

"Damn!" Berlin exclaimed. "You think any of 'em will be able to talk about where we're camped?"

Blue Owl shook his head. "No. They were all hit real hard. I don't think any of them will be talking to anybody ever again, leastways, not in this life."

Berlin glanced up at John Ashby and Moses Johnson. "Either of you boys hurt?" he asked.

They shook their heads.

"Come on into the cabin an' we'll see about gettin' that hand fixed up," he said to Blue Owl. "You boys go on over to the other cabin an' get yourselves some grub," he said to Ashby and Johnson.

After Blue Owl's hand was cleansed and bandaged, Berlin lit a cigar and poured himself and Blue Owl a glass of whiskey.

"We really needed those supplies," he said, his eyes staring out the window of the cabin.

"I know, Boss," Blue Owl replied after taking a large swallow of his whiskey. "We did all we could, but it was as if they was waiting for us."

Berlin nodded. "I suspect the word has got out to all the towns around this area by now."

Blue Owl nodded his agreement.

"Well, there's nothin' else we can do. The men gotta eat, an' pretty soon we're gonna need more ammunition."

"Guess we're gonna have to find some ranches or mines nearby to replenish our stock," Blue Owl said.

"Yep. After you get some hot food into your gullet an' a good night's sleep, why don't you and me take a little ride around the area first thing in the morning an' see what we can find?"

"Sounds good to me," Blue Owl agreed, finishing off his glass of whiskey and getting to his feet.

After a good night's sleep and a hearty breakfast fixed by Sally, Smoke and Cal and Pearlie saddled up their horses for the trip into the high lonesome.

Smoke decided to take their best horses this time, so he told Cal and Pearlie to bring out Joker, Silver, and Cold, the crosses from Smoke's Palouse mares and Joey Wells's big strawberry roan stud Red. The legendary gunman, Joey Wells, and his wife had bought the old Rocking C ranch in Pueblo, Colorado, after killing Murdock, the man who'd owned it. Sally, as a gift to Joey's wife, had given them some Palouse mares to breed with Red and start their remuda.*

The offspring Joey had sent to the Sugarloaf were all beautiful animals that had inherited their father's big size and strength and the Palouses' speed and endurance.

Smoke's stud was a blanket-hipped Palouse, red or roan-colored in front with hips of snow white, without the usual spots of a Palouse. Smoke had named him Joker because of his funny coloring.

Pearlie's descendant of Red was a gray and white Palouse he'd named Cold. When Smoke asked him why he'd named him that, Pearlie said it was because the horse was cold-backed in the morning and bucked for the first ten minutes every day when Pearlie saddled him up.

**Honor of the Mountain Man*

Cal's mount was a quicksilver gray, and was actually lmost pure white, differing from a true albino by having ray in front with snow-white hips, also without the usual alouse spots. Cal had named him Silver, and the two eemed to have a bond that was as close as any Smoke ad seen between animal and man.

As they saddled the animals, Cal looked over at Smoke. Saddlin' these broncs reminds me, Smoke," he said. Why didn't you look up Joey an' see if he'd help us while e were over near Pueblo?"

Smoke shook his head. "I thought of that, Cal, but oey's settled down with a wife and family now. He's been rancher a long time, and the last word Sally got from is wife said he'd hung up his guns for good. I respect he wishes of a man who wants to change his way of life, nd I certainly wouldn't want to be the one to ask him to trap his guns back on after all these years."

Pearlie grinned. "Plus, if you asked him to ride with us n' somethin' happened to him, Sally'd have your ears," e said.

Smoke laughed. "I won't say that thought didn't cross ny mind too, Pearlie."

Once the horses and pack animals were saddled and eady to go, Smoke stepped into the house. He found ally busily washing dishes from breakfast.

When he turned her around, he saw tears in her eyes. "What's the matter, darling?" he asked.

She threw her arms around his neck. "I'm just being a illy wife, Smoke. I'm worried that this may be the last ime I ever see you."

He leaned back and stared into her eyes. "Now, don't ou fret, Sally. I promise to be careful, and I promise to ave Cal and Pearlie watch my back at all times."

She put a finger on his nose. "I'm telling you right ow, Smoke Jensen," she said sternly. "If you're not back ere inside of a month, or I don't hear from you, I'm oing to ride up into the mountains and find out why."

"We'll be back before then, Sally," Smoke said, taking

her finger off his nose and kissing it gently. "If this thing can't be done in a month, then it can't be done at all."

"You sure you don't need more men?" she asked.

He shook his head. "No, this is a job best done by as few men as possible. The more men I have along, the more chance the outlaws will know we're coming. This thing is best done by stealth, as I told Cal and Pearlie, not by brute strength."

"So, you plan to pick them off one at a time?"

"If everything goes as planned," he answered.

"When was the last time everything went as you planned?"

He laughed. "Never, now that you mention it."

"I'll keep the bed warm for you, mountain man."

"You do that, lady," he said, bending and giving her a long, serious kiss. "'Cause just the thought of that will make me be sure to come back."

Sally and Smoke walked out onto the porch, her arm around his back.

"Cal, Pearlie," she said to the boys sitting in their saddles in front of the house.

"Yes, ma'am," they answered.

"I'm counting on you two to make sure this big galoot doesn't get anything vital shot off, you hear me?"

Both Cal and Pearlie blushed and smiled. Sometimes, even as well as they knew Sally, her plainspoken ways shocked their Western ideas of women.

"Yes, ma'am," Pearlie said, touching the brim of his new black Stetson. "I'll make sure he don't take no unnecessary chances."

"That'll be the day," Cal murmured, causing both Smoke and Pearlie to give him hard looks.

Sally laughed. "If you can manage that, Pearlie, it'll be the first time in his life Smoke Jensen has ever played it safe."

30

Fully rested after a good sleep, Ozark Jack Berlin and Blue Owl headed out searching for a nearby ranch or mining camp to raid for food and supplies.

As they rode out of the outlaws' camp, Berlin glanced at Blue Owl's right hand. "How's the hand this mornin'?" he asked, noticing the way the Modoc was favoring it.

Blue Owl held his hand up and looked at the blood-soaked bandage. "It hurts and the fingers are so swollen I don't think they'll fit in my trigger guard."

"Can you still use that scattergun in your rifle boot?" Berlin asked.

"Yeah. If I need to, I can fire it left-handed."

"Good, 'cause I'd hate to think you wouldn't be any good to me in a fight."

"Don't worry about that," Blue Owl growled. "If need be, I'll hold up my end if we get in a fracas."

Berlin nodded, and led the way down a snow-covered trail out of the valley of their camp.

After a while, Blue Owl spoke again. "You know something, Jack?"

"What?"

"I think one of those men who attacked us back in Big Rock was Smoke Jensen."

"Smoke Jensen? The gunslick? Are you sure?"

"Yeah, I'm sure. I saw him once in a gunfight over near Tucson. He went up against three men who all slapped leather before he did."

"Yeah?" Berlin asked.

"That's right, and not one of the men managed to clear leather before he'd planted 'em all forked-end-up."

"Why in hell would a man like Smoke Jensen take up arms against you? He wasn't wearin' a badge or anything, was he?"

Blue Owl shook his head. "No, but he was sure as hell standing there on the boardwalk next to a fancy-lookin' gent and they both drew down on the boys."

"That's interesting," Berlin said, his lips pursed in thought.

"I heard a while back that Jensen hung up his guns and settled in some hick town in the mountains. Maybe he considers Big Rock his home."

Berlin scowled. "Well, if he gets in our way again, his home's gonna be six feet under Boot Hill."

Blue Owl chuckled. "There was also this lady involved."

"A lady?"

"Yeah, a right pretty little thing with long black hair. She stepped out of a doorway with this little bitty old pistol in her hand and blew half of George Carver's head off while he was riding by at a full gallop."

"That's pretty good shootin' for a lady," Berlin mused, shaking his head.

"Hell, that's damn good shooting for anybody, man, woman, or child."

"Did you take her out?" Berlin asked, glancing at Blue Owl, his eyes narrowed.

"I was fixing to when somebody shot the gun right outta my hand with an express gun." He paused a moment, thinking back on the event. "It's funny too. She was out of bullets and saw me aiming right at her gullet, and she never ducked nor flinched at all . . . just stood there staring at me with those big eyes."

"Probably too scared to move," Berlin said.

Blue Owl shook his head. "Nope. Far as I could tell, this woman wasn't afraid of nothing nor nobody."

Berlin laughed. "Well, Blue Owl, I wouldn't go repeatin' that story to the men. We don't want them thinkin' women an' children are gettin' the best of us."

Blue Owl nodded, then pointed up ahead over a small rise in the trail. "Hey, look there, Jack. A ranch."

Berlin reined his horse to a stop on the crest of the hill overlooking a small valley below. Smack in the middle was a large ranch house, corral, barn, and what looked like a smaller bunkhouse off to one side.

As they sat there staring down at the ranch, a voice came from off to one side. "Howdy, gents."

Both men whirled in their saddles, hands going to pistol butts.

An older man, who looked to be in his midfifties, held up his hands. "Whoa, hold on there," he said with a smile. "Didn't mean to startle you. My name's Jim Morrow, and that's my spread down there."

Berlin let his hand relax and forced a smile on his face. "Howdy, Mr. Morrow. My friend and I were just headin' cross-country from Pueblo toward Big Rock. We seem to have gotten lost in the snowstorm yesterday."

Morrow grinned. "You certainly are. Big Rock's off in that direction, 'bout ten miles or so."

He looked at them, his face curious. "I don't see no supplies on your mounts. You trying to get to Big Rock without any food along?"

Berlin grinned sheepishly. "No, sir. Our packhorse slipped his lines and ran off during that storm. Truth of the matter is, we're 'bout starved to death."

"Well, come on down. I'll have my wife fix you up some vittles to eat right now, an' I'll pack you some to take along. It's doubtful you'll make Big Rock in less than two days, as deep as the snow is."

"We're much obliged, Mr. Morrow," Berlin said, winking at Blue Owl when the rancher couldn't see.

* * *

While Bess Morrow, Jim's wife, fixed the men some breakfast, Jim took them out to the barn. He opened a door to a large storeroom.

Stacked inside were stacks of canned goods, several sides of beef and pork hanging from hooks in the ceiling, and many large sacks of flour, beans, and other sundry dry goods.

Berlin whistled softly. "Looks like you got near enough food here to feed an army, Mr. Morrow," he said, glancing out of the corner of his eye at Blue Owl, who was similarly impressed with the amount of food before them.

Morrow laughed. "Yeah, you're right, Mr. Jones," he said, using the fake name Berlin had given him.

"You see, we're quite a ways from the nearest general store. It's a good three-day trip to Big Rock by buckboard. Not an easy journey in the winter, so we stock up with all we think we'll need to get through the winter while the weather's still good," Morrow explained.

"You need this much to feed your hands?" Blue Owl asked, trying to figure out how many men they might have to kill to get the food.

"Not during the winter," Morrow said. "We let most of the hands go this time of year. There just ain't enough work to keep 'em on year-round. Spring comes, I go down to Big Rock and hire however many I need for the spring calving and branding. Otherwise, there's just me, the missus, and Hank, our foreman."

Berlin nodded while Morrow began to pack an empty burlap sack with enough food to last two men the two days it would take to get them to Big Rock.

While he was working, Berlin and Blue Owl wandered out of the barn to light up cigarettes.

"You think we ought'a take them now?" Blue Owl asked.

Berlin shook his head. "No. We're gonna need several of the men to help us carry off all this stuff, so it'd be better to come back later in force an' take what we need then."

Morrow came out of the barn, the gunnysack over his shoulder. "This ought'a get you to Big Rock, all right. Once we've eaten, you can be on your way," he said, handing the sack to Blue Owl.

Smoke and Cal and Pearlie swung to the east on their way up the mountain. Smoke wanted to go by Johnny and Belle North's spread on the way and let them know about the outlaws being in the area.

As they approached the North ranch house, Belle came out on the porch, wiping her hands on an apron around her waist.

"Howdy, men," she said. "Come on in out of the cold and have some coffee."

"Is Johnny around, Belle?" Smoke asked as he stepped up on the porch.

"Yes," she replied, looking over her shoulder at the barn out behind the house. "He's out in the barn." She grinned. "Probably smoking one of those big black cigars I won't let him light up in the house."

"Cal, you and Pearlie go on in," Smoke said. "I want to talk to Johnny for a spell."

Johnny North was sitting behind the barn on a bale of hay, a cup of coffee in one hand and a long, black cheroot in the other.

His face broke out in a wide grin when he saw Smoke walking around the corner of the barn.

"Howdy, Smoke," he said. "Long time no see."

Smoke smiled and shook Johnny's hand. "It has been a while, Johnny," he said. "Sally's always after me to invite you and Belle up for a meal, but . . ."

"I know," Johnny said. "Seems there's always something

to do around a ranch that keeps you from visiting your friends."

Smoke laughed. "You miss the owlhoot trail, Johnny?" he asked. He was referring to Johnny's past, when he was a notorious gunfighter who hired his gun out to the highest bidder. He'd been hired years ago by a man who went up against Smoke and the town of Big Rock, but Johnny couldn't tolerate the methods of the man, and he'd switched sides. Soon thereafter, he'd met and fallen in love with the Widow Colby, Belle, and they'd been peaceful ranchers ever since.

Johnny shook his head. "Not for a minute, Smoke. How about you?"

Smoke shook his head. "No. Same as you, Johnny, a good woman saved me from that life forever."

"Ain't that the truth," Johnny agreed.

"The reason I'm here, Johnny, is to warn you."

"Warn me? About what?"

Smoke went on to tell Johnny about the outlaws' escape and that they'd been sighted in the mountains just above Big Rock and the North ranch.

"How many we talking about?" Johnny asked, his eyes worried.

"Between twenty and thirty," Smoke said. "They tried to get supplies in Big Rock the other day and we managed to kill four of them, but there's plenty more up in the hills."

"So, you figure they'll be raiding some ranches looking for supplies and such?"

"That'd be my guess," Smoke said. "I just wanted you and Belle to be on the lookout for anyone you don't know."

Johnny nodded. "Will do, Smoke. I'll get my guns all loaded and board up the windows of the house until they're caught, or move on."

"You think you and Belle will be safe out here all by yourselves?" Smoke asked. "You're welcome to head on over to the Sugarloaf and stay with Sally. I've kept most of my hands on, so there'll be some extra guns in case they're needed."

Johnny shook his head. "No, thanks, Smoke. Belle is right handy with a Winchester, and I haven't lost all of my abilities. We'll do just fine now that you've warned us to be on the lookout for strangers."

"Anybody else you can think of needs warning?" Smoke asked.

Johnny scratched his face for a moment, thinking. "Yeah, you might swing on by the Morrow place. Jim and Bess only keep the one hand on during the winter, and their place is a mite closer to the mountain than mine."

Smoke thought for a moment. "Their place is over by Slaughter Creek, isn't it?"

"Yeah, in that little valley just before you start up the steep slope to the peak over yonder," Johnny said, pointing at a snow-covered peak in the distance.

"Soon's you finish that wolf-turd you're smoking, come on in the house," Smoke said, grinning. "Belle's making fresh coffee."

Johnny stubbed the cigar out on his boot heel, then put it in his shirt pocket. "I'll just save it for later," he said.

"Times getting that tough you got to save your old cigar stubs, Johnny?" Smoke asked, only half-kidding.

Johnny grinned. "No, but come winter, with all the snow and storms and such, being married to a woman who won't let you smoke in the house is kind'a tough. After a while, a man gets cabin fever stuck in the house. Sometimes, you just need a good excuse to get away from one another for a while. Otherwise, you get to griping and fighting and life gets hard."

"I can't imagine you and Belle fighting," Smoke said, thinking the Norths' marriage was one of the best he'd ever seen, outside of his and Sally's.

Johnny's face became serious for a moment. "Oh, I ain't saying it's Belle's fault, Smoke. A finer woman never lived. But, even after all these years as a rancher, I'm still an ornery old cuss, and sometimes the meanness just comes out if I'm cooped up too long."

Smoke nodded, understanding completely. "I know, Johnny. After all the years we spent on the owlhoot trail, sometimes you get to feeling trapped when you stay in one place too long."

"That's it, exactly, Smoke."

31

When Ozark Jack Berlin and Blue Owl arrived back at the camp, the men wanted to know what they'd found.

"An old codger an' his wife have a ranch 'bout five or six miles off to the east," Berlin told them as he unpacked the supplies Jim Morrow had given them.

"They got enough food to last us the rest of the winter stashed in their barn up there," Blue Owl added.

Moses Johnson grinned and rubbed his stomach. "That's good, Boss, 'cause we been on such short rations lately, my stomach thinks my throat's been cut."

"Well," Berlin said with an evil laugh, "we'll have plenty to eat after tomorrow."

"Why not go an' get it now?" Dan Gilbert asked.

Berlin glanced at the sky, where dark clouds roiled over the peaks to the north. "'Cause it's gonna be dark soon, an' it looks like there's another storm on the way. I wouldn't want you men to get lost if a blizzard hits," he said.

Jesus Santiago shivered and flapped his arms around his chest. "Me, I'm getting very tired of this cold," he complained, glancing at the sky.

"I tell you what, Jesus," Berlin said roughly. "If you're tired of the weather, we can send you back to Utah. I'm sure the warden still has your old cell kept nice and warm for you."

Santiago grinned, showing a gleaming gold tooth in his mouth. "That is all right, Señor Berlin. I believe I can stand the cold for a little while longer."

"Then quit your gripin'," Berlin said. "By tomorrow, we'll have all the food and whiskey we can drink, an' by this time next year, we'll have enough gold to take us clear to Mexico, where you'll never have to see snow again."

"That will be a good day indeed," Santiago said, stepping over to the campfire to warm his hands.

The next morning, Berlin called all the gang together. "Since Sam Cook ain't around and probably got killed, I want Dan Gilbert to take over as squad leader."

Dan Gilbert nodded, and stepped to the front of the group of men. "No problem, Boss," he said, looking around to see if any of the men disagreed.

They all nodded, accepting Berlin's judgment in the matter.

"Now, I want some of you to head on over to that ranch an' get us those supplies," Berlin said, glancing at the sky. The threatened storm of the night before had never materialized, though the north wind was raw and cold. "I figure you'll have just enough time to get there, load up the goods, an' get back before dark."

"Who do you want to go?" Blue Owl asked.

Berlin nodded at Gilbert. "Dan, this will be a good chance for you to show you're ready to lead. Why don't you choose four men for your squad and take them along, along with Blue Owl to show you the way?"

"Sure, Boss," Gilbert agreed, turning to point out four men and telling them to saddle up.

"You think six men will be enough?" Berlin asked Blue Owl.

"Sure," the Indian said. "We're only going up against two old men and a woman."

"You thought the trip to Big Rock was going to be easy too," Berlin said with a sneer. "An' look what happened."

Blue Owl's red face got even redder. "That was different, Boss," he said. "They was expecting us. That old rancher don't know nothing about us, so it ought to be as easy as shooting fish in a barrel."

Smoke, Cal, and Pearlie were riding cross-country through snow almost up to their mounts' chests.

"That was a damn good idea of yours, Smoke," Pearlie said, "puttin' burlap around the horses' legs so's they wouldn't get too cold in this snow."

"Just another trick I learned from Preacher," Smoke said, referring to the man who'd taught him all he knew of living in the high lonesome.

"He learn you 'bout usin' this bootblack under our eyes too?" Cal asked, referring to the smears of black boot polish Smoke had put on their cheeks just under their eyes.

"Yes," Smoke replied. "It helps to ward off snow blindness from the glare of the sun off the snow."

"Sure feels foolish, though," Pearlie said, glancing at Cal, who had black polish smeared all over his face.

"Better to feel foolish than to go blind out in the open," Smoke said. "I've seen pilgrims who didn't know what they were doing wander around, blind as bats, until they froze to death in their saddles."

Pearlie pointed at a rise in front of them. "If Johnny was right about the Morrows' place, it ought'a be just over that next hill," he said.

Smoke was about to reply, when the sound of a gunshot echoed across the hills.

"Damn!" he exclaimed. "I hope we're not too late."

The three men spurred their horses forward until they crested the hill in front of them.

Almost a thousand yards below, they could see a group of men sitting on horses in front of the Morrow ranch house.

Smoke jumped down off his horse and pulled his

Sharps fifty-caliber rifle out of his saddle boot in one swift motion.

Pearlie grabbed his binoculars out of his saddlebag and put them to his eyes. "Looks like they got the drop on the Morrows, Smoke," he said.

He could see five men with guns drawn, covering a man and a woman on the porch, who stood with their hands in the air. Lying flat on his face on the porch was another man, who looked like he'd been shot.

Smoke eared back the hammer on the Sharps and flopped down on his stomach in the snow.

He took careful aim, remembering what Preacher had taught him about shooting at a distance when the targets were downhill.

He raised the vernier sight on top of the rifle and adjusted the range to a thousand yards, raising his head to feel which way the wind was blowing before sighting in on the man in the front of the group.

While he was doing that, Cal and Pearlie, who'd remained in their saddles, pulled Winchester rifles out of their saddle boots and jacked shells into the chambers.

"I'm going to take out the lead man," Smoke said. "As soon as I fire, you two hightail it down toward the ranch house. I may be able to get another one or two before you get in range. As soon as you start firing, I'll get up on Joker and join you."

"You think you can get them 'fore they kill the Morrows?" Pearlie asked.

"I don't know," Smoke said, "but it's their only chance, so here goes. . . ."

He gently squeezed the trigger. The big fifty-caliber rifle exploded, kicking back and turning Smoke halfway around as flame and smoke erupted from the barrel.

As soon as he fired, Cal and Pearlie leaned over their saddle horns and kicked their mounts forward. They rode as Smoke had taught them, reins in their mouths, steering their horses with their knees as they brought their rifles up to their shoulders.

With Smoke's shot, the man in the front of the group was knocked off his horse as if he'd been hit by a cannonball, arms flailing, hat flying.

The other men on horseback looked wildly around to see where the shot had come from as Smoke, without waiting, jacked another shell into the Sharps and took aim again.

When the outlaw was blown off his horse, Jim Morrow whirled around and shoved his wife through the door of their cabin, diving after her as fast as he could.

One of the outlaws snapped a shot at him, hitting him in the back of his left shoulder and driving him to the floor just inside the door.

Bess Morrow reached down and grabbed him by the shirt, dragging him inside and slamming the door just as more bullets pocked the wood of the door frame.

Smoke's second shot was low, missing the man he aimed at but hitting his horse in the chest, knocking it to its knees as blood spurted from its hide.

By then, Cal and Pearlie were in range, and began to fire and load and fire again as fast as they could, peppering the group of outlaws with .44-caliber slugs.

Two more men were hit, flying off their mounts to lie dying in the snow.

In the barn, Blue Owl was busily loading sacks of supplies and sides of beef on the back of a packhorse when he heard the booming explosion of the Sharps.

"Goddamnit!" he exclaimed. "What now?"

He ran to the door of the barn and saw three of his men down, the others trying to stay in their saddles as their mounts crow-hopped and jumped around, frightened by the gunfire.

"Shit!" Blue Owl said, running back into the barn and jumping into his saddle, grabbing the dally rope of the packhorse and galloping off toward the mountain, trying to keep the barn between him and the attackers as he raced for their camp.

Smoke swung onto Joker's back, stuffing the Sharps into his saddle boot as he urged the big stud down the hill.

The lone remaining outlaw on horseback leaned over his saddle horn and made tracks away from the cabin, while the man on the downed horse struggled to his feet and began to fire his pistol at Cal and Pearlie as they rode toward him.

The cabin door opened and Bess Morrow stepped out on the porch, a long-barreled shotgun cradled in her arms.

She leveled the scattergun at the outlaw's back and let go with both barrels.

He was thrown facedown in the snow, cut almost in two by the buckshot in her loads, dead in his boots.

Pearlie slowed Cold to a stop, took careful aim with his Winchester, and fired.

The man on horseback straightened, flung his arms out to the side, and toppled off his mount onto the ground, a hole in the middle of his back.

By the time Smoke got to the house, it was all over. Five men lay dead or dying in the snow in front of the ranch house.

He looked up in time to see a distant figure, trailing a packhorse, disappear into the pine trees on the mountain slope north of the house.

Cal whirled around, breathing heavily from his ride. "You want me to go after him, Smoke?" he asked, inclining his head toward the man riding off.

Smoke shook his head. "No, he's got too big a lead, Cal. Besides, we can use his tracks to lead us to the gang's hideout."

Bess Morrow, seeing all the outlaws down, turned and went back inside the house.

Smoke and Cal and Pearlie followed her in. On the way, Pearlie knelt by the man on the porch to check him.

He glanced up as Smoke walked by. "He's had it, Smoke."

Smoke nodded and opened the door. Bess was kneeling

next to her husband, wrapping her apron around his bleeding shoulder.

She glanced up. "Smoke Jensen," she said, "you're a sight for sore eyes!"

"Howdy, Mrs. Morrow," he said, stepping to her side. "Is Jim going to be all right?"

Jim Morrow groaned and rolled on his side, sticking his right hand out toward Smoke. "I want to thank you for what you did, Smoke," he said. "If you and your men hadn't showed up, we'd've been goners for sure."

Smoke tilted his head toward the front porch. "I'm sorry about your man. He's dead," Smoke said.

Bess shook her head, tears in her eyes. "Good ol' Hank," she said. "He tried to draw on them men, never mind the odds."

Smoke bent and examined the wound on Jim's shoulder. "You're lucky, Jim. Looks like the bullet passed through clean without hitting the bone.

"Cal, Pearlie, help me get him onto the bed," Smoke said.

Once Jim Morrow was situated on the bed, his head propped up by pillows, Bess wiped her hands on her skirt.

"You boys gonna go after that galoot?" she asked.

"Not tonight," Smoke said. "It'd be too easy for him to ambush us in the dark by the time we got up onto the mountain. I'd rather give him time to get to the outlaws' camp and think he's safe."

He glanced out the window. "Besides, we need to help you bury Hank, and clean up that mess in your front yard."

She nodded. "I'd appreciate the help with Hank," she said. Then her voice got hard. "As far as that other trash, you can just haul their bodies up the hill a ways and let the wolves and coyotes have 'em."

32

After Dan Gilbert and Blue Owl took their men and left the camp to go and get Jim Morrow's supplies, Ozark Jack Berlin joined his men around the campfire for some coffee mixed with whiskey to ward off the chill.

Berlin glanced around the group sitting or standing near the fire. There were fourteen, counting himself, left in camp. "Damn," he muttered to himself, thinking the loss of Sam Cook and his men and the four Blue Owl lost in Big Rock was whittling down his gang from more than thirty to less than twenty.

He smiled to himself grimly. If this keeps up, he thought, we won't need near so much grub to get through the winter, and the gold we steal will go a lot further.

Wiley Gottlieb walked over to stand next to Berlin. "Jack," he said, glancing over his shoulder at a group of men huddled near the fire.

"Yeah?"

"The men are gettin' kind'a restless, just sitting around here trying to keep their fingers from freezing off. What say we make a little run around the area today and see if we can find something to do?"

Berlin looked up at him. "Something to do? You mean, somebody to rob an' kill?"

Gottlieb grinned slyly. "The men need a little excitement, Jack. Otherwise, 'fore too long, they're gonna be at each other's throats."

Berlin thought about it for a few minutes. Gottlieb was right. These were not the sort of men to stay idle too long before their natural aggressiveness began to cause trouble in the camp.

"You're right, Wiley," Berlin said, getting to his feet and dusting the seat of his pants off. "Tell the men to saddle up. We're goin' huntin'."

Three hours later, after following winding mountain trails that cut back and forth across the side of the mountain, Berlin raised his hand to bring his band to a halt.

Down the trail in front of them were three small cabins made of logs and chalked with mud in the chinks between the logs.

The cabins were by the side of a small, bubbling stream that ran down the side of the mountain. About a quarter mile up the slope, a hole could be seen cut in the rock of the mountain, with some wooden steps arranged on the steepest part of the slope.

Berlin pointed at the cabins, then at the hole in the rock. "Looks like we found us a mine, boys." He grinned as he looked from one to the other. "Let's hope these miners have had a good run of luck this year . . . 'cause their luck is gonna take a sudden turn for the worse.

"Get down off your mounts an' spread out. We'll go in on foot. These miners have been known to not take kindly to somebody takin' their gold," Berlin ordered as he stepped out of his saddle.

Berlin took a Henry rifle from his saddle boot and levered a shell into the chamber, then, crouching, began to walk down the trail toward the cabins.

Behind him, his men spread out and filtered into the piney woods on either side of the trail, guns drawn, grinning at the prospect of both action and gold.

When Berlin was fifty yards from the first cabin, the

door opened and a man with a bushy, black beard walked out and moved toward the stream, a coffeepot in his hands. He was dressed in the canvas pants favored by miners who spend a lot of time on their knees, and when he got to the stream, he squatted next to the water. As he bent over and began to fill the coffeepot, Tony Cassidy stepped from behind a pine tree and shot him in the face.

When Cassidy's gun exploded, four more men ran from the cabins, and three came out of the mine on the mountainside.

The outlaws opened fire, dropping the men before they had time to get off more than a couple of wild shots.

As the smoke, which hung in the air like ground fog, began to clear, Berlin reloaded his Henry and walked toward the cabins.

"Get their guns an' ammunition, men. Then we'll check out the cabins to see where they hid their gold."

An hour later, Berlin and his men stepped from the cabins. They'd found six pounds of gold dust and nuggets hidden beneath the bunk beds in the houses. Another ten ounces was still in the mine where it'd just been dug up.

Berlin bounced a canvas sack of dust in his hand, grinning. "Not a bad mornin's work, huh, boys?" he asked, looking around at his men.

As he looked, he noticed a figure sitting on a horse on top of a ridge above the mine, several hundred yards away.

Berlin quickly shielded his eyes and glared up the slope at the man. The man appeared to be dressed in buckskins, and was sitting on a paint pony, a long rifle cradled in his arms. He had some sort of fur hat on his head, and he was glaring down at the outlaws.

Berlin pointed at the man and hollered, "Hey, you!"

As the outlaw gang all turned to look, the man shook his head and slowly rode out of sight without looking back.

"What the hell?" Moses Johnson asked, his eyes wide. "You think that was a spook, Boss?"

Berlin shook his head, a curious look on his face. "Naw. Probably an old mountain man. I've heard there are still some of 'em up in these parts."

"You think we ought'a go after him?" Billy Bartlett asked, his hand dropping to the butt of his pistol.

Berlin shook his head. "No. From what I hear, those old coots tend to mind their own business. It's a wonder we even seen him."

Spotted Dog looked worried. "If we saw him, Jack, it is because he wanted us to see him. My people say the mountain men can become invisible if they wish."

"What?" Moses asked, his mouth open.

"It is true," Spotted Dog persisted. "I have been in camp with my people when a mountain man walked right past our fires without anyone seeing him. We only knew he'd been there by his tracks the next morning."

"That's bullshit, Dog," Berlin said. "He's just an old man who's outlived his usefulness. He won't give us any trouble."

Spotted Dog shook his head, his face a mask of fear. "I hope not, Jack. The sort of trouble a mountain man gives you is usually fatal."

"Come on, boys," Berlin said, trying to lighten the mood. "Let's get on back to camp with our gold. Blue Owl and the others ought to be there soon, so we can put on the feed bag and have ourselves a little party tonight."

The men walked back up the trail to their horses. As they climbed in the saddle, Spotted Dog looked over his shoulder up the mountain where the strange man had been seen. He shivered as he thought he saw a shadow moving among the trees and bushes there, as if it were following them.

33

Once Hank was buried, the outlaws' bodies were moved away from the Morrows' ranch house, and Jim's wound was treated, Bess Morrow insisted on fixing some fresh food for Smoke and the boys to take on their quest after the gang.

She handed a large sack of fresh-fried chicken to Pearlie with a wink. "I've seen the way you eat, son, so I know you'll take good care of this little snack."

Pearlie opened the sack, took a deep sniff, and rolled his eyes as if he were in heaven. "Yes, ma'am, you can be sure of that," Pearlie said, carefully rolling the top of the sack over to keep the chicken fresh and putting it reverently in his saddlebags.

Cal looked at Pearlie, "You know, Pearlie, that there chicken is for *all* of us, not just for you."

Pearlie gave him a look. "Of course, Cal, an' if you're a good lad, I may share the neck and wings with you."

Smoke took Bess's hand. "Are you sure you and Jim will be all right if we leave?"

"Smoke, you don't live on a ranch twenty miles from nowhere without learning how to care for a little old bullet wound. We'll be fine." She narrowed her eyes. "You just find those . . . outlaws and give them what they got coming for what they did to Hank. I know he'll rest easier knowing they ain't gonna get away with what they done."

"You can count on that, Bess," Smoke said, climbing up on Joker. He tipped his hat. "Give my best to Jim. We'll check back in on you on our way back to the Sugarloaf."

"Good luck, boys," Bess said, waving as they rode off up the slope of the mountainside, following the tracks Blue Owl had left when he'd hightailed it away from the ranch the day before.

Four hours later, when they were well within the thick pine and maple forest of the mountain, Smoke slowed Joker and said, "I guess it's about time we took our nooning."

"I thought you'd never say that," Pearlie said. "That chicken's been callin' to me for the past five miles."

Smoke ground-reined the horses and walked over into a small copse of maple trees, where the branches had kept the snowfall to a minimum.

"Gather up some wood for the fire, Pearlie. No need to eat a cold lunch when we've got plenty of time."

After the fire was going, using dry wood at Smoke's suggestion so it wouldn't smoke so much as to give their position away, Smoke melted some snow for the coffee and heated up some beans in a skillet to go with the chicken. Cal found a sack of day-old biscuits and put them in a pan to steam them soft.

Once the water was boiling for the coffee, Smoke added a couple of handfuls of coffee grounds to the mixture, causing a wonderful aroma to percolate into the air.

He raised his head and said in a loud voice, "If the smell of that coffee doesn't bring you into camp, nothing will, Bear Tooth."

Pearlie and Cal looked up from where they squatted next to the fire.

"Bear Tooth?" Cal asked. "Is he out there?"

Smoke grinned. "He's been dogging our trail for the past two hours. Didn't you notice?"

Cal's face blushed a bright red. "No, sir. I didn't see nothin'."

Pearlie laughed. "I guess we weren't supposed to, Cal. Like Smoke always said, the only time you'll see a mountain man is when he wants you to see him."

A gruff voice came from the woods off to their right. "You sure you put enough coffee in that mix, young'un?" he said to Smoke.

"I know," Smoke replied with a grin. "Good coffee don't take near as much water as you think it do," he said, quoting an old mountain man saying.

A tall, hulking man well over six feet tall walked into the clearing, leading a smallish pinto pony by its reins. He was dressed in buckskins and was wearing a bearskin coat that gave off an odor, as if he hadn't been too particular about curing it before fashioning it into a coat. He wore a coonskin hat, and was cradling a Sharps Big Fifty in his right arm. His face was covered with a matted, tangled, scraggly black beard, with quite a bit more gray in it than the last time they'd seen him.

His voice, when he spoke, was husky and rough, as if he didn't get much practice talking.

"How do, boys," he said with a grin to Cal and Pearlie. "I see Smoke's taught you enough to keep you alive these past few years."

"Howdy, Bear Tooth," both Cal and Pearlie called, happy to see the old mountain man they'd befriended a while back while on the trail of Big Jim Slaughter.*

The pinto pony balked at the sight of the men around the fire, and pulled back on its reins.

"Goddamnit, Buck," Bear Tooth growled, jerking on the reins until the pony moved up closer to the camp.

"I thought you never gave a name to your horses,

**Heart of the Mountain Man*

'cause you might have to eat 'em someday," Pearlie said, his eyebrows raised.

"I changed my mind after our last meetin'," Bear Tooth said in his deep voice. "Once you told me Puma Buck had crossed the last mountain, I named this misbegotten beast after him, 'cause he's just as ornery an' mean an' stubborn as ol' Puma was."

"Set and have some *cafecito,*" Smoke offered, handing Bear Tooth a mug of steaming black coffee.

"Don't mind if'n I do, Smoke," he replied, squatting on his heels and taking the cup in both hands. He breathed deep of the aroma, then took a deep sip.

He looked up, grinning and showing a mouthful of yellowed stubs of teeth. "I been livin' on acorn-nut coffee for the past six months. This is right special."

"Why don't you go into Pueblo or Big Rock an' get some of the real thing?" Cal asked.

"Too damn many pilgrims for my taste," Bear Tooth said with disgust. "If'n I did that, they'd probably expect me to bathe first, an' I ain't due for my annual bathin' for another six months."

"How's the trapping this year?" Smoke asked.

Bear Tooth shrugged as he dipped his head and sampled the coffee again. "Not near as many as last year, or the year before," he said. "Damn miners run 'em all off with their diggin' an' blastin' an' such."

While Cal stirred the beans and moved the biscuits off the fire, Pearlie unwrapped the sack of chicken and began to hand pieces out to everyone.

"My God Aw'mighty," Bear Tooth exclaimed. "Fried chicken!"

"Enjoy," Smoke said. "There's plenty for everyone."

"Long as you eat fast, 'fore Pearlie has a chance to eat it all up," Cal remarked, spooning beans onto plates.

As they ate, Bear Tooth grunting with satisfaction over the meal, Smoke asked him, "Have you heard from or seen Muskrat Calhoon lately?"

Bear Tooth nodded. "Yep. He was up this way last year for

our annual mountain man gatherin' at Pagosa Springs." He grinned again. "He tole us 'bout all the fun you boys had over at Jackson Hole. Said he hadn't enjoyed hisself so much since that winter he had a squaw share his camp with him."

"He doing all right?" Smoke asked.

Bear Tooth frowned. "Oh, all right, I guess. The rheumatiz' is startin' to freeze his joints up a mite, but that happens to all of us livin' up here in the high country sooner or later."

He stared at Smoke for a moment. "The old beavers missed you at this year's gatherin', Smoke. You ain't forgot your roots, have you?"

Smoke shook his head. "No. I was down in Texas, getting some beeves and horses for my ranch. Got involved in a little fracas down there, and it took me longer to get home than I thought."

"Texas, huh?" Bear Tooth said with distaste. "Never cared much for Texas, or Texicans neither for that matter. Place is too damned flat for my taste."

He held his mug out for more coffee, and as Smoke filled it, Bear Tooth peered at him from under bushy eyebrows. "What brings up to the high country this time, young'un?"

Smoke told him of the escape of the outlaws and how they were riding roughshod over the ranches and towns of the area. When he told him about what they'd done to the women on the train, the old mountain man scowled.

"While I ain't got much use for womenfolk generally, man that does that ought'a be turned into a steer."

"Have you seen any sign of the outlaws, Bear Tooth?" Pearlie asked around a chicken leg bone still in his mouth.

Smoke chuckled as Bear Tooth bristled. "Have I seen 'em? Course I have, you young beaver. Bear Tooth sees ever'thing that happens up here."

"Where'd you see them last?" Smoke asked, leaning back and building himself a cigarette.

When Cal pulled out his makin's, Bear Tooth leaned

over and stuck out his hand. "It's only good manners, young'un, to offer to share your tabaccy with a guest."

As Cal blushed, Smoke got to his feet. "Wait a minute, Bear Tooth. I brought you something from town."

He walked over to their packhorse, dug in the packages on its back for a minute, then brought out a box wrapped in waxed paper. He stepped back to the fire and handed it to Bear Tooth.

The old man raised his eyebrows. "Is it Christmas already?"

"That's for helping us out last time we were up here," Smoke said.

Bear Tooth opened the package to find a box of long, black cigars and a two-pound tin of Arbuckle's coffee.

He took one of the cigars, bit the end off, and used a burning twig from the fire to light it. "Damn," he sighed, "a good cigar, real coffee . . . life just don't get no better than this."

"About the outlaws," Smoke reminded him.

Bear Tooth nodded. "Yeah, saw 'em yesterday. They attacked a mining camp 'bout four mile from here. Killed seven men an' took all their gold."

"Yesterday?" Smoke asked.

Bear Tooth nodded. "Took me most of the night to get the bodies all under the ground. I don't have no love fer miners, but a man's entitled to a decent buryin' nevertheless."

"You know where the outlaws are camped?" Smoke asked, his jaw tight at the thought of another seven men to add to the list of victims of the outlaw gang.

"Shore. They're camped out over at the hot springs."

Smoke looked surprised. "The hot springs? But I kind'a thought they'd be someplace where there were some cabins. Nothing over at the springs 'cept those old caves."

Bear Tooth shook his head. "Been too long since you been up here to visit, Smoke. Some miners built theyselves some cabins up at the springs two year ago. When the mine played out, they left 'em to rot."

Smoke thought for a moment, letting smoke trickle from his nose. "As I recall, the springs are in a little natural valley between two sheer cliffs that rise to about two hundred feet."

Bear Tooth nodded. "Nothin' wrong with your memory, Smoke."

Smoke glanced at Cal and Pearlie. "That's perfect, boys. And the springs are less than a day's ride from here."

Bear Tooth narrowed his eyes. "You men plannin' on goin' after those coyotes?"

Smoke nodded. "They attacked the Morrow place yesterday, Bear Tooth. Killed the hired hand Hank, and wounded Jim Morrow."

"They wounded ol' Jim?" Bear Tooth asked. "How 'bout Bess? They didn't mess with her none, did they?"

"No," Smoke said. "We got there in time to stop them before they were able to finish what they started."

"The Morrows are good people," Bear Tooth said. "Couple'a year ago I had me a helluva toothache. Bess, Mrs. Morrow, yanked it out with a pair of fence pliers, an' then made me take some of their supplies to get me through the winter."

"They're special people, all right," Smoke said. "That's why I'm going to rid the mountain of those pond scum before they can hurt anyone else up here."

Bear Tooth nodded. "There's a passel of 'em, Smoke, more'n fifteen or so. You want some help?"

"I'd be obliged, Bear Tooth," Smoke said. "A man can always use another Sharps in a fracas like this."

"I don't normally get involved in flatlanders' troubles, but"—he grinned—"like you say, this is my mountain an' I'm right particular who gets to stay up here. I figure the neighborhood can use a little cleanin' up."

Pearlie grinned and handed Bear Tooth another piece of chicken. "Have another piece, Bear Tooth."

"Don't mind if'n I do, young'un."

"And maybe, while we're riding with you, you can

teach these young beavers something about living on the mountain," Smoke said.

"You mean, like Preacher did you?" he asked with a smile.

Smoke nodded. "I figure they need to learn from the best."

Bear Tooth's eyes lit up. "Then that'd be me," he said with the typical egotism of the confirmed mountain man.

34

Ozark Jack Berlin was in the main cabin at the hot springs camp, counting out and weighing the gold they'd stolen from the miners. He was grinning, and the men surrounding him were laughing with delight at the fortune they'd managed to accumulate since their escape from prison.

"Boys," he said, a wide smile on his face as he glanced around at the men in the cabin, "we're gonna live like kings in Mexico on this loot."

Jack McGraw, who was standing near the window to the cabin, uttered an oath. "Uh-oh, Boss," he said in his gravely voice. "You ain't gonna like this."

"What is it, Jack?" Berlin said, frowning. "I'm busy countin' our money here."

"Looks like Blue Owl's back," McGraw said. "An' he's all by himself."

"What?" Berlin said, jumping to his feet and hurrying out the door.

"Where the hell are the rest of the boys?" he asked, anger deep in his voice at the sight of Blue Owl sitting on his horse alone.

Blue Owl swung down out of the saddle and handed the reins of the packhorse carrying the supplies from the Morrow ranch to Billy Bartlett.

"I suspect they're coyote food by now," Blue Owl said, his face grim.

"What the hell happened?" Berlin asked, striding over to stand next to the Indian. "You and five men couldn't handle a couple of old farts an' a woman?"

"I need a drink," Blue Owl said, walking over to the campfire and pouring some coffee into a mug, to which he added a generous supply of whiskey from a bottle in his vest pocket.

"Goddamnit! Tell me what happened," Berlin shouted.

"We was doing all right," Blue Owl began after taking a deep swallow of the whiskey and coffee. "Had the hired hand down and had the old man and his wife covered, when all of a sudden, out of the blue, somebody started shooting the men right out of their saddles."

"Who?" Berlin asked. "There wasn't but the three of them at the ranch."

Blue Owl shrugged. "Don't know for certain," he said, "but it sure looked like that gunslick Smoke Jensen to me."

"You let one man shoot up the lot of you?"

Blue Owl shook his head. "Not one man. He had two other gents with him, and they was right handy with their rifles. Jensen must've been six hundred yards or more away when he shot the first two, then those other boys rode down on us hell-bent for leather, shooting as they rode. They took out the rest."

"How'd you manage to get away during all this?" Wiley Gottlieb asked suspiciously.

"I was back in the barn, loading up the pack animal with the supplies we went there for. When I saw the boys dropping like flies, I lit out and never looked back."

"And they didn't come after you?" Berlin asked, his face thoughtful.

Blue Owl shook his head. "They were too busy with the Morrows, I guess. Like I said, we killed the hired hand and wounded the ranch man. They must've stayed behind to take care of them."

"And all of the others were killed?" McGraw asked, shaking his head.

"They sure looked dead to me, unless you can live with a hole in your chest and your head blown off."

Berlin took a deep breath, trying to calm himself. "Well, at least you got the supplies."

"Yeah, but it cost us five men to do it," Gottlieb observed drily.

Berlin tried to make the best of it. "'Course, that means the gold we got will go further."

"What gold?" Blue Owl asked.

Berlin threw his arm around Blue Owl's shoulders. "Come on in the cabin and rest up while I tell you about it."

"Uh, Jack," Wiley Gottlieb said, "maybe we ought'a post some guards around the camp, just in case those shooters decide to follow Blue Owl here."

"That's a good idea, Wiley. Why don't you take care of it while I show Blue Owl our gold?"

Smoke and Cal and Pearlie followed Bear Tooth in single file up the side of the mountain, taking trails that were almost invisible to the naked eye, trails that only a man who lived on the mountain would know about.

"I'm gonna take you up the back way to the springs," Bear Tooth called over his shoulder. "That way, if'n they're smart enough to post lookouts, they won't see us comin'"

"There's no need to hurry," Smoke replied. "I don't plan to do anything until after dark anyway."

"Moon won't set till midnight or so," Bear Tooth said, glancing at the sky, "an' it appears there's another storm on the way."

Cal and Pearlie looked up, and seeing no clouds in the sky, they looked at Smoke. "How's he know that?" Pearlie asked. "I don't see no storm clouds."

Smoke smiled. "He can smell it, and so can I. When

snow's on the way, the air has a different smell to it, kind'a damp and stingy to the nose."

Cal and Pearlie both sniffed loudly through their noses. "I don't smell nothin'," Cal said.

"You spend enough time up here, you will," Bear Tooth replied without looking back.

Just after sunset, Bear Tooth reined in his pony. "Whoa, Buck. This looks like a good enough place to make camp."

"How much farther?" Cal asked.

Bear Tooth shook his head. "Not too far, little beaver, but we want to camp on this side of the slope so's we can make a fire without bein' seen by those men. That is, unless you wanna make a cold camp?"

Cal shook his head. "No, sir," he said. "I'm 'bout frozen clear through. I need some hot coffee."

"Don't call me sir nor mister, young'un. Name's Bear Tooth, or just Bear."

"Yes, sir . . . uh, I mean, all right, Bear," Cal said, hurrying off his horse and beginning to gather wood for the fire.

Bear Tooth grinned and winked at Smoke. "They know 'bout not gettin' no green wood?"

Smoke nodded. "Yes, they've learned that much at least."

"Good. Now, I'll show 'em how to build a fire 'tween some rocks so the smoke don't go straight up an' signal our enemies where we are."

"While you do that, I'll get the grub ready," Smoke said, smiling to himself at the valuable lessons the boys were going to learn from the old mountain man.

Soon, Bear Tooth had a fire going up next to several boulders where the smoke was funneled in several different directions and couldn't be seen from more than a dozen yards away.

"Now, young'uns," he said, dumping a double handful of coffee grounds into the pot, "as far as makin' good coffee goes, if it's not thick enough to float a horseshoe, it's too weak."

"Hell," Pearlie said, "we won't need cups for that. We can just spoon it outta the pot."

Smoke flipped Bear Tooth something. "Here, Bear Tooth," he said.

"What's that, Smoke?" Cal asked.

"I saved some egg shells from this morning's breakfast."

"You put 'em in the pot to settle the grounds, boy," Bear Tooth said to Cal. "What are you, a pilgrim?"

"Miss Sally says cold water does just as good," Pearlie observed.

"Yeah, but that waters down the brew, boys, an' up here you need coffee strong enough to keep the winter chill off."

"You have any secrets for beans?" Cal asked as he stirred the skillet.

"Only that you can't cook 'em too long," Bear Tooth said. "That, an' a couple'a pieces of fatback, helps give 'em a right nice flavor."

"All right," Cal said, and reached into the saddlebags to get some bacon out. He sliced off a generous chunk and placed it in the skillet with the beans.

"We're gonna have you boys eatin' like mountain men 'fore this trip is over, ain't we, Smoke?"

Smoke laughed. "If we do that, it'll spoil them for any other food," he said.

After they finished supper, the men sat around the fire. Cal and Pearlie and Smoke made cigarettes while Bear Tooth enjoyed one of the cigars Smoke had brought him.

"Do you remember the springs well enough to draw us a map of the area?" Smoke asked Bear Tooth.

The mountain man nodded, took a stick, and began to draw in the snow next to him. "It's a circular valley," he said, "surrounded on three sides by sheer cliffs goin' straight up. There's an openin' on the south where the trail enters it, an' a smaller one on the north where the stream enters that feeds the springs," he said, making the appropriate marks in the snow.

He made three X's near the line for the stream. "Right here's the three cabins the miners built."

"What about the caves?" Smoke asked.

Bear Tooth nodded, and made two more marks next to the cliffs. "They're right here, but I don't know nothin' much 'bout 'em, how deep they is an' such."

Cal glanced at the mountain man. "Didn't you ever use the caves as shelter?" he asked.

Bear Tooth shook his head. "Never cared much fer caves. If'n I can't see the stars, I get to feelin' trapped an' hemmed in."

Cal nodded as the mountain man continued. "'Cept for the winter of sixty-six, I believe it was."

"What happened then?" Pearlie asked, leaning forward to pitch his cigarette butt in the fire.

"'Twas the coldest winter I recollect," Bear Tooth said, leaning back and looking at the sky. "It was so cold, when you took a piss, you had to break it off 'cause it froze 'fore it hit the ground."

Smoke smiled, knowing another mountain-man tall tale was coming.

"Yep, that winter I decided to take refuge in a cave over on the north side of the mountain. Trouble is, an ol' bear had the same idee."

"Did you have to kill it?" Pearlie asked, wide-eyed.

"Hell, no," Bear Tooth replied. "It was so cold, we was both glad of the company. I just snuggled down to that old critter, and it wrapped its arms around me like an ol' squaw, an' we slept the winter through."

"Gosh," Cal said, "don't bears stink somethin' awful?"

Bear Tooth nodded. "Well, I must say, he was a mite gamy, but I'll tell you the truth, little beaver. I didn't think he'd take to kindly to me suggestin' he take a bath, so we both put up with the smell best we could."

Smoke and Pearlie laughed out loud; then Cal joined in when he realized the old man was having fun with him.

"Bear Tooth," Smoke said, "I haven't heard such a tall tale since Puma Buck was alive."

Bear Tooth looked offended. "You mean you don't believe me?" he asked.

"Is that the same year Puma talked about?" Smoke asked. "When it was so cold you had to thaw your words out in a skillet so's you could hear what the other men were saying?"

Bear Tooth smiled and shook his head. "No, now that sounds like somethin' Puma would've said. That man never told the truth a day in his life." He hesitated. "But it was the year I had a campfire freeze on me one night. Damn thing didn't start burnin' again till the next day when the sun came out an' the temperature rose to fifty below."

"On that note, I think I'll get some shut-eye," Smoke said, chuckling. "We've got to get up around midnight and ride over and take a look at the springs when the moon goes down."

"How're you gonna wake up when it's time?" Cal asked.

Bear Tooth looked at Cal as if he couldn't believe what he'd asked.

"You mean you haven't learned to wake up whenever you want yet?"

"Uh, no, sir . . . I mean, no, Bear."

"Why, you just set your mind to the time an' pretty soon, you'll just naturally get up when you're supposed to."

"Is that the truth, Smoke?" Cal asked.

"Maybe for Bear Tooth," Smoke replied, "but as for me, I'm gonna set this pocket watch Sally gave me. It'll ring a bell when midnight comes."

"Oh," Cal said.

"Cal, I swear you're dumber'n a rock," Pearlie said.

Bear Tooth shook his head. "Now you just wait an' see, boys. When that little trinket of Smoke's goes off, I'll be up an' waitin' for you."

35

In spite of what he'd told Cal, Smoke woke up just before midnight, before the tiny alarm in his pocket watch had a chance to go off.

Like most mountain men, he came fully awake in seconds. One minute, he was sound asleep; the next, his eyes were open and checking his surroundings for danger before his body moved at all.

He turned his head and saw Bear Tooth, squatted next to a small, hat-sized fire among the boulders next to their camp. He had a pot of coffee warming on the coals of the fire, which was giving off no smoke whatsoever.

"Mornin', Smoke," the old man whispered, pouring an additional mug of coffee and handing it to Smoke when he crawled out of his sleeping blanket.

Smoke glanced at Cal and Pearlie, still snoring softly across the clearing.

"Time to wake the young'uns up," Bear Tooth said, inclining his head toward the sleeping men.

Smoke fished a couple of pine cones out of the snow and pitched them onto the sleeping bodies.

Cal and Pearlie snorted awake, both men instinctively going for their guns.

"Easy, boys," Bear Tooth growled with a smile. "Breakfast time."

Pearlie yawned and stretched. "Them's music to my ears, Bear," he said, his voice still husky with sleep.

Cal just groaned and rubbed his eyes as Smoke handed them both steaming mugs of coffee.

Pearlie glanced around at the fire. "I don't see no breakfast cookin'," he said.

"You're drinkin' it, beaver," Bear Tooth said.

Smoke finished his coffee and walked over to Joker. He took several pair of moccasins out of his saddlebags and threw them over to Cal and Pearlie. "Here, put these on," he said.

"Moccasins?" Cal asked.

"Yes, we're gonna be going right up to the outlaw camp," Smoke said. "I don't want any spurs or sounds of leather on wood or stone to alert them to our presence."

He took one of the tins of bootblack out of his saddlebag and smeared some on his face before passing the tin to the boys.

"How 'bout Bear Tooth?" Pearlie asked. "Doesn't he need some of this?"

Smoke shook his head. "No, that beard of his is black enough to keep his face hidden in the dark."

"What's the plan, Smoke?" Bear Tooth asked. "I mean, are we gonna show these dogs any mercy?"

Smoke shook his head. "No quarter, no mercy. There'll be no prisoners taken by us this trip. These bastards have already escaped from one prison, and it cost a lot of good people their lives." He patted the butt of his revolver. "I think we'll rely on Mr. Colt for all the justice these sons of bitches deserve."

Bear Tooth nodded, a grim smile on his face. "Good. I never was one for tellin' a man to put his hands up."

"If you can get us up on the cliffs overlooking the outlaws' camp," said Smoke, "the first thing we'll have to do is take out any sentries they have posted."

"Won't they hear the gunshots?" Cal asked.

Smoke shook his head and pulled out his Bowie knife.

"No, 'cause we're not going to shoot them." He passed the blade next to his throat in explanation.

Pearlie began to build a cigarette, but Bear Tooth shook his head. "Uh-uh, son," he said gently, "not 'fore battle. We don't want the smell of tabaccy on us when we're sneakin' up on a man."

Pearlie glanced at the mountain man, wondering if he was going to go without his smelly bearskin coat, but decided not to say anything.

Smoke squatted next to the fire, addressing his men. "Now, when we get to the camp, we're gonna have to split up and each take a different side of the valley. In case things go to hell and there's a commotion, we'll each make our way back to this camp, so be sure and pay attention on the way up so's you can find your way back down here in the dark."

"What if one of us gets in trouble?" Cal asked.

Smoke stared into Cal's eyes. "This is war, Cal, and we're all on our own. We could all get killed rushing in to try and save another and the outlaws would win."

Bear Tooth nodded. "So, be careful an' get the job done right the first time. Don't go gettin' softhearted an' even think of givin' the man you're after an even break, 'cause thinkin' like that'll get you killed."

"Now, after the sentries are all taken out, I'm going to pay the camp itself a little visit," said Smoke.

"You're goin' down there alone?" Pearlie asked. "Why?"

"Because there's nothing that makes a man more nervous than waking up and finding his friend lying next to him with his throat cut and his scalp gone." Smoke grinned through bared teeth. "Makes sleeping the next night awfully hard, and sleepy, tired men don't think or fight too well."

They left their horses behind and made their way up the mountain toward the outlaws' camp on foot, to minimize any sound they might make. Smoke carried on his back a large burlap bag of surprises for the outlaws.

The storm Bear Tooth had predicted began with a light snowfall, but thankfully, the wind stayed down and the temperature didn't drop too much.

"This is good," Bear Tooth whispered over his shoulder to the men following him. "The new snowfall will cushion our feet an' keep the noise down."

Once they got to the top of the trail, he squatted and pointed across the mountainside.

"The valley of the springs is right over there, past that clump of trees."

"You make out any of the sentries?" Smoke whispered.

Bear Tooth nodded, pointing again.

A bright orange speck of light could be seen off to one side where one of the sentries was smoking a cigarette.

Bear Tooth shifted his weight and pointed off in another direction, where a dark figure could be seen outlined against the lighter darkness of the sky.

"I'll take the one on the left," Smoke said. "Pearlie, you take the one on the right."

"What about me?" Cal asked.

"You go with Bear Tooth and circle around to the other side of the valley. There'll probably be a couple more over there."

Walking on the soles of his feet in a low crouch, Smoke moved as silently as the wind toward the sentry, who had finished his cigarette and was leaning back against the bole of a tree, trying to stay out of the falling snow.

Smoke slipped his knife out of its scabbard and eased up to the far side of the tree. When he heard the man yawn, he moved quickly in front of him, slashing backhanded with the Bowie knife.

The razor-sharp blade severed throat, trachea, and carotid arteries as easily as if they were made of soft butter.

The only sound the man made was a soft gurgle as he

strangled on his own blood. Smoke caught him when he toppled, and laid his dead body gently in the snow. After looking at it for a moment, he grinned as a thought occurred to him. He bent and quickly arranged the body so it was sitting with its back against the tree. He put the man's hat on his head and lowered the brim so it looked like he was sleeping.

"Someone's gonna get a big surprise when they try and wake him up," Smoke said to himself.

Pearlie's job wasn't so easy. His man was standing out in the open, with no nearby cover for Pearlie to use in his approach.

Pearlie considered throwing his knife, but decided not to because if he didn't get a clean kill, the man might be able to shout a warning or get a shot off.

Finally, an idea occurred to him. He searched until he found a fist-sized rock, and heaved it over the man's head. When it landed on the side of the sentry away from Pearlie, the man grabbed his rifle and turned in that direction.

Pearlie took several running steps and was on the man before he had time to react. Pearlie's knife entered the man's back just below the ribs on the left, at an upward angle as Smoke had taught him. The point went through spleen and diaphragm on its way to savage the man's heart. Pearlie's left arm was around his neck so he couldn't cry out as he died.

The only sound was the slight noise the man's rifle made when it fell to the ground. Pearlie dragged his body into the bushes and covered it with fallen tree limbs and snow. Then he made his way to the edge of the cliff overlooking the camp to see what was going to happen next.

Bear Tooth and Cal found only one sentry on their side of the valley. Once Cal had pointed the man out, Bear Tooth nodded at Cal to go get him.

Cal, surprised and delighted that the mountain man trusted him, pulled his skinning knife from its scabbard and moved quietly toward the man, who was bent over building a cigarette.

Cal was shorter than the sentry, even bent over, as he slipped up behind him and tapped him on the shoulder.

When the man grunted in surprise and whirled around, Cal swung his hand in an uppercut with the point of his knife pointed at the sky. The knife entered the man's throat just under his jaw and drove upward to lodge in his hard palate, pinning his tongue so he couldn't make a sound.

When the man struggled, both hands at his throat, Cal grunted and pushed harder, driving the knife blade upward into the man's brain, killing him instantly.

Cal had to put his foot on the man's head to get his knife out of the man's skull.

When Bear Tooth walked up, Cal asked him, "Why'd you let me do that?"

Bear Tooth grinned and whispered, "Since the rheumatiz has hit my legs, my knees pop somethin' fierce when I walk. I didn't want the sound to give us away."

"Oh," Cal said, wiping his blade on the dead man's shirt.

Bear Tooth squatted, and sure enough, the sound of his knees cracking was like a twig breaking. He pulled out a knife that was so long it was almost a machete, and proceeded to scalp the dead man.

The sight made Cal's stomach roll, so he turned away and looked down into the camp while the mountain man finished his grisly work.

Smoke had no trouble following his sentry's tracks back down the trail leading to the camp in the valley. The outlaws' campfire had burned itself down to just coals, so there was very little light to give him away as he scurried across the open space toward the cabins.

All of the outlaws were sleeping in the cabins, and

none were outside where Smoke could get to them. He stood there a moment, undecided if he should take the chance of going into one of the cabins, when his eyes fell on several empty whiskey bottles lying next to the fire.

He smiled to himself, knowing if they'd been drinking that much, sooner or later one would have to come outside to relieve himself.

He walked to the back of one of the cabins and found what he was looking for, a small outhouse twenty yards from the cabin.

He stepped behind it and settled down to wait.

Fifteen minutes later, the door to the cabin opened and a man stumbled toward the outhouse, coughing and trying to clear phlegm out of his throat.

Smoke waited for him to get inside and get his pants down. Then he jerked the door open and drove his knife in the man's heart where he sat.

Then Smoke made a quick slice around the man's skull and yanked his scalp off, leaving his bloody skull bone exposed.

Once that was done, Smoke took a bundle of four sticks of dynamite he'd tied together and walked back to the fire. Brushing aside the snow a few feet away, he buried the dynamite, leaving a four-foot length of fuse. He put the end of the fuse near a half-burned log on the fire and covered it with snow mixed with mud. When the outlaws built up the fire the next morning, they were going to be in for a surprise.

Smoke then walked to where the outlaws' horses were grouped in a makeshift corral in the corner of the valley. He opened the gates and walked among them, shooing them out so they'd wander off during the night. He knew some would stay put, but others would walk off in search of grass to graze on, leaving many of the outlaws afoot.

Figuring he'd done enough for one night, he climbed back up the trail and headed back to their camp.

He'd heard no outcries, so he knew Cal and Pearlie and Bear Tooth had done their jobs to perfection.

36

Once they'd all made it back to their camp, Smoke told them, "We've got time for about three hours sleep. Then we need to be on the cliffs overlooking the camp when they wake up."

Just before dawn, Bear Tooth filled eight canteens with fresh coffee and handed two to each of the men. "You're gonna need this *cafecito* to keep you alert," he said. "It figgers to be a long day."

Smoke handed each of the men a sack filled with bundles of dynamite sticks with short fuses. He then handed them each a cigar. "Light these when you see the outlaws stirring," he said. "Use them for the fuses, but be careful. You'll only have about fifteen seconds after the fuse is lit before it goes off."

"Try for the cabins first," Bear Tooth advised. "That way they won't have no cover to hide behind once the shootin' starts."

"And remember, you'll be shooting downhill," Smoke said, "so aim a little low; otherwise, you'll overshoot your targets."

He nodded at Bear Tooth. "Bear, you take Pearlie with

you. I'll take Cal with me. That way, we'll have them surrounded."

"Smoke," Pearlie said, "make sure you tell Cal to keep his damn head down. I'm gettin' tired of pickin' lead outta his carcass."

"You do the same, Pearlie," Cal advised. "I'd hate to have to eat all those bear sign Miss Sally makes by myself. I'd get big as a horse."

Bear Tooth laughed. "I'll say one thing 'bout these young beavers of your'n, Smoke. They don't scare easy."

"They've been to the river and back a few times, Bear. They'll handle themselves all right, take my word for it."

By the time the sun began to lighten the sky to the east, Smoke and his band were ensconced on all sides of the valley.

Smoke showed Cal how to lay his ammunition out in a line on one side next to where he lay, so as to be able to grab it and reload in a minimum of time. The bundles of dynamite were similarly laid out on the other side within easy reach. The cigar was to be lit at the first sign of movement below.

Ozark Jack Berlin came out of his cabin and stretched, checking the sky to see what the weather was going to be.

The storm of the night before had passed, and the sky was orange and purple with the first light of day.

"Good, no snow," he muttered to himself, thinking how glad he was going to be to get to Mexico, where the sun was as hot as the *señoritas,* and where the tequila flowed like water.

He walked over to the fire, which was down to a few smoldering coals. He threw some fresh wood on the coals, placed a pot of water next to them, and walked toward the outhouse.

As he walked, he glanced up at the cliffs overlooking the

valley, wondering where the sentries were. They usually were the first in line for coffee after a night standing guard.

"Lazy bastards probably sleepin'," he muttered as he opened the door to the outhouse.

"Goddamn!" he almost shouted, seeing the bloody mess of one of his men sitting on the board over the shit-pit.

He whirled, reaching for his pistol, realizing something was terribly wrong. As he ran toward his cabin, he looked to the side, and saw only three horses standing near the open corral gate. The others were all gone.

"Son of a bitch," he yelled, pulling his pistol and firing once in the air to wake up his men.

Within minutes the cabin doors opened and men boiled out into the early morning sun, some still in long underwear with their pants around their knees as they tried to get dressed on the run.

"What the hell's going on?" Blue Owl shouted, running toward Berlin with his rifle in his hands.

Just as Berlin got next to the now-roaring fire, he saw a trail of fire burning away from the coals toward the snow.

"What the hell?" he thought, then realized it was a fuse.

"Hit the dirt!" he shouted, and dove facedown in the snow twenty feet from the fire.

The dynamite went off with a loud explosion, sending logs and burning wood in all directions.

Billy Bartlett, nearest to the fire, was blown fifteen feet in the air, a piece of burning pine log protruding from his chest and his face blown off down to the bone.

Jack McGraw's left arm was shredded by wooden splinters, spinning him around and throwing him against the cabin wall.

A loud, booming explosion from Smoke's Sharps sounded from above. Wiley Gottlieb was knocked to his knees, a hole the size of a bucket in his chest from front to back. He had time to glance down at it before his eyes clouded over and he toppled over onto his face.

Another explosion from Bear Tooth's Big Fifty sounded,

and Jesus Santiago's right leg was blown completely off just above the knee, causing the Mexican to begin to scream in Spanish as he thrashed around on the ground, trying to staunch the spurting stream of crimson from his stump.

Berlin rolled to the side just as the snow where he'd been was pocked by several shots from Cal's Winchester. Berlin scrambled to his feet, firing wildly upward without aiming as he ran full out toward one of the caves.

Tony Cassidy ran in a low crouch toward one of the horses near the corral, firing as he ran. He vaulted up on the bronc's back and kicked its flanks, trying to get to the head of the valley.

Pearlie calmly aimed and fired, his bullet taking the outlaw square between his shoulder blades, throwing him over the horse's head to tumble and roll several times. He died from a broken neck before he bled to death from the bullet hole.

Joe Wyatt aimed his rifle at the cliff tops and fired as fast as he could lever shells into the chamber, spinning on his heels trying to get a clear shot.

Cal ended his life by shooting him in the face, tearing his jaw off and ripping a hole in his throat. He fell into what was left of the fire and began to burn.

The rest of the men ran back into the cabins, trying to get under cover, except for Blue Owl. He saw Berlin headed for the caves, and followed as fast as he could, running almost bent double to make a smaller target.

Bear Tooth took a shot at him with the Sharps, but the bullet missed by inches and tore a hole in the wall of the outhouse, hitting the dead man inside and decapitating him.

Smoke stood up where Bear and Pearlie could see him, and held a bundle of dynamite up for a second. Then he lit it from his cigar and made a long toss toward one of the cabins.

Cal followed suit, as did Bear Tooth and Pearlie.

Four bundles of dynamite hit at almost the same time.

Bear Tooth's fell short, and did little damage other than blowing snow and mud and dirt into the air.

The others landed square on the cabins' roofs, exploding and blowing them into splinters, along with some of the men inside.

Jack McGraw had crawled away from the cabin, cradling his ruined left arm with his right. He was twenty yards away when the cabin exploded. He rolled over onto his back, thanking his lucky stars he hadn't crawled inside, when a shadow appeared overhead. He looked up in time to see a fifteen-foot log tumbling down toward him. He barely had time to scream before it crushed him into the dirt, breaking every bone in his body.

Spotted Dog and John Ashby were blown out of their cabin to land twenty feet away. Spotted Dog's left ear and half his face were blown completely off, along with his left eye. He stumbled to his feet, screaming and yelling with his right hand to his face, firing his pistol blindly with his left hand.

Cal and Pearlie both shot at the same time, blowing him onto his back, his mouth open but no sound coming from it as blood pumped from twin holes in his chest.

Smoke, who'd seen Berlin and Blue Owl disappear into the cave, put down his Sharps and scrambled down the path on the side of the cliff to follow them.

John Ashby, his thigh bone sticking out of his leg like a piece of alabaster china, crawled toward the head of the valley, as if he could crawl to safety.

Bear Tooth stood up, took careful aim, and blew his spine in half. Ashby grunted once, then let his head fall as he died on his stomach.

Moses Johnson, buried in the rubble of a cabin, lay still, figuring he'd play dead and see what happened.

Smoke entered the cave, crouching to make a smaller target, and walked forward, his Colt in his hand, to see if he could find the two men who'd entered moments before.

* * *

Bear Tooth, Cal, and Pearlie made their way down the cliffs until they were on the valley floor. Dead men and pieces of dead men were scattered all over the area. A couple of the men moaned and cried weakly for help, but none looked as if they were going to survive the assault.

The three men moved among the bodies, checking them to make sure they'd cause no more trouble.

Bear Tooth searched the rubble of the cabins, finding the large sack of gold nuggets and dust in the main room.

"Hey, boys, looky here," he said, holding up the bag and grinning.

Suddenly, from behind him, the remains of a wooden table moved and a huge black man stood up, a pistol in his hand aimed at Bear Tooth's back.

In an instant, Cal and Pearlie drew and fired, their shots sounding as one.

Bear Tooth ducked as twin bullets whizzed past his head, missing him by inches.

Moses Johnson screamed, "Jesus!" as the bullets hit him on either side of his chest, almost directly over his nipples.

He dropped his pistol and looked down at the blood oozing from his shirt, then looked up, a quizzical expression on his face.

"You boys done kilt me," he said, almost in disbelief.

Bear Tooth whirled around, whipped his long knife out, and shouted, "No, son, *I* did," and threw the knife.

It spun three times in the air and hit Johnson right between the eyes, snapping his head back and burying itself in his brain.

The big man toppled like a tree that'd been cut, falling directly onto his back.

Bear Tooth turned back to Cal and Pearlie, a gap-toothed grin on his face. "Damn if you young beavers didn't save ol' Bear Tooth's hide."

As Cal and Pearlie smiled, Bear Tooth threw his arm around their shoulders and said, "Thank yee kindly, boys."

Pearlie wrinkled his nose and said, "I'll call it even if you'll take that bearskin coat off and burn it."

Cal looked around. "Say, where's Smoke?" he asked, a note of alarm in his voice.

Bear Tooth pointed to the cave. "Last I saw, he was headed into that cave over yonder after two of them outlaws."

Cal and Pearlie drew their pistols and ran toward the cave as fast as they could, hoping they wouldn't be too late.

Bear Tooth followed at a slower rate. "Don't you worry none 'bout Smoke Jensen, boys," he drawled. "A mountain man like Smoke Jensen's more'n a match for just two pond scum like them fellers."

37

Smoke made his way cautiously through the cave, finally seeing a square of light ahead in the darkness.

Slowly, carefully, he squeezed out of the opening and got to his feet.

Twenty yards away, he saw Ozark Jack Berlin and Blue Owl getting their supplies together and getting ready to get on two horses they had tied to a tree.

Smoke stepped out into the open, his right hand near the butt of his Colt .45 Peacemaker on his right hip.

"You boys thinking of leaving this little party?" he asked in a low, hard voice.

The two men whirled around, their eyes wide with surprise.

Berlin smiled slowly and turned to square off facing Smoke. "You must be the famous Smoke Jensen I've been hearin' so much about," he growled.

Smoke smiled lazily back at him. "One and the same."

"You as fast with that six-killer as they say you are?" Berlin asked, his hand moving toward the pistol on his hip.

"You're about to find out, Mr. Berlin," he answered.

Berlin's hand moved and he slapped the butt of his gun, his teeth bared in a grimace of hatred.

Smoke waited a second, then drew in a movement so fast, Berlin's pistol was still in the leather when he fired.

His bullet took Ozark Jack Berlin in the middle of his forehead, snapping his head back and blowing brains and hair and blood all over the horse behind him.

The outlaw's eyes widened in surprise before they clouded over and stared the long stare into eternity.

Blue Owl jumped to the side and raised his hands. "I don't have a gun, Jensen," he said, a pleading whine in his voice. "You'll have to arrest me and take me to jail."

Smoke slowly shook his head. "I'm not an officer of the law," he said in a hard voice. "And you're not going anywhere."

"But . . . but . . . you wouldn't shoot an unarmed man, would you?" Blue Owl pleaded.

Just then, Cal, Pearlie, and Bear Tooth crawled out of the cave behind Smoke.

Smoke nodded at the knife in Blue Owl's belt. "That the knife you used on those women?" he asked.

A strange light gleamed in Blue Owl's eyes. "Yeah, it is. You want a taste of my blade, white eyes?" he asked scornfully.

Smoke took a deep breath. "I think it only fitting you die the way you killed so many others, breed."

"I'm not a breed!" Blue Owl said heatedly. "I'm a full-blooded Modoc."

Smoke unbuckled his belt and let his guns fall to the ground, pulling out his Bowie knife in the same motion. "Then you know what I'm going to do to you, Indian. I'm going to kill you, then I'm going to cut your eyes out so you'll wander the afterlife blind for all eternity."

"We'll see, Jensen, we'll see," the Modoc said, pulling his knife and spreading his arms in the classic knife-fighter's stance.

"Smoke," Cal called fearfully.

"Hush, boy," Bear Tooth said, grinning. "Watch, an' learn."

The two men circled each other warily, Blue Owl occasionally sweeping his knife before him to keep Smoke away as he looked for an opening.

Suddenly, he yelled and jumped forward, slashing viciously in a wide arc.

Smoke didn't retreat as the Indian thought he would, but merely leaned back, letting the point of the attacker's knife graze his chest, slicing his buckskin shirt and drawing a thin line of blood across his chest.

While Blue Owl was off balance and leaning forward, Smoke's knife moved so fast it was a blur, back and forth across Blue Owl's face, laying both his cheeks open to the bone.

Blue Owl staggered back, lowering his knife. "I've had enough," he said, as if defeated. "You win."

"No," Smoke said calmly. "It won't be over until one of us is dead, like all those women you killed."

"Bastard!" Blue Owl screamed and lunged forward, his knife outstretched.

Smoke leaned to the side and let the knife pass harmlessly by his face, bringing his blade up with all his strength.

The blade impaled Blue Owl just below his belly button, and he hung there, his eyes bulging in pain and terror as Smoke stared into his face, inches away.

With a grunt, Smoke lifted his knife with all his might, bringing the blade slicing upward through Blue Owl's belly all the way up to his chest.

Smoke stepped back and let the Indian sink to his knees, his bowels flopping out of the long hole in his abdomen to writhe like purple snakes on the ground in front of Blue Owl.

As the Indian sat there, helpless, Smoke stepped forward and with a quick double slash, took his eyes.

Blue Owl screamed and let go of his intestines to grab his face.

Smoke turned his back and walked away, leaving Blue Owl screaming in pain.

"Aren't you gonna finish him off, Smoke?" Pearlie asked.

Smoke shook his head. "Let's go home, boys. Let him suffer for a while, like all the women he cut up did. With any luck, he'll last a couple of days before the wolves find him."

Bear Tooth put his arms around Cal and Pearlie's shoulders again as they turned to go.

"Let that be a lesson to you, boys. Don't never make a mountain man mad."

"Uh, Bear," Pearlie said, "about that coat . . ."

WARPATH OF THE MOUNTAIN MAN

1

Smoke Jensen was in front of the hardware store, looping the reins of his horse around the hitching rail, when he heard the gunshot. Sometimes, in drunken play, shots were fired into the floor or in the air. Most of the citizens of Big Rock had learned to tell the difference between the sound of a shot fired in play and one fired in anger.

This shot, fired at ten-fifteen A.M. on a Tuesday morning in October, was fired in anger.

Suddenly, a man burst from the front door of the bank, which was located about two blocks west of the hardware store. It was Rich Flowers, one of the bank tellers.

"They're robbing the bank! They're robbing the bank!" Flowers shouted. "Help, somebody, they're . . ."

That was as far he got before a masked man appeared in the doorway of the bank, clutching a bag in one hand and a pistol in the other. The masked man raised his pistol and fired at Flowers, hitting him in the back. Flowers fell facedown in the dirt.

Up and down the street there were screams and shouts of fear and alarm. Citizens of the town scrambled to get out of the way: running into nearby doorways, ducking behind watering troughs or around the corners of buildings. Three more masked men appeared in the bank door, firing their weapons indiscriminately. There was a scream

from inside Mrs. Pynchon's dress shop. The crash of glas
followed as a woman tumbled through the window and fel
onto the boardwalk, bleeding from her wound.

"Clear the street, clear the street!" one of the bank rob
bers shouted, waving his pistol. "Everybody get off th
street!" He punctuated his demand with more pistol shot

Although most of the citizens obeyed the bank rob
bers' orders, Smoke Jensen did not. Instead he strolled
almost casually, to his horse, and pulled his rifle from it
saddle holster. Then, jacking a shell into the chambe
he stepped out into the middle of the street, raised th
rifle to his shoulder, and fired at one of the bank rob
bers. The bank robber went down.

"What the hell!" one of the other robbers shouted
"Where did that come from?"

"Down there!" another said, pointing to Smoke.

The robber aimed at Smoke and fired, but he wa
using a pistol, and he missed. Smoke returned fire, an
didn't miss.

Now there were only two of the robbers left.

"Get the money and let's get out of here!" one of th
two shouted. The other robber tried to retrieve th
money bag from the hands of one of the two robber
Smoke had killed, but Smoke put a bullet in his leg an
he went down.

The last robber, now seeing that he was alone and ou
gunned by the man with the rifle, threw his pistol dow
and put his hands up.

"Don't shoot! Don't shoot!" he shouted. "I quit!"

Keeping the robber covered, Smoke walked towar
him. By now, most of the townspeople realized tha
Smoke had everything under control. They starte
coming back into the street, heading toward the ban
and the two robbers who were left alive: one standin
with his hands up, the other, groaning and bleeding
lying in the dirt.

"Who are you, mister?" the one who was still standin
asked.

"Why do you need to know?" Smoke replied. "It's not like we're going to be friends, or anything."

Some of the citizens of the town, now close enough to hear the exchange, laughed.

"Mister, you just been brought down by Smoke Jensen," someone said. "And if it's any consolation to you, he's beaten many a man better than you."

By now, Sheriff Monte Carson was also on the scene, and he took the two robbers into custody.

"What about my leg?" the wounded robber asked. "I got me a bullet in my leg. I need a doctor. I'm your prisoner, and the law says you got to get me a doctor."

"We've only got one doctor in this town, mister," Monte replied. "And right now he's seeing to Mrs. Pynchon and Mr. Flowers. You better hope neither one of them dies, 'cause if either of them does, you'll both be hung for murder. Let's go." Monte made a motion toward the jail.

"I can't walk on this leg, I tell you."

"'Couple you men . . . help him," Monte said.

With assistance from two onlookers, the wounded man and his uninjured partner crossed the street and entered the jail.

"We've got two nice rooms just waiting for you," Monte said, opening the doors to adjacent jail cells.

"When's the doctor going to look at my leg?"

"When he gets around to it," Monte replied. "In the meantime, if I were you, I'd just lie on the bunk there and take it easy."

"It hurts," the wounded prisoner insisted.

"Yeah, I reckon it does. What are your names?" Monte asked.

"I'm Jack Tatum," the uninjured man said. He nodded toward the other robber, who had taken Monte's advice and was now lying on the bunk. "His name is Billy Petrie."

"Tatum?" Monte said. "I've seen that name." He opened the drawer of his desk and took out a pile of wanted posters. After looking through several of them, he pulled one out. "Ah, here it is. This is you, isn't it?"

Monte turned the poster so Tatum could see it.

WANTED
JACK TATUM
For Murder and Robbery
$5,000
Reward to be paid
DEAD OR ALIVE

"Only five thousand? They're a bunch of skinflints, Tatum snorted. "Hell, I'm worth more than that."

"Proud of it, are you?" Monte asked. He pulled out a tablet and began writing. "I reckon I'd better get a telegram off. No doubt some folks are going to be happy to hear that you are out of business."

"Sheriff, what are you going to do about that fella that murdered my two friends?" Tatum asked.

Monte looked up from his desk. "I beg your pardon Did you say murdered?"

"Yeah, I said murdered, 'cause that's what he done We wasn't shootin' anybody, we was just shootin' in the air to clear the street. Next thing I know, that bank teller was down, then that woman come crashin' through the window, then Fuller and Howard, then Billy was shot The fella doing the shooting—Jensen, I think someone said—was a crazy man, sending bullets flying everywhere. You ask me, he's the one who should be locked up in here."

"Are you trying to tell me that you didn't have anything to do with shooting Mr. Flowers or Mrs. Pynchon?

"That's what I'm telling you," Tatum said.

"I'll give you this, Tatum. You've got gall, telling a lie like that when the whole town saw what you did."

"Well, now, some folks may have seen it one way and some the other," Tatum replied. "We are going to get a trial, aren't we? Or do you plan to just hang us?"

"You'll get a fair trial," Monte replied. He paused for a moment, then chuckled. "Then we'll hang you."

Dr. Spaulding came into Monte's office then, and set his bag on the corner of Monte's desk.

"How's Mrs. Pynchon?" Monte asked.

"She'll be all right. The bullet went all the way through her upper arm, but it didn't hit any bones."

"Rich Flowers?"

Doc Spaulding shook his head. "Dead. He was dead before I even got to him."

"That's a shame. Flowers was a nice man."

"Yes, he was. And the really sad thing is, Edna, his wife, is going to have a baby."

"Damn, that's a shame. What about the two bank robbers? Both dead?"

"Yes."

"Listen, Doc, I want you to do me a favor. Take the bullets out of the bodies. No doubt the court will need them for evidence."

"All right. I understand one of your prisoners is wounded?"

"Yeah, he's on his cot back there. He took a bullet in his leg."

"I'll take a look at it," Spaulding said, picking up his bag and heading toward the cell.

"Sheriff," Tatum called.

Sighing, Monte looked up at him. "What is it now, Tatum?"

"I want to see a lawyer. That's my right, ain't it? To see a lawyer?"

"You have that right," Monte agreed.

"And if I don't have one, you have to appoint him?"

"That's right."

"Then appoint a lawyer for me and get him over here," Tatum demanded.

In the cell next to Tatum, Billy Petrie started screaming.

"Hold still, young man," Doc Spaulding said. "If I don't get this bullet out, you're likely to lose that leg. Here, here's some laudanum."

The laudanum took effect, and the prisoner's screams turned to a few moans and groans. Doc Spaulding, ever the caregiver, spoke in quiet, reassuring tones as he worked on Petrie.

Monte was just finishing the telegram he was going to send when Dewey Wallace, a recently hired deputy, came in.

"Whoowee, the town is really buzzing over all the excitement this morning," Wallace said, walking over to the little stove to pour himself a cup of coffee.

"Is Welch seeing to the bodies yet?" Monte asked.

"You bet. He had his measuring tape out before they were cold. Want a cup of coffee?"

"No, thanks," Monte said. He tore the sheet of paper off his pad. "As soon as you finish your coffee, take this down to the telegraph office."

"All right," Wallace said. Sipping the coffee, he looked at the sheriff's message, then whistled. "You think they'll pay Smoke Jensen that reward?"

"I don't know why they shouldn't," Monte said.

Wallace walked over to the jail cells and stood just outside the bars, looking at the two prisoners as he drank his coffee. "So, what were you fellas thinkin'?" Wallace asked. "Did you think we're such a small town you could just come in here and rob our bank, then leave without so much as a fare-thee-well?"

Tatum glared at the deputy, but said nothing.

"Quiet, huh?" Wallace said, chuckling. "Well, I reckon you won't be so quiet when we string you up." Holding his hand beside his neck to represent a rope, he made a jerking motion, then gave his impression of a death rattle. He followed that with a laugh. "Yeah, you won't be so quiet then," he said.

"Wallace, get the hell away from the cells and quit bothering the prisoners," Monte said. "Take that telegram down to Western Union like I told you."

"All right, Sheriff. Whatever you say," Wallace said, draining the rest of his coffee.

As Wallace was leaving, Doc Spaulding came back from Petrie's cell.

"I don't know what I was thinking when I hired that boy," Monte said.

"Ahh, he'll come around," Spaulding said. He dropped a small piece of lead on the corner of Monte's desk. "Here's the bullet I took from his leg."

"What is it? A .44-40?"

"Is that what Jensen was shooting?"

"Yes."

"Then that's what it is. Of course, it's pretty hard to tell the difference between a .44 and .44-40, seeing as they are so close to the same size and weight."

"That's true," Monte agreed. He had opened a small notebook and was looking through it. Then, when he found what he was looking for, he groaned. "Jensen's not going to like this."

"Who's not going to like what?" Doc Spaulding asked as he closed his bag.

"Sam Covington is next in line to be the public defender."

Doc Spaulding chuckled. "You're right," he said. "He's not going to like it."

"I'll tell you who else won't like it. Norton, the prosecuting attorney. If anyone can make a case out of this, it will be Sam Covington."

"Covington's good, all right."

"Good has nothing to do with it. As far as I know, every lawyer in the county is good. But Covington is more than good, he is ruthless. He'll do anything it takes to win a case, any case. It doesn't matter to Covington whether something is right or wrong or whether someone is guilty or innocent. All that matters to him is who wins and who loses."

When Smoke Jensen returned home to Sugarloaf, he dismounted and untied a sack from the pommel. He had gone into town to get a few things at the hardware store, and despite the excitement of the morning, he had not lost sight of his objective.

The aroma of fried chicken assailed his nostrils as he entered the house, and going into the kitchen, he saw Sally standing over the stove. He stepped up behind and put his arms around her, then pulled her to him, nuzzling his cheek against hers. She leaned back into him.

"Uhmm-uhm, that smells good," he said.

"What smells good?" Sally replied. "The fried chicken, or the five-dollar-an-ounce perfume I'm wearing?"

"Uh . . . the, uh . . . perfume of course," Smoke stammered. "Well, the chicken too, but definitely the perfume."

Sally laughed. "You are the biggest liar I know. Not only am I not wearing any perfume, you know full well that I would never be foolish enough to spend five dollars for one ounce. Especially when I could put essence of fried chicken behind my ears and accomplish the same thing, as far as you are concerned."

"Well, as far as I'm concerned, you don't need perfume or fried chicken," Smoke said. "To me, you always smell good."

"Uh-huh, don't you try and butter me up now, Mr. Smoke Jensen. Especially after what happened in town today. You go into town to make a simple purchase at the hardware store and you wind up in a gunfight."

Smoke picked up a drumstick from the platter of chicken that was already done and began eating. "How'd you hear about it so fast?"

"Well, I'm glad to see that you aren't going to deny it. Mrs. Fremont was in town and she saw the whole thing. You better believe she couldn't wait to stop by and tell me about it."

"She always was a busybody."

"You can't blame her. She figures that is her purpose in life."

"Then you also heard about Rich Flowers?"

Sally nodded. "Yes, I heard. And poor Edna is pregnant. Pregnant and a widow. It's terrible. But you had no business putting yourself on the line like that. One man against four? Did you want to make me a widow too? What were you thinking?"

"I don't know. It just seemed like the thing to do at the time," Smoke said.

Smoke knew that Sally's bark was worse than her bite, because he knew that had she been there, she quite likely would have joined him. Sally was as good with a gun as just about any man Smoke had ever met. She was lightning fast and deadly accurate with a pistol. A trick she liked to do was to put a pie pan on the ground at her feet and a steel washer on the back of her hand, then hold her arm out straight and go for her pistol. Of course the moment she turned her hand, the washer would start to fall and, as it was falling, Sally would begin her draw. She could pull the pistol, fire, and hit her target, before the washer hit the pie pan. And with a rifle she was even deadlier, for she could drill a dime from a fifty yards.

"You aren't mad, are you?" he asked.

Sally chuckled. "Do I get mad at a raindrop for getting my hair wet? Some things are just acts of nature. And when you see someone in trouble, you have just naturally got to come to their rescue. It's who you are."

"You're a good woman, Sally. I don't know how I was ever lucky enough to find you, or why you were foolish enough to marry me. All I know is, you are the best thing that ever happened to me."

"Better be careful, cowboy," Sally said with a seductive smile. "Talk like that will get you . . ."

"Whooeee, am I starved!" a voice suddenly shouted from the front of the house. "And does that ever smell good."

"Damn, Pearlie, if you don't have the worst timing in the world," Smoke said.

"The timing seems pretty good to me," Pearlie said. "I mean, the food's about ready, isn't it?"

Smoke and Sally laughed.

"Yes, it's ready," Sally said. "Wash up, I'll have it on the table shortly."

Pearlie, a young man just past twenty, was the acting foreman of Sugarloaf, having come to work for Smoke after a stint as a hired gun. But the concept of being a hired gun had soured when some of the men Pearlie was working with had raped and killed a young girl. Pearlie had quit that job and thrown in with Smoke, whose ranch had been the target of the man Pearlie was working for at the time. Since then, Pearlie had proven to be one of the most loyal—and hungry—people Smoke had ever known.

Cal came into the house right behind Pearlie. Cal was a couple of years younger than Pearlie, and while his appetite wasn't quite as large, his loyalty to Smoke and Sally was just as intense.

Smoke and Sally had no children of their own, but if they had, they would have wanted them to be exactly like the two young men.

"Wish I'd been with you for the little fracas in town," Cal said as they all sat down to eat.

"Why?" Pearlie asked as he spooned a pile of mashed potatoes onto his plate. "What could you have done that Smoke didn't do?"

"Watch," Cal said simply.

The others laughed.

2

While Big Rock did not have a courthouse, it did have a city administration building, with an area that was set aside specifically to be used as a courthouse when the occasion demanded. However, there was no permanently sitting judge. Because of that, there was a two-day delay while they waited for Harry Tutwyler, circuit judge of the third judicial district, to come to town to conduct the trial. The judge was met by Sheriff Monte Carson; Abner Norton, the prosecuting attorney; and Emil Bartholmew, the president of the bank. In addition, there were several other townspeople on hand because the upcoming trial was a big event for the small town of Big Rock.

The judge, a man of considerable girth, was wheezing from exertion as he stepped down from the train. "Have you made arrangements for my accommodations?" he asked.

"Yes, Your Honor," Monte replied. "We've put you up at the Homestead Hotel."

"Is there a restaurant nearby?"

"Yes, sir, the City Pig is right next door. It's a very fine restaurant, and I have arranged for the town to pick up your tab."

"Thank you," Tutwyler said. "I take it that everything is ready for the trial?"

"Oh, yes, we're all ready for it," Monte said.

"Do the accused men have a lawyer? I'm not going to conduct the trial if they don't have a qualified attorney representing them."

Monte and Norton looked at each other for a moment. Seeing their hesitation, Judge Tutwyler stopped. "Don't tell me they aren't represented?"

"Oh, they're represented, all right," said Norton. "Sam Covington is their lawyer."

Tutwyler looked at Norton with an expression of surprise on his face. "Sam Covington? Isn't he the governor's man?"

"Hand in glove."

"How did he wind up representing a couple of bank robbers and murderers?"

"It was his turn, Your Honor. As you know, every lawyer in the county is on a roster and must take his turn representing the indigent. Covington's name came up."

"From what I know of Covington, Mr. Norton, you can be sure that he will be a powerful adversary. He doesn't like to lose at anything."

"No, sir."

"Well, if you gentlemen will show me to the hotel, I'll freshen up, have some dinner, then retire for the night. Court will convene sharply at nine tomorrow morning. Please make certain that all interested parties are so informed."

"Yes, sir," Monte said.

The next morning, Smoke, Sallie, Cal, and Pearlie came to town to watch the trial of Jack Tatum and Billy Petrie. It wasn't mere curiosity that brought them to town, because Smoke had been subpoenaed as a witness for the prosecution.

The four of them arrived in a trap that was driven by

Cal. Pearlie sat beside him on the front seat, Smoke and Sallie on the backseat.

"What time does the trial start?" Pearlie asked.

"Nine o'clock," Smoke answered.

"It's just now a little after eight. Maybe we could get something to eat while we're waiting."

"Heavens, Pearlie, after that huge breakfast you had, you are still hungry?" Sally asked. Then, almost immediately, she laughed. "What am I saying? Of course you are still hungry. I don't think there is ever a time when you aren't hungry."

"I could use a cup of coffee myself," Smoke said.

The four went into the City Pig and found a table.

"Good morning, Mr. Jensen, Mrs. Jensen," Kathy said, coming over to the table. "Are you folks in town for the trial?"

"Yes," Smoke said without elaboration.

"It seems that everyone is. We've never been so busy. Oh, and everyone is talking about what a hero you were."

"Yes, well, people talk too much," Smoke said, self-conscious at being the recipient of such accolades.

"Well, what can I get for you?" Kathy asked, realizing that she was embarrassing him. "Our pancakes are awfully good this morning."

"Thanks, but we've had breakfast," Sally said. "We're just waiting around until the trial starts. All I want is coffee."

"That'll do for me," Smoke said.

Cal also ordered only coffee, but when Kathy got to Pearlie, he was still studying the menu.

"Pearlie?" she asked.

"Uh, I had breakfast too," Pearlie said, "but it was fairly light."

Sally gasped, then looked at Smoke and Cal. All three laughed.

"Well, I mean, it wasn't all that heavy," Pearlie said. "So I might have just a little something to tide me over until lunch. Maybe a stack of pancakes, three eggs, 'bout half a pound of sausage, some biscuits and gravy ought to do it."

"I'll get a work crew started on it right away," Kathy said, laughing as she started toward the kitchen.

Forty-five minutes later, Smoke, Sally, Pearlie, and Cal were in the courthouse, sitting in the second row of seats. They were there when Monte and Deputy Wallace brought in the prisoners, Jack Tatum and Billy Petrie.

Jack Tatum looked out over the gallery. The courtroom was packed for the show, and he intended to give them one. No stranger to court appearances, Tatum was a man who had spent at least half of his forty-two years in various jails and prisons.

He had a misshapen eye, the result of a knife fight that left him permanently scarred, and his adversary permanently dead. There were few laws he hadn't broken, and none he wouldn't. He had started his life of crime when, at the age of fourteen, he sneaked into his mother's bedroom, killed the man she was sleeping with, took his money, and ran away into the night. He had neither seen nor contacted his mother since then, and neither knew nor cared whether she was dead or alive.

Billy Petrie was considerably younger than Tatum. Petrie's mother, a soiled dove, died when he was twelve. He never knew who his father was, so when he was orphaned, he became a ward of the state. They put Petrie in a reform school because there was no room for him in the orphanage. He broke out of reform school when he was sixteen, and had lived a life of crime ever since.

Although the bullet had been removed from Petrie's leg, the wound was still bothering him. He was limping noticeably as the prisoners were brought into court to await the arrival of the judge. It also didn't help matters that he and Tatum were chained together.

Sitting at the defendants' table, and greeting them when they arrived, was Samuel B. Covington, appointed by the court as counsel for the defense.

Covington was a dapper, distinguished-looking man exceptionally well dressed, complete with vest and gold watch chain. His hair was dark, except at the temples, where it was gray. He had a small, well trimmed mustache.

Sam Covington was a well-known lawyer who was very active in politics. In the most recent election, he had directed the successful campaign of the sitting governor. As a result, he was now one of the most powerful men in the state, with the governor's ear any time he wanted it.

Mrs. Edna Flowers was in court, the grief over the recent loss evident in her face. The widow's weeds she was wearing did little to hide the fact that she was pregnant. Margaret Pynchon was in court as well, sitting next to Mrs. Flowers. Mrs. Pynchon's arm was in a sling, and both she and Mrs. Flowers glared at the defendants as they were brought in.

Before the judge entered the court, Smoke and Sally went back to speak to the two ladies who had suffered most from the aborted bank robbery.

"Edna, I was so sorry to hear about Rich," Sally said. "The entire town will feel his loss deeply. If there is anything I can do for you, please let me know."

"Thank you, Mrs. Jensen," Edna said, dabbing at her eyes. "Everyone has been so kind."

"And that goes for you as well, Margaret. I know with your arm hurt like that, you can't work. So if you need anything, please let me know, would you?"

"Thank you," Margaret said. "Dr. Spaulding said he was sure I could get back to work in a couple of days, so I'm sure everything will be all right."

At that moment the bailiff came into the courtroom. "All rise!"

The court fell silent as everyone stood.

"Oyez, oyez, oyez, this court is now in session, the Honorable Harry Tutwyler presiding. All who have business with this honorable court draw near and listen. God bless this honorable court, and God bless the United States of America. Order in the court!"

Judge Tutwyler, wearing black robes, came in and

stood behind the bench for a moment, then sat. Not until then did everyone else sit.

"Who comes now before this court?" said Tutwyler.

"Your Honor, before this honorable court comes the case of the state against Jack Tatum and William, also known as Billy, Petrie. They are charged with murder in the first degree, aggravated assault with the intent to commit murder, bank robbery, and conspiracy to commit bank robbery."

"Will the defendants please stand?"

At Covington's urging, both Tatum and Petrie stood.

"You have heard the charges against you," Judge Tutwyler said. "How do you plead? Guilty, or not guilty?"

"We didn't do all them things that was just said," Tatum said. "I mean, to listen to all that, you'd think . . ." That was as far Tatum got before Covington was able to put his hand out toward his client to quiet him.

"The defendants plead not guilty, Your Honor," Covington said.

"The plead of not guilty is entered," the judge said.

After they spent nearly an hour selecting the jury, the judge finally turned to Norton and said, "Mr. Prosecutor, make your case, sir."

Norton gave his opening remarks, called upon witnesses from the bank, then called his star witness, Smoke Jensen.

Reaching over to pat Sally's hand, Smoke walked up to the front of the courtroom, where he was sworn in.

"Mr. Jensen, would you please, in your own words, tell the court what happened on the morning of the fourteenth of last month?"

Without elaboration, Smoke told the story of being in front of the hardware store when he heard the shooting. He told of watching Mr. Flowers shot down in the street before he himself joined the action. His statement was concise but complete, with no self-aggrandizement.

"Your witness, Counselor," Norton said as he walked back to his table.

Covington approached Jensen, looked at him for a long moment without saying a word, then moved over to stand in front of the jury.

"Mr. Jensen, how many men have you killed?"

"Objection, Your Honor!" Norton shouted, leaping up from his own chair. "That question is inflammatory and irrelevant!"

"Your Honor, by definition, anytime someone is killed, it is inflammatory," Covington replied. "But if you will allow me to pursue this course, I will be able to establish the relevance."

"I will allow the question, Counselor, but be cautioned, I will be keeping an eye on you. And if I see you misusing my generosity, I'll withdraw permission in a heartbeat."

"Thank you, Your Honor," Covington said. He turned back to Smoke. "How many men have you killed?"

"I'm not sure," Smoke replied.

"You're not sure? You mean the act of killing another human being is so insignificant to you that you can't even remember how many you have sent to their Maker?"

"I've never killed anyone who wasn't trying to kill me."

"Would you say you have killed more than ten men?"

"Yes."

"More than twenty?"

"Your Honor, I object. The witness has answered the question. He has killed more than ten men. I see no reason for carrying this any further," Norton protested.

"Objection sustained. Continue the cross-examination."

"I am curious, Mr. Jensen. When you killed Mr. Fuller and Mr. Howard, did you pause to reflect upon it?"

"I'm not sure what you mean."

"Before you pulled the trigger that sent Mr. Fuller and Mr. Howard hurling into eternity . . . did you hesitate, even for a moment?"

"No."

"Did you not even ask yourself if you were doing the right thing?"

"Mr. Covington, much is said about the speed of a

gunfighter's draw. But in reality it isn't the speed of drawing the gun as much as it is the speed of making the right decision. Once I realized what was going on, I made the decision to intervene. I knew it was right and I didn't have to reconsider."

"I see. Mr. Jensen, what caliber bullets were you shooting on the day in question?"

"The rifle I fired used .44-40-caliber ammunition."

"Are you aware that the shots that killed Fuller and Howard were made from a distance of one hundred seventy-five yards?"

"I didn't measure the distance," Smoke said.

"I did. Given the distance of the shot, don't you think some hesitation might have been prudent? Especially since Richmond Flowers and Mrs. Pynchon were both struck by bullets that are consistent with the caliber of the bullets you were shooting?"

"Objection! Is defense trying to suggest that Smoke Jensen shot Mr. Flowers and Mrs. Pynchon?" Norton asked.

"Your Honor, I am making no such claim," Covington said quickly. "I am merely making the observation that Mr. Flowers was killed and Mrs. Pynchon was wounded by bullets that are consistent with the caliber of the bullets Mr. Jensen was shooting. It goes to establishing doubt."

"Objection overruled."

"Thank you, Your Honor." Turning back to Smoke, Covington continued with his cross-examination. "Mr. Jensen, you do admit to killing Howard and Fuller, do you not? I mean, that issue is not in doubt?"

"I killed them," Smoke said.

"Would it be fair to say then that, on that day, you were their judge, jury, and executioner?"

"Objection, Your Honor. Inflammatory," Norton protested.

"Sustained."

"Withdraw the question. Mr. Jensen, are you an officer of the law?"

"No."

"Would you consider yourself a vigilante?"

"No."

"Then, by what right did you kill Fuller and Howard?"

"Objection, Your Honor, the witness is not on trial here. Jack Tatum and Billy Petrie are on trial. It is clear to anyone with reason that, by his actions, Mr. Jensen saved more innocent lives. I'll not have him browbeaten like this."

"Your Honor, this goes to witness credibility," Covington said. "As far as I know, there has been no hearing to determine whether or not Mr. Jensen's homicide was justifiable. And unless or until that happens, any testimony Mr. Jensen may give this court could be said to be self-serving."

"Objection sustained," Judge Tutwyler said. "Unless you can prove that the witness has perjured himself, his testimony will be given relevant weight. Now, please continue."

"I have no more questions for this . . ." Covington turned his back on Smoke as if disgusted, then added in a derisive tone, "Witness."

"Redirect?" the judge asked Norton.

"No redirect, sir. And, as Mr. Jensen was my last witness, prosecution rests."

3

"Prosecution having rested, you may now present your case, Mr. Covington."

"Thank you. Your Honor, defense wishes to call Sheriff Monte Carson to the stand."

There was a buzz of curiosity throughout the courtroom as Monte was called. He had been one of the prime witnesses for the prosecution, and everyone wondered what use Covington could make of him for the defense.

"Sheriff, I remind you that you are still under oath," the bailiff said as Monte took the stand.

"I understand," Monte replied.

"In the course of your investigation of the events on the fourteenth of October, were you presented with the bullet that killed Mr. Flowers?"

"I was."

"And I believe you testified that it was a .44-caliber bullet?"

"It was."

"And the bullet that wounded Mrs. Pynchon? Also a .44-caliber?"

"It was."

"And, under questioning from prosecution, you stated that the pistols you took from the defendants, Jack Tatum and Billy Petrie, were also .44-caliber?"

"They were."

"Now, Sheriff, I would like to ask you a question that prosecution did not ask you. Did you also take the pistols from the two men that Smoke Jensen killed?"

"Yes."

"What caliber were they?"

"The pistols were Colt .44's."

"And the bullet that Dr. Spaulding took from Mrs. Pynchon's shoulder, as well as the bullet he took from Mr. Flowers's body, what caliber were they?"

"The bullets were .44-caliber."

"What about the bullets taken from the bodies of Mr. Howard and Mr. Fuller?"

"They were .44-40."

Covington walked over to his table and picked up two envelopes. Returning to the witness stand, he held the envelopes in front of him. "Your Honor, I have defense exhibits marked A and B. I beg permission to perform an experiment."

"You may proceed."

"Sheriff Carson, would you hold your left hand out, please?"

Monte did as directed.

"I am removing an object from the envelope marked A and placing it in your hand. Would you identify it for the court, please?"

He placed a small piece of lead in Monte's hand.

"It is a spent bullet," Monte said.

"Caliber?"

Monte hefted it, and examined it closely. "I'd say it was a .44-caliber."

"And now this one?" Covington put another bullet in Monte's right hand.

"It's also a bullet."

"Caliber?"

"It's a .44-caliber."

"You are correct, Sheriff, this is a .44-caliber bullet."

Monte smiled and nodded at the jury.

"But the bullet you are holding in your left hand is a .44-40."

The gallery reacted with a buzz of wonder and surprise.

"Thank you, Sheriff Carson. No further questions," Covington said. "Defense calls Mr. Jack Tatum to the stand."

The bailiff held the Bible out toward Tatum, who looked it for a second, then placed his hand on it.

"Do you swear to tell the truth, the whole truth, and nothing but the truth, so help you God?"

"Yeah, yeah, sure," Tatum snorted.

"Be seated, please."

Tatum took his seat.

"Mr. Tatum, on the fourteenth of October, at approximately ten-fifteen in the morning, did you, Mr. Petrie, Mr. Howard, and Mr. Fuller attempt to rob the bank of Big Rock?"

"Yeah, we tried," Tatum said.

"Your Honor, if he is confessing to this, why are we continuing with the trial?" Norton called from the prosecutor's table."

"Your Honor, if the court will indulge," Covington said quickly. "There is a greater purpose to this."

"Continue the questioning," the judge said.

"Tell the court, in your own words, what happened that morning," Covington said.

"Yeah, well, like I said, me, Petrie, Howard, and Fuller was robbin' the bank. And everything was goin' along just fine. I mean, nobody was getting hurt or anything like that, and nobody was going to get hurt. Then, when we come out of the bank, someone started shooting at us. First thing I know after that, the bank teller went down. I yelled out to Fuller and Howard, 'What'd you shoot him for?' But instead of answerin' me, I seen that they was shootin' at Jensen. That's when I first found out that Jensen was the one shootin' at us."

"Did either you or Petrie return fire?"

"We shot at Jensen in self-defense, but only at Jensen.

And we didn't even do that until he started shooting first. Then I seen that he was out of range, so I yelled at Petrie to just forget the money so we could get out of there! But that's when he got shot in the leg. I figured then that we'd better surrender before anyone else got hurt, or maybe kilt. This Jensen fella was goin' wild, you know what I mean? He was just shootin' up the whole town. I admit I come to town to steal money, but I never had it in mind to hurt anyone. When I seen what Jensen was doin', I figured the only way to keep anyone else from getting shot was if I surrendered."

Billy Petrie's testimony was almost an exact duplicate of Jack Tatum's. According to Petrie, Smoke Jensen started the shooting. The bank teller was killed, not intentionally, but by a wild shot. Mrs. Pynchon was also hit with a wild shot. Neither of them was shot, Petrie insisted, until after the shooting was started by Smoke Jensen. He added one more thing to his testimony. Looking directly at Mrs. Flowers and Mrs. Pynchon, he said, "Ladies, didn't none of us want anyone hurt. I'm sorry you lost your husband, Mrs. Flowers, and I'm sorry you got shot, Mrs. Pynchon, but wasn't neither one of us that done it."

When Petrie stepped down, Covington presented his closing argument.

"Some may regard Smoke Jensen as a hero for what he did. I don't share that opinion of Mr. Jensen," Covington began. "By opening fire in an otherwise peaceful street, he placed the lives of everyone in town in mortal danger. Did my clients kill Mr. Flowers?" Covington paused for a moment, then nodded. "They may have. It is entirely possible. They were shooting, and so were Mr. Howard and Mr. Fuller. Bullets from one or more of their guns may well have killed Richmond Flowers and wounded Mrs. Pynchon.

"However, it is also possible that Smoke Jensen killed Richmond Flowers." From his pocket, Covington held up two unfired bullets.

"Here you see an unfired .44-40 rifle bullet, and an unfired .44-caliber pistol bullet. When they are like this, it is easy to tell the difference. Ahh, but the spent bullets"—returning to his table, Covington picked up the two chunks of lead he had shown to Sheriff Carson—"are a different story. Not even Sheriff Carson, who everyone will concede is an expert in these matters, was able to tell, for certain, which bullet was which. And though I am not saying with certainty that Smoke Jensen killed Mr. Flowers, I am proving to you that it is possible that he did.

"Now, why would a man like Smoke Jensen open fire when doing so would place ordinary people in danger? That's a good question, and I think it deserves an answer. Smoke Jensen is a successful rancher to whom money is everything. To such a man, money means more than the life of an ordinary person.

"What, exactly, is an ordinary person? Rich Flowers was a simple teller, so he was an ordinary person. Mrs. Pynchon is a simple tailor, so she is an ordinary person."

Covington walked away from the jury, and fixed his gaze upon Mrs. Flowers and Mrs. Pynchon.

"Our government was founded upon the principle of the sovereignty of the ordinary person. People like these two noble ladies." He took them in with a wave of his hand, milking the moment. Then he walked away from them to stand just across the railing from Smoke Jensen. He glared at Smoke. "In Jensen's world, such people as Rich Flowers and Margaret Pynchon are unimportant." He turned to the jury. "In Smoke Jensen's world, you the gentlemen of this jury, are all ordinary people. Thus you are unimportant."

After a pause to let his point sink in, Covington continued. "But those of us who are unimportant know something that people like Smoke Jensen will never understand. We know that, while money can be replaced human life cannot.

"It wasn't lives Jensen thought to save that terrible Tuesday morning. It was money. After all, Jensen's own money is kept in that bank, so he did have a vested interest in stopping the robbery. Incensed by the idea that his money might be stolen, Smoke Jensen began shooting, and now we all know the sad and tragic consequences of that action. Gentlemen of the jury, I do not have to prove that Jack Tatum and Billy Petrie are innocent beyond a shadow of a doubt." He paused for a moment, and held up his finger. "But the prosecution must prove they are *guilty* beyond a shadow of a doubt. So, think about that. You heard Sheriff Monte Carson testify that Fuller and Howard were carrying .44-caliber pistols. In order to find Jack Tatum and Billy Petrie guilty beyond the shadow of a doubt, you must be absolutely certain that it was one of their bullets that killed Mr. Flowers—not a bullet fired by Fuller, nor a bullet fired by Howard, nor even a bullet fired by Smoke Jensen. Because it is entirely possible that Mr. Flowers was killed by one of those three. And if that is the case, then you have no choice but to find these defendants *not guilty.* Defense rests, Your Honor."

Abner Norton stood at his table, then looked toward the jury.

"Mr. Covington has just made a brilliant closing argument for his case, and I applaud him for his attempt to spin straw into gold. My closing won't take long. We have seven witnesses who testified about what they saw that day. Their stories varied somewhat, but no more than could be expected in relating accounts of such horrifying events. But all of them agreed on one thing. Smoke Jensen only fired three times, and all three of those bullets are accounted for. One killed Howard, one killed Fuller, and the third was taken from Billy Petrie's leg.

"Finally, it does not matter whether the bullet that killed Rich Flowers was fired by Howard or Fuller. Legally, the act by any one of the four men who attempted to rob that bank is shared equally by all four parties. And if anyone is killed resulting from *mala in se,* which is a legal term meaning an act of malice, then that killing—whether by intent or accident—is murder.

"There is only one finding you can return, and that is the finding of guilty. Prosecution rests, Your Honor."

When the jury retired for deliberation, Smoke, Sally, Cal, and Pearlie went back to the same restaurant where they had had their morning coffee.

"Do you think Mr. Covington really believes everything he said?" Sally asked.

"If he does believe it, then he is an even bigger fool than he looks," Pearlie said, shoveling a large piece of pie into his mouth.

"He is a lawyer. His job is to get his clients off by whatever means possible," Smoke said, trying to placate Sally, who had been bristling with anger ever since Covington had started attacking her husband.

"Well, he doesn't have to lie about it, does he?"

Smoke chuckled. "Well, I don't think we have much to worry about. Abner did a pretty good job of taking Covington's argument apart. And let's not forget that Tom Burke is foreman of the jury. I can tell you for a fact that he won't be buying any of Covington's bluster."

Just down the street from the restaurant, in the defendants' room of the courthouse, Tatum and Petrie sat across a table from Covington.

"So, what do you think?" Tatum asked. "Will the jury let us go free?"

"Let you go free?" Covington replied. "Are you insane? You were caught red-handed robbing the bank. You even admitted as much from the stand. The best you can possibly hope for is that you don't hang. Either way you're going to prison."

"Prison?" Tatum said. "I thought you were supposed to be such a good lawyer."

"There's not a lawyer alive who could get you declared not guilty," Covington said. "As it is, I've alienated everyone in town by the way I've attacked Smoke Jensen. He is held in very high regard by folks in these parts."

"Yeah? Well, he's not held in high regard by me," Tatum said. "If it hadn't been for him we'd be in New Mexico now, spending our money."

There was a quick knock on the door; then the bailiff stuck his head in.

"Jury's in," he said.

After taking his seat at the bench, Judge Harry Tutwyler adjusted the glasses on the end of his nose, then cleared his throat.

"Would the bailiff please bring the prisoners before the bench?"

The bailiff, who was leaning against the railing with his arms folded across his chest, spat a quid of tobacco into the brass spittoon and looked over toward Tatum and Petrie.

"Get up, you two," he growled. "Present yourselves before the judge."

Tatum and Petrie were handcuffed together, and they had shackles on their ankles. They shuffled up to stand in front of the judge.

"Mr. Foreman of the Jury, have you reached a verdict?" the judge asked.

"We have, Your Honor," Tom Burke replied.

"What is the verdict?"

"Your Honor, we have found these guilty sons of bitches guilty," Tom Burke said.

"You damn well better have!" someone shouted from the court.

The judge banged his gavel on the table.

"Order!" he called. "I will have order in my court." He looked over at the foreman. "So say you all?" he asked.

"So say we all," Tom replied.

The judge took off his glasses and began polishing them as he studied the two prisoners before him.

"Jack Tatum and Billy Petrie, you have been tried by a jury of your peers and you have been found guilty of the crimes of robbery and murder. Before this court passes sentence, have you anything to say?"

"What? You mean like beg for mercy or something like that?" Tatum asked. He laughed, an evil cackle without mirth. "Go on, you fat-assed son of a bitch. Sentence us and get it over with."

There were several shocked gasps from the gallery, followed by an outbreak of shouts and curses. Judge Tutwyler had to use the gavel to restore order. Finally, everyone was quiet for the sentencing.

"Jack Tatum and Billy Petrie, it is the sentence of this court that you be taken from this place and put in jail just long enough to witness one more night pass from this mortal coil. At a time to be fixed by the sheriff, though no later than noon on the morrow, you are to be removed from jail and transported to a place where you will be hanged by the neck until you are dead."

"Your Honor, we can't hang 'em in the mornin'. We don't have a gallows yet," Monte said.

Judge Tutwyler held up his hand to silence Monte, indicating that he had already taken that into consideration. "This court authorizes the use of a tree, a lamppost, a hay-loading stanchion, or any other device, fixture, apparatus, contrivance, agent, or means as may be sufficient to suspend the prisoners' carcasses above the ground, bringing about the effect of breaking their necks, collapsing their windpipes, and in any and all ways, squeezing the last breath of life from their worthless, vile, and miserable bodies."

4

Deputy Wallace had been napping at his desk in Monte's office when something—a noise, or perhaps a dream—awakened him.

"What?" he asked, startled awake. "What is it?" He opened his eyes and looked around the inside of Monte's office. The room was dimly lit by a low-burning kerosene lantern. A plethora of wanted posters fluttered from the bulletin board. A pot of aromatic coffee sat on a small wood-burning stove. The Regulator clock on the wall swept its pendulum back and forth in a measured tick-tock, the hands on the face pointing to ten minutes after two in the morning. Wallace rubbed his eyes, then stood up and stretched. He went to the stove to pour himself a cup of coffee, then stepped over to the jail cell to look inside. Expecting to see the prisoners asleep, he was startled to see that both Tatum and Petrie were wide awake, sitting on the edges of their bunks.

"What's the matter?" Wallace asked. He took a slurping drink of his coffee. "Can't you fellas sleep any?"

"No," Tatum growled.

"Well, I wouldn't worry about it," Wallace said. He took another drink of coffee. "In just about four more hours or so, you won't have no trouble at all goin' to sleep. You'll be sleepin' forever!" He laughed at his joke, then took another swallow of his coffee.

"Ahh," he said. "Coffee is one of the sweetest pleasures of life, don't you think? But then, life itself is sweet, ain't it?" He laughed again, then turned away from the cell.

Wallace gasped in surprise at seeing a Mexican standing between him and his desk. He had not heard the Mexican come in. The Mexican was wearing an oversized sombrero, and had a dark mustache, which curved down along each side of his mouth.

"What the hell are you doin' in here, Mex?" Wallace asked gruffly. "You aren't supposed to be in here."

"I have come to work, *señor,*" the Mexican said. He made a motion as if he were sweeping the floor. "Sweep floor."

"Sweep the floor at two o'clock in the morning? Are you crazy? Get the hell out of here!"

"Deputy?" Tatum called.

"Now what do you want?" Wallace asked, turning back toward the jail cell. He was surprised to see both Tatum and Petrie smiling broadly.

"I want you to be nice to our friend Senor Sanchez," Tatum said.

"Your friend?" Wallace asked, confused by the strange remark. Suddenly, he realized what he had done! He had just turned his back on the Mexican.

Too late, Wallace felt the Mexican's hand come around to clasp over his mouth. Wallace dropped his cup of coffee and started reaching for his gun. That was a mistake, for even as his fingers wrapped around the grip of his pistol, he felt something sharp at his throat. The Mexican's hand flashed quickly across his neck. There was a stinging sensation, then a wetness at his collar. The Mexican let go of him and stepped back. Wallace felt his legs turn to rubber, and he fell to the floor. He put his hand up to his neck, then pulled it away and looked in horror at the blood on his fingers. He tried to call out, but could not because his windpipe had been cut. He could make no sound at all, save the silent scream in his head.

As he was losing consciousness, he saw the Mexican opening the cell doors. Tatum and Petrie hurried out. Tatum came over to look down at him.

"Deputy, when you get to hell, tell ole Fuller an' Howard hello for us, will you?" he asked.

"Horses in alley behind calaboose," Sanchez said. "Come."

"Not yet. We got us a little job to take care of," Tatum said.

"What's that?" Petrie asked.

"The judge is stayin' over in the hotel till after the hangin'. We need to give him our regrets, tell 'im we're sorry but we can't make it."

Petrie laughed.

The three men left the jail, then slipped through the shadows down the street to the hotel. Moving in through the front door, they walked quietly over to the counter. As the desk clerk snored loudly, they checked the registration book.

"He's in two-oh-three," Tatum whispered.

Taking the spare key to the room, the three men left the desk clerk undisturbed, then moved quickly and quietly up to the second floor. They walked down the carpeted hallway until they found the door. Slowly, Tatum unlocked the door and pushed it open.

The judge was snoring loudly.

"The son of bitch ain't losin' no sleep over sentencin' us to hang, is he?" Tatum whispered. He pulled his gun.

"*No, señor,*" Sanchez said, shaking his head. He put his finger over his mouth to indicate the need for silence.

"Sanchez is right," Petrie whispered. "You use the gun it's goin' to make too much noise."

"I kill him for you," Sanchez offered. Pulling his knife, Sanchez stepped over to the judge's bed.

"Wait!" Tatum said. "I want the son of a bitch to wake up long enough to know what happened to him."

Sanchez nodded.

Tatum put his hand on the judge's shoulder.

"Judge. Judge, wake up," he said.

The judge snorted, then opened his eyes.

"What is it? Who is there?"

"It's a couple of friends of yours, Judge. Jack Tatum and Billy Petrie. We just killed the deputy and broke jail. We've come to tell you good-bye."

"What?" the judge gasped. He started to sit up, but before he was halfway in the upright position, Sanchez's knife flashed quickly across his neck. The judge's eyes opened wide in shock and fear, and he put his hands up to his throat, then fell back down onto the pillow.

"Let's get out of here," Petrie said.

Tatum started looking around the room.

"Come on!" Petrie said. "What the hell are you lookin' for? You know this old fart doesn't have any money. Let's go, before someone hears us!"

"This is what I was lookin' for," Tatum said a moment later, holding something up that gleamed softly in the dim light.

"What is that?"

"The judge's gavel," Tatum said triumphantly. "I want something to remember him by."

The three men went downstairs, walking quietly so as not to awaken any of the guests. When they passed through the lobby the clerk was still sleeping behind the desk. Slipping down through the alley, they mounted their horses and rode off into the night.

When Monte walked down to the jailhouse at just after seven o'clock the next morning, he passed the carpenters who were working on the gallows. Because of the time constraints, and the fact that the judge had authorized the hanging to be from any such contrivance as they might be able to find, Monte and a few others had come up with an ingenious solution. The stoutest of any of the pillars in town holding a porch roof were the pillars of the hardware store. Thus it was there that they decided to attach a crosspiece that would protrude out into the street.

At the street end of the protruding crosspiece, a second post was placed to support it, resulting in an upside-down U. Underneath the U, there was a plank for Tatum and Petrie to stand on. When the support post for the plank was suddenly removed, the drop would be sufficient to break the necks of the condemned men.

Several people were already gathered around the makeshift gallows, watching and talking.

"What time is the hangin' to be, Sheriff?" someone asked.

"Eight-thirty," Monte said. He took out his watch, opened it, and glanced at the time. "About another hour and a half. Has anyone seen the judge this morning?"

"No, and we don't think we will. A highfalutin fella like the judge don't get out of bed *this* time o' day. He said any time before noon. My thinkin' is, he was hopin' that's about when you would do it so he wouldn't lose any sleep."

The others laughed at the observation.

"Well, if any of you see him, tell him I'm down at the jail," Monte said. "I'm going down to relieve Wallace so he can get some breakfast."

"We'll tell him, Monte," someone said. Then, as Monte walked away, he heard the same voice saying, "You better put another brace right there if you don't want this whole thing to come crashing down on you."

"Now, who's building this contraption, Paul, you or me?" the carpenter replied.

"Well, you are, I reckon. You just ain't doin' that good a job with it, that's all."

"It's just temporary. How good does it have to be?"

"Good enough to get these fellas hung, and the way you're doin' it, might not get the job done."

"Would you like to test it out, Paul?"

Monte grinned as he heard the others laugh at the

carpenter's retort. He reached the jailhouse door and tried to open it, but was surprised to find it locked. He tapped on it.

"Dewey? Dewey, you in there?" He tapped on the door again. "Why have you got the door locked?"

When he got no answer, he fished in his pocket until he pulled out his own key. Then, opening the door, he stepped into the jail. "Dewey, I'm here," he called. "If you want any breakfast you'd better . . ." That was as far as he got. Even from the door he could see blood on the floor, and when he stepped around the desk for a better look, he saw his deputy lying in a pool of blood, his throat cut and his eyes open, opaque now, but still reflecting the horror of his last moment on earth.

"Jesus, Dewey," Monte said quietly. He didn't know if it was prayer or a curse.

Monte hurried back down the walk toward the hotel. He passed the carpenters and their audience on his way.

"You forget something, Monte?" one of the men asked.

Monte stopped. They might as well know it now as later. He drew a deep breath, then sighed. "Deputy Wallace is dead," he said. "The prisoners are gone."

"The hell you say. How did it happen?"

Monte shook his head. "He's lying on the floor with his throat cut," he said. He shook his head. "The judge isn't going to like this."

Monte hurried down to the City Pig, figuring to catch the judge at breakfast. When he came in, Kathy walked over to him. "You mean Mary's going to let you have breakfast with us this morning?" Kathy teased. Kathy and the sheriff's wife, Mary, were good friends.

Monte shook his head. "No, I'm looking for the judge. Has he come in for breakfast yet?"

"I haven't seen him."

"Hmm, I would've thought he would have been here by now. All right, I'll check the hotel. If I miss him and you see him, would you tell him I'm looking for him?"

"Sure thing, Monte," Kathy promised.

When Monte crossed through the lobby of the hotel, he saw the clerk sweeping the lobby floor.

"Has the judge come down yet?"

"Not yet."

"What's his room number?"

"Two-oh-three."

Monte went upstairs. When he reached the second floor, he stepped over to Room 203 and knocked on the door.

"Judge? Judge Tutwyler, you awake? Judge?" Monte knocked again, more loudly this time. "Judge, wake up!"

When the judge still didn't answer, Monte went back downstairs. "Do you have an extra key to the judge's room?" he asked.

"Yes," the clerk said, starting back toward the registration desk. He reached up toward a large board covered with nails from which keys were hanging. His hand started toward 203, then stopped. That nail was empty. "That's funny."

"What's funny? What is it? What's wrong?"

"The extra key is gone."

"You sure? You sure you didn't give two keys to the judge?"

"I'm positive. The extra key was hanging right here," the clerk said. "I know it was here last night because I saw it. I don't have the slightest idea what happened to it."

"Damn," Monte said. "I'm afraid I do." Turning, Monte went back up the stairs, this time taking them two at a time, although he knew in his gut that any need for hurrying was long over.

Puzzled by the sheriff's strange behavior, the hotel clerk hurried up behind him.

This time Monte made no effort to knock on the door, or even try the doorknob. Instead he backed away from it, then raised his foot and kicked hard right beside the knob.

"Here, what are you doing!" the clerk asked in alarm.

The door popped open, along with part of the door frame. Monte took one step into the room, then stopped.

"Holy shit," he said.

The bed on which the judge was lying was soaked in blood. Like Deputy Wallace, the judge's eyes were open and opaque. And like Wallace's eyes, these too reflected the horror of his death.

Jack Tatum had met Raul Sanchez six months earlier when the Mexican came to him with information about a shipment of rifles to the Mexican Army. Tatum, Sanchez, and a half-dozen others had hit the freight wagon, killed the Mexican Army guards, and taken the shipment of repeating rifles. Their initial plan had been to sell it to one of the several revolutionary groups operating in northern Sonora, but none of the groups had enough money to make the deal worthwhile. So Tatum came up with a new plan, a particularly ambitious one, which would require several more men. After breaking Tatum and Petrie out of jail, Raul Sanchez went his own way, intending to round up the men they would need to carry out Tatum's plan. Sanchez and Tatum had agreed to meet in Risco, a tiny town in northern New Mexico Territory.

Tatum was pulled out of his reverie by a call from Billie Petrie, who was riding behind him.

"Jack," Petrie called. "Jack." His voice was strained and filled with pain.

Twisting in his saddle, Tatum saw that Petrie had fallen from his horse. With a disgusted sigh, Tatum rode back to look down at him.

"We ain't makin' no time with you fallin' off your horse ever' mile or so," he said.

"I can't help it, Jack," Petrie said in a pained voice. "This here leg is killin' me. The wound has festered."

Tatum dismounted, then pulled a knife, knelt down by Petrie and ripped his pants leg open. The leg was swollen and blue. He put his hand on the leg near the bullet entry wound and felt its heat.

"You're in bad shape," Tatum said matter-of-factly.

"I'll be all right soon's I get to where I can rest a little," Petrie insisted.

"No, you ain't going to get all right."

"Maybe a doctor could . . ."

"There ain't no doctor in Risco," Tatum said. "And even if there was, 'bout the only thing he could do for you is take the leg off."

"No," Petrie said, shaking his head. "I ain't goin' let no doctor do that."

Tatum turned away from Petrie and started back toward his horse. "Think you can get mounted?" he asked.

"Yeah," Petrie said. Painfully, he got up, then reached for the saddle horn. He tried to pull himself up into the saddle, but he couldn't do it. Then, with a mighty effort, he heaved himself up, only to fall from the other side.

"Sorry, Billy, but I ain't got time to take care of you," Tatum said.

"Don't you worry about me," Petrie said.

"Oh, I ain't worried," Tatum said. There was something about the tone of Tatum's voice that caused Petrie to look up at him. When he did, he saw that Petrie was holding a gun on him.

"Jack, no!" Petrie said. "What are you going to do?"

"It's best this way, Billy. You wouldn't want to go through the rest of your life without a leg now, would you?"

"Listen, Jack, no, don't—" That was as far he got before Tatum pulled the trigger. The bullet hit Petrie in his heart, stopping it instantly.

Tatum started to leave him there, then looking down, saw the snakeskin boots Petrie was so proud of.

"No sense in lettin' these go to waste," he said. "I'll just take 'em with me—as a keepsake, so to speak." Kneeling at Petrie's feet, he pulled the snakeskin boots off, one at a time. Then, taking the reins of Petrie's horse, he rode off, even as the vultures were circling.

5

Tom Burke, the man who had acted as foreman for the jury that convicted Tatum and Petrie, gave a barbecue on his ranch, Timber Notch. It was a gala event, with half a steer turning on a spit over an open fire, tended to by a couple of Tom's hired hands. He had invited everyone who served with him on the jury, as well as the sheriff, the bailiff, and all his neighboring ranchers. Sugarloaf was adjacent to Timber Notch, which meant that Smoke, Sally, Pearlie, and Cal were included in the invitation.

The barbecue was given as a way of getting everyone together and settled back down again after the events of the recent past: the attempted bank robbery, the killing of Richmond Flowers, and more recently, the killings of Deputy Wallace and Judge Tutwyler.

The party was supposed to help people put everything behind them, but throughout the large house there were little groups of guests all talking about the same thing: the events of the recent past. Not until one of the hands came in, carrying a large joint of beef, did the subject change.

"Here's the first carving, folks!" Tom said. "If you'll get in line at the table there, when you get to the meat, I'll serve you."

Although the steer had been cooked over an outdoor

pit, it was a little cold outside, so the serving was inside. A long table, laden with vegetables and salads, provided the side dishes. There were at least forty people in attendance, and they were going down each side of the table, loading their plates with the salads and vegetables. Then they took their plates to another table where Tom was carving the meat. As Tom carved the meat, his wife, Jo Ellen, served.

Jo Ellen was wearing a gold chain, from which hung a sparkling diamond. It was an anniversary gift from Tom, and she had been showing it off proudly.

"Have you seen my new diamond?" she asked as Smoke held his plate out to be served.

"It's pretty, all right," Smoke agreed. "But I'd just as soon you not be showing it off to Sally. Next thing you know, she'll be wantin' one."

"Hah! As if you wouldn't get it for her, Smoke Jensen," Jo Ellen said. "I know you. You'd do anything Sally asked you to do. And why wouldn't you? She's a wonderful woman."

"Well, I reckon I'll confess to that," Smoke agreed with a little laugh.

Pearlie was right behind Smoke, and he held his plate out to Jo Ellen while she put a generous portion of beef on it. When Pearlie looked a little disappointed, she smiled at him.

"Would you like a little more?"

Grinning broadly, Pearlie held his plate out again. "Yes, ma'am, if you don't mind," he said.

"Say when." Jo Ellen put another large slice of beef on his plate, and when he didn't pull it back, she put another.

"Damn, Smoke, you didn't tell me I was going to have to butcher half my herd just to feed Pearlie," Tom said, laughing.

"The boy does have an appetite," Smoke agreed.

"Appetite? He doesn't have an appetite, he has a bottomless pit."

After Tom had carved enough meat, he got his own

plate, then found Smoke and joined him. Tom had recently announced that he would soon be going to Texas to buy blooded bulls, and some of the other ranchers were already making arrangements to buy stud service from him.

"When are you leaving, and how long do you think you'll be gone?" Smoke asked.

"I'll be leaving sometime in the next two weeks," Tom replied. "It'll take me two days to get there by train, maybe a week to find the bulls, and two days back. So, make it about two weeks that I'll be gone."

Tom's young son brought his own plate over and sat down beside them.

"What are you doing here, Buddy? I thought all the kids were outside, playing down at the pond," Tom said.

"They're running around putting frogs down the girls' dresses," Buddy said disgustedly. "I don't have time for that kid stuff."

Tom laughed. "You're twelve years old. If you don't have time for it now, when will you have time for it?"

"Never," Buddy said. "Anyway, you're talkin' about goin' to Texas to get the bulls, aren't you?"

"Yes."

"That's more interesting than playing with frogs."

"Buddy, would you please come take this plate over to Mrs. Pynchon?" Jo Ellen Burke called.

"Yes, ma'am," Buddy replied, putting his own plate down and going over to do his mother's bidding.

Pearlie pointed to him as he walked away. "That kid acts older'n you do, Cal," he teased.

"Jo Ellen and I are convinced that Buddy's not really a kid," Tom said, laughing. "We think he's a full-grown man, passing himself off as a kid."

"Well, look at it this way. If he keeps up his interest in the ranch, you'll have a home-grown foreman in no time at all," Smoke suggested.

"Did you read that letter in the paper from Judge

Tutwyler's wife, thankin' the town for the flowers it sent to his funeral?" Tom asked.

"Yes. It was a nice letter," Smoke said.

"It's a shame, what happened to him and the deputy."

"You should've killed both those sons of bitches while you had the chance," Pearlie said.

"It would've been better if I had," Smoke agreed.

"Where do you think they are now?" Cal asked.

"If I were them, I'd be in California," Tom said. "Or Washington State maybe. Anywhere, as long as it's somewhere far away from here."

It was after midnight when Tatum rode into the tiny town of Risco, in northern New Mexico Territory. It had been six days since he escaped, and four days since he left Billy Petrie dead on the desert floor. Using some of the money he had stolen from the deputy and the judge, he bought a bottle of tequila at the cantina, then picked up a Mexican whore, taking her as much for her bed as for any of the special services she could provide for him.

Risco was a scattering of flyblown, crumbling adobe buildings laid out around a dusty plaza. What made it attractive to people like Tatum was the fact that it had neither constable nor sheriff, and visitations by law officers from elsewhere in the territory were strongly discouraged. In fact, there was a place in the town cemetery prominently marked as "Lawman's Plot." There, two deputy sheriffs, one deputy U.S. marshal, and an Arizona Ranger—all uninvited visitors to the town—lay buried.

Tatum woke up the next morning with a ravenous hunger and a raging need to urinate. The *puta* was still asleep beside him. The covers were askew, exposing one enormous, pillow-sized, blue-veined breast and a fat leg that dangled over the edge of the bed. She was snoring loudly, and a bit of spittle drooled from her vibrating lips. She didn't wake up when Tatum crawled over her to get out of bed and get dressed.

There was an outhouse twenty feet behind the little adobe crib, but Tatum chose not to go inside, peeing against the outside wall instead.

Finished, Tatum went back in to get dressed. He looked at the snakeskin boots, then smiled as he pulled them on. They were every bit as comfortable as Petrie had said they were. "Hell, if I'd known the boots felt this good, I'd'a shot you a long time ago," Tatum said quietly, laughing at his little joke. Dressed now, he walked over to the table where he had seen the woman put the money last night. He took his money back, then let himself out and went downstairs.

Tatum was sitting at a table in the back of the cantina, having a breakfast of beans, tortillas, and beer, when Pigiron McCord came in. Pigiron wasn't very tall, but he was a powerfully built man, bald, with a prominent brow ridge, thick lips, and heavily muscled arms that seemed too long for his body. Seeing Tatum, Pigiron came back to join him.

"Sanchez told me you would be here," he said.

"Did he tell you what I've got in mind?"

"He said you were going to sell guns to the Indians."

"That's right."

Pigiron shook his head. "You ain't going to make no money that way. The Indians have gone straight. They've got their own money; they can buy guns anytime they want. Hell, they can even order them from a catalogue."

Tatum shook his head. "The treaty allows them to buy guns for hunting purposes only, and there is a limit to how many they can buy."

"Why would they want any more than they can buy?"

"Because they are going to be in a war," Tatum said. "And you can't fight a war if you don't have enough guns."

"Hell, Tatum, you been in jail too long," Pigiron said with a snort. "Except for a few Sioux and their Ghost Dancers, there ain't no Indians nowhere that's on the warpath."

"That's the way it is now," Tatum said. "But it don't have to stay that way."

"What do you mean?"

"Soon's we get through causing trouble, there will be Indians on the warpath. I guarantee it." Tatum concluded his comment by shoving half a bean-loaded tortilla into his mouth. When bean juice ran down his chin, he wiped it off with his shirt cuff, then licked the juice from the accumulation of filth that was on his sleeve.

"What are we going to do?" Pigiron asked.

"You let me worry about that. In the meantime we're going to need some men. Think you can round a few up?"

"Sure, if they don't all have to be white Anglos."

"They don't. In fact, I already got me a couple of half-breed Injuns goin' to throw in with us. We need them to make the plan work."

"How soon you want me to get 'em?"

"Soon as you can. Is there any paper out on you up in Colorado?"

"No, not that I know of."

"Good. Soon as you get a few men rounded up, I want you to take one of them with you and go on up to Big Rock to have a look around. Wait for me up there. I'll join you soon as everything's ready."

"All right." Pigiron was silent for a moment. "You said take a look around. What am I lookin' for?" he asked.

"The man who was the foreman on the jury that convicted me is named Tom Burke. I understand he has a ranch somewhere near to Big Rock. I want you to find out where it is and how many men he's got workin' for him. 'Cause the first thing I aim to do after I get back up there is pay that son of a bitch a little visit."

When Pigiron McCord and Jason Harding rode into Big Rock some days later, they rode right past Tom Burke, though, never having seen him, they didn't realize it. Pigiron and Harding headed straight for Longmont's Saloon, while the buckboard they had just passed, containing Tom Burke and his family, continued on toward the railroad station. Tom had driven in from Timber Notch so he could catch the afternoon train.

Tom's ten-year-old daughter, Sue Ann, had been bribed by the promise of a sarsaparilla, but Buddy had needed no inducement. He'd come willingly. When they reached the depot, Tom stopped the team and set the brakes on the buckboard. He left for a few minutes to check his suitcase and buy his ticket, then came back to sit on the buckboard and wait for the train with his family.

Because trains were the town's contact with the rest of the world, nearly every arrival and departure were major events. Therefore, the depot platform was crowded with men, women, and children. There was nearly always someone there to take advantage of the crowd: a musician, an artist, or even a public speaker looking for an audience. Today a juggler was entertaining the crowd by keeping brightly colored balls in the air, in exchange for whatever coins might be tossed in his hat. Getting permission, Sue Ann got down from the buckboard and went over for a closer look. She'd asked Buddy to come with her, but he'd declined, concentrating instead on the purpose of his father's visit to Texas.

"Pop, I know bulls near 'bout as good as you do. You sure you don't want me to come along?"

"Not this time, Buddy," Tom said. "Maybe next year."

"All right, next year," Buddy said, pleased by the concession. "You think I won't remember that, but I will."

Tom chuckled. "Oh, I've no doubt but that you will remember."

In the distance they heard a whistle and looking north saw smoke in the sky.

"Well, here it comes," someone called, though as everyone had heard the whistle and seen the smoke in the sky, no such announcement was necessary.

Tom stepped down from the buckboard, stretched, then reached for a small valise. He saw his suitcase, along with a dozen other bags, on the little steel-wheeled cart that was being rolled out to the track, where it would be loaded onto the baggage car.

Tom stood alongside the buckboard as the train arrived. When it drew even with him, he could feel the pounding of the big driver wheels rolling against the track as wisps of spent steam spewed out of the actuating cylinder. The train slowed, then stopped, with the cars alongside the platform while the engine, venting steam and popping and snapping as the metal cooled, sat on the far side of the depot.

"Well, this is it," Tom said. He kissed Jo Ellen and Sue Ann good-bye. Then he put his hand on Buddy's shoulder. "Take care of them while I'm gone," he said.

"I will, Pop," Buddy said.

Tom started toward the train, but Jo Ellen called out to him. "Tom?"

He turned.

"Kiss me good-bye again?"

Tom chuckled, then came back and kissed her. During the embrace she held him very hard.

"Easy, darlin'," Tom said gently. "I'm only going to be gone a couple of weeks."

"I know," Jo Ellen said.

Tom kissed her once more, then walked out to the train. Jo Ellen and her two children watched as Tom climbed onto the train and disappeared inside. The conductor called all aboard, and the train began to pull away from the station. Jo Ellen could no longer see him, but just in case he could see them, she wanted them to all be there when he took his last look back. For that reason they stayed right where they were until all that could be seen of the departing train was its smoke, hanging in the distant sky.

"Mom? Mom, aren't we going to get my sarsaparilla?" Sue Ann asked.

"What?"

"You promised me a sarsaparilla, remember?"

"Oh, yes," Jo Ellen said. "Of course."

Suddenly, and unexpectedly, Jo Ellen's body quaked

as she shivered. Sue Ann laughed. "Why did you do that?" she asked.

"Oh, no reason," Jo Ellen replied.

"Ben says when you shiver like that, it means someone just stepped on your grave," Buddy said.

"Don't be saying such things," Jo Ellen said more harshly than she intended.

"It's just a joke, Mom."

"Well, it's not a very funny one," Jo Ellen said. For some reason she had a strange feeling of foreboding that she couldn't shake.

6

By coincidence, Smoke Jensen was in town the same afternoon that Tom Burke left for Texas. And though he had come to run a few errands, he allowed himself enough time to stop by Longmont's to have a drink.

The owner of the saloon, Louis Longmont, was a lean, hawk-faced man, with strong, slender, always clean hands and long fingers with nails that were carefully manicured. Louis had been Smoke's friend for many years, and though he was sitting at his special table in the back, he got up and came over to the bar specifically to serve Smoke, pouring his drink from a special bottle he kept just for his friend.

Louis was dressed in a black suit with white shirt and dark ascot. He wore low-heeled boots and a pistol hung in a tied-down holster on his right side. The saloon owner was an enigma to many people. On first glance, he was just another dandy. But in fact, he was worth a great deal of money, and in addition to the saloon, owned a large ranch up in Wyoming, several businesses in San Francisco, and a rather significant share of a railroad.

"Did you hear about Billy Petrie?" Louis asked as he poured the drink.

"No, what about him?"

"They found his body about fifty miles south of here."

"His body?"

"Yes, he'd been shot. Sheriff took the noon train down to see about it. Looks like Tatum may have shot him to keep him from slowin' him down. So much for friendship."

"I'm not all that surprised," Smoke said. "Tatum struck me as the type of person who might do something like that."

"You crazy bitch!" someone shouted. The shout was followed by the sound of a slap, and when Smoke looked around, he saw that a big man had just hit one of the bar girls.

"You come back here!" the big man bellowed when the girl ran from him.

"Who is that?" Smoke asked.

"He gave his name as Pigiron McCord," Longmont answered. "He's a stranger in town, must've just come in today." Louis started to pull his pistol, but Smoke put out his hand to stop him.

"Wait, no need for that yet."

When the big man started toward the girl a second time, Smoke called out to him.

"Leave the girl alone, McCord."

The big man looked toward Smoke in surprise. "How'd you know my name?"

Smoke didn't answer.

The man chuckled. "So, you've heard of ole Pigiron McCord, have you? What have you heard? That I'm not someone you mess with?"

"What makes you think I would have heard of a worthless pile of shit like you?"

The smile left Pigiron's face. "Well, you will have heard of me by the time I get through with you. Then I'm goin' to settle accounts with that whore."

Pigiron started toward Smoke, but he was stopped when Smoke snapped a quick, slashing left into Pigiron's face. It was a good, well-placed blow, but Pigiron just flinched once, then laughed, a low, evil laugh.

"Fight!" someone shouted across the batwing doors of the saloon. "Smoke Jensen and some big bastard are havin' a fight in the saloon!"

Within a few seconds, there were twice as many people in the saloon as there had been when Smoke came in, and though Smoke was concentrating on the task at hand, in the back of his mind he couldn't help but wonder where all the people had come from. It wasn't as if they were out on the street, and yet here everyone was, gathered in a large circle to watch Smoke Jensen and the stranger going against each other.

"Ole Smoke may of bit off more'n he can chew this time," someone said.

"I know. Did you see a moment ago when Smoke hit him? Hell, it would'a laid just about anyone in here out, but that big bastard hardly blinked."

Pigiron rushed Smoke, and Smoke stepped to one side, causing Pigiron to slam into the bar. With a roar like an angry bull, Pigiron ran his arm down the bar, clearing it of a half-dozen glasses or more. Then he turned to face Smoke a second time.

"Why don't you stay in one place, you yellow-bellied bastard?" Pigiron asked, his words a low growl.

"I haven't gone anywhere," Smoke said. He held his left hand out, palm up, curling his fingers in invitation. "Come on, if you want me, come get me. I'm right here."

Again Pigiron lunged, and again he missed. Finally, he gave that up as a fruitless tactic and, panting heavily now, raised his fists in front of his face. For the next few minutes, the two men circled each other, holding their fists doubled in front of them, each trying to test the mettle of the other.

Pigiron swung, a clublike swing that Smoke leaned away from. Smoke counterpunched, and scored, but again, Pigiron laughed it off. As the fight went on Smoke continued to score, and though Pigiron had laughed off his early blows, he was beginning to show some effect from the punches. His eyes began to puff up, and there was a nasty cut on his lip. Then Smoke landed a punch that broke Pigiorn's nose, causing blood to flow.

So far Pigiron hadn't landed a single blow, and Smoke was glad. He had a feeling that if just one of Pigiron's blows landed, it would be like getting kicked by a mule.

Then Smoke saw an opening, and took it. He timed it just right, and landed a solid right on Pigiron's already smashed nose. He hit it perfectly, and had the satisfaction of hearing a bellow of pain from Pigiron for the first time.

Then, when Pigiron put both hands over his nose, Smoke drove his fist hard into Pigiron's solar plexus. As Pigiron bent over, stunned by the blow, Smoke finished it with a roundhouse right to the jaw. Pigiron went down and out.

Pearlie was standing in the crowd with the others, watching the fight as he ate boiled eggs he had scooped from the jar on the bar. When Smoke scored his telling blow, Pearlie started to cheer along with the others. His cheer was interrupted when he saw a man in front of him slip his pistol from his holster, aiming it at Smoke.

Dropping his eggs, Pearlie pulled his own pistol, then brought it down hard on the man's head. The would-be shooter fell forward across Pigiron's prostrate form, the pistol in his hand clattering to the floor.

"Damn!" Pearlie said. "The son of a bitch made me drop my boiled eggs."

Smoke and the others laughed. "Come on home," Smoke said to his friend. "I'll have Sally boil you up a dozen. I reckon you've earned them."

"Smoke," Louis called. "What do you think we should do about these two? Monte's gone."

"Ah, throw a bucket of water over 'em and let 'em go," Smoke said. "I don't think they'll bother anyone else. I seem to be the one that pissed them off."

"What about me?" the bar girl asked.

"Yeah," Smoke said. "Well, maybe you'd better stay out of sight until they're both gone."

When Smoke and Pearlie stepped out in front of the

saloon, Smoke saw that Pearlie had picked up three of the dropped boiled eggs. He was blowing on them, brushing them against his shirt.

"I thought you dropped those."

"Yeah, I did, but the floor wasn't that dirty."

Smoke laughed. "Tobacco quids, ground-out cigarette and cigar butts, spilt beer, whiskey, and other things I don't even want to know about, and you say it isn't that dirty?"

Pearlie was about to take a bite of one of the refurbished eggs, but he got a funny expression on his face, and pulled the egg away from his mouth.

"Yeah," he said. "Yeah, you're right. They're probably pretty dirty, aren't they?"

"I'd say they were."

Seeing a stray dog under the porch, Pearlie tossed the eggs to the animal. "You'll have Sally cook me a dozen eggs, you say?"

"An even dozen," Smoke promised as he mounted his horse.

"Those will probably be better anyway."

Smoke laughed. "I'm sure she will be flattered that you think so."

Smoke and Pearlie rode out of town as an unsteady Pigiron McCord and his equally groggy partner were tossed out of the saloon.

It was dark by the time Pigiron and Jason reached the mesa where Tatum had told them he would meet them.

"You sure this is the place?" Jason asked, looking around. "I don't see no one here."

"You think they're going to put up a sign or something?" Pigiron replied. He put his hand on his jaw and worked it back and forth a couple of times. "That son of a bitch nearly broke my jaw."

Jason rubbed the top of his head. "Yeah, and whoever hit me nearly broke my head," he said. "What the hell did you start that fight for in the first place?"

"I didn't start it. That fella Jensen did. All I was doing was having a little fun with one of the whores. Next thing I know he was comin' after me, like I'd stepped on his boots, or somethin'."

Their conversation was interrupted by the quiet hooting of an owl.

"Did you hear that?" Pigiron asked.

"What, that owl?"

"That ain't no owl," Pigiron said. "Like as not, it's one of Tatum's half-breeds."

The owl sounded again.

"That's an owl," Jason insisted.

Looking back at him, Pigiron smiled, then raised his hands to his lips. He made an owl call that almost perfectly duplicated the one they had just heard. A moment later, a man appeared out of the darkness. He was obviously an Indian, and his appearance startled Jason, who jumped—but Pigiron held his hand out to stop him.

"This is Russell Swift Bear," Pigiron said. Then Pigiron asked the Indian, "Where's Tatum?"

"Come," was all Swift Bear said in reply.

Pigiron and Tatum followed Swift Bear for a short distance until they came to a little draw. There, several shadowy figures sat around a flickering campfire. Tatum came over to greet the two men.

"Did you find out what I wanted to know?" he asked Pigiron.

"About Tom Burke? Yeah, I found his ranch. It's about seven miles northwest of Big Rock. Burke ain't there, though."

"Burke ain't there? What do you mean, he ain't there? Where is he?"

"He went down into Texas."

"Damn! He's moved?"

"No, he ain't moved. He just went to Texas to get some bulls, they was sayin'. His family is still there at the ranch. It's a placed called Timber Notch."

"His family? Who's he got in his family?"

"Don't know, didn't get all that. Just heard that his wife and kids were staying back at the ranch."

"How many hands working at the ranch?"

"Didn't find that out," Pigiron said.

"How do you expect me to plan anything if you don't get all the information I need to . . ." Tatum stopped and looked more closely at Pigiron's face. "What the hell happened to you?"

"What do you mean?" Pigiron asked, self-consciously putting his hand to his nose.

"I mean, you've always been an ugly son of a bitch, but damn if you ain't uglier now than you was last time I saw you." Tatum put his hand out and touched the puffed up bruise on Pigiron's jaw. "You been beat up."

"He got into a fight with Smoke Jensen," Jason said.

Tatum laughed. "You let him whip you like that?"

"He got in a lucky punch," Pigiron said.

"Yeah, well now we both got a case against Smoke Jensen," Tatum said. "He's the one killed Fuller and Howard. He killed Billy too."

"You ask me, he's the one we should go after, instead of Tom Burke."

"Not yet. I'll get around to taking care of him when the time comes, but that time ain't here yet. Did you boys eat any supper?"

"No."

"They's prob'ly some beans left in the pot."

Getting their kits from their saddlebags, Pigiron and Jason went over to the little black pot that was suspended over the fire and helped themselves.

Tatum climbed up on a rock and looked toward the distant horizon, approximately where he thought Burke's ranch might be.

Tomorrow, he would put his plan into operation. It was a good plan, and the beauty of it was, it didn't matter whether Burke was there or not. In fact, this might even be better.

7

The morning sun, a bright red orb just beginning t
gather warmth and brilliance, rose in the east. A dar
gray haze was still hanging in the notches, though it wa
already beginning to dissipate, like drifting smoke. Tim
bered foothills, covered with blue pine and golden aspen
marched down from the higher elevations. One of th
mountains, scarred by some ancient cataclysmic even
of geology, shone blue-green in the early morning light
On Timber Notch, a cock crowed. In the barn of th
neatly laid-out ranch, a horse whickered. A cow, anxiou
to be milked, moved nervously in her stall. The mornin
air was perfumed by the smell of coffee, frying bacon
and baking biscuits.

"Buddy, don't forget, you need to get that cow milked,
a woman's voice called.

"I'm going to do it, Mom, soon as I'm dressed," Budd
answered.

"And put on a coat. It's cold this morning."

From a bunkhouse adjacent to the big house, a cow
hand came outside carrying a handful of paper wit
him, his breath creating puffs of vapor in the bris
morning air. The door to the outhouse creaked as h
opened it. He stepped inside, then slammed the doo
shut behind him.

In the corral a windmill answered a slight freshening and turned into the breeze, its fan blades spinning. The actuating piston rattled as water spewed from the pump's wide mouth and splashed into a big, wooden trough.

Unnoticed by any of the residents of the ranch, ten riders sloped down the side of a nearby hill, their appearance making an ugly scar on this idyllic scene. The leader of the group was Jack Tatum.

Raul Sanchez was riding directly behind Tatum. Although he wasn't technically second in command, because Tatum knew that some of his men wouldn't accept a Mexican as second in command, he was probably the one Tatum depended on more than any other.

Behind Sanchez rode Pigiron McCord. Pigiron's face still showed signs of the beating he had taken the day before. One eye was swollen shut, his nose was flattened, his lips were puffy and deformed, and there were scars on his chin and jaw.

The next three in the line of riders who were coming single file down the side of the mountain were Jason Harding, Orville Clinton, and Dirk Wheeler. They were petty outlaws who had been in and out of jail several times over the years, but even though all three were wanted men, the government didn't consider any of them important enough to go to the expense of having reward posters printed for them.

Like Pigiron, Jason had been in town the day before, and also, like Pigiron, he was showing the effects. He had a large knot on top of his head, the result of a pistol being brought down hard on his cranium.

In addition to Raul Sanchez, there was another Mexican in the group, Paco Arino. Perry Blue Horses and Russell Swift Bear rode just behind Raul Sanchez. Blue Horses and Swift Bear were half-breed Indians who were equally unwelcome in both Indian and white society. The last rider in the group was a man known simply as Jim. Jim was completely alone, not only within this group, but in most of the territory he roamed, for he was black. Jim was a big, muscular man who seldom spok but whose eyes and demeanor did little to hide th hatred that smoldered within him.

When they reached a rock outcropping that was n more than one hundred yards from the house and ou buildings, Tatum gave silent hand signals to put his me in place.

"All right, boys, get ready," he said once they were i position.

All but Blue Horses and Swift Bear raised rifles to thei shoulders, waiting for an order from Tatum. Blue Horse and Swift Bear also had rifles, though for this particula operation they were using bows and arrows.

The door to the outhouse opened, and the man wh had entered it a few moments earlier now exited, hool ing his suspenders over his shoulders as he did so.

"Now," Tatum shouted, and everyone opened fire.

Blue Horses aimed for the man at the outhouse, an had the satisfaction of following his arrow in its swi flight, all the way across the open space between them until it buried itself in the man's chest. Swift Bear's arro plunked into the wall beside the door of the outhouse

"Indians!" someone shouted. "Get your guns, boy and get to shootin'!"

Now Blue Horses and Swift Bear were shooting fir arrows into the compound. The bunkhouse and bar were quickly enveloped in flames. Within a few minute the hired hands ran from the bunkhouse, coughing an gasping for breath. That was exactly what Tatum wante and he and the others directed their firing at the me who were so devastated by smoke inhalation that the were unable to put up any kind of effective respons Within moments, all were down.

"Hold it! Hold it!" Tatum shouted to his men. "Sto firing. I think we've got 'em all."

"What about from the house?" McCord asked.

"Anyone hear any shootin' come from the house? Tatum asked.

"I didn't hear nothin'," Clinton said.

"You boys hear anything?" Tatum asked the Indians. Both responded in the negative.

"Could be they're already dead. Or maybe, nobody was there in the first place."

"How do we find out?" McCord asked.

"We'll surround the house," Tatum replied. "Pigiron, you, Jason, and Wheeler go round front and bust in through the front door. Sanchez, Arino, you two go in through windows there on the left side of the house. Jim, you, Blue Horses, and Swift Bear go in through windows on the right. Me'n Clinton will bust in through the back door."

Tatum led his men down to the main house. There were four bodies on the ground: the hand who was killed as he left the outhouse and the three who had run out from the bunkhouse. The outlaws approached the main house cautiously, not sure of who was still inside, or even if whoever was inside was still alive.

Tatum gave the signal, and his men moved into the positions he had assigned them.

"All right, boys! Let's go!" he shouted. He started toward the back door, then stepped to one side, indicating that Clinton should go in first. Clinton hesitated for just a moment, then he burst in through the door. As he did so, he caught a charge of double-ought buckshot from a ten-gauge Greener shotgun. The blast knocked him back outside, and he fell on the porch with his guts ripped open and his head hanging halfway down the steps. Looking cautiously around the door frame, Tatum saw a boy of about twelve trying desperately to reload the shotgun he had just fired.

"Hold it right there, boy!" Tatum shouted, jumping in through the door and pointing his gun at Buddy. "You're pretty damn handy with that scattergun."

"Not handy enough," Buddy said. "If I was, you'd be dead too."

"You've got a big mouth. Where are the others?"

"What others? There ain't no one here but me."

"You expect me to believe you are all alone here?"

"That's what I said."

"Where's your pa?"

"He's down in Texas, buying bulls."

"What about your ma?"

"I told you, nobody else is here."

Looking over toward the sideboard, Tatum saw a plate of biscuits and bacon. "You plannin' on eatin' all this yourself, were you?" Tatum said. He broke apart a biscuit, laid several pieces of bacon on it, then making a sandwich of it, began eating.

"Let me go!" a woman's voice said from the front of the house. "Who are you people? What are you doing here?"

An attractive woman and a young girl were dragged into the kitchen.

"Look what we found," McCord said.

"Are you Mrs. Burke?" Tatum asked, his words muffled by the fact that his mouth was full of biscuit and bacon.

"It's none of your business who I am," Jo Ellen answered defiantly.

Almost distractedly, Tatum backhanded Sue Ann, knocking the little girl against the wall. She slid down to the floor, her nose and mouth bleeding. Immediately, she began crying.

"What are you doing?" Jo Ellen screamed in rage.

"If you don't want the little girl hit anymore, answer the question, woman. Are you the wife of the jury foreman who sentenced me to hang?"

"Yes," Jo Ellen said. "I'm only sorry that the state didn't get the job done."

"Good. That's all I wanted to know," Tatum said. He took another bite of his biscuit sandwich.

"What do we do with them?" McCord asked.

"Kill 'em," Tatum said, his words muffled by the fact that his mouth was full of biscuit and bacon.

"You sure? Seems to me like if we keep the woman alive, we could have a little fun with her," McCord said.

But almost before he could finish his statement, Tatum drew his own pistol and shot the woman.

"Mama!" Sue Ann screamed. Tatum's next shot stopped the little girl in mid-cry.

"You son of a bitch!" Buddy shouted.

Tatum pointed his gun at the boy. "I saved you till last so you could watch your mama and sister die," he said evilly.

Buddy glared at him.

"I guess you think your mama and sister are in heaven, huh?"

"I know they are."

"Then look at it this way. You won't be apart very long, because I'm about to send you to heaven to be with them."

Buddy shook his head. "Uh-uh. I'll get around to going heaven," he said. "But first I'm going to wait for you in hell so I can soak your ass in kerosene and watch you burn, you sorry son of a bitch."

"Ha, ha! Gutsy little shit, ain't he?" Pigiron said, laughing.

"Like I said, kid, you've got a big mouth." Tatum shot Buddy in the heart. Then, holstering his pistol, he made himself another bacon and biscuit sandwich. Some of the others started to eat as well, but Tatum waved them away.

"We ain't got time to eat," he said. "Get busy. Remember, this has to look like the work of Indians."

Tatum looked back toward Jo Ellen's body. That was when he saw, for the first time, the gold chain with diamond pendant that was around her neck.

"I reckon I'll just take that as a little souvenir," he said. He grabbed the chain, then hung it around his own neck. "All right, let's go, get busy. We can't hang around here all day," he shouted to the others.

There was a little grumbling about not getting to enjoy the grub, but the men went to work as ordered, scalping and mutilating the bodies. Perry Blue Horses and Russell Swift Bear left a few more arrows around.

"Hey, Jack, ole Clinton here is still alive," Wheeler called from the back porch.

"He can't still be alive. Hell, that Greener purt' nigh took out all his innards."

"Yeah, it did that, all right. But he's still groanin'. What'll we do with him?"

"Leave him, he'll die soon enough," McCord said.

"No, we can't leave him here. This is supposed to be the work of Indians, remember?" Tatum said. "Drag 'im back to the horses, then throw him belly down across his. We'll take him somewhere else to get rid of him."

After a few more minutes of leaving Indian sign, Tatum ordered his men away and, dragging the nearly lifeless body of Clinton with them, they mounted and rode off. Three quarters of an hour later they were ten miles south.

It was Cal who discovered the carnage at Timber Notch Ranch. He had been riding the fence line when he saw the smoke. Realizing that so much smoke had to mean a burning building, he rode hard to get there. From the looks of the smoke the fire had a pretty good start, so he wasn't sure he would be able to do anything to help once he arrived, but he intended to be there to help nevertheless.

His first suspicion that something was wrong was when he reached the place and saw that, while the fire outside was still raging, no one was attempting to fight it. The barn was burning and the stock was still in the corral, gathered in a frightened bunch at the far end. The horses were wild-eyed and restless; the milk cows were milling about as if dazed. Although the barn, bunkhouse, and granary were on fire, the main house and the outhouse were not. It was then that he saw someone lying on the ground near the outhouse. Urging his horse to a gallop, he crossed the remaining distance very quickly, then dismounted.

"Oh, shit!" he said aloud. The man on the ground was the foreman of Timber Notch, Ben Goodpasture. Ben had an arrow sticking from his body, and he had been scalped. In various positions around the burning bunkhouse lay the bodies of Tom Burke's remaining ranch hands.

"Mrs. Burke!" Cal shouted, running toward the house. "Mrs. Burke, are you here?"

Cal darted up the steps and into the kitchen. There, just inside the kitchen door, he saw young Buddy's body. Like the hands outside, Buddy had been scalped. Mrs. Burke had been scalped as well as mutilated. Both breasts had been cut off. Only the little girl was neither scalped nor mutilated, though there was blood on her face, as if she had been beaten before she was shot.

Cal felt sick, and he turned and went back outside, then walked over to the edge of the porch, where he grabbed hold of one of the supporting posts. He stood there for a long moment, breathing deeply and trying hard to force the image of what he had just seen out of his mind. Then, when he was no longer afraid he was about to throw up, he walked back out to his horse, mounted, and started the long ride back to Sugarloaf.

It was nearly noon by the time he got back. Smoke, Sally, and Pearlie were just sitting down to eat when Cal came in.

"Cal, good, you're just in time," Sally started. "Wash up and . . ." Sally stopped in mid-sentence as she stared at Cal. "Good heavens, Cal, what is it? You look as if you have seen a ghost."

"It's Mrs. Burke," Cal said.

"Jo Ellen? She's here?"

Cal shook his head. "Not just Mrs. Burke. It's her, the boy, the little girl, Ben, and all the hands. All of them. Every one of them." Cal stopped for a moment, then took a deep breath. "They're dead."

"What?" Sally asked with a gasp.

"They're dead. Every one of them," Cal said. "I just got back from their place. Looks like they were attacked by Indians."

"Indians? That's impossible. There aren't any warring Indians around here," Smoke said.

"They burned the barn, the bunkhouse, the granary. There's arrows all over the place and every one of them have been scalped."

"Oh, God in heaven, Smoke, what will we do?" Sally asked.

"If it's already done, there's nothing we can do," Smoke replied. "Except see to it that Tom gets the word."

"Oh, that poor man," Sally said.

The lunch Sally had just put on the table went uneaten. Even Pearlie had no appetite for this meal.

8

It had been three days since the massacre at Timber Notch. Smoke Jensen, wearing a black suit and black bolo tie, was leaning against the wall in the kitchen of his house with his arms folded across his chest. Sally, who was wearing a black hat, was fussing with the veil, part of the funeral ensemble she was wearing. Pearlie was sitting at the table eating a piece of pie left over from supper the night before. Pearlie didn't own a black suit, but he was wearing a brown suit and a white shirt. The door opened and Cal came in. Cal didn't have a suit of any kind, but he was wearing clean jeans and a clean and pressed white shirt, complete with closed collar and a bolo tie he had borrowed from Smoke.

"The surrey is all hitched up, Smoke," Cal said.

"Thanks, Cal. If we can pull Pearlie away from the pie, we're ready."

"Uhmm, if you're waiting on me, you're backing up," Pearlie said, making a point to jump up quickly. He took one step away from the table, then reached back, picked up the last piece of pie, and shoved it in his mouth as they started toward the door.

"Has anyone heard from Tom Burke yet?" Pearlie asked as they climbed into the surrey. Pearlie rode in the front seat alongside Cal, who was driving. Smoke helped Sally into the backseat, then got in beside her.

"Tom wired back that he would be on the five o'clock train this morning," Smoke said. "So I suspect he's already here."

"How awful this must be for him," Sally said. "There he was down in Texas, buying cattle, when he gets the telegram that his family and all his hired hands were killed by Indians."

"If it was Indians," Smoke said.

Cal snapped the reins and the team pulled the surrey away smartly. As it rolled up the road, its wheels singing on the hard-packed dirt, Smoke turned to look back. The house and buildings of his own ranch gleamed brightly in the morning sun. It was a neatly kept, well-laid-out ranch that spoke well of Smoke's success, and even more of Sally's industry and creativity, for it was she who had made Sugarloaf the showplace that it was.

Seeing his ranch made Smoke feel an even greater sense of sympathy for his friend Tom Burke, for Tom had been every bit as proud of Timber Notch as Smoke was of Sugarloaf. Now, with his family dead, what was the purpose?

There were scores of buggies, surreys, buckboards, wagons, carriages, and horses around the cemetery in Big Rock, for Tom Burke was a well-liked and highly respected man in the area. Ben Goodpasture and one of the hired hands who had been killed at Tom's ranch had been buried the day before. Even before Tom returned, he'd made arrangements, by telegram, to pay for their funerals. The other two hired hands had been sent, by train, back to their families, one in St. Louis, the other in Memphis, also at Tom's expense. The funeral today was for Jo Ellen, Tom Jr.—who was called Buddy by everyone—and Sue Ann.

Cal parked the surrey behind one of the several long lines of conveyances that were arrayed around the cemetery; then the four climbed down and walked up he path toward the three open graves. There were nore than five hundred people gathered for the funeral. That number included nearly everyone from Big Rock as well as people from all over the Las Animas County. When Smoke and his companions reached the op of the hill where the three were to be buried, Smoke saw Tom Burke sitting in a chair next to the open graves. Tom's uncovered head was bowed, his silver hair shining. Smoke knew that the loss of his amily was a particularly cruel blow for Tom, because amily life had come late to him.

"Oh, Smoke," Sally said, putting her hand on his arm. "Look at the poor man. Have you ever seen anything so sad? We must speak to him."

"All right," Smoke agreed.

The four moved through the crowd until they reached Tom. From this position they could see the hree coffins waiting to be lowered into the openings, one full-sized and two smaller ones. The air was redolent with the many floral arrangements that were scattered around, including a full bouquet of roses on op of the larger coffin, and a single rose on top of each of the two smaller coffins, red for Sue Ann, yellow for Buddy.

"Oh, Tom, I am so sorry about this," Sally said as she leaned down to embrace their friend and neighbor.

"Thank you," Tom mumbled.

"Tom," Smoke said, taking his friend's hand. It was all he could think to say.

"Smoke, I don't aim to just let this go," Tom said.

Smoke shook his head. "No, I didn't expect you would."

"Can I count on you?"

Smoke felt, rather than saw, Sally's quick glance oward him.

"Yes, of course you can," he said.

Pearlie and Cal paid their respects as well; then the four of them moved away from the bereaved rancher, finding a nearby place to stand that would keep them away from the crowd, yet afford them a good view.

"What was that all about?" Sally asked.

"What?" Smoke replied innocently, though he knew exactly what she meant.

"He said he wasn't going to let it go. Then he asked if he could count on you. You said, and I quote, 'Yes, of course you can.'"

"I'm sure he intends to go after whoever did this," Smoke said.

"Why? Going after the murderers isn't going to bring Tom's family back."

"I know it won't, but that's not the point," Smoke said. He put his arm around Sally and pulled her closer to him. "I don't quite know how to explain it, Sally, but leaving Sugarloaf this morning, I looked back at it and thought about it, and you and . . . well, I reckon it just gave me a deeper feeling about what Tom's going through right now. I know we can't bring his family back, but getting the ones who did it and making them pay? That can go a long way toward bringing him some peace of mind. And if there's any way I can help him do that, I aim to do it. I hope you understand."

"Whether I understand or not, you're going to help him find the renegade Indians who did this, aren't you?"

"I reckon I am," Smoke said. "But it would set a lot easier with me if you understood and approved."

Sally sighed. "Of course I understand," she said. "You have a tremendous generosity of spirit, Smoke Jensen. I think that is one of the reasons I fell in love with you."

The preacher stood up then and the buzz of conversation halted. The tall, gaunt man looked out over the assembled mourners, giving them a moment to interrupt their conversations and focus on the task at hand, that of burying some of their own.

Once he had their attention, the preacher delivered a

homily invoking God's wrath upon the evil savages who would perpetrate such a thing. After that, he reminded everyone of the promise of a joyous reunion in the hereafter. Finally, after the coffins were lowered into the grave, the preacher invited Tom to drop a handful of earth onto each of them. As Tom did so, the preacher intoned his final prayer.

"For as much as it hath pleased Almighty God in his wise providence to take out of this world the souls of Jo Ellen, Sue Ann, and Thomas Jr., we therefore commit their bodies to the ground; earth to earth, ashes to ashes, dust to dust; looking for the general Resurrection in the last day, and the life of the world to come through Our Lord Jesus Christ; at whose second coming in glorious majesty to judge the world, the earth and the sea shall give up their dead; and the corruptible bodies of those who sleep in him shall be changed, and made like unto his own glorious body; according to the mighty working whereby he is able to subdue all things unto himself. Amen."

When the funeral was over, the mourners began leaving the cemetery, walking quietly through the nearly one hundred tombstones that marked the last resting places of the late citizens of Big Rock. Like the living citizens of a town, the deceased ran the gamut from innocent children to murderers who were there because they had paid the ultimate penalty to the state. Four of the graves were so recent that the pile of dirt was still fresh over them. Those were the graves for the two would-be bank robbers, and for Richmond Flowers and Deputy Wallace.

One by one the mourners went their own way, some on foot, others on horseback, and still others by buggy, surrey, carriage, buckboard, or wagon. The quiet cemetery echoed with the sounds of subdued conversation, the scratch of horse hooves on the ground, and the creaking roll of wheels.

"He is still there, isn't he?" Sally asked as she climbed into the surrey. "He's all alone."

Settling into his own seat, Smoke looked back toward the three graves. Only one person remained, and that was Tom Burke, still sitting in the chair that had been put there for him by Nunley Welch, the undertaker.

"Looks like it," Smoke said.

"Oh, Smoke, I feel so sorry for him. I wish there was something we could do for him."

"There's nothing we can do to bring back his family," Smoke said.

"Do you think it was Indians?"

"I don't know," Smoke said. "I do know this. If it was Indians, it had to be a band of renegades. I'm sure it wasn't any of the regular tribes. We haven't had any Indian trouble in years. Soon as I can get around to it, I plan to have a good, long look around over there."

"Then you're going after whoever did it?"

"I am as soon as Tom feels up to going. I don't think he's quite finished saying good-bye yet."

"I'm glad you are going with him, Smoke. I only wish I could go."

Smoke reached over and patted her hand. "Don't think I don't believe for one minute that you couldn't handle it," he said. "But I think I would rather you and Cal stay back to watch the ranch."

"Wait a minute!" Cal said sharply. "You mean you aren't going to let me go with you?"

"Cal," was all Smoke said.

Cal looked down for a moment, then nodded contritely. "Sure, I'll stay here," he said.

"I knew I could count on you."

As the last mourner left the cemetery, Angus Pugh, the grave digger, stuck a wad of tobacco in his mouth, then glanced over at Nunley Welch.

"He's still there, Mr. Welch. Still just sittin' in that chair over there. Do you think maybe I ought to go start closing the grave anyway?"

Welch shook his head. "We don't let our people see the dirt thrown in on their loved ones," he said. "It's just too painful. Give him a little more time."

"How much time should I give him?"

"As much time as he needs," Welch answered. "He isn't like one of our normal bereaved. He has lost his entire family."

"Yes, sir, I know that."

"Then we will give him as much time as it takes."

"Yes, sir."

Sam Covington went straight from the funeral to the telegraph office. The Indian attack on Tom Burke's ranch was a tragedy of tremendous proportions. In fact, Covington could not recall any other incident in the brief history of the little town, or the even longer history of the county, that could quite compare with it. Covington was sorry it happened, but it had happened, so it just didn't make sense not to take advantage of the situation.

Covington was a man with political ambition, and he made no effort to hide that ambition. He wasn't that great an admirer of Governor Cooper. In fact, when Cooper was running for election, Covington chose to support him only because Cooper was obviously losing, and if Covington could turn it around, it would put Cooper deeply in his debt. Covington did turn it around, running a brilliant campaign for Cooper which ultimately snatched victory from the jaws of defeat. And now he was still calling the shots for Cooper.

Cooper was going to be a one-term governor, Covington would see to that. Then, after Cooper stepped down, Covington intended to run for governor. And in

Covington's grand scheme of things, he too would be a one-term governor, but would persuade the legislature to send him to the U.S. Senate. From the Senate there was only one more step up the ladder, to the office of President of the United States. And who was to say that Covington couldn't take that step?

Fred Dunn, the Western Union clerk, looked up as Covington went into his office. "Is the funeral over?" Fred asked.

"Yes."

"I thought it must be, when I saw all the traffic out on the road. I wish I could've gone to pay my respects, but the wire has to be manned twenty-four hours a day."

"And it's a fine job you're doing too," Covington said. "Has there been any reply to the wire I sent this morning?"

"Oh, yes, here it is," Fred said, picking up an envelope from a small pile that was on the desk.

Covington received the envelope, then tore it open quickly and began to read:

> YOU ARE HEREBY APPOINTED TO RANK OF FULL COLONEL IN STATE MILITIA STOP INCUMBENT WITH RANK IS AUTHORITY TO RAISE AND EQUIP ONE CAVALRY REGIMENT STOP ONCE REGIMENT IS RAISED AND READY YOU ARE TO EMBARK ON CAMPAIGN AGAINST INDIANS WHO ATTACKED TOM BURKE RANCH STOP YOU ARE FURTHER AUTHORIZED TO USE ALL FORCE REQUIRED END

The telegram had been sent by Gerald Cooper, the governor.

Smiling, Covington put the telegram back in its envelope, then put the envelope in his pocket.

"So, am I to call you Colonel now?" Fred asked, reserving any comment on the contents of the telegram until after Covington read it.

"Yes . . . for now," Covington replied. Although he didn't say it aloud, he thought that if things went well—and so far they had gone very well—Fred and everyone else would be calling him Governor.

9

After taking Sally back home, Smoke got out of his suit, put on his jeans and a shirt, then changed from the surrey to the buckboard for a drive back to town. Before he could leave on an extended campaign with Tom Burke, he would need some things from the store. Going into the hardware store, he gave his list to the clerk.

"Whew," the clerk whistled. "You've got quite a list here, Smoke. Three boxes of .44-caliber bullets, three boxes of .44-40, ten sticks of dynamite, two boxes of lucifers, a gallon of kerosene, rope . . ." There were many more items listed, but he stopped reading aloud. "What are you going to do with all this stuff?"

"Pay for it," Smoke joked. "That is, if you've got it and will get it packed for me."

The clerk laughed. "That's what I get for being too nosy, I guess. Yes, sir, I've got it. It'll take me a good half hour or so to get it all gathered and packed, though."

"I can wait. I'll be over at Longmont's," Smoke said.

Leaving the store, Smoke saw someone posting a circular, and curious, he went over to read it.

* * *

Attention!
INDIAN FIGHTERS
Having been authorized by GOVERNOR COOPER OF COLORADO to raise a MILITIA COMPANY OF CAVALRY for immediate service against hostile Indians, I call upon all who wish to engage in such service to contact me soonest for the purpose of enrolling your names and joining your friends and neighbors for this great adventure. Weapons and uniforms will be furnished by the State. Pay and rations will be the same as U.S. Army. Those who volunteer shall be entitled to all horses and other plunder as may be confiscated from the Indians.

COLONEL SAMUEL B. COVINGTON
COVINGTON'S MILITIA
COMMANDING

Longmont's saloon was more crowded than normal for this time of day. That was understandable, though, since nearly every ranch hand within fifty miles of town had been given the day off in order to attend the funeral. And, as might be expected, the conversation was about the funeral and what had happened out at Timber Notch.

"What I don't understand is why them fellas there at the ranch didn't put up any more of a fight than they done," one of the men was saying. "Hell, if I'd been there, there would'a be dead Injuns lying all over the place."

"We don't know that there weren't any Indians killed," one of the other patrons said. "Indians tend to carry away their dead."

"Yeah? Well, if I had been there, I would'a killed so damn many of them redskin bastards, they couldn't of carried them away."

"Dingo, you're full of shit," someone said, and all laughed.

"You think I haven't killed my share of Indians? I fought against the Apaches."

"Well, if you still have it in you to kill Indians, you can always join the militia cavalry," still another suggested. "Covington is sittin' back there at a table, signing up folks right now."

"By God, maybe I'll just do that," Dingo said.

Seeing Smoke standing at the bar, Louis came over to see him.

"It was a very impressive funeral, didn't you think?" Louis asked.

"Yes, it was," Smoke replied.

"Tom took it real hard," Louis said. "Of course, under the circumstances, I can see why. Smoke, is he going to be all right? Do you think there's anything I can do for him?"

"He'll be all right," Smoke said. "He's just got to get through this." Smoke nodded toward a table in the back corner where half a dozen men were standing in line. Sam Covington, normally a lawyer, was sitting at the table wearing the uniform and insignia of an Army colonel. "I see Mr. Covington is busy."

"Oh, hell, it's Colonel Covington now, and don't think he isn't quick to let you know that," Louis replied with a little laugh. "Yesterday he was a lawyer, foreclosing on widows and orphans, and today he is their savior."

"How did he ever talk the governor into giving him a commission in the first place? What does he know about the military?"

"About the military? Not a blasted thing," Louis replied. "But he doesn't need to know anything. Don't forget, he was the governor's right-hand man during the last election."

"If I had known the governor's character judgment was so weak, I never would have voted for him," Smoke said. Then he chuckled. "Hell, now that I think of it, I *didn't* vote for him."

Louis laughed with him. "I can't find anybody who did vote for him, or at least, who will own up to it now. But there he is, sitting up in Denver as our governor, and here is Sam Covington, colonel of militia."

"Well, I don't guess it can hurt anything for them to dress up like soldiers, then ride around in the countryside for a while," Smoke said.

"If that's all that happens, I agree with you," Louis said. "But knowing Covington, there's no telling what that dumb bastard might stir up."

Although he was too far away to know he was being talked about, Covington looked up from his table and saw Smoke and Louis standing together at the bar.

"Excuse me, boys," Covington said, getting up.

"Wait a minute, where you a-goin'?" Dingo asked. "I aim to sign up here."

"I'll be right back," Covington replied with a wave of his hand. "There's plenty of time and room for all of you to sign up. Don't worry."

Stepping up to the bar, Covington slapped a coin down. "Mr. Longmont, another for Mr. Jensen, if you don't mind."

Nodding, Louis poured another drink for Smoke.

"Thanks," Smoke said, holding his glass up.

"Mr. Jensen, I hope you have no hard feelings about the things I said during the trial," Covington said. "I was just trying to win the case."

"You lost," Smoke said simply.

"Yes, I did," Covington admitted. "And though I hate to lose anything, I must confess that I'm glad Tatum isn't free because of me. Who would've thought he would do something like kill Deputy Wallace and the judge? That was a terrible thing, absolutely terrible."

"Yeah," Smoke said, indicating by the tone of his voice that he wasn't buying what Covington was trying to sell.

"Well, enough about Mr. Tatum. He'll wind up in custody again somewhere. His kind always does. And I won't be defending him next time."

"No, I don't suppose so," Smoke replied.

"Anyway, right now, we have an even bigger problem on our hands."

"What problem would that be?" Smoke asked.

Covington looked at Smoke with a surprised expres
sion on his face. "What do you mean, what problem.
Why, Indians of course," he replied. "My God, man, yo
know what happened out at Timber Notch."

"No, I don't know," Smoke replied.

"What do you mean you don't know?" Covingto
replied, the expression on his face growing even mor
confused. "You were at the funeral. I saw you there."

"Yes, I was. Tom Burke is a close, personal friend o
mine."

"Then I don't understand. Why do you say you don'
know what happened out there?"

"Because I don't know. At this point, I don't thin
anyone knows."

"Of course we know. Everyone knows. The ranch wa
attacked by Indians."

"Is that a fact?"

"Of course it is. Everyone knows that it was Indian
who murdered Tom Burke's family and hands."

"Covington, do you have any idea how long it ha
been since we've had any Indian trouble in these parts?

"Quite a while, I'm sure. Do you know anything abou
volcanoes, Mr. Jensen? Sometimes they remain dorman
for hundreds of years before they erupt."

Smoke chuckled. "And you are suggesting that the In
dians are what? Like a volcano?"

"The comparison isn't strained," Covington said. "W
all know what the Indians are capable of. And don'
think for one minute that they aren't living out there i
their reservation villages envious of the life we lead an
seething inside with hate and resentment. I've alway
known they could break out of the reservation someda
Well, they have. And now it's our duty to punish them se
verely enough that they will think long and hard befor
they ever try anything like that again. So, what do yo
say, Mr. Jensen?"

"What do I say about what?"

"I'm asking you to join my militia as a scout. The ran

of major comes with it. That would put you second in command."

"And allow me a share of the booty?"

"Yes, indeed," Covington said, smiling broadly in the belief that he was winning Smoke over.

Smoke finished his drink and looked at Covington. He stared at him for such a long time that Covington's smile faded. He got nervous and began to fidget under Smoke's gaze. Finally, Smoke wiped the back of his hand across his mouth.

"No, thanks," he said.

"What?" Covington asked in surprise. "Jensen, do you realize that by your action, you are showing that you don't care about what happened to poor Tom Burke?"

Smoke sighed in disgust. "You do have a way with words, don't you, Covington? You don't let truth bother you. I suppose that's what makes you a good lawyer."

"It's just that I am surprised that you don't want to help your friend."

"I am going to help him," Smoke said. "But I'm going to do it in my own way."

"What does that mean? In your own way?" Covington asked.

"It means I have no intention of running around with a bunch of fools in pretend-Army uniforms who'll probably get lost before they get more than ten miles out of town."

"You need have no fear about that," Covington said, sputtering. "I'll be leading them."

Smoke laughed. "My point exactly. Using both hands and a compass, you couldn't find your own ass."

Covington's face became purple, and the vein in his temple began to pulsate. "We'll just see about that," he said. "After we make a couple of successful scouts and kill us a few Indians, we'll bring this uprising to a halt."

"Uprising? There is no uprising," Smoke said.

"No? How do you explain what happened out at Tom Burke's ranch?"

"If it was Indians, it was a party of renegades at best," Smoke said. "I hardly think we have an Indian war on our hands."

"An Indian is an Indian. And you might remember that a famous general once said, 'The only good Indian is a dead Indian,'" Covington said. He paused for a moment, then smiled and held his hand out, offering to shake with Smoke. "Anyway, we shouldn't be arguing about this, you and I," he said in a conciliatory voice. "After all, we are the natural leaders of this community. We should be allies in this noble endeavor. So, what do you say, man? Will you join us?"

Instead of taking Covington's proffered hand, Smoke reached for his glass and took another drink, staring over the rim at Covington. "I thank you for the drink," he said, and there was such a finality to his voice that it stopped all further conversation between the two men.

Covington stared at Smoke for a moment longer, then turned and walked back to his table.

"You think he finally got the message?" Louis asked.

"Maybe. But it takes a while for anything to get through a head as thick as his is."

All right, men!" Covington called out to the others in the saloon. "I'm still signing up volunteers for the cavalry. Who's next?"

"I am," Dingo said.

"Your full name?" Covington asked.

"Marcus W. Dingo."

"Do you have any military experience, Mr. Dingo?"

"Yes, sir. I was a sergeant with General Miles when we fought the Apache."

Covington looked up from the paper he was writing on. "You were a sergeant, you say?"

"Yes, sir."

"Why did you leave the Army?"

"After we whupped the Apache, there wasn't nothin' else to do 'cept drill and the like. So when it come time, I took my discharge and moved on."

"But you are willing to come back in now? To serve in whatever capacity I assign you, and to recognize the authority of the officers appointed over you?"

"Yes, sir," Dingo said. "I know what armyin' is all about."

"Why do you want to serve now?"

"Well, sir, I don't know 'bout the rest of these boys, but after what them heathens did to Mrs. Burke and those children, I'm by God ready to start killin' me some Injuns."

"Hold up your right hand," Covington said.

Dingo did as instructed.

"You swear to follow the orders of those in authority over you, and to defend your state and your fellow citizens against all enemies, foreign and domestic?"

"Yeah, that is, yes, sir, I do," Dingo said.

Covington stuck his hand out to shake with Dingo. "Welcome to Covington's militia, First Sergeant Dingo."

Dingo grinned broadly. "First Sergeant?"

"Yes, First Sergeant. I feel that is the best way to utilize your experience."

At the far end of the bar, a small man with weasel eyes finished the rest of his beer, then wiped his mouth with his sleeve.

"Another one?" the bartender asked.

"No," the small man replied. "I've got to go." Turning, he left the bar, then pushed through the batwing doors and walked out into the street. As he headed toward the livery, he took out a plug of chewing tobacco and stuck it in his mouth. As a result, he had worked up a good spit by the time he got there.

Standing just inside a Dutch door, looking through the open top, was Pigiron McCord.

"Did you see him, Wheeler?" Pigiron asked.

"Yeah, I seen him. Jensen's in there, all right."

Pigiron smiled broadly. "Good. Good. Now it's time to pay him back for what he did."

"Pigiron, you sure you want to do this? I mean, Tatum

told us to just hang around to see what was goin' on, then get back to him. He didn't say nothin' 'bout killin' anyone."

"If you got no stomach for it you can go on back, far as I'm concerned," Pigiron said. "But I aim to kill that bastard Smoke Jensen." Pigiron opened the door so Wheeler could come into the livery.

The three men in the livery stable were Pigiron McCloud, Jason Harding, and Dirk Wheeler. Because Pigiron didn't want to be recognized, he'd sent Wheeler into the saloon to see if Jensen was there. Harding, who had had his own run-in in the saloon, had also stayed away. He was stretched out on the barn floor, his head on a sack of grain and his hat pulled down over his eyes.

"Seems to me like killin' a man is a long way to go just to get back at him for whuppin' you," Wheeler said.

"Well, now, that's just 'cause you didn't see how bad ole Pigiron here got his ass whupped," Harding said from under his hat.

"I told you, he got in a lucky punch," Pigiron said, turning away from the open window and glaring at Harding. "Besides which, you ain't got a lot of room to talk. Seems to me like you got your head bashed in as well. Hell, I'd think you would be with me on this."

"I am with you," Harding said. "I'm here with you, ain't I? I just want to make sure nothin' goes wrong. I asked some of the boys back at Risco about Smoke Jensen. And from what they tell me, he ain't a man you want to mess with. And I don't aim to get myself kilt before we get some of that money Tatum's been talkin' about."

"There ain't none of us goin' to get kilt if we all stick together," Pigiron said.

"What's goin' on over there in that saloon anyhow?" Pigiron asked. "They's an awful lot of people just goin' in and out."

"They're raisin' an army," Wheeler said. "hey's a man there in a Army suit signin' folks up to go fight the Injuns."

Pigiron laughed. "Is that a fact? Well, you got to hand

it to ole Tatum. He was right about that. After these fellas get all dressed up in their Army suits and march around an' salute for a while, they're goin' to get tired of playin' army. When that happens, they're goin' to attack some Injuns some'ers. And soon as they do that, well, we got us some customers for our rifles."

"Yeah, well, I wish Jensen would get back out here so we can get this over with. I'm hungry," Harding said.

"You're always hungry, or sleepy, or thirsty, or gotta piss or somethin'," Pigiron said. "I swear, you'd bitch if they hung you with a new rope."

Harding stood up and dusted himself off. "I seen Muley Thomas hung with a new rope," he said. "Ole Muley didn't bitch about it. He didn't do nothin', 'cept maybe twitch a little."

Wheeler shuddered. "Don't talk like that," he said. "I don't like to hear that kind'a talk."

Harding held his fist alongside his neck, then tilted his head and ran his tongue out in a mockery of someone being hanged, while making the sound of a death rattle. He laughed at his own impression.

"I said, I don't like that kind'a talk!" Wheeler said.

"Shhh!" Pigiron hissed. "Quiet! Here he comes."

"We goin' to shoot him, Pigiron? Or are we goin' to brace him?" Wheeler asked.

Harding raised his pistol and aimed it at Smoke. "I say let's just shoot the son of a bitch and be done with it," he said.

"No," Pigiron said. "I want him to know who it was shot him. I want my ugly face to be the last thing that son of a bitch sees before he dies."

"Pigiron, I don't know," Harding said. "I told you, I've heard a lot about him since we run into him. They say he's faster'n greased lightning."

"I ain't no virgin in this business," Pigiron said. "I think I can beat him."

"You thought you could whup him too," Harding said. "But look what happened."

"I told you, he got in a lucky punch. Anyway, there are three of us. I don't care how fast the son of a bitch is. He can't take all three of us. I say we brace him."

"You brace him," Wheeler said. "I ain't goin' to."

"What?"

"You want to kill the son of a bitch from here, I'm with you," Wheeler said. "But if you're countin' on me walkin' out there in the street and callin' him out, you goin' to have to do it without me."

"And without me," Harding added.

"You two yellow-bellied bastards!" Pigiron swore.

"We kill him from here, or you go it alone," Harding said.

In frustration, Pigiron pinched the bridge of his nose. "All right," he finally said. "If that's the way it is to be, then that's the way it'll be. I don't care how we kill the son of a bitch, as long as we kill him."

The three men, in agreement now as to their tactics, walked back to the Dutch door and looked through the top window. Jensen was nowhere to be seen.

"What the hell? What happened to him?" Pigiron asked.

"There he is over there, going into the hardware store," Wheeler said.

By the time Pigiron saw him, Jensen was just going into the store, with the door closing behind him.

"All right, we'll get him when he comes out," Pigiron said.

10

"I've got everything you asked for, Smoke," the hardware clerk said. "Beans, bacon, coffee, sugar, salt, flour, three boxes of .44's, three boxes of .44-40's, and two boxes of lucifers. That comes to three dollars and twenty-five cents." The clerk put everything into two boxes. "Will you need help carrying that out to your buckboard?"

"No, thank you, I can get it," Smoke said. He paid for his purchases, then picked up the two boxes and headed for the door. The clerk beat him to the door and held it open for him.

"Here he comes!" Pigiron said to the others, and they pulled the hammers back on their pistols as they took aim. "Wait until he gets into the buckboard. It'll be a closer shot."

They watched as Smoke put his boxes in back, then untied the reins and climbed into the driver's seat.

Suddenly, the stagecoach rolled into town, the six-team hitch sweating and breathing hard as they trotted the final hundred yards. The stage was filled with passengers and piled high on top with luggage and cargo. Its route to the stage depot went between the livery and the hardware store.

"Damn it!" Pigiron swore, lowering his pistol until the

stage passed. They waited for a moment. Then when the stage was gone, they raised their pistols again, but Smoke wasn't there.

"What the hell? Where is he? What happened to him?" Pigiron asked.

"There he is, down there," Wheeler said.

Smoke had driven away, matching the speed of the stagecoach all the way down to the depot. As a result, he had been shielded by the coach until he was now too far down the street for any kind of a shot.

"Now what?" Wheeler asked.

Sighing in disgust, Pigiron put the pistol back in his holster. "Let's get on over to the saloon and see what we can find out about this army they're raisin'," he said.

"Thought you didn't want to go to the saloon," Wheeler said.

"I said I didn't want to be seen by Jensen. Now that he's gone, it don't matter whether I'm seen or not."

"The saloon sounds good to me," Harding said. He rubbed his mouth with the back of his hand. "Yeah, I like that idea. In fact, it's your best idea yet."

When Louis Longmont saw Pigiron and Harding come into his saloon, he got up from his table and walked over to confront them.

"I'll take your money, McCord," he said, "but I won't take anything from *you*. Stay away from my girls, and don't start anything."

"All me 'n my pards want is a couple of drinks," Pigiron said. "We ain't lookin' for no trouble."

Louis looked toward the bartender, then nodded. "You can serve them," he said.

As the three stood at the bar drinking, they listened to several of the conversations, hoping to hear something they could take back to Tatum. Much of the conversation was about the militia company being formed, but Pigiron heard something that caught his attention right away.

"I would'a thought Smoke Jensen would'a joined up with the militia," someone said. "Him an' ole Tom Burke been friends for a long time."

"You heard him say he was goin' to help in his own way, didn't you?"

"Yeah, but I don't know what that means."

"I figure it means he'll be goin' out on his own to find whoever done this."

"On his own? What can he do by his ownself?"

"What can he do? He can track, hunt, shoot, and live out in the mountains better'n anyone I ever heard of. If I was the one that done this, I'd rather have two companies of milita after me than to have Smoke Jensen doggin' my trail."

"When you think he'll leave?"

"He's probably left by now. I was over to the hardware store while ago, and Mr. Clark told me that Smoke bought a lot of provisions to take with him."

"What about Mrs. Jensen? You think she'll stay out at the ranch by herself? Or will she come stay in town till he gets back."

"Sally? Oh, she'll stay out there and run the ranch." The speaker chuckled. "And probably do as good a job with it as any man would."

"Probably. I'll say this for her. She's a good-lookin' woman."

The first speaker chuckled. "I agree, but if you ever say that around Smoke, you better make damn certain he don't misunderstand it."

The second speaker chuckled as well. "You didn't have to tell me that. You think I'm some kind of fool?"

"Well, now," Pigiron said very quietly, "That's good information to know."

"Beg pardon?" Wheeler asked.

"Never mind," Pigiron said. "We'll talk about it later."

* * *

As Smoke and Pearlie were saddling their horses, Cal was leaning against the fence, his arms folded across his chest, looking on with an expression of disappointment.

"Cal, did anyone ever tell you that if you make a bad face, it could freeze like that?" Pearlie asked with a laugh. "Cheer up."

"Easy for you to say. You're going," Cal said. "I have to stay here."

Smoke tightened his cinch, then sighing, looked over at Cal. "I've explained it to you, Cal," he said. "Whoever did this, whether it's renegade Indians or just a gang of outlaws, might still be around. If they double back while we're tracking them, we could miss them. That would leave Sugarloaf vulnerable. I'd feel a lot better if you were here with Sally."

"I know," Cal said. "And I'm honored that you trust me with it. But if nothing happens here, and you find them, then I'm going to miss out on it."

"I'll tell you all about it," Pearlie promised.

"I'd rather hear it from Smoke. If you tell it, no doubt it will be a pack of lies."

"Well, yeah, it probably will be," Pearlie said. "But it'll be a lot better story than you can get from a dime novel."

All three laughed.

"What is this?" Sally asked, coming out to join them. "Here I expected to see long faces, sad because you're going away. Instead, you are laughing. Are you that happy to get away from me?"

"You know better than that," Smoke said, putting his arm around her. They kissed, then Sally held up a little bag.

"I thought you might like a sack full of sinkers for your trip."

"You made doughnuts?" Pearlie asked, reaching for the sack.

"I did. If I told you to go easy on them, to try and make them last a couple of days, would I just be wasting my breath?"

"Ma'am?" Pearlie replied, the word muffled by a mouthful of doughnut. Even as he answered, he was reaching for a second one.

Sally laughed. "Never mind. Smoke, if you plan on getting any of those, you'd better carry the sack yourself."

"Looks that way, doesn't it?" Smoke said, taking the sack from Pearlie and sticking it down into his own saddlebag.

"Don't worry, Cal, I held some back for us," she said.

Cal grinned broadly. "Well, for once I won't have to fight Pearlie for them."

Smoke and Sally kissed again. Then Smoke swung into the saddle. He looked down at his wife.

"I don't have any idea when I'll be back," he said. "Just look for me when you see me. And take care."

"I will," Sally replied. "Smoke?"

Smoke had just started to turn his horse and he stopped to look back at her.

"Be careful?"

"Careful? Damn, now there's an idea. I hadn't even thought about that," he said, teasing her.

"Oh!" Sally said in an exasperated tone of voice. "Go on, the sooner you leave the better."

Laughing, Smoke urged his horse ahead and it broke quickly and easily into a trot.

Smoke and Pearlie were over at Timber Notch, preparing to leave on their hunt for whoever had raided the ranch. Pearlie was sitting on the edge of the porch of the Burke house, already into the little bag of doughnuts Sally had made for them. Tom Burke was cinching up the saddle on his horse, while Smoke was kneeling by the steps of the porch, studying the dirt.

Reaching down, he picked something up, then examined it closely. "Well, now. It looks like they didn't get away clean," Smoke said.

"What have you found?" Tom asked.

"Do you have a shotgun in the house?"

"Yes, a double-barreled Greener ten-gauge. At first I thought maybe they stole it, but I found it out by what's left of the barn."

"Did you keep it loaded with double-aught buck?"

"As a matter of fact I did. Why?"

"Because this shot is double-aught buck," Smoke said holding out his hand. There were three large shotgun pellets in his palm. "And if you look close enough, you can see that they are bloodstained."

"So one of them is wounded?" Pearlie asked.

Smoke shook his head. "I doubt that. Whoever caugh a bellyful of these pellets is more'n likely dead."

"I hope so."

"There's something else about these pellets," Smoke said. He held something up. "This thread was sticking to one of them. It's red and black."

"Red and black thread. Came from a shirt maybe?" Tom asked.

"That would be my guess. But the question is, wha would an Indian on a raiding party be doing wearing a white man's shirt?"

"That doesn't seem all that unusual to me, Smoke," Pearlie said. "Since they've all started getting paid for a lowing grazing on their land, most of the Indians hav more money than most of the cowboys I know. They bu all sorts of white men's things."

"That's true," Smoke agreed. "But let's think about it for a moment. These Indians were out on a war part right? Now, it's been a long time since any of our Indian around here were hostile. They've got no reason to be It's like you say, most of them are making more mone than most of the cowboys as it is. So the only reason I ca think of that Indians might be on the warpath would b for some holy reason known only to them. If they'r goin' to war for some holy reason, then they would wan it to be in the old way. That means they would paint the face, wear feathers and traditional warrior getup. And t tell the truth, I have a hard time picturing a warrior in a red and black plaid shirt."

"Maybe they aren't out to make medicine," Tom said. "Maybe they're just out to steal what they can."

"Are you missing anything, Tom? Anything that the Indians might want?"

Tom shook his head. "The only thing that was taken was that gold chain and diamond I had given to Jo Ellen. You remember it, don't you?"

"Yes, of course I do."

"That was gone, but nothing else was missing. Not any of the horses. Not even the shotgun. Come to think of it, none of the guns were taken from my hired hands either."

"Have you thought about that?" Smoke asked. He walked over to mount his horse. Tom and Pearlie mounted as well.

"Sort of curious, isn't it," Tom replied.

"Very curious," Smoke agreed. "I mean, here we find arrows all over the place, which means they were armed with bows. Wouldn't you think they would want to replace those bows with guns?"

"So, what do you think all this means?"

"I believe it means someone wants us to think it was Indians."

"Think we'll be able to follow the trial, Smoke?" Cal asked.

"I don't see why not. They didn't make any effort to cover it up," Smoke said. "Let's see where it leads us."

11

The sun was high overhead at Sugarloaf, a brilliant white orb fixed in the bright blue sky. Pigiron McCord, Jason Harding, and Dirk Wheeler looked down on the ranch from atop a nearby hill. As they watched, a woman came out onto the back porch. There, in broad daylight, she took off her shirt, and would have been naked from the waist up had it not been for the fact that she was wearing a camisole.

"Goddamn!" Pigiron said, nearly choking on the word. "Look at that!"

The woman poured water into a basin, then began washing her hair.

"Is that Jensen's woman?" Wheeler asked.

"Who else would it be?" Pigiron replied.

"You think she's alone?"

"'Course she is. If they was some hired hands here, you think she'd be out on the back porch damn near nekkid?" Pigiron chuckled.

"What is it?" Wheeler asked. "What are you laughing about?"

"I'm laughing about Jensen," Pigiron said. "He's out looking for us, and we're here with his woman." Pigiron rubbed himself. "You know what? I think I'm going to enjoy this more than I would have enjoyed killing Jensen back in town."

"We goin' to take turns with her, aren't we?" Harding asked.

"Yeah," Wheeler said. "We are going to take turns, aren't we? I mean, I ain't plannin' on just standin' by and watchin' you have all the fun. I figure to get in on it too."

"Don't worry, you will. We'll take turns," Pigiron said. "Long as you boys both know that I'm first."

Sally looked at the pile of towels she had brought out onto the back porch with her. Under the top towel was a loaded pistol. She looked at it to reassure herself by its presence, then, without being too obvious, checked the progress of the three riders who were coming toward the house.

What Pigiron and the others didn't realize was that Sally and Cal knew they were there. A few minutes earlier Cal had gone up into the loft of the barn to push down a couple of bales of hay. While he was up there, he just happened to walk over and stand in the attic opening to have a look back toward the distant tree line. He didn't know what made him walk over there, or what made him look, but whatever it was was fortuitous, because that was when he saw the three riders coming.

The way they were approaching—avoiding the road, staying back in the trees, and never crossing a hill in silhouette—told Cal that whoever they were, they were up to no good. He hurried to the house to tell Sally.

"Cal, do you think you could manage to get around behind them without being seen?" Sally asked.

Cal nodded. "Yeah, I think I can. I can get across to the ridgeline before they are close enough to see me cross in the open. The ridge will give me cover until I reach Bushy Draw. By then, they'll be beyond Bushy Draw, which will put me behind them."

"All right, you do that. And while you're sneaking around behind them, I'll do something to keep their attention here."

Cal hurried back to the barn, saddled his horse quickly, then rode hard to get across a field that would let him go along the back side of the ridge. He figured to come back down behind them about the time they hit the edge of the south pasture.

Sally decided to get their attention by washing her hair. And to make certain that she kept their attention, she upped the ante a little by taking off her shirt. It would also give her the opportunity to carry a pistol outside without anyone knowing she had it, by slipping the revolver in between the towels.

In the meantime, Cal reached Bushy Draw, a pass through the ridgeline. Bushy Draw was so well protected by vegetation that unless someone knew it was there, they would never see it. In fact, even knowing it was there, one had to be right on it to see it. Because of that, Cal was able to get within twenty yards of the riders, close enough to hear them talking.

"They said she was a good-lookin' woman," one of the men said. "I reckon I just didn't know how good-lookin' she was until I seen her."

One of the others laughed. "Hell, Wheeler, what difference does it make to you whether or not she's a good-lookin' woman? I've seen you with women that was so ugly they'd gag a maggot on the gut wagon."

"Yeah, but just once, I'd like to have me a good-lookin' woman," the one called Wheeler replied.

"Well, you boys better enjoy her while you can," the third man said. "'Cause I don't aim to leave her alive."

"You goin' to kill a good-lookin' woman like that? Why? Seems to me like we could take her with us. That way, anytime we wanted to, why, we could just take our pleasure with her."

"Nah, she'd just be getting in the way all the time. And I don't aim to leave her here where she can talk."

"Yeah, I reckon you're right."

Cal pulled his pistol. "You fellas just hold it right there," he called.

"What the hell? Where'd you come from?" Harding hissed, startled by Cal's sudden appearance.

"Who are you?" Cal asked.

"What's it to you?" Harding asked.

Cal fired at Harding. His bullet clipped Harding's earlobe, sending out a misty spray of blood and leaving a bloody wound.

"Ahhh!" Harding yelled in pain, slapping his hand to his ear. "Are you crazy, mister?"

"If somebody doesn't answer me really quick, I'm going to take off another earlobe," Cal said. He smiled. "Only, I'm going to let you three guess which earlobe it will be. Am I going to take your other one?" He pointed his pistol at Harding. "Or one of yours?" He pointed to the other two. "Now, I'm askin' again. Who are you?"

Suddenly there was an angry buzz, then the *thocking* sound of a heavy bullet tearing into flesh. A fountain of blood squirted up from the neck of Cal's horse and the animal went down on its front knees, then collapsed onto its right side. It was a good half second after the strike of the bullet before the heavy boom of a distant rifle reached Cal's ears.

The fall pinned Cal's leg under his horse. He also dropped his pistol on the way down, and now it lay just out of reach of his grasping fingers.

"What the hell? Who's that shooting?" Wheeler shouted, pulling hard on the reins of his horse, which, though not hit, was spooked by seeing another horse go down.

"Who the hell cares?" Harding shouted back. "Look at him! He's pinned down!" Harding drew his gun and fired at Cal.

Though Cal's right leg was still pinned, he was able to flip his left leg over the saddle and lay down behind his horse, thus providing himself with some cover. Harding's bullet dug into his saddle and sent up a little puff of dust, but did no further damage.

"Shit!" Harding said. "I can't get to him from this angle."

"Come on, let's get the woman and get out of here!" Pigiron shouted.

"Not till I put a bullet in that son of a bitch!" Harding insisted. "The son of a bitch shot off my ear!" Harding slapped his legs against the side of his horse and moved around to get a better shot at Cal.

Cal made one more desperate grab for his pistol, but it was still out of reach. His rifle, however, was in the saddle sheath on the side of the horse that was on the ground, and Call could see about six inches of the stock sticking out. He grabbed it, gratified when it pulled free. He jerked it from the sheath and jacked a shell into the chamber, just as Harding came around to get into position to shoot him.

"Good-bye, asshole!" Harding said, raising his pistol and taking careful aim. The smile left his face as he saw the business end of Cal's rifle come up and spit a finger of flame. The bullet from Cal's rifle hit Harding just under the chin, then exited the back of his head, taking with it a pink spray of blood and bone as Harding tumbled off his horse.

"He got Jason!" Wheeler shouted.

"Let's get out of here!" Pigiron shouted.

Pigiron and Wheeler started riding away hard now, forgetting all about their original intention of going after Jensen's wife. They didn't even bother to look back to see what happened to Harding. In the meantime, another bullet whistled by from the distant rifle. When Cal located the source of the shooting, he saw a mounted man with one leg thrown casually across his saddle. Using that leg to provide a stable firing platform, the shooter raised his rifle to fire again. There was a flash of light, the man rolled back from the recoil, then the bullet whizzed by so close to Cal's head that it made his ears pop. All this before the report of the rifle actually reached him. With a gasp of disbelief, Cal realized that the man was shooting at him from over five hundred yards away.

Suddenly Cal heard hoofbeats and, looking around, he saw Sally riding hard toward him.

"No! Sally, get back!" he shouted.

The distant rifleman also saw Sally approaching, and his next shot went toward her. Cal watched with alarm as dust puffed up from her hat, and he was sure she had been hit. He was greatly relieved when she reached his fallen horse, leaped down with a rifle in her hand, and slapped her own animal on the rump to get him out of the way. She dropped to the ground behind Cal's horse.

"Thank God you weren't hit!" Cal said. "When I saw that bullet hit your hat, I thought you were a goner."

"The bullet hit my hat?" Sally asked. Reaching up to pull it off, she saw the hole in the felt. "Oh, my, that was very close, wasn't it?"

Another bullet whizzed by, this one so close that both of them could hear the air pop as it passed.

"We've got to get you out from under that horse and over on this side," Sally said.

Cal tried to pull his leg free, but couldn't. Then he got an idea. He stuck the stock of the rifle just under the horse's side and grabbed the barrel. Using the rifle as a lever, he pushed up and wedged just enough space between the horse's flesh and the ground to allow him to slip his leg free.

"Is your leg broken?" Sally asked.

Cal felt it. "No, I don't think so. But the blood circulation was cut off and now it's numb."

"Let's try and make it over to the dry streambed," Sally suggested, pointing to a depression that snaked its way across the ground. Only in the freshet season was the channel a stream. Then it caught the runoff waters from the snow of the higher elevations. Now it was just a low spot in the ground, but if they could reach it, it would give them more protection from the distant shooter.

Crawling on their bellies, Sally and Cal slithered and twisted their way down to the dry streambed. They reached the bank and rolled over behind the berm just as another bullet ploughed into the dirt beside them. Then they twisted around behind the bank and looked back up toward the place where the shots were coming from.

"Well, with this cover and the rifles, we aren't easy targets," Sally said. "And if he tries to come any closer, he'll be playing with our deck of cards."

The shooter, whoever he was, had come to the same realization, because he put his rifle back in the saddle sheath, then turned and rode away as casually as if he were riding down Main Street. And why not? There was no way Cal and Sally could reach him from where they were.

As Pigiron and Wheeler got close to the rifleman who had rescued them, they recognized him. He was easy to recognize. His skin shone black in the sun.

"Jim!" Pigiron said. "What are you doing here?"

"Tatum sent me after you."

"What does he want?"

"He didn't say," Jim said.

"Well, I'm glad you come when you did," Wheeler said. "I reckon we owe you."

Jim, always a man of few words, didn't answer.

12

Pigiron and the others rejoined Tatum just before dark that night. Tatum was sitting on a fallen log near a fire, eating beans. He looked up as they arrived.

"Find out anything?"

"Yeah," Pigiron said. "They've raised 'em an army. A fella by the name of Covington is leading it."

"Covington?" Tatum asked. "A lawyer?"

"Yeah, a lawyer."

Tatum laughed out loud. "Well, what do you know. My lawyer leading the army. Why, this couldn't have worked out better if I'd planned it."

Tatum looked around, as if just noticing that someone was missing. "Where is Harding?" he asked.

Pigiron and Wheeler glanced at each other, hesitant to answer.

"I said, where's Harding?" Tatum repeated.

"We, uh, run into some trouble," Pigiron finally said.

"What kind of trouble? I told you to lay low when you were in town. Last time you were there you got yourself whipped by Smoke Jensen, as I recall. So what happened, did you run across him again?"

"Not exactly," Pigiron replied.

"Not exactly. What the hell is that supposed to mean?"

"Well, Jim was there, weren't you, Jim?" Wheeler said.

Jim just stared at Wheeler with an absolutely emotionless expression. Then, without saying a word, he got his kit from his saddlebag, went over to the pot, and spooned out a serving of beans.

"Hah!" Tatum said. "I can just see the kind of fracas Jim might get into, him being black and so talkative and all. Now I'm going to ask you one last time to tell me what the hell happened to Harding."

"We went out to Smoke Jensen's ranch," Pigiron said.

"Did I tell you to go to his ranch? No. What I said was hang around town and see what was going on."

"I know you didn't tell us to, but I figured maybe we could find out something out there too."

"Bullshit, Pigiron. You figured you would get even with him for beating you up," Tatum said. "Hell, I don't blame you none for that. Truth is, I'd like to see the son of a bitch dead myself, and when all this is over, I may just arrange that. So, did you kill him?"

"He wasn't there," Pigiron replied. "There wasn't no one there except his wife and some hired hand, a kid."

"Well, did you kill them?"

"No," Pigiron admitted.

"Wait a minute," Tatum said, stroking his chin. "Let me get this straight. There was no one there except Jensen's wife and a kid, but Harding is the one who wound up gettin' hisself kilt?"

"Yeah," Pigiron said. "That's about the size of it."

"What did Jim have to do with it?"

"Well, the kid . . . uh . . . he got the drop on Harding. . . ."

"He got the drop on Harding?"

"Yeah, he got the drop on Harding, and when he did, well, he sort of had us over a barrel too. He was going to kill Harding unless we give up to him."

"So you let him kill Harding," Tatum said. "Yeah, I can see that. Two for one, that's a pretty good exchange."

This wasn't at all where Pigiron was going with the story, but when Tatum accepted it this way, Pigiron looked over at Wheeler in a silent suggestion that they let him believe it this way.

"Yeah," Wheeler said, catching on quickly. "That's exactly the way it happened. Then, ole Jim here come along with his rifle and he kilt the kid's horse. That gave us a chance to get away."

"Get away? You didn't kill the kid?"

"No. Jensen's wife was comin' by then. She had a long gun, we only had pistols. We didn't have no choice but to leave."

Some miles away, Smoke, Pearlie, and Tom Burke were also sitting around the fire. They had eaten well tonight, for Smoke had killed a turkey, and the aroma of its cooking still hung in the air. Tom was cleaning his .52-caliber Spencer rifle.

"I'll be damned," Smoke said, nodding toward the rifle. "You've still got that rifle."

"Yep," Tom answered.

"What rifle?" Pearlie asked.

"The rifle he made the shot with," Smoke answered.

"The shot?"

"You mean you've never heard about the shot? The shot that won the battle of Adobe Springs?" Smoke asked. "How far was it, Tom?"

"They measured it later, said it was twelve hundred yards."

"Wait a minute," Pearlie said. "Are you trying to tell us he made a shot from twelve hundred yards?"

"At least that far," Smoke said. "To tell the truth, it looked even farther to me."

"To you? Wait a minute, you mean you were there too?"

"Oh, yes," Smoke replied. He looked at Pearlie. "I can't believe I've never told you the story."

"No, but I have a feeling I'm going to hear about it now," Pearlie said, smiling.

"Tom was a buffer then, and from time to time I would do a little of it myself."

"A buffer?" Pearlie asked.

"That's what they called buffalo hunters," Smoke explained. "Anyway, about fifteen of us just happened to wind up in a stage depot called Adobe Springs."

As Smoke told the story, he did so with such vivid imagery that Pearlie could almost see himself in the little adobe trading post where the fifteen buffalo hunters had come together.

It was early in the morning and Smoke had just awakened. Spread out all over the floor of the little stage way station were the bedrolls of other buffers who had gathered there. Some of them had whiskey and one of them had a guitar. In addition, there were two women passengers from the stagecoach, headed for Denver. They were saloon girls, known to nearly all the buffalo hunters, so most had stayed awake, drinking and singing far into the night. As a result, nearly everyone else was still asleep this morning.

Smoke went outside to relieve himself, and was just finishing when he saw a large group of mounted Indians advancing slowly toward them.

"Indians!" he shouted, running back inside.

Barricading the door, Smoke ran to the window and looked outside. The Indians weren't approaching as they normally did, either by stealth or by riding back and forth. Instead, they were heading straight for the building in a massive charge, their horses leaping over obstacles, feathered bonnets flying in the breeze.

By now everyone else in the building had responded to Smoke's warning and rushed to the windows. There was the sound of glass breaking as the defenders cleared the way for them to shoot.

Nobody gave the order to fire, because no one was in charge. Instead, the defenders fired at targets of opportunity, and the opening salvo was devastating. Half-a-dozen Indians went down. Stunned by the unexpected volley, the Indians withdrew about two hundred yards, then formed for a second attack.

"Anyone get hit?" Smoke called.

"Yeah, Johnny got hit, but I don't think it's bad," Tom said.

"I'll look after him," Jo Ellen offered. Jo Ellen was the more attractive of the two prostitutes who had come in on the stage.

The Indians came again, three abreast this time, galloping through the dust, shouting and whooping their war cries. They charged all the way up to the building, firing from horseback, shooting arrows and bullets at the cracks between the logs. They hurled lances toward the open windows. Two of them jumped down from their horses and tried to force the door open by hitting against it with the butts of their rifles.

Once again, the buffalo hunters took very careful aim, making every shot count. Several Indians went down, and their riderless horses whirled and retreated, leaving their riders dead or dying on the ground behind them. The rest of the Indians waited a few minutes, then launched a third attack.

"Here they come again," someone shouted and, once more, the defenders fired at targets of opportunity.

This time, however, the Indians made a much more traditional approach. Using a stone wall and a barn as cover, they were almost on top of the defenders before anyone could get a shot at them. The Indians fired through the windows, and bullets buzzed about like angry hornets.

Three more of the defenders were hit, including Lily, the other woman.

"Lily!" Jo Ellen shouted, running to her friend. She sat on the floor and held her friend's head in her lap.

"Never figured I'd go out this way," Lily said, smiling up at Jo Ellen. "I always thought some drunken cowboy would shoot me in a jealous rage."

"Hang on, Lily, you'll be . . ." Jo Ellen said, but Lily's head fell to one side and her open eyes began to glass over.

Suddenly, fire arrows came streaking in through the window, starting several small fires.

"Get 'em out, quick!" Smoke shouted.

Grabbing blankets and rugs, the defenders managed to beat out all the arrows but one, which continued to burn out of control.

"We're going to need water!" someone yelled, and another grabbed the water bucket and with it, finally got the upper hand over the last fire arrow.

"Was that our drinking water?" someone asked.

"Yeah," Tom said.

"We're going to get awful thirsty."

"Where's the well?" Smoke asked.

"Out there," the depot manager said, pointing to the well out in the front yard. Anyone who went after water would be completely exposed to the Indians.

"I'll go," someone said, grabbing the bucket.

"Speaker, no!" Smoke shouted, but Speaker was out before anyone could stop him, and he dashed across the open space toward the well.

Watching through the window, Smoke saw a puff of dust fly up, then a gush of blood spurt from Speaker's shirt. He went down and the bucket rolled, clanging, across the yard.

"I wish he hadn't done that," Smoke said.

"Yeah, he should've thought more about it. He never had a chance," Tom said.

"That's not the only thing," Smoke replied. "Now the Indians know we are out of water. All they have to do is wait us out."

That's exactly what the Indians did. They did not launch another attack. Instead, they waited just out of range. The afternoon grew long and very thirsty, aggravatingly so when the Indians, who had plenty of water, would appear, just out of range, and pour gourds of water over their heads.

The Indians didn't leave during the night. From every window, the defenders could see campfires. They could also hear the drums and singing.

"We've got to have water," someone said. "I'm going out to get the bucket."

"You won't make it," Smoke said.

"I might. It's dark, they might not see me."

"Do you think they don't know we need water?" Smoke replied. "You saw how they were pouring water over themselves today, tantalizing us. They're waiting at the well for anyone who is crazy enough to try."

"We've got to do something. We can't make it another day without water."

"How long can we last?" Jo Ellen asked, and Tom was surprised to see that she had come up to stand right beside him.

"Maybe another day," Tom replied.

Tom looked out across the open ground toward the ridge where the Indians were. Though the fires had mostly burned down, he could still see faint glowings here and there. There was also enough of a moon that he didn't think the Indians could sneak up on them, even if they wanted too.

"You're going to think I'm crazy," Jo Ellen said. "But I'm glad this happened. That is, if I live through it, I'm glad it happened."

Tom chuckled. "Well, I don't know as I think you're crazy. But that is a curious outlook."

"I reckon it is. But I aim to change my life after this. I don't plan on being a whore anymore."

"Good for you," Tom said.

"What about you? You plan to go on being a buffalo hunter?"

"Doesn't make much difference whether I plan to or not," Tom replied. "There aren't many buffalo left. The truth is, I'm going to have to get into some other line of work pretty soon."

"You ever thought about ranching?"

"Thought about it. I wouldn't mind owning a ranch, but I don't think I'd care to cowboy for someone else."

"I own a ranch," Jo Ellen said.

"What?"

"That is, I own some land. It's out in Colorado. A . . . uh . . . friend left it to me."

"He must've been a good friend."

"He was," Jo Ellen said without elaborating.

"Have you ever seen it?"

"No, but I know it's there. The county clerk sent me a letter describing it to me. And I've kept the taxes up. You aren't married, are you, Mr. Burke?"

"No, I'm not."

"You think you could marry someone who was once a whore?"

Tom stared at Jo Ellen for a long moment. "Jo Ellen, are you asking me to marry you?" he asked in surprise.

"I reckon I am," Jo Ellen replied. "That is, if we get out of here. The way I look at it, we're both going to be making some big changes in our life. Seems to me like it might be easier if we made those changes together."

Tom laughed out loud.

"I'm sorry," Jo Ellen said, her face burning in embarrassment. "I had no right to . . ."

"No," Tom said, reaching out to her. "You don't understand. I'm not laughing at you. I'm laughing because I never thought anything like this would happen to me. Yes, I'll marry you."

Shortly after dawn, when everyone was awake, Tom told the others that during the night he and Jo Ellen had made plans to get married.

"When?" someone asked.

"Soon's we get out of here," Tom replied.

"Then you're both goin' to die single, 'cause there ain't no way we're ever goin' to get out of here. Them Indians out there are just goin' to wait us out till we either die of thirst or go crazy and start runnin' toward the well," someone said.

"Maybe not," Tom suggested.

"Maybe not? What do you mean, maybe not?"

"Well, I've been doin' some thinking." Tom walked back over to the window and looked out toward the Indians who were still there on the distant ridge. He studied them through a pair of binoculars, and took two large-caliber bullets from his bullet bag. Separating the bullets from the cartridges, he began pouring the powder from one of the cartridges into the other cartridge.

"What are you doing?" someone asked.

"I'm double-loading a shell," Tom said. He nodded toward the binoculars. "If you take a look through those glasses, you'll see some fancy-dressed son of a bitch up there givin' orders to the rest of the Indians. Seems to me like if someone was to kill him, the others might go home. So, that's what I plan to do."

"You mean next time he comes down here?"

"No, I mean now," Tom said.

"Hell, man, he's a thousand yards away if he's a foot. What are you talking about?"

"Light that candle for me, would you?"

Shaking his head, the man lit the candle, then handed it to Tom, who tapped the bullet back into the cartridge, then used the dripping wax to help seal it. After that, he loaded his rifle, then stepped back up to the window.

"You're wasting a bullet."

"Maybe not," Smoke said.

"Wait a minute, are you saying you think he can do it?"

"I've seen him shoot," Smoke said. "He's got a place to rest his rifle, and the target is right up on top of the ridgeline. Yeah, I think it's possible. At least it's worth a chance."

Tom picked up the rifle then and rested the barrel on the windowsill. He aimed, then lowered the rifle and adjusted his sights, lifted it up, aimed again, then lowered it for another adjustment.

No one said a word.

Tom aimed a third time. This time the rifle roared and bucked against his shoulder.

One of the others had been looking at Tom's target through the binoculars. "Missed," he called.

"I told you he couldn't—"

"Wait!" Smoke shouted. "You got him!"

Everyone rushed to the window then to watch as, far in the distance, the fancy-dressed Indian fell from his horse.

"They left after that," Smoke said. "All of the Indians turned and rode away."

"And the woman?" Pearlie asked. "Wait a minute, you said her name was Jo Ellen. You mean that's where you met Mrs. Burke?"

"Yes, Pearlie. Jo Ellen was a former whore," Tom said. "But I will tell you this. No man could have ever asked for a better woman." He had been quiet during the telling of the story, and now he used a burning brand from the fire to light his pipe. Walking away from the fire, he found a place to be alone for a while.

13

The Comanche village was near the Purgatory River and for this reason, the little settlement was called Purgatory by the white men, though not by the Comanche. The Indians had no specific name for their village. It was just where they lived, a part of them, and they would not think to name it, any more than they would give a name to the water they drank and the air they breathed. Here, an old chief sat in the center of a circle of men, women, and children.

"Listen," the old chief said, "and I will tell you the story of the Comanche."

Those who were around him, including the elders of the council and the young men, drew closer to hear his words. The one who held the attention of the others was Stone Eagle, the traditional chief of the Comanche. Stone Eagle was an old man who had fought many battles when he was younger. Because of that, he had the respect and admiration of everyone in the tribe.

The women and children grew quiet, not only because it was forbidden to make noise while stories were being told around the campfires, but because they knew it would be a good story, and it filled them with excitement to hear it.

"Once there was a young man," Stone Eagle said. He

held up his finger and wagged it slowly back and forth
"He was not Comanche, he was not Kiowa, he was no
Crow, and he was not Lakota."

"What was he, Grandfather?" one of the childre
asked. It was a term of respect. Stone Eagle wasn't reall
his grandfather.

"He was before," Stone Eagle said. "He was in the tim
of the beginning, before the winter-counts, when me
could speak with the animals and the spirits of the earth
fire, wind, and water. Now the young man did not kno
this was unusual, because he had always been able to d
so and it seemed a natural thing for him to do. Then, on
day as he stood watching an eagle fly, he thought that pe
haps he would try and fly too, so he leaped into the ai
and he beat his arms like the wings of an eagle, but h
could not fly and he fell to the ground . . . *ker-whump.*"

Stone Eagle made the *ker-whump* sound in such a wa
as to amuse the children, and they all laughed.

"'Foolish one, you cannot fly,' the eagle taunted, an
he soared through the air and laughed at the young mar

"Then the young man saw a coyote running swiftly, s
swiftly across the plains, and he ran after the coyote, think
ing to catch him, but he couldn't. 'Foolish one, did yo
think you could run as swiftly as I?' the coyote mocked.

"Then the young man saw a bear. The bear smelle
honey in a comb that was high in a tree, and the bea
with his great strength, pushed the tree over so he coul
have the honey. The young man was very impressed wit
the bear's great strength, so he too tried to push a tre
over, but he could not. The bear, who was enjoying h
honey, saw the young man, and he teased the young ma
and called him a weakling, and told him he had no bus
ness trying to push over a mighty tree in the first place.

Stone Eagle shook his head sadly, and clucked h
tongue.

"What did the young man do next, Grandpa?"

"Oh, the young man felt very bad," Stone Eagle sai
"He tore out his hair, and he gashed his face with rock

and he cried out in anger and in despair. 'I cannot fly like the eagle,' the young man said. 'I cannot run as swiftly as the coyote, nor do I have the strength of the bear. Why am I on earth if I cannot do any of these things?'

"Suddenly, the young man heard a strange-sounding voice, carried on the wind. 'Go . . . to . . . the . . . mountain,' the voice said."

Stone Eagle made his voice wail in a terrible sound, and the smaller children were frightened. Some cried, and others clutched the hands of their mothers tightly. The older children were frightened too, but they welcomed the fright because it made them feel brave to listen to the story without betraying their own fear.

"The young man climbed the mountain," Stone Eagle went on. "And as he climbed, the voice in the wind continued to speak to him. 'You are a worm,' the voice in the wind said. 'You are a blade of grass. You are an ant, a mote of dust. You are nothing. You cannot fly, you cannot run swiftly, you have no strength. Climb to the top of the mountain.'

"'Why should I climb to the top of the mountain?' the young man asked.

"'You will know why when you get there,' the voice in the wind answered.

"The young man began to do as he was instructed, but he did so with a heavy heart. He believed that the voice had instructed him to climb the mountain so he could jump off and kill himself. He was frightened and sad, but he felt that he must do what the voice told him to do."

"And did he climb to the top of the mountain and jump off, Grandpa?"

Stone Eagle held up a finger, as if to caution the young questioner against impatience, then went on with his story. "As the young man climbed, a strange thing happened. He grew hungry and, looking for something to eat, he saw the buds of the peyote cactus. He ate the peyote buds and as he did, he began to see things he could not see before. He was no longer frightened, or confused, or ashamed. Only truth remained in his body, and with truth, he understood all.

"It was true, he thought, he could not fly like an eagle, but an eagle could not use his wings as hands. It was true he could not run as swiftly as a coyote, but a coyote could not walk upright. It was true he did not have the strength of the bear, but the bear could not make poems or music or dance to the rhythm of the drums. When the young man reached the top of the mountain, he thought of all this and he spread his arms wide and looked over the valley, far below.

"'Why don't you jump?' a voice asked, and the young man looked around and there he saw a warrior, wearing many feathers and shining as bright as the sun."

"Who was the warrior, Grandpa?"

"Some say it was he who is called Shining Warrior, a messenger from the Great Spirit, and that is what I believe," Stone Eagle replied.

"And did the young man jump?"

Again, Stone Eagle held up a finger, calling for quiet.

"'No,' the young man said. 'I will not jump. I am not a worm, I am not a blade of grass, I am not an ant or a mote of dust. I am a man!'

"'Now,' Shining Warrior said. 'Now your period of trial is over. Now you have the gift of the peyote and the sacred wisdom, and from this day forth you will be the master over all the animals and over all the things of nature. You shall have a name and your name shall be called Comanche, and your people shall be many, and they will be mighty hunters and warriors.'

"'But wait,' the young man called. 'Wait, I have questions to ask. There are many things I do not know. How will I learn what is needed to know to be worthy of the fine name you have given me?'

"'I have given you the gift of the peyote,' Shining Warrior said. 'Now I tell you, when you wish to attain wisdom you need only to build a sweat lodge. Go into the swea lodge and build a fire so that you may sweat as you chew the peyote.'

"And that is why, even today, wise men of our people use peyote to gain knowledge and to know the truth," Stone Eagle said.

"What happened next, Grandpa?"

"The young man left the mountain and returned to the valley below. When he returned, he discovered that all the animals had been struck dumb as their punishment for mocking Comanche. The animals could no longer speak to him. They couldn't even speak to each other, and every animal had to go for all time after that unable even to speak to their own kind."

"Is that why men can speak to each other, but animals cannot speak?"

"Yes," Stone Eagle said. "For it was intended for man to rule over the animals."

"And what happened to Comanche after that?" another child asked.

"Comanche took a wife and had many children, and the children took wives and had many children and those children took wives and had many children. I am the child of one of those children, just as you are the children of my children. And that is why we are known as Comanche."

After Stone Eagle finished his story, there were others who told stories as well. If the story was to be a story of bravery in battle, the one who spoke would walk over to the lodge pole and strike it with his coup stick. Then everyone would know that he was going to tell a story of an enemy killed in battle. Such stories were only told by the older men of the tribe, for it had been a long time since the Comanche had been in battle and none of the younger men could make such boasts. In such stories, the enemy warriors were always brave and skilled, because that made the warrior's own exploits all the greater.

Not all the stories were of enemies killed in battle. Some of the stories were of hunting exploits, and these stories could be told by the younger men. Some stories were even of things that had happened in the time of their father's father's father, which had been handed down through the generations to be preserved as a part of their history.

One of the men who had listened intently to all the stories was Quinntanna. Quinntanna was the nephew of Stone Eagle, though, as Quinntanna's father had died many years ago, Stone Eagle was more a father than an uncle.

Quinntanna, a handsome man with a broad chest, powerful arms, strong legs, had listened to all the stories because he hoped to find—in one of them—the answer to a troubling and recurring dream.

In the dream, Quinntanna had seen many people walking through a pall of smoke. The people were weeping, but they were not weeping because smoke was in their eyes. They were weeping from sadness. Quinntanna asked why they were sad, but he always awoke before anyone could answer him.

At first, Quinntanna was disappointed because he did not find the answer in any of the stories. Then, as he thought about it, he realized that perhaps he had. The story of Comanche was the story of the origin of the use of peyote buttons.

Only once before had Quinntanna used the peyote. Perhaps if he used it now, he would understand the meaning of this strange and disturbing dream. That night, before he went to sleep, Quinntanna mentioned his dream, and what he had decided to do about it, to his wife, Sasheena.

"Does that mean you will not go with the hunters then?" Sasheena asked as she nursed their baby.

"Ho!" Quinntanna laughed. "Do you think I would stay here, only to listen to the stories the others will tell when they return? Were I to do that, Teykano would have me believe that he took every animal with his bare hands. No, I will make the hunt, then when I return, I will seek the knowledge of the peyote."

"I will sleep cold until you return, my husband," Sasheena said.

Quinntanna, who was already lying in the bed of blankets and robes, turned back the top blanket for her. "That is true," he said, smiling at her. "But you will not sleep cold tonight."

Putting the baby in its own bed, Sasheena removed her dress, then slipped naked into the bed alongside her husband.

14

Smoke Jensen stopped at the edge of a grassy meadow where he saw hoofprints. Then, seeing some elk droppings, he squatted to get a closer look at them. The droppings were soft, which meant they had been made less than an hour ago. That meant that the elk was close by, more than likely in the clump of trees just ahead.

Smoke knew that the elk would think himself safe in the woods, but those same trees would also allow Smoke to get closer without being seen, provided he made no noise as he approached. For most men that would be difficult or impossible, but Smoke had learned from the old mountain man, Preacher, how to choose his steps so carefully that he could walk on a carpet of fallen leaves without being heard. He knew too to stay downwind of his prey.

A small bush, its limbs bare but for a few brown leaves, rattled dryly in the wind. The bush stood just on the edge of the open meadow, the last piece of vegetation between the woods and a small, swiftly running stream. Smoke was certain that when the elk left the woods for water, it would come this way. Smoke crouched behind a rock and waited.

He had been there for about thirty minutes when he saw a bull elk's head stick out from between a couple of trees. The animal stood perfectly still for a long time, its eyes sweeping over the open meadow, its nose twitching, its ears cocked. The elk was not about to commit itself until it had examined every possible danger.

Moving as slowly and quietly as he could, Smoke raised his rifle to his shoulder and took aim.

The elk started out into the open. It moved slowly and cautiously down to the edge of the stream, then stopped. The elk's head popped up, its rack held high. It stared for a long moment, remaining perfectly still as it did so. Smoke held his breath.

The creature's eyes twitched, and Smoke wondered what sound it had heard, for he had made no noise at all. The elk listened, then decided that whatever it had heard represented no danger. It stuck its head down into the stream and began to drink.

Smoke sighted down the barrel of his rifle, finding a target just above and behind the elk's left foreleg. He tightened the finger on the trigger.

At almost the precise moment he squeezed off his shot, he thought he saw something flying out of the trees toward the elk. But the white puff of smoke that billowed from the end of the rifle barrel so obscured his vision that he decided what he had seen was nothing more than a trick of light, or a moving shadow.

The boom of his shot echoed back from the trees just as the elk fell to its front knees. It got back up and tried to run, but could go no more than a few steps before it fell again.

Smoke got up and ran across the open field toward the still-twitching elk. When he reached the animal, he stopped cold and stared at it in surprise. It was lying on its left side with its legs stretched straight out in front. Sticking up from just behind the right foreleg was an arrow.

"It is my kill!" a voice shouted.

When Smoke looked toward the sound of the voice, he saw an Indian coming toward him from the edge of the woods. He was tall for an Indian, and he was wearing traditional Indian dress.

"My elk," the Indian said again, pointing to the fallen animal.

"No," Smoke said. "It was my shot that killed it."

"My arrow," the Indian insisted, pointing to the shaft sticking up from the flesh of the animal.

Smoke turned the animal over, then pointed to the bullet hole. "My bullet," he said. They were quiet for a moment. Then Smoke offered the Indian his hand. "I am Smoke Jensen."

"You are Smoke Jensen?"

"Yes."

"I have heard of you." The Indian stuck out his hand. "I am Quinntanna."

Smoke smiled. "I have heard of you, Quinntanna. By the way, there is a way to settle this, if you are interested."

"Yes, I am interested. What is the way you would settle this?"

"Well, I'm looking for meat, and I reckon you are too. And the way I look at it, half an elk is better than no elk at all. We could cut the animal in half."

"I want the front half," Quinntanna said. "And I want the heart."

Smoke chuckled. "All right, you can have the front half."

"I will cut the elk in two pieces," Quinntanna offered, dropping to one knee beside the slain animal. He took out his knife and began cutting.

"Why are you hunting with a bow and arrow?"

"We wanted to make this hunt in the way of our fathers and their fathers," Quinntanna answered.

"If you went on the warpath now, would you go on the warpath in the way of your fathers?" Smoke asked.

Quinntanna looked up at Smoke and laughed. "Warpath? Why would we go on the warpath now? The days of war are over."

"For you perhaps, but not for everyone," Smoke said.

"Yes, I have heard of the Sioux and their Ghost Dancers and medicine shirts. They think they can bring back the buffalo, but I know they cannot."

"No, I'm not talking about the Sioux," Smoke said. "I am talking about the Comanche."

Quinntanna snorted. "It is not true. There are no Comanche on the warpath."

"Perhaps some who are renegades?" Smoke suggested. "Evil young men who have left your village?"

Quinntanna shook his head. "I know where every young man from my village is. Why do you ask this?"

"Because recently, some Indians attacked a ranch. They killed everyone on the ranch—the rancher's wife, his children, and those who worked for him. Then they burned the barn and the outbuildings."

"And people think we did it?" Quinntanna asked.

"The arrows did have Comanche markings."

"I do not understand this," Quinntanna said. "It is not good that a white man's ranch was attacked. And it is not good that people think Comanche attacked the ranch."

"So you are telling me that you know nothing about this?"

"I know nothing," Quinntanna repeated.

"I didn't think you did," Smoke said. "Truth to tell, I've thought all along it might be someone else, Comancheros perhaps, who wanted to make it look like Indians attacked."

"Yes, that would be smart," Quinntanna said. "They could take what they wanted from the ranch, but people would think it was the Indians."

"No," Smoke said.

"No?"

"That is the strange part. The people who did this took nothing. They only killed and burned."

Quinntanna shook his head. "Such people I do not understand," he said. By now the elk was in two parts, and Quinntanna stuck the knife into the open cavity of the front half. He carved for a moment, then pulled out the elk's heart. "Make a fire," he said. "We will eat the heart together."

Smoke smiled. "Good idea," he said. "I was getting a little hungry anyway."

While Smoke made a fire, Quinntanna found two forked sticks. Then he peeled the bark of a third stick and used that as a skewer for the heart. With the flames dancing, Quinntanna placed the skewer across the forked sticks so that the heart was in the fire. Within a few moments the juices, dripping into the fire from the roasting heart, snapped and popped and perfumed the air with their aroma.

Smoke and Quinntanna talked of inconsequential things until finally, Quinntanna stood up and carved off a piece of the meat. It was too hot to hold in one hand, so he passed it back and forth between his hands as he gave it over to Smoke. Laughing, Smoke also passed it back and forth between his hands for a moment until he could hold it.

"Here, I have some salt," Smoke said, taking a little paper envelope from his pocket. He gave a pinch to Quinntanna, then salted his own meat before he took a bite. He smiled as the juices filled his mouth and ran down his chin.

"It is good," Quinntanna said.

"Yes," Smoke agreed.

"To eat the heart of the animal you kill is a good thing," Quintanna explained. He took a big bite and began chewing. "If it is a male animal, you will have his strength, and"—Quinntanna rubbed himself and smiled, then added—"that which makes him a male."

"Oh," Smoke said. "What if it is a female?"

Quinntanna laughed out loud. "Do not worry," he said. "From the female we get courage and cunning. And that which makes us male is not harmed."

"I'm glad of that," Smoke said with a laugh. "For I have eaten many female elk and deer."

The two men finished eating the heart. Afterward,

they held their hands up to each other in the sign of peace; then each took his half of the elk and went his own way.

"Would you mind tellin' me how you managed to kill half an elk?" Tom asked with a chuckle when Smoke rode back into their camp carrying the elk's haunch. "And the back half at that?"

Smoke told Tom and Pearlie of his encounter with Quinntanna.

"You sound more than ever convinced that they didn't have anything to do with the raid on Tom's ranch," Pearlie said.

"Practically the whole tribe is out on some sort of ritual hunt," Smoke said. "They don't even have any weapons with them, except for bows and arrows. If they were the ones who had attacked the ranch, they sure wouldn't be wandering around without guns."

"I think Smoke's right," Tom said.

"I almost wish I wasn't right," Smoke declared.

"Why's that?"

"Because if we were after Indians, we would at least have some idea of what we are up against. Now, we don't know. The only thing we know about whoever did this is that they are pure evil."

Camp Covington, as Covington called it, was located just outside Big Rock. There, in a wide meadow, tents were pitched and a military camp was born. Covington had insisted that all those who signed up leave their homes, ranches, and hotel rooms in order to come together as a military unit.

Covington had absolutely no military experience, so he knew nothing about drilling. However, Marcus Dingo, who Covington had appointed as his first sergeant, did know drilling, and he spent a couple of days "whipping the troops into shape."

This was particularly rewarding for Dingo. Dingo was the kind of man who had a difficult time hanging onto a job. As a result, he was often unemployed, which meant that sometimes he had to accept the most self-demeaning of tasks just to keep body and soul together. When he was sweeping the barroom floor, or emptying the spittoons, it was easy for the others to make fun of him. Now the situation was changed. As first sergeant of Covington's Company, Dingo was someone who could, and did, demand and receive respect from the same men who used to tease him.

For three days Dingo drilled the men, taking special delight in making life difficult for those who, but a week earlier, had regarded him as their inferior. Throughout the three days, there was a great deal of talk and complaining from the men, who insisted they had not joined the company to drill, they had joined to fight. Covington kept them in line by quoting an old military adage: "Ten men wisely led are worth a hundred without a head."

"What that means," he explained, "is that without discipline and structure, we are nothing. But with discipline, structure, and tactics, combined with a willingness to follow orders, we will fight the Indians and we will beat them."

Finally, Covington called his troops together in order to give them word that on the next day, they would go after the Indians.

Breakfast the next morning was coffee, bacon, and biscuits. After breakfast, the order was given to strike tents, followed by Boots and Saddles. The latter called for them to saddle their mounts. Then, the order was given "To horse!" This put every soldier standing at the head of his horse. Finally, they were ordered to mount, then to move out.

* * *

The march continued on through the day. Because they were a newly activated unit, poorly led and with no economy of motion, the march was difficult and tiring. For twenty minutes of every hour the men dismounted and led their horses for ten minutes, then let them rest for ten minutes.

For miles upon miles, Covington's Cavalry moved toward the Purgatory River, on which was located the Indian village that Covington was convinced was responsible for the raid on the Burke ranch. Finally, just before nightfall, a stream of water was found and Covington gave the order that this would be their bivouac. A handful of hardtack crackers supplemented the coffee and served as their supper.

While the men were eating, Covington sent Dingo ahead on a little scouting expedition. Dingo returned less than an hour later with word that he had located the village.

"Good," Covington said with a broad smile. "We will attack it tomorrow."

"Tomorrow?" Dingo replied.

"Yes. We'll hit them just before dawn," Covington said. "I want to catch the heathen redskins before they get out of bed."

"Get up," Dingo said, shaking the shoulder of one of the men.

"Get up? What fer? Hell, it's two or three hours 'till dawn."

"We want an early start," Dingo said. "Wake up the others in your platoon."

One by one the orders passed through the command, rousting everyone from their bedrolls. Then, in the darkness, they saddled their horses and made them ready to go. They did it quietly, for from the point of their bivouac to the Indian village itself was no more than two miles, and any unnatural noise could give them away.

Finally, when the bivouac was struck and all the men were mounted, Covington ordered the men forward.

15

Even though all its young men were gone, leaving the village virtually defenseless, the people of the village were enjoying the peaceful sleep of the innocent. They were completely unaware that less than two hundred yards from the village's outer ring, in the lower reaches of a great pine forest, shadows were emerging from the darkness, and that these shadows represented danger to them.

The emerging shadows were the men of Covington's Militia, and they began to take up their positions around the village in accordance with Colonel Covington's instructions. Their horses moved silently, with only their movement and the vapor of their breathing giving any indication of life.

It was cold in the predawn darkness, and Colonel Covington and his staff officers moved to the crest of a small hill to stare down at the Comanche village. All the teepees appeared to be tightly shut against the cold, and no one was moving anywhere. Wisps of smoke curled up through the smoke vents in the top of all the tepees, and the smell of wood smoke mixed with the aroma of last night's cooking, clear indications of habitation.

"Are you sure the Indians who raided Tom Burke's ranch came from Purgatory, Colonel?" Captain Roach asked.

Normally, Roach was teamster for a wagon-freight line, but he had joined Covington's Company of Indian fighters.

"Of course they came from Purgatory," Covington said. "This is the closest Indian village, isn't it?"

"Yes, sir, but that's my point," Roach said. "It just don't seem likely to me that they would shit so close to their home nest."

"Did it ever occur to you, that is exactly what they want us to think? What do you think about it, First Sergeant?" Covington asked. He rubbed his hands together and blew against them, warming them with his breath.

"I figure it's more'n likely these here Injuns is the ones who done it," Dingo said. "But even if it ain't these, it don't matter, 'cause once this here war gets started, all Injuns is going to be the same."

"I think you are right, First Sergeant," Covington replied. "Captain Roach, how long will it take you to get your men to the other side?"

"Half an hour," Roach said.

"Then get your men into position, Captain. It looks like we have caught them completely by surprise, and I want to attack before it's light."

"Yes, sir. Uh, Colonel, what about the women and children in the camp? By attacking while it is still dark, I am afraid we will be putting them at great risk."

"Will we now?"

"Yes, sir."

"What about the women and children at Mr. Burke's ranch? Were they at risk?" Covington asked.

Roach was silent for a moment, then nodded. "Yes, sir. I guess I see what you mean."

"Once your men are in position, fire one shot," Covington ordered. "That will be our signal to attack from both sides."

"Yes, sir."

A small clinking sound of metal on metal came from somewhere among the soldiers. The sound was an unnatural intrusion into the soft whisper of wind in the trees. In her tepee in the village, Sasheena heard the sound while in the deepest recesses of her sleep, and her eyes came open as she wondered what it might have been. Automatically, she looked over toward her baby. He was sleeping nearby, dimly visible in the soft golden glow of the coals that still gleamed in the warming tepee fire. She felt the place beside her, empty now because Quinntanna and nearly every other young man in the village had gone hunting.

Sasheena smiled as she remembered the excitement her husband felt over the expedition.

"Why do you hunt for meat?" she had asked him. *"Our village has enough money from leasing grazing rights to the white man to buy all the pork, beef, lamb, and chicken that we need."*

"You are a woman, and I do not expect a woman to understand," Quinntanna had replied. *"But the traditional hunt is something a man must do. I only wish there were buffalo to hunt."*

The bed robes were warm, and Sasheena realized she must have dreamed the unusual sound. She closed her eyes, and quickly dropped off to sleep again.

Outside, the silent horses and the quiet men were now in position. They stayed motionless for several minutes. Then they heard what they were waiting for: the crack of a rifle shot echoing from the far side of the village.

"All right. Attack, men, attack!" Covington yelled. "Remember the Burke ranch!"

At Covington's orders, the militiamen galloped forward from both sides of the Indian camp, firing as rapidly as they could at the conical tepees that rose up in the darkness before them.

It had been so long since there was any battle between Indians and whites in this area that many of the Indian residents of the village hadn't even been born then. Because of that, the sleeping villagers had no instinctive responses to call upon. They poured out of the tepees, not to join in the fight, but to see what was going on.

"Keep calm, men," Covington shouted to his troops. "Keep calm and fire low."

Though the Indians were totally surprised by the unexpected attack on their village, they realized quickly that they were in mortal danger. Many of them tried to run, only to be cut down by the gunfire. One young Indian in his early teens suddenly burst out of one of the tepees and jumped on an unsaddled and unbridled pony. Covington started after him, not realizing that the boy was armed. The boy whirled around and fired, the bullet whizzing by Covington's ear. Then the boy, displaying unusual courage, rode directly toward Covington, firing twice more, but missing both times. Covington returned fire, killing the boy with one shot.

Sasheena had awakened as quickly as the others, and when she moved to the door flap of her tepee to look outside, she saw the swirling melee of soldiers and Indians. At first she was as confused as everyone else in the village. Then, looking around, she saw Stone Eagle going toward the soldiers, holding an American flag over his head. As a young girl she had heard stories around the council fires of the flag, for it had been given to Stone Eagle by the Great White Father in Washington, the man the whites called President Grant.

"Do not shoot!" Stone Eagle was shouting, waving the flag over his head and trying to be heard above the rattle of musketry. "We are friends to the white man! I am friend of Grant!"

Stone Eagle was shot down within twenty yards of his tepee. But it wasn't only Stone Eagle, for Sasheena could see old men, women, and children being shot as well, slaughtered by the indiscriminate firing of the soldiers. Suddenly, a fusillade of bullets punched through her tepee, and she knew she had to leave.

Grabbing a robe, Sasheena wrapped it around her naked body. Then she picked up her baby and left the tepee, running toward the edge of the trees. Two soldiers on horseback galloped after her. One of them reached down and grabbed the robe, then jerked it away.

Sasheena screamed, and tried, in vain, to cover her exposed body.

"I'll be damned! She's naked!"

"Hey, she ain't bad-lookin'! Get the kid away from her!" the other said. "Get the kid away from her, and we'll have us some fun."

"No!" Sasheena screamed, trying to keep the baby from being taken.

"Hell, don't fight her, Ed, just kill the damn kid."

Using the butt of his pistol, the first soldier hit the baby on the head, crushing its skull. Shocked almost senseless by the brutality, Sasheena felt the life leave her child. She screamed in anger and grief.

"Now, let's see what this little ole Injun gal can do for us," the other soldier said, dismounting and coming toward her, unbuttoning his pants as he did so.

Suddenly a shot rang out, and a bullet hit Sasheena right between the eyes.

"What the hell?" Ed said, looking around to see who'd shot her. He saw Dingo.

"We're here to kill Injuns," Dingo said. "Not make some half-breed brats that we'll have to deal with in the future. You want a woman, get yourself a whore like ever'one else."

"There ain't nothin' says we can't have a little fun now," one of the two men said.

"Yeah, there is somethin' says that," Dingo replied. He pointed to himself. "Me. I say it."

"The first sergeant is quite right," Covington said,

arriving to see what the discussion was about. "We are here to conduct war against these people, not commit rape and other atrocities. You will conduct yourselves with dignity. Now, get on with it."

"Yes, sir," the two soldiers replied contritely.

"Good work, First Sergeant," Covington said. "It's a shame the young woman had to be killed, but it is serving a higher purpose." Covington turned his horse then, and rode back into the swirling melee of dust, running, screaming Indians, and mounted cavalrymen.

Very soon thereafter, most of the shooting had stopped, simply because there were no more targets of opportunity. Covington held up his hand, then described a circle, calling all his men together. The ground was strewn with Indians. Most were dead, though a few were still groaning.

"All right, men, I congratulate you on a fine victory here today. Surely this will go down in history as one of the greatest Indian battles of all time. Now I want you to search all the tepees and remove anything of value, especially any weapons that you might find. And bear in mind that you are liberating contraband, not for yourself, but for the entire company. We will make a fair and balanced division of plunder once we return to Big Rock."

"Some of these people are still alive," Captain Roach said. "What do we do about them?"

"Shoot them, I guess," Covington said, almost in an offhand way. "That would be the humane thing to do. No sense in letting them lie here and suffer."

"What about the tepees?" Dingo asked.

"Burn them."

For the next several minutes the men of Covington's Militia moved through the encampment, removing blankets, cooking utensils, knives, furs, and anything else of value they could find, including, in several cases, money. There was an excited babble of voices as they displayed their treasure to one another, interrupted only by the occasional sound of a gunshot as the wounded Indians were killed.

"Colonel, I suggest that we not stay around much onger," Roach said.

"Why is that?"

"Have you noticed that there are no young men among the dead?"

"What are you suggesting, Captain?"

"I'm saying that, for some reason, all the young men are gone. If they come back from wherever they are, and ee us here with all this"—he took in the camp with a weep of his arm—"they aren't going to take it very well. And we would be very vulnerable right now."

Covington stroked his cheek, then nodded. "A most astute observation, Captain Roach. Very well, give the order to withdraw back to Big Rock."

"Yes, sir," Roach said.

A few minutes later, with most of the tepees burning behind them, Covington led his militia back into the woods from which they had come. The bodies of 137 old men, women, and children lay on the ground, while the fires of scores of tepees sent a large column of smoke climbing into the air above them.

16

The travois of several horses were laden with the results of the hunt: deer, elk, wild turkey, and other game. It had been a good hunt, and as Quinntanna led the hunting party back to the village, he was thinking of the celebration they would have on their return. The meat would be put on spits and turned slowly over a fire, and the smell would cause everyone's appetite to grow. They would tell stories of the hunt, and some of the older men would speak of the early days when buffalo were plentiful.

Quinntanna could remember when, as a young boy, he had gone on a buffalo hunt. That had been one of the last hunts to actually take a buffalo, because the herds were all gone now. For hundreds of years the buffalo had served the Comanche. Then the white men had come and within one lifetime, the buffalo were gone.

None of the others were thinking about the vanished buffalo. They were thinking only about the last two days and the success of their hunt. They talked about it, reliving certain shots and honing the stories they would tell around the campfires. Everyone bragged of their exploits except Quinntanna.

"Quinntanna, have you no stories to tell?" Teykano asked. "We are all waiting to hear how it is that you killed only one half of an elk."

"Yes," one of the others said. "Is the back half still running around somewhere in the woods, waiting to be taken at the next hunt?"

The others laughed.

"I will tell my story when there are better ears to hear it," Quinntanna teased. "Such a story to ears as yours would be a terrible waste."

"Quinntanna," Teykano said, pointing ahead. "Look ahead. There is smoke. Is it a forest fire?"

The hunting party stopped for a moment to study the smoke. Then Quinntanna shook his head. "I think it is not a forest fire," he said. "If many trees were burning there would be much more smoke."

"Grass, perhaps?"

"Perhaps it is grass, though it does not seem to me that the smoke is wide enough for a grass fire."

"Then what is the cause of this strange thing?"

"I don't know," Quinntanna admitted.

Quinntanna urged his horse ahead, and the hunting party followed him, riding quickly toward the smoke that rose before them. Though he didn't share it with the others, there was something about this that he found extremely troubling.

Then, when they reached the meadow where the village had been, Quinntanna realized what was bothering him. This was his dream, come to life, his worst fear realized. Ahead of him he saw several blackened circles. He also saw about fifty people moving through the pall of smoke. He wasn't close enough to see whether or not they were crying, but he knew without a doubt that they were.

Then he saw something that he had not seen in his dreams, even though he had always known they were there. He saw several bodies stretched out on the ground.

With a scream of rage, Quinntanna slapped his legs against the side of his horse. The steed bolted into a gallop, closing the remaining distance in but a few seconds. When he arrived, he leaped down from his horse and started searching for Sasheena.

"Sasheena!" he called. "Sasheena, where are you?"

"Quinntanna," an old man said. "Your woman and your child are here."

The old man who called him was Isataka, Sasheena's grandfather. Quinntanna looked down at the two bodies. The baby's head had been smashed like a gourd. Sasheena's face was deformed by the effect of the bullet that had ended her life. With grief and confusion in his eyes, Quinntanna looked up at Isataka, who had summoned him.

"Who?" he asked. "Who did this?"

"It was white soldiers," Isataka replied.

"Soldiers?" Quinntanna was shocked by the answer. "Soldiers of the white man's army did this?"

"Yes. They came before light this morning, and began firing. Stone Eagle was going to reason with them, to ask them why they are doing this thing, but they shot him down before he could get to them. Then there was much confusion. Some of us got away during the confusion, and we hid in the forest and watched as they slaughtered those who did not get away."

Suddenly, Quinntanna recalled his conversation with Smoke Jensen. Jensen had told him that someone had attacked the family of a white rancher.

"I think I know why the white soldiers attacked," Quinntanna said.

"Why?" Isataka asked.

"The home of a white rancher was attacked, and the rancher's wife and children were killed. According to the sign left, the attack was made by Comanche."

"That cannot be true," the old man said. "There are no Comanche on the warpath."

"We know that, but the whites do not. And I can think of no other reason why they would attack our village."

"I think they do not need a reason," Isataka said. "There is an evil in the white man that cannot be kept down. It has been many years since there was any trouble between our people. Perhaps the evil could wait no longer."

From all over what had been the village, Quinntanna

heard the wails of grief and anger from the young men of the hunting party who were returning to find their own families slaughtered.

"Quinntanna, we must do battle with the white man," Teykano said angrily. Like Quinntanna, Teykano had lost his wife. He'd also lost two children.

"We can't fight the white man," Quinntanna said. "There are too many of them. There are as many white men as there are blades of grass. If we make war against them, we will all be killed."

"Better to be killed fighting than to die a coward. And that is what we will be if we do nothing," Teykano insisted.

"We will do something," Quinntanna promised.

"What? What will we do, Quinntanna?"

"I will talk with the spirits," Quinntanna said. "It is for the spirits to decide what we must do."

Quinntanna buried his wife and child, then went into the mountains to consult with the spirits. He took neither water nor food with him, for the nourishment he sought was for his soul, not his body. And to nourish his soul, he took a supply of peyote buttons.

He went high into the mountains, above the snow line, and there he sat, wrapped in a buffalo robe, looking out over the valley below. He didn't know how long he had been there when he saw a warrior mounted on a horse. The warrior was wearing a headdress of many feathers that stretched all the way to the ground. He also wore a shirt and trousers of beaded buckskin, and there was a glow around him that was so bright that it hurt Quinntanna's eyes to look at him.

"Shining Warrior!" Quinntanna said.

Shining Warrior looked at Quinntanna for a moment, but he didn't speak. Instead, he uttered a war cry, then urged his horse into a gallop. Shining Warrior rode for some distance away, then turned and rode back toward Quinntanna. As he galloped toward him, Shining

Warrior held his war club over his head and leaned to one side as if he were going to strike Quinntanna. Quinntanna was frightened, but he knew, instinctively, that he must not flinch. Shining Warrior let forth a mighty yell, and swinging the club at Quinntanna's head, stopped it just inches away from smashing his skull.

Then Quinntanna noticed a very strange thing. Even though the horse had galloped back and forth across the snow-covered plain, it had left no tracks. Except for the footprints Quinntanna had left, the snow was completely pristine.

Shining Warrior leaned down then to put his hand on Quinntanna's forehead. Quinntanna shut his eyes, and when he did, he saw a vision of what was left of his people. In the vision, he saw that his people were being attacked yet again by soldiers.

"No!" Quinntanna shouted.

When Quinntanna opened his eyes, Shining Warrior was gone. There was no sign of his having been there at all, for the snow was still undisturbed. And now, amazingly, even his own footprints were gone. There had not been a fresh snowfall, yet the surface of the snow was brilliantly white, fresh, clean, and absolutely unblemished.

The Indians were still cleaning up the mess of what had been their village when Quinntanna returned from his sojourn into the mountains. He was met by Teykano and others.

"You have returned," Teykano said.

"Yes."

"And did you have a vision?"

"Yes. Teykano, Shining Warrior came to me," Quinntanna said.

"Shining Warrior?" Teykano repeated in awe. "Ayiee, your medicine is very strong. I have known many who wished to see him, but I have known none who have. What did he look like?"

"Like a warrior of old," Quinntanna said. "He looks like the warrior who visited Comanche in the story Stone Eagle told."

"What did he say to you?"

"He did not speak."

"He came to you, but he did not speak?" Teykano replied in a surprised voice.

"He did not speak to me with words, but he made me see here, and here," Quinntanna said, touching his forehead and his heart.

By now the other young men had gathered to hear what Quinntanna was saying.

"When we ride on the path of war . . ."

Hearing Quinntanna proclaim that they would be riding on the path of war, the others suddenly shouted and howled in excitement, elated over the prospect of getting revenge for what was visited upon their village.

"When we ride on the path of war," Quinntanna said again, "our horses will leave no sign. Not even the most skilled of trackers will be able to find us."

"All creatures leave tracks," Teykano said. "Even an ant leaves a track."

"A bird leaves no track because it does not touch the ground," Quinntanna said. "We will be like the bird. The hooves of our horses will not touch the ground."

"How can this be? How can our horses travel without touching the ground?"

"I do not know," Quinntanna admitted. "But Shining Warrior showed me that it could be done." Quinntanna described the amazing sight of seeing Shining Warrior's horse galloping back and forth, yet leaving no mark upon the snow. Then he told how his own tracks had disappeared, even though there was no snowfall to cover them. "Perhaps it will appear to us as if our horses are touching the ground, but the sign will be invisible to everyone else."

"Yes," one of the other young men said. "If Shining Warrior has said it will be so, then I believe it will be so."

Quinntanna looked over to where the survivors were busy rebuilding as much of their village as they could.

"What are they doing?" Quinntanna asked.

Teykano took in the village with a motion of his hand. "Look. The village still lives. The lodges that weren't burned by fire have been put up again, and soon new lodges will take the place of those that were destroyed."

"No, our people must not rebuild here," Quinntanna said. "We must move the village."

"Why?"

"In my vision, I saw more soldiers come to this place. Many more of our people were killed."

"If you have seen it in your vision, then it is to be so and there is nothing we can do about it."

Quinntanna shook his head. "I do not believe this. I believe that I was shown the vision so that it could be changed. If the village is moved, then the soldiers cannot find it."

"Come," Teykano said to the others. "We will move our people."

"What about guns?" one of the others asked. "While we hunted with bows and arrows, our guns were left behind and the soldiers who killed our families stole our guns."

"Yes. Did Shining Warrior show you how we would get guns?" Teykano asked.

"No," Quinntanna said. "But I believe a way to get the guns will be shown to us."

Even as Quinntanna made that statement, they saw two riders approaching. Two of the hunters, still angry and grief-stricken, raised their bows and drew the string to shoot the visitors, but Quinntanna held out his hand to stop them.

"Wait. These are not soldiers. We will see what they want." As the two riders came closer, the villagers saw that they were Indian.

As they approached, the riders held up their right

hands, palms out, in a sign of peace. Quinntanna returned the sign as a signal that they could enter without fear.

"I am Perry Blue Horses," one of the riders said. He pointed to the other. "This is Russell Swift Bear."

"You have white and Indian names," Quinntanna said.

"We have white and Indian blood," Blue Horses replied. He looked around at the destroyed village. "This was done by the white man?"

"Yes."

"I am shamed by my white blood," Blue Horses said.

"All the men were away," Quinntanna said. "When we returned, we learned that soldiers had attacked our village and killed our women and children and our old men."

"Are you at war with the whites?" Blue Horses asked.

Quinntanna nodded. "I think we are at war now," he replied. "For many years our people and the whites have been at peace. We lease our land to white ranchers so they may graze their cattle. We keep the money they pay us in the white man's bank. But some people attacked and killed a white rancher and his family. The whites think we did it."

"What?" Teykano replied. "A ranch was attacked? When did this happen? I know nothing of this."

"I think it happened a short time ago," Quinntanna said.

"Then we must go to the whites and tell them that we did not do such a thing. Perhaps then there will be no war," one of the older Indians said.

"I think they will not listen," Quinntanna said.

"Will you make war against the white men who did this?" Swift Bear asked.

"When we went away to hunt, we hunted in the old way, with the bow and arrow, as did our ancestors. Our rifles and bullets stayed behind. Now all our guns are gone, taken by the white soldiers when they attacked."

"We can get weapons for you," Blue Horses said, taking in Swift Bear with a wave of his hand.

"How?"

"Because of our blood, we can do business with the white man."

Quinntanna smiled broadly and looked at the others. "Did I not say that Shining Warrior would show the way?"

"Get guns for us," Teykano said. "Rifles and bullets. We will need these things."

"Fifty rifles with bullets will cost two thousand five hundred dollars in white man's money," Swift Bear said.

"How can we pay this? Our money is in the white man's bank."

"It is your money. Go to the bank and take it out," Swift Bear said.

"All right. I will get the money. When will we get the guns?"

"I will talk to the one who has them," Blue Horses said. "We will come with the guns when you have the money."

As Blue Horses and Swift Bear rode away, the others gathered around Quinntanna.

"Quinntanna, you will get the money?" one of them asked.

"Yes," Quinntanna said. "I will get the money."

"If you lead, we will follow," Teykano said.

17

The citizens of the small town of Stonewall weren't particularly surprised to see an Indian riding into town. The Indians frequently did business in the town, and though they had heard that renegades attacked a ranch over near Big Rock, they certainly didn't expect any trouble from their Indians. After all, the Indians did do a great deal of *their* business in Stonewall: everything from keeping their money on deposit in the Stonewall bank to buying goods from the local merchants. And because the Indians spent freely, the merchants often went out of their way to make certain that the Indians understood that their money was welcome in the town's stores.

The Indians had money because their great chief Quanah Parker had negotiated the grazing rights for all Comanches and Kiowa within a 240,000-square-mile area. With millions of acres to work with, Quanah Parker had arranged to lease pasturage to wealthy stockmen so they could run their cattle on Indian land. That brought in hundreds of thousands of dollars per year, and though the village of Quinntanna was much smaller, and had less land to lease, their percentage was enough to provide an income for every Comanche in the village.

Quinntanna was extremely cautious as he rode into town. Although he had made a deal to buy rifles for 2,500

dollars, he had discussed the issue with Teykano, anc
they'd decided that he had better take five thousand dol
lars from the bank. They'd come to that decision becaus
they didn't know when, or even if, they would get anothe
chance to make a withdrawal. They had even discusse
taking all their money from the bank, but decided that i
they did that, there might be some sort of negative re
sponse to their action. And until all was ready, they wante
to minimize any chance of trouble with the whites.

If all whites believed that the Comanche were respon
sible for the attack on the ranch, then even the citizen
of Stonewall, who were normally very receptive, migh
be antagonistic, and an attempt to close the accoun
could set them off. Quinntanna also realized that the cit
izens of Stonewall might already consider themselves a
war, so he was observant of everyone and everything. H
kept his eyes on the roofs and second floors of the build
ings, looking for any would-be shooters. To his surprise
no one seemed particularly interested in him.

He stopped in front of the bank, looped the rein
around the hitching post, then went inside. There was stil
no reaction. But how could this be? Surely they have hear
of the raid against his people by the soldiers. And yet, the
gave no indication that anything was other than normal.

Quinntanna stepped up to the teller's window.

"Yes, sir, and what can the Bank of Stonewall do fo
our Indian customers today?" the teller asked, a wide
professional smile on his face.

"I want to sign paper to get five thousand dollars,
Quinntanna said.

"Five thousand dollars? Oh, my, that is a great deal o
money," the teller said. Checking a ledger, he looked u
and smiled. "However, your village does have enoug
money in the account to cover it," he said. "In fact, yo
have much more than that. But in order to withdraw fron
the account, you will have to have the signature of eithe
Mr. Running Deer or Mr. Stone Eagle. I'm afraid they ar
the only two names on the signature card."

"Dead," Quinntanna said.

"I beg your pardon?"

"Running Deer and Stone Eagle are dead."

"Both of them?"

"Yes."

"Oh, my," the teller said, clicking his tongue. "Oh, my. Well, this does complicate things."

"I am Quinntanna. I will sign paper for money."

The teller shook his head. "No, Mr. Quinntanna, I'm afraid that won't do. You can't get the money."

"It is money of the Indian people of my village, is it not?" Quinntanna asked.

"Yes, indeed it is," the teller said. "But surely you understand that, in order to keep just any Indian from coming in here and getting the money, only certain people are authorized to make a withdrawal. It is for your own protection. And the only ones who can take money from the account are Mr. Running Deer and Mr. Stone Eagle."

"Dead," Quinntanna said again.

"Yes, yes, so you told me. Wait here for a moment while I go to talk to Mr. Freeman. I'm sure he will know what to do."

The teller left the window and walked to the back of the bank to speak to an older man who was sitting behind a desk. As he spoke, he pointed back toward Quinntanna, and the man at the desk looked up toward Quinntanna.

Quinntanna saw the man, whom the teller had identified as Mr. Freeman, shake his head, then go back to work. The teller returned to the window.

"I'm sorry, Mr. Quinntanna, but Mr. Freeman says we can't give the money to you. Now if you will have Mr. Running Deer or Mr. Stone Eagle come into the bank, we will be glad to give them as much money as there is in the account."

"They are dead," Quinntanna said again, as if explaining something to a child.

"Yes, but they are the only ones who can withdraw money, you see."

Quinntanna nodded, then, without further comment, turned and walked away.

"The nerve of that Indian," the teller said after Quinntanna left the bank. "I suppose he thought he could just come in here and take money out as if this were his own private bank."

The others in the bank laughed.

Outside the bank, Quinntanna had started to mount his horse when he saw the stock of a rifle protruding from the saddle holster of another horse that was tied to the same hitching rail. Without a second thought, Quinntanna pulled the rifle from its scabbard, jacked a round into the chamber, then went back inside. As soon as he stepped through the door, he fired at the table in the middle of the room, hitting the ink bottle. The bottle shattered, sending a spray of black ink spewing up into the air, then splashing back down on everyone. Women screamed and men shouted in alarm. Quinntanna jacked another shell into the rifle, then stepped up to the same window he had been at before.

"Give me money," he said, handing a buckskin pouch to the teller.

"Y-yes sir," the teller replied. With shaking hands, he began taking money from his cash drawer and stuffing it into the pouch.

Quinntanna stuck his hand out to stop the teller. "I don't want all money. I only want five thousand dollars of Indian money."

"Five thousand dollars. Yes, sir," the teller said.

"Write on paper that I, Quinntanna, took five thousand dollars of Indian money."

"Yes, sir." Quickly, and with nervous hands, the banker did as he was instructed.

Quinntanna signed the paper, then taking the money pouch, he backed out of the bank, pointing the rifle at everyone inside. Once outside, he jumped onto his horse, then with several whoops and shouts, rode out of town.

"The bank!" Freeman yelled, running out into the street a moment later. "The bank has been robbed!"

Freeman began firing his pistol down the street toward the fleeing Quinntanna. His bullets were going wild, ricocheting off the walls and whizzing by innocent citizens.

"Freeman, you dumb shit! Stop shooting!" a deputy shouted, running toward him. "You're going to kill someone."

"That Indian just robbed the bank!" Freeman shouted.

With Quinntanna in the lead, the village left the reservation. As they traveled, they took special pains to cover their tracks—sometimes moving across rock where no tracks could be left, other times using routes that were so well traveled that their tracks could not be discerned from those already on the ground.

A few of the young men wanted to let the villagers travel on their own. Now that they had money for guns, they wanted to meet with Blue Horses and Swift Bear, buy the guns, and go on the warpath; however, Quinntanna insisted that their first obligation was to the safety of the old people, women, and children who had managed to survive the attack.

Joe Mayberry, editor of the *Big Rock Sentinel*, removed the paper from the press, then took it over to the composition table to look at it. Big Rock was the fourth town in which Joe had started a newspaper. Joe had a history of coming into a town, starting a newspaper, then when the paper was going well, getting restless, selling it, and moving on. An indication of how solid a newspaperman Joe was was the fact that all of the previous newspapers were still going, being run by the people who had bought Joe out.

Joe wasn't afraid to take an unpopular stand, and often upset his readers with his pointed editorials. He had the notion that this editorial would be one of those.

WAS THE RAID ON THE INDIAN
VILLAGE NECESSARY?

All of Big Rock, if not the entire state, knows about the tragic attack against the ranch of Tom Burke. And while most suspect that Indians were responsible for the attack, nearly everyone concedes that the attack had to be carried out, not by the law-abiding Indians we have come to know over the last several years, but by renegade Indians.

Last week Sam Covington, in his recently appointed guise as a colonel in the state militia, led a company of volunteer cavalry in a raid against Purgatory, the Comanche village that is nearest Big Rock. The number of Indians killed was quite substantial, whereas not one of Colonel Covington's men received so much as a scratch. Colonel Covington is hailing it as a very big victory.

But how big a victory is it? It is now known that most, if not all, of the Indians killed were women, children, and the elderly. There were no young men present at the time of the attack; therefore, the attack was virtually unopposed. What that means is, the "Battle" of Purgatory wasn't a battle at all. It was a slaughter, a slaughter of helpless and innocent Indians.

Yes, I said innocent, for even if those scoundrels who raided the Burke ranch were Indians, they were acting on their own. And a peaceful Indian village shouldn't be any more responsible for their outlaws than we are for ours. If justice is to be done here, let it be done against those who are truly responsible for the evil deeds done. For to do otherwise is to shift the evil from the Indians to ourselves.

When Covington finished reading the article, he let out a roar of displeasure and wadding the newspaper up, threw it into his trash can. The campaign against the Indians had not generated the kind of publicity Covington had hoped it would. It was barely mentioned in the newspapers in the state, and when it was mentioned, the articles were often as unflattering as this editorial was.

He wasn't sure that any out-of-state paper had carried any news about the campaign. Why this was, he had no idea. It wasn't too long ago that every Indian campaign, regardless of how small it might be, would receive national coverage. In fact, people were still talking about Custer's debacle, and that was over ten years ago. As a matter of fact, from the intensity of the interest in Custer still ongoing, Covington was willing to bet they would be talking about the Battle of Little Big Horn one hundred years from now.

So, why weren't they discussing the Battle of Purgatory? Unlike the Battle of Little Big Horn, where every soldier in Custer's command had been killed, in the Battle of Purgatory Covington had lost not one man. By all that was right, Covington should be regarded as a hero throughout the state.

Maybe he just wasn't well enough known yet. Yes, he thought, that had to be it. So, what could he do about it? Maybe he could arrange a speaking tour, telling of the dangers everyone in the state was facing today by being so complacent about the Indians. Yes, that would do it. He would write to Denver and secure the governor's sponsorship for a tour of the state. He knew that some photos had been taken out at Timber Notch Ranch. He could use those gruesome photos to arrange a magic lantern show to illustrate his talk.

He would call his talk "The Cost of Neglect," and he would use the graphic photographs to illustrate what could happen due to a lack of vigilance with regard to the Indians. At that moment, Covington's musing was interrupted by Dingo.

"Yes, First Sergeant," Covington said, "what can I do for you?"

"I was just wonderin' if you had heard about what happened over in Stonewall?"

"Something happened at Stonewall? No, what happened?"

"The Injuns come into a bank with guns blazing. Then they robbed it."

Covington looked up. "You don't say?" he asked, his interest stirred by the news. "The Indians, you say. Are you sure?"

"Yes, sir, I'm sure."

"Where did you hear this?"

"Why, you can hear about it all over town," Dingo replied. "And they're especially talking about it over in Longmont's Saloon."

"Has Sheriff Carson gotten word of it?"

"I reckon he has," Dingo said. "I figure that's how ever'one else found out about it."

"He got word, and he didn't tell me," Covington replied, the tone of his voice showing his anger. "That's not right. The sheriff is obligated to tell me of any incident involving Indians. I think perhaps it is time I paid a little visit to our noble sheriff," Covington said, reaching for his hat.

"Yes, sir, I thought you might be interested in doing that."

18

"What do you mean, why weren't you informed?" Monte Carson replied, answering Covington's angry question. "It was a bank robbery. It has nothing to do with you."

"Oh, but I'm afraid it does, Sheriff," Covington replied. "You see, if the Indians robbed—"

"It wasn't Indians, it was one Indian. And the funny thing is, he didn't really rob the bank."

"What do you mean, he didn't rob the bank? You just told me that he did rob it."

"Technically, I suppose he did," Sheriff Carson admitted. "In that he took the money without proper authority. However, the money he took, five thousand dollars, was from the Indians' own account. He tried to write a draft for the money, but he couldn't because the only two men authorized to sign for the money, Stone Eagle and Running Deer, are both dead. You killed them, Covington."

"Are you telling me the Indians had five thousand dollars in their account?" Covington asked.

"Oh, yes. From what I understand, they have nearly fifteen thousand dollars in the account. Quinntanna merely tried to make a withdrawal, and when they wouldn't give the money to him, he took it at gunpoint."

Monte chuckled. "And get this. He didn't rob them. He just forced them to accept his draft."

"Yes, well, it doesn't matter. If the person who took the money isn't on the signature card, then the draft is not valid. And if the draft isn't valid, then taking the money at gunpoint is bank robbery. He did take it by force, didn't he?" Covington said, rubbing his hands together excitedly.

"I'll be damned, Covington, if you don't look happy about it," Monte said.

"I'm happy only in that it will wake the people up. I think everyone needs to be aware of the dangers the Indians still present to the peaceful citizens of this great state."

"Bullshit," Monte said. "You're just wantin' an excuse to mount another campaign against them. Only, I don't think you will be able to steal anything from them this time."

"Steal from them?"

"That's what you did, isn't it?"

"It is not what I did. I made a legal confiscation of contraband," Covington said.

"Uh-huh. And if you had done that anywhere other than an Indian reservation, I'd have you in jail right now."

"Yes, well, that's the point, isn't it? I did do it on an Indian reservation."

"I don't know what you plan to take from them now. I'm sure that the Indians don't have anything left. I heard that, in addition to everything else, you also stole a thousand dollars in cash from them."

"As I informed you, Sheriff, the money wasn't stolen. It was part of the legal spoils of war," Covington said.

"Spoils of war," Monte said.

"You say it was Quinntanna who took the money from the bank?"

"Yes. But for the life of me, I can't see why you are so interested. Even if it was a bank robbery, and there is some question as to whether it was, it is a civil affair and has nothing to do with you."

"It does if Quinntanna's action is a direct result of the punitive raid we conducted against Purgatory. And such a reaction on the part of a principal member of the village means that the issue is still unsettled. I'm afraid this moves things to the next step."

"The next step? What do you mean, the next step?"

Covington pulled himself to attention. "Sheriff Carson, it is my unpleasant but necessary duty to inform you that, as of now, Big Rock and all of Las Animas and Costilla Counties are, and will continue to be until further notice, under martial law. From now on, you, your deputies, the mayor, and the city council will be responsible to me. No city or law enforcement business can, or will, be conducted without my express permission."

"What? Have you gone crazy? You can't declare martial law," Monte said in an exasperated and disbelieving tone of voice.

"Oh, but I can, and I have. My commission from the governor is very specific about that. If you have any questions, contact the governor."

"You are doing all this because of the act of one Indian?" Monte asked in disbelief.

"Indians are like cockroaches, Sheriff. Where there is one, there are many." Covington started to leave, but as he got to the door, he turned back to the sheriff. "Oh, please inform the mayor of my decision to declare martial law."

"I shall do so," Monte said. "I shall definitely do so."

Covington left a frustrated and disgusted sheriff behind as he walked quickly down the street to the telegraph office. When he pushed inside, the little bell that was attached to the top of the door rang merrily.

"Be right with you," Fred called from a room at the rear of the office. A moment later he came into the office, wiping his hands on a napkin. "I was just having my lunch," he said. "What can I do for you, Mr. Covington?"

"It is Colonel Covington for the duration," Covington replied.

"Duration? Duration of what?"

"The Indian uprising," Covington said. "But as for what you can do for me, I have a few regulations I am putting into effect."

"Go ahead," Fred invited.

"Effective immediately, you will send no telegram unless the sender has my express, written permission."

"What? I can't do that," Fred said.

"Also, no telegram will be delivered to anyone in town without my clearance. That means that all incoming telegrams must come to me first."

"Mr. Cov—"

"I told you, it is *Colonel,*" Covington said resolutely.

"*Colonel* Covington. I can't do what you ask. The rules and regulations of Western Union are quite specific. Our customers have the absolute right of privacy of communication. If we start running all incoming and outgoing messages through some official somewhere, people will no longer trust us."

"That's Western Union's problem, not mine," Covington said. "You will do what I say, or I will close your office."

"Yes, sir," Fred said contritely.

Leaving the Western Union office, Covington made his next stop the *Big Rock Sentinel.* Joe Mayberry was sitting at the composing desk, setting type. Because his back was to the door, he didn't see who came in.

"If you have a news story, put it in the basket on the right. If it's an ad, put it in the basket on the left," Joe said without turning around.

"It is neither," Covington said.

Recognizing Covington's voice, Joe sighed and turned toward him. "What is it, Covington?" he asked.

"I did not appreciate the editorial you wrote about our operation," Covington said. "You impugned the action of many brave men."

"Brave?" Joe replied, scoffing. "What is so brave about

going into a village in the middle of the night and killing sleeping women, children, and old men?"

"I wouldn't expect someone like you to understand. This was a military matter. What do you know of the military?"

"Sonny, where were you in the first week of July 1863?" Joe asked.

"July 1863? Why, I don't know," Covington replied. "Anyway, what is so significant about that date?"

"I was at Gettysburg, with the First Missouri Brigade," Joe said. "And unlike your midnight murder, Gettysburg was a real battle."

"All right, you were at Gettysburg. I admit that those who fought at Gettysburg may have faced more danger than we faced at the Battle of Purgatory. But unless you have had a command of your own, I still submit that you aren't qualified to discuss things of a military nature."

"Oh, I had a command," Joe said.

"You had a command? What was your command?"

"The First Missouri Brigade."

"Yes, yes, you told me that. What was your command within the brigade?"

A wry smile spread across Joe's face. "The brigade was my command," he said.

Covington gasped. "You?" he asked. "You are a brigadier general?"

"I *used* to be a brigadier general," Joe answered. "Now I'm a newspaperman. Now, are you here just to complain about my editorial? Or do you have something else in mind? What are you doing here?"

For a moment it looked as if Covington was still trying to absorb the fact that this man who published a weekly newspaper in a small Colorado town was once a brigadier general in the greatest war in America's history. "What?" Covington asked, almost distractedly.

"I asked what are you doing here," Joe repeated. "What do you want?"

"Oh, yes," Covington said, regaining his composure.

"I want you to print an announcement for me. Effective immediately, all of Las Animas and Costilla Counties are under martial law."

"Martial law? Why?"

"I should think the reason would be obvious to you, Mr. Mayberry. We are in the midst of an Indian uprising. Martial law is necessary to protect the lives of our citizens."

"What exactly are the terms of this martial law?"

"Well, to begin with, I am establishing a ten P.M. curfew. No guns can be carried within the city limits. No guns can be sold without my permission. All legal matters, both criminal and civil, will come through my office. The text of all telegrams, sent and received, must be approved by me. Any gathering of ten or more people shall be construed as an unlawful assembly and those participating in such a gathering will be arrested."

"Are you going to arrest people for going to church?" Joe asked.

"Churches are exempt."

"That's big of you. Schools?"

"Yes, of course, schools are also exempt."

"What about Longmont's? On a good night, he'll have as many as forty patrons. Are you going to close Longmonts?"

"I will allow Longmont's to stay open in order to conduct its normal business. But the patrons of Longmont's will be put on notice that they will not be permitted to conduct a meeting of any sort. And the establishment will be closed by ten P.M."

"You don't really expect to make any of this stick, do you?" Joe asked.

"I do indeed. And finally, Mr. Mayberry, I want it understood by you that any article you print from now on is subject to military censorship."

"What?" Joe exploded in anger. "You can't do that! That is a direct violation of the First Amendment!"

"Disabuse yourself of any idea that you are covered by the Constitution or the Bill of Rights. Those are elements of civil law and authority. Big Rock is now under military law and authority and those personal rights normally guaranteed are withdrawn for the duration of the Indian emergency. I have the authority to prevent assemblies, suspend habeas corpus, close church and school, ban firearms, and censor the press, and I intend to do just that. Do I make myself clear, Mr. Mayberry?"

"Painfully clear," Joe replied.

"Good. See to it that this information is published at once. Don't wait for your next issue. Get an extra edition out."

Before nightfall that very day, an extra edition of the *Sentinel* was published and distributed. In addition, Covington had signs printed and posted all over town:

To all seeing these greetings
be it known that a state of
EMERGENCY EXISTS BETWEEN OUR
CITIZENS AND HOSTILE INDIANS
Resulting in the Declaration of
MARTIAL
LAW
To be administered by
SAMUEL COVINGTON
COLONEL, CMNDG

One such poster was placed on the batwing doors leading into Longmont's Saloon. Also prominently displayed was notice that a ten o'clock curfew was in effect, and would remain in effect for the duration of the emergency.

As a result of the implementation of martial law, the mood inside Longmont's was somber. Gone was the laughter that was normal when patrons gathered for drinks and friendly card games. Instead of conversation and congenial banter, there were mutterings and complaints about the new order.

"What gets me is why Monte Carson don't do nothin' about it," one of the patrons said.

"What can he do?" another replied. "Since martial law, he ain't actually the sheriff no more."

"Then why don't he send a telegram to the governor and get this changed?"

"Have you forgotten? Any telegram sent out of here has to be approved by Covington. It ain't likely Covington would let that kind of telegram go through."

"I hear tell the militia's getting ready to go after the Injuns again."

"They say they are."

"Well, I never thought I'd hear myself say it, but by God when it comes to Covington and the Injuns, damned if I wouldn't be on the side of the Injuns."

The comment brought laughter, a rare commodity on this night.

19

Quinntanna and Teykano watched as Blue Horses and Swift Bear rode toward them, leading two packhorses. Word spread quickly that the weapons had arrived, and by the time the two gunrunners were on the scene, nearly all the young men of Quinntanna's group had gathered around, waiting anxiously for the opportunity to get their hands on a rifle again.

As soon as Blue Horses and Swift Bear arrived, the Indians rushed toward the packhorses and began opening the parcels, disclosing the rifles tied together in bundles of five.

"Ayieee!" one of the Indians shouted in excitement, grabbing a Winchester and holding it over his head in triumph. He pumped his arm and shouted again, his shout igniting excitement in the others.

"You have kept your promise," Quinntanna said.

"You have the money?" Blue Horses asked.

Quinntanna held out the sack of money he had taken from the bank. "Two thousand five hundred dollars. That is what you asked for."

Blue Horses took the money as the Indians began unpacking everything. The excitement waned somewhat when they saw the ammunition.

"Quinntanna, there are not many bullets," Teykano

said, looking at the pitifully few boxes. "There are not even enough bullets to fill all the guns."

"Why is this?" Quinntanna asked angrily. "We have given you much money, all that you asked for."

"This was all the bullets we could get this time," Blue Horses said. "But for one thousand dollars more, we can get many bullets."

"You did not speak of one thousand dollars more," Quinntanna said. "You spoke only of two thousand five-hundred dollars."

"Maybe we will kill you and take the money back," Teykano said, pointing his rifle at the two.

Blue Horses and Swift Bear reacted in fear, but Quinntanna held up his hand. "No," he said. "If we are to make war, we will need bullets and they are the only ones who can bring bullets to us." Then, to Blue Horses, he said, "Bring more bullets. But don't bring them here. We are going to leave this place."

"You will have one thousand dollars more?"

"Yes."

"Where do we bring them?"

"Do you know the place of Howling Winds?"

"Howling Winds is high in the mountains, near Raton Pass," Blue Horses said.

"Yes."

"It is not good to go high in the mountains now. There will be much snow there. Nobody goes high in the mountains when there is much snow."

"That is why we go. There, our people will be safe from the soldiers. If you want to sell more bullets, you must come there."

Blue Horses and Swift Bear looked at each other for a moment. Then Blue Horses nodded. He turned back to Quinntanna. "We will bring bullets to the place of Howling Winds."

As Cal approached the edge of town, two men came out into the road, holding up their hands to stop him.

They were wearing military uniforms. Curious, Cal hauled back on the reins, stopping the team.

"What's going on?" he asked.

"We'll take your gun," one of the soldiers said.

"The hell you will," Cal answered. "Why should I give you my gun?"

"It's the law."

Cal shook his head. "I've lived here a long time," he said. "And I've never heard of such a law. In fact, I don't think Sheriff Carson would even let such a law get passed."

One of the men spat a wad of tobacco at the wheel of the buckboard, then wiped his lips with the cuff of his shirtsleeve.

"Carson ain't got nothin' to do with it," the tobacco-spitting soldier said. "This here town is under martial law."

"Martial law? What does that mean?"

"It means you do exactly what we tell you to do, or else."

"Or else what?"

"Or else you go to jail. Now, you goin' to give us the gun, or not?"

"Take it," Cal said menacingly.

One of the soldiers made a move toward Cal, but almost quicker than he could see it happen, a gun appeared in Cal's hand. The other soldier raised his rifle and started to jack a shell into the chamber, but even as he was operating the lever, Cal was firing. His bullet hit the rifle stock, right in front of the soldier's hand, causing him to drop the weapon.

Both soldiers were stunned into submission.

"You," Cal said, looking at the soldier who still had his rifle, though he wasn't holding it in a threatening way. "Jack out all the shells."

The soldier pumped the lever several times.

"Gun empty?" Cal asked.

"Yeah," the soldier replied.

"Good. Point it at your friend here, and pull the trigger."

"What?"

"You heard me."

The soldier pointed his rifle at his friend.

"Amon, no! What are you going to do?"

Amon hesitated for a second, then jacked the lever one more time. Another cartridge flipped out. He pulled the trigger, and there was a snapping sound as the hammer fell on an empty chamber.

"Now, empty the other rifle and do the same thing."

Again the lever was jacked up and down several times, until a metallic click of the hammer falling on an empty chamber proved that the rifles were empty.

"Pick up the shells and put them in the back of the buckboard," Cal ordered.

The soldiers responded and a moment later, there were fourteen shells lying in the back of the buckboard.

Cal's next move was to make them drop their rifles in a nearby watering trough. Then, and only then, did he feel safe enough to present his back to the two soldiers as he drove into town.

Cal left the buckboard in front of the general store, provided the store clerk with a grocery list, then walked across the street to Longmont's Saloon. He had just greeted Louis Longmont when four armed soldiers suddenly rushed into the room behind him. All had their guns drawn.

"Put you hands up, mister!" one of the soldiers said gruffly. "You are under arrest."

"For what?" Cal said, turning toward them.

The soldiers considered the abrupt turn threatening, and the one nearest Cal slammed the butt of his rifle into Cal's face. Cal went down and out.

Sally wasn't too worried when Cal didn't come back right away. He was young, and enjoyed getting into town, so she figured he had found something to occupy his time. When she happened to look outside late in the afternoon, she saw the buckboard coming up the lane. She smiled and stepped out onto the porch, intending to ask Cal if he'd had a good time. But the smile left her face when she saw that the team wasn't being driven. The horses had returned to the ranch on their own.

The team headed straight for the barn, then stopped. Sally hurried out to the buckboard and looked around. She saw no sign of foul play, but neither did she see any sign of Cal.

"Cal?" she said aloud. "Cal, are you hiding somewhere, playing a trick on me? Because if you are, it isn't funny."

One of the horses whickered, and stamped his foot. Sally went over to him, and patted him gently. "You've been in harness all day, haven't you, boy?" she said gently. "Let me get you out of there."

Sally unhitched the team and turned then into the corral. Then she went back inside and changed out of her dress and into a pair of denim trousers and a red wool shirt. She tied up her hair, then covered it with an old felt hat. After strapping on her Colt .44, she topped the ensemble off with a sheepskin coat. The coat not only provided warmth against the bracing chill, it also completed the picture so that, on casual glance, one would think they were seeing a young man. That was exactly the way Sally wanted it.

It was dark by the time she reached Big Rock. She was just riding past Josh Dobbins's livery when she was challenged.

"Halt!" a voice commanded.

"Halt? Did you say halt?" Sally replied, surprised by the call. She pitched her voice low.

Two men, dressed as soldiers, stepped out of the shadows of the livery. "You packin', mister?"

"What's going on here?"

"We're askin' the questions," the talkative soldier replied. "Are you carrying a gun?"

"Yes."

"Take it out real slow-like, and drop it in the dirt."

"Why should I?"

The talkative soldier jacked a shell into the chamber

of his rifle. "Because, by God, I told you to," he said. "Now, do you have any more questions?"

"No," Sally replied quickly. "I'd say that pretty well does it for me." Sally slipped the pistol from its holster and let it fall. She had another one in the pocket of the jacket, but she made no move toward it, nor did she mention it.

"Case you're wonderin' about things, this here town is under martial law."

"Martial law?"

"Yeah. Case you ain't heard, we got us a Injun war goin' on."

"No," Sally said. "I haven't heard anything about it."

"Colonel Covington, he's done took over ever'thing—sheriff's office, telegraph office, the newspaper even. You goin' to spend any time in this town, you better watch your p's and q's."

"Yes," Sally said, still keeping her voice low. "Thanks." She started on into town.

"And whatever it is that you're a-doin', best you have it done before ten o'clock. That's curfew."

As Sally rode down the middle of the street, the sound of her horse's footsteps echoed back from the dark buildings. She had been in Big Rock after dark many times before, but the entire town seemed changed now. It took her a moment to figure it out; then she realized what it was. There was very little sound coming from any of the saloons, no boisterous conversation, and most noticeable of all . . . no laughter.

Sally dismounted in front of Longmont's. Ordinarily she wouldn't go into a saloon alone, especially at night even a place like Longmont's. But this wasn't an ordinary situation. Looping the reins around the hitching rail, she went inside.

Longmont's was doing a brisk business, but it didn' look as if anyone was enjoying himself. Rather, the customers were all sitting around with glum expressions or their faces, drinking almost mechanically. Even the ba irls, who normally flitted around like brightly colored utterflies, were sitting together at one table, engaged n quiet conversation. The only animation came from he half-dozen or so men who were in military uniforms.

As usual, Louis was sitting at his table in the back of he room. He was playing solitaire, and he dealt three ards, facedown, then studied the layout in front of him. ally walked straight to his table.

"What can I do for you, mister?" Louis said, without ooking up.

"Louis," Sally said. It was all she said.

Looking up, Louis recognized her, and his face became nimated and he started to say something, but was autioned against it by a small, almost imperceptible nod om Sally.

"Uh, sit down, mister," Louis said.

Sally sat across the table from him. "Louis, have you een Cal?" she asked.

Louis nodded. "They've got him in jail."

"Monte has Cal in jail?"

Louis shook his head. "Not Monte. The Army. We're nder martial law now."

"Yes, that's what the men said at the edge of town hen I rode in. They took my gun."

"One of the first things Covington did was declare that o guns could be carried by anyone but members of the ilitia."

"What about Monte? Where does he fit into all this?"

"He doesn't fit," Louie said. "In fact, he's not even in own now. He took the afternoon train to Denver to see he governor."

"Why didn't he just send a telegram?"

Louis shook his head. "No telegrams can come or go ithout Covington's permission."

"Why is Cal in jail? What did he do?"

"Far as I know, the only thing he did was not give up is gun when they asked for it."

"Smoke gave him that gun," Sally said. "He's not likely

to give it up to anyone without a fight." She sighed. "I'n
going to get him out. Do you know if bail has been set?
"Bail? I doubt if Covington will allow bail."
"Well, bail or no bail, I'm going to get him out. I can'
let him stay there."
"How do you plan to do that?"
"I don't know yet," Sally replied. "But if you've got an
ideas, I'd be more than happy to listen to them."
"I've got one idea," Louis said, breaking into a broa
smile.

Fifteen minutes later, Louis Longmont was standin
in the dark just outside town, behind an old tanner
building. The building was unoccupied now, and ha
been for a few years, ever since the tanning operatio
went out of business. Now there was nothing left of th
once-thriving business, except four walls and a caved-i
roof. Louis had bought the property and had plans t
build a boot store there, as soon as he cleared the ol
building away. Tonight was the night he decided to clea
the building away.

Louis was holding a bow and four arrows. Each arro
was wrapped in cloth, and each of the cloth wrapping
had been soaked in kerosene. Louis lit one of the arrow
fitted it to his bow, pulled the string back, then let th
arrow fly. The arrow described a long, high, beautifu
flaming arc through the sky. It landed on what was left
the shake roof of the old tannery building, and almost in
mediately, the building began burning.

Louis let out a long, bloodcurdling scream, yelling th
way he perceived an Indian would yell. Another flan
ing arrow arced through the dark sky.

"Indians!" someone shouted. "Help, someone! We'r
being attacked by Indians."

Louis changed positions before he launched th
third arrow.

"Where's our guns? Give us our guns so we can defend ourselves!"

A fourth flaming arrow arced through the night sky and though no one in town realized it, this would be the last arrow of the "Indian" attack.

Suddenly, those who did have guns, the militamen, began shooting out into the dark, toward the direction from which the arrows had been launched. Louis was in no danger, however, because by the time the militia got organized enough to return fire, he was gone. He could hear the ripple of fire as he stepped up onto the porch of his saloon.

"I see 'em!" someone shouted. "There's hundreds of them!"

"Yeah, I see them too!" someone else shouted.

The gunfire increased as the soldiers fired into the woods just out of town. Now, every shadow was an Indian and every branch a warrior, waiting to take their scalp. As Louis stepped into his saloon, he saw Covington running up the middle of the street, heading toward his panicked men.

Louis laughed as he sat back down to the card game.

"All right, Sally, girl, the rest is up to you," he said quietly.

Sally waited in the dark behind the jail. When she heard the shooting, she moved through the shadows to the jail window.

"Cal?" she called. "Cal, you in there?"

"Sally!" Cal said. His head appeared in the window. "What's goin' on? What's all the shooting?"

"Don't worry about it," Sally said. "Anyone else in here?"

"No. The fellas who were here ran outside when the shooting started.

"Any other prisoners?"

"No."

"Good," Sally said. "Get away from the wall, far as you can. Take the mattress off your bed and get under it."

"What are you going to do?"

Sally held up a stick of dynamite. "I'm going to get you out of here," she said.

"I hope you know what you're doing."

"What is there to it besides lighting the fuse?" Sally replied. She struck a match, then held a flame to the fuse. When the fuse started sputtering, she looked up and saw that Cal was still at the window, watching with great interest. "If I were you, I'd get back," she said calmly.

"Oh, shit! I nearly forgot!" Cal said, scurrying to get to the far side of the room. Sally too hurried to get out of the way.

The fuse snapped and sputtered for a moment; then the stick of dynamite exploded with a flash of light and a loud boom. A substantial part of the back wall of the jail came tumbling down.

Sally ran to the wall, then started waving her hand against the smoke and the dust. "Cal!" she called. "Cal, you all right?"

Cal appeared then, coughing and wheezing. "Yeah," he said. "Yeah, I'm fine."

"Let's go."

Cal picked his way through the rubble.

"We're going to have to ride double," she said.

"Wait," Cal said.

"Wait? Wait for what? We've got to get out of here!"

"I ain't goin' anywhere without my pistol," Cal said. "Smoke give me that gun and I'm not leavin' it."

"Cal, don't be an idiot. We can get it later."

"I don't trust these sons of bitches," Cal said, moving along the side of the jailhouse, heading for the front. "I'm going to get it back."

"All right, get it," Sally said. "But hurry up!"

The shooting was still going on at the far end of town, augmented by the shouts of the soldiers and even a few townspeople. The old tannery was burning fiercely by now and half the street was lit by the wavering orange glow. Cal sneaked around the corner of the jailhouse, then slipped inside. He jerked open the desk drawer, removed his pistol, and strapped it on.

"What are you doing?" Someone said suddenly, and Cal looked up to see that one of the men who had been watching the jail was back. He was standing in the door, pointing his gun at Cal. "Get back in the . . ." When he saw the entire back wall gone from the jail, he gasped. "What in the hell? How did that . . . *uhng!*" He was interrupted in mid-sentence by a blow to his head. He fell to the floor unconscious. There, behind him, stood Sally, her pistol in her hand.

"Come on, let's go," Sally said. "I don't know how long he'll be out."

"You're really something, Sally," he said. "If you weren't already married and if you weren't so old, I'd marry you."

"Old?" Sally said sharply. "How'd you like to walk home?"

Cal laughed out loud. "I was teasing, Sally. I was just teasing," he said.

Hurrying out front, both of them mounted Sally's horse. Then she urged it into a gallop. Even though it was carrying double, the horse responded quickly, and they were out of town before anyone knew they were gone.

20

Jack Tatum lay on a flat rock halfway up a hill that overlooked a stage depot known as Miller's Switch, named after Tony Miller, the man who ran it. He watched as the coach from Stonewall to San Luis pulled into the station. Even when the stage was several hundred feet away, he could see the horses' sides heaving and the clouds of steam from their nostrils, evidence of the effort they had put out pulling the stage up the long hill. The driver brought the team to a halt, then set the brake.

A middle-aged, heavyset man came out of the way station to meet them.

"Hi, Tony," the driver said to the man who had come to greet them.

"Hey, George," Tony replied. "You made good time this morning. You're about fifteen minutes early."

"It's a good, strong team," George replied.

"Keep this up, you'll be into San Luis before three. How many passengers you carrying?"

"Just four this trip."

"Hope they're all hungry. The missus cooked for eight passengers. You all go on inside, I'll take care of the team."

"Thanks," George replied. Then, yelling down to the coach, he added, "Okay, folks, we'll change teams here.

There's food inside for anyone that wants to eat, and the facilities are out back."

George climbed down from the box. The shotgun guard climbed down as well, leaving his gun under the seat. When the coach door opened, four passengers got out: three women and a man.

From his position on the rock, Tatum watched them cross the yard toward the main building, where they were met at the door by a woman wearing an apron.

"Welcome folks," Tatum heard the woman say. "Come on in. We've got baked chicken and dumplin's today."

Two liverymen who worked at the way station joined Tony then, and the three of them started unhooking the horses so they could change the team.

Tatum slid back down from his position on the rock.

"What's it look like down there?" Pigiron asked.

Tatum smiled. "Looks like we're going to have chicken and dumplin's for dinner," he said.

"That's good, because I'm getting plenty tired of beans, I don't mind telling you."

"Let's go," Tatum said as he mounted his horse.

Tatum and the others moved in single file down the narrow trail that led to the road and Miller's Switch below. They rode by the coach, which was now standing empty and devoid of its team, and headed straight toward the corral. Just inside the corral fence, Tony and his two workers had rounded up fresh horses and were just beginning to put them in harness.

Tony looked up as the riders approached. The expression on his face showed that in addition to his curiosity as to why they were there, he was also a little wary of them.

"Something I can do for you gents?" he asked.

"Yeah," Tatum answered. He pulled his pistol. "You can die." He pulled the trigger and Tony went down.

"What the hell?" one of the liverymen yelled, and both of them started running toward the main house. Tatum's men started shooting at them, and they were hit half-a-dozen times each. One fell facedown in a horse

pile in the middle of the paddock; the other made it a
far as the fence before he was hit. He fell onto the fenc
and hung there, half over.

Hearing the shooting outside, George and his shotgu
guard came running out of the way station to see wha
was going on. Although both had drawn their pistols, ne
ther got off a shot, as they were cut down by gunfir
almost as soon as they set foot on the front porch.

"Let's go get us somethin' to eat," Tatum said, ridin
over toward the main house.

The men dismounted in front, tied their horses to th
porch-roof support posts, then went inside. Four wome
and an old man were cowering against the wall on the op
posite side of the room, having gotten up from the dinin
table. The table itself was filled with food-laden plates.

"Who . . . who are you?" the woman with the apro
asked, her voice quivering with fear. "And what have yo
done with Tony?"

"Tony? Would that be the name of the man who run
this place?"

"Yes. Tony Miller. I am Mrs. Miller. This is Miller'
Switch and we are host and hostess here. Where is Tony
I want to see him."

"Oh, we shot him," Tatum said matter-of-factly.

"No!" Mrs. Miller cried out. She started toward th
door.

"Pigiron," Tatum said, and Pigiron grabbed Mrs. Mille
then pushed her back toward the wall by the others.

"Please, let me help my husband," Mrs. Miller pleade

"Lady, there ain't no helpin' him left," Tatum said. "
told you, we shot him. He's dead."

Mrs. Miller hung her head and began weeping quiet

"See here," the male passenger said, speaking for th
first time. "This is an outrage. An outrage. Do you kno
who I am?"

"No, old man. Who are you?"

"I am John Pierpoint Northington, a member of th
State Legislature."

"Is that a fact?" Tatum asked.

"It certainly is a fact, sir."

"What is that supposed to mean to me? You expect me o vote for you?" Tatum joked. The others laughed.

"It means that I intend to see to it that you are arrested, rought to trial, and sentenced," Northington said.

"You mean, you don't even intend to bargain for your ife?"

"I do not," Northington said.

"Then there is no sense in going on with this conver-ation, is there?" Tatum pulled his pistol and shot Northington between the eyes. The women screamed as Northington's body was thrown back, then slid down to he floor, leaving a smear of blood on the wall behind im. The old legislator sat on the floor, almost as if it were y design, with his arms down to each side, his palms up, nd his eyes open. It was only the ugly black hole in his orehead that belied the tranquil scene.

"My, oh, my, this looks good," Tatum said, putting his istol away and taking a piece of chicken from one of the lates. He popped the chicken into his mouth. "Uhm, it s good," he said.

"You can't eat that," Mrs. Miller said quietly. "That ood is for the coach passengers, the driver and shotgun uard, and those who work here."

"Is it? Well, doesn't look like any of the menfolk are round to enjoy it, does it?" Tatum asked.

"Please, if you'll just wait a short spell, I'll cook some-hing for you and your men."

"Oh, you would do that for us, would you?" Tatum sked. "Well now, that's very . . . Christian . . . of you," e said, laughing at his choice of words. "Especially hen we haven't been what you might call friendly since e arrived."

"I'd do it just to get rid of you," Mrs. Miller replied.

Tatum broke out in loud, raucous laughter. "Well, I'll ive you this. You don't hold back your thoughts none. nd it's a right generous thing you're doin, offerin' to

feed us all, particular seein' as I got me a Mexican, tw
Injuns, and a colored fella ridin' with me," Tatum saic
"Are you tellin' me you'd serve their kind in here?"

"Yes," Mrs. Miller said nervously. "If you'll just give m
time to do it, I'll serve you and all your friends."

Tatum laughed. "Did you hear that, Jim?" he asked th
black man, who was standing back by the wall with hi
arms folded across his chest. "She called you my friend.

Jim just stared impassively.

"Hell, lady, Jim's no more a friend of mine than you ar
He's a colored man who just threw in with us, that's all.

"What are we goin' to do with 'em, Tatum?" Pigiro
asked.

"Kill 'em," Tatum said.

The room echoed with the sound of gunfire as Tatu
sat at the table and began eating from the plate in fro
of him.

At first it was just a thin wisp, like nothing more than
column of dust in the distance. But as Smoke, Pearli
and Tom drew closer, the wisp of dust took on more su
stance until it became a column of smoke, growin
thicker and heavier until finally it was a heavy, blac
cloud, filled with glowing embers and roiling into the sk

The fire was still burning and snapping when th
three reached Miller's Switch, but there was little left
burn. The main building, the barn, and the outhous
were nothing more than collapsed piles of blackene
timbers, with just enough wood remaining to suppo
the dying flames. Not even the stagecoach had escape
for it sat in front of what remained of the depot, burne
down to the wheels.

In addition to the fires, there had been a wantc
slaughter of the replacement teams. A dozen horses l
dead in the corral, and there were even several pi
killed. Animals weren't the only victims. They four

half-a-dozen bodies lying around as well, including two that were burned beyond recognition.

"Help! Help me, somebody." The voice that called was strained with pain.

"George!" Smoke said, running toward the stagecoach driver, finding him on the ground near the watering trough.

"When did this happen?"

"'Bout noon," George said.

"Who did it? Was it Indians?"

George shook his head. "Don't know exactly who or what they were. They was whites, Injuns, Mexicans. They even had 'em a colored man with 'em."

"Comancheros," Smoke said. "I knew it. Same as hit your ranch, Tom."

"What happened?" Tom asked.

"I don't rightly know," George replied. "Me'n Pete was inside havin' lunch when we heard someone shootin'. We come out here to see what was goin' on, and the next thing you know, they shot us. I must'a passed out then, 'cause when I come to some later, everything was on fire."

"So you didn't see which way they went?" Smoke asked.

George shook his head. "I don't have the foggiest idea," he answered. "But I can tell you the name of the fella that was leadin' 'em. I was sort of in and out, but I heard 'em talkin'. They called him Tatum."

"Jack Tatum," Tom said. "Yes, it figures now."

Smoke looked George over. He had at least three bullet holes in him, two in the thigh and one in the arm. They were painful, and he had lost a lot of blood, but he would probably live.

"Pearlie, get him patched up as well as you can," Smoke said. "I'm going to look around for sign. This is the closest we've been to those bastards, and I don't plan to let them get away."

"What'll we do with him after I get him patched up?" Pearlie asked.

"George, what time is the next stage due through here?" Smoke asked.

"If nothin' has happened to it, it ought to be here before supper time," George replied.

"We'll wait here with him until then," Smoke said. "Then we'll put him on the stage and send him back to Stonewall."

While Pearlie attended to his patient, Smoke began looking around. After a few minutes, Tom came over to stand beside him.

"Find something?"

"They came down this way," Smoke said, pointing to the place where a small trail joined the road. "And they left that way," he added, pointing toward another climbing trail.

"Into the Sangre de Cristo range?" Tom asked. "They're going higher into the mountains? That's sort of dumb, isn't it? Nobody goes up there this time of year."

"That's what they are counting on," Smoke said. "They plan to get over on the other side before the pass is closed. If they can do that, they'll get away."

"Lord, I'd hate to think of those murderin' bastards getting away."

"Then don't think about it," Smoke said with a wry smile. "Because they aren't going to get away. We're going to find them, and they are going to pay."

"Now you're talkin'."

21

Quinntanna sat astride his horse and watched as the little band in his charge moved slowly by. Some rode horses, some walked, while others—the very old, and those who had been wounded but survived the attack—rode on travois that were pulled behind the horses. All were bundled against the cold. As the people passed by, they looked neither right nor left, but stared straight ahead as they moved laboriously toward the mountains rising in the distance.

Quinntanna had arranged to meet Blue Horses and Swift Bear at the place of the Howling Winds because it was on the trail and it fit in conveniently with his plans. He intended to move the entire village, or at least what was left of it, to the other side of Culebra Peak in the Sangre de Cristo mountain range. If he could get them over the top before the heaviest of the winter storms came, all the passes would then be closed by snow and his people would be safe. But getting them there was easier said than done.

The little party of travelers made a pitiful sight, for there was scarcely one among them who had not lost one or more members of his or her family. There were dozens of children without mothers, mothers without their children, as well as old men and women who had survived the attack but now had no one left to care for them. Quinntanna saw Teykano coming toward him.

"The trail is clear," Teykano said.

"Will we get through before nightfall?" Quinntanna asked.

Teykano shook his head. "I think not. The top is too far away and our people are not moving quickly enough."

"They can't go any faster. They are old, weak, and tired. Some are sick and injured."

"I know," Teykano said. "Some of the others, the young men, want to leave now. They want to find the white men who did this and fight them."

"They would abandon our people?" Quinntanna asked.

"They say we can leave two or three to help our people get across the mountains. The rest can fight. We have guns now."

"What do you think?" Quinntanna asked.

"I think if we did this, who would we leave behind? All want to go, but some must stay because our people cannot get over the mountain alone."

"We will all stay until the people are safe. Then we will all go," Quinntanna said.

Teykano smiled. "I told the young men that you would say this."

"And do they understand?"

"Yes. They did not like it, but they understand."

"Good."

"We will get revenge against the evil ones who did this won't we?" Teykano asked.

Quinntanna sighed. "How will we get revenge?"

"How? We have guns and some bullets. We are not helpless the way the people of our village were. We will fight the whites."

"Someone attacked the ranch of a white man and killed many of their people. The whites thought Indians did it, so they attacked our village and killed our people. They didn't know who did it, but their blood was hot so they killed. Would you have us kill innocent whites?"

"Yes!" Teykano replied without hesitation.

"What is to be gained by that? If we kill the innocent, and the guilty go unpunished, how is our revenge satisfied?"

"We must do something, Quinntanna," Teykano insisted. "Our young men have blood that is hot. We cannot tell them that they cannot seek revenge."

"I will find a way to kill the ones who are responsible," Quinntanna promised.

"How will you do this?"

"I don't know," Quinntanna replied. "But if you will tell our young warriors to trust me, I will find a way."

"You are my friend, Quinntanna, and I will trust you," Teykano said. "I will counsel the others to trust you as well. But look into your heart and into your mind and find a way to do this thing you say."

"I will find a way," Quinntanna said again, though even as he was saying the words, he was searching for some way to carry out his promise.

Quinntanna knew about the place where the white man's people-wagons stopped on their journeys between Stonewall and San Luis. It was called Miller's Switch, and it was located just as the trail started climbing into the mountains. He was certain that by now the people at Miller's Switch would have gotten word that a white ranch was attacked and burned. If so, like everyone else, they would believe the Indians were responsible.

If he could have done so, he would have gone around the way station, but because they were following the only passable trail up into the mountain range, that wasn't possible. Therefore, the only thing he could do would be to scout the way station, then pass by as quietly as possible and hope they weren't seen. Informing the villagers to stay where they were for a while, he and Teykano went ahead to check out the depot. When they moved to the edge of the woods, they were surprised to see nothing but burned-out buildings and a burned-out stage.

"Ayiee, what happened here?" Teykano asked.

"I believe the ones who attacked and burned the white ranch did this," Quinntanna said.

"It does not matter who did it. The whites will think we did."

"Yes," Quinntanna. "That is why we must . . ." Quinntanna stopped in mid-sentence. "Teykano, here is where we will get our revenge," he said.

"Here?"

"Yes. It is as you said. It does not matter who attacked here. The whites will think we did it. I believe they will send their soldiers here. I believe they will send the same soldiers here who attacked our village and murdered our people."

Teykano smiled. "And when the soldiers come, we will be here, waiting for them."

"Yes. In the meadow beyond the first rise."

"That is a good plan, my friend," Teykano said. "That is a plan worthy of the warriors of old. But what will we do with our people?"

"We will find somewhere for them to stay. Then we will come back to the meadow and wait for the soldiers."

As soon as the coach rolled into Big Rock, the driver hurried down to the sheriff's office.

"Monte," he called, stepping inside. "Monte, where are you?" When he saw the big hole in the back wall, he let out a low whistle. Covington was standing inside the open cell, supervising the repair work on the wall. "Oh my, what happened here?" the driver said.

"We had a prisoner escape."

"I'll say you did."

"What can I do for you?" Covington asked.

"I'm looking for the sheriff."

"He's in Denver. I'm in charge here now."

"You're in charge? Who are you?" the driver asked.

"Colonel Sam Covington, temporarily the military administrator for Las Animas and Costilla Counties."

"Military administrator? I've never heard of such a thing."

"I've placed both counties under martial law," Covington said. "Now, I'll ask you again. What did you want with the sheriff?"

"Well, since you're in charge, I suppose I can tell you," the driver said. "Miller's Switch has been hit."

"Hit?"

"Attacked and burned. Miller, his wife, the men who worked for them, all the coach passengers were killed. Jeb, the shotgun guard was also killed, but looks like the driver might pull through. I dropped him off at the doc's office back in Stonewall."

"We've got 'em!" Covington said, hitting his fist in his hand and grinning broadly. "First Sergeant Dingo, assemble the troop! We're going to Miller's Switch."

"What about these two?" Dingo asked, indicating the two men who were laying brick to patch the hole in the back wall.

"Them too," Covington said. "We'll let Sheriff Carson worry about his wall. I don't intend to let these Indian bastards get away from us."

"Yes, sir," Dingo said. "Come on, men, help me round everyone up."

"Excuse me," the driver said after the others left. "Did you say you didn't intend to let the Indians get away with this?"

"That's right."

The driver shook his head. "It wasn't Injuns."

"What wasn't Indians?"

"Them people that hit Miller's Switch. They wasn't Injuns."

"What makes you say that?"

"George told me. He was there, he seen it all. He said they was just a bunch of outlaws."

"Are you trying to tell me that it wasn't Indians who did this?" Covington asked.

"George said they might have been one or two Injuns with 'em, but it was white folks, Mexicans, they even had 'em a colored man with 'em."

"And Indians," Covington insisted.

"Well, yeah, that's what I said. But accordin' to George, there was only one or two of 'em was Injuns."

"That's good enough for me," Covington said. "One Indian, one hundred Indians, far as I'm concerned, they're the ones behind it."

"Yeah, well, whatever you say. I've got to get back over to the depot. The stage is goin' on through to Trinidad."

The driver started toward the door, but Covington called to him. "What's your name, driver?"

"Simpson. Arnold Simpson."

"Simpson, you keep quiet about what you have told me here. I don't want you shooting your mouth off to anyone."

"You mean about it not being Injuns?" Simpson replied.

"I mean I want you keep your mouth shut, period. This is a military matter now, and if I find that you have been shooting off your mouth, you could wind up on the gallows."

"On the gallows?" Simpson replied. "What the hell have I done that you can threaten to hang me?"

"If you start spouting off military information, some of it might get back to the Indians we are going after," Covington said. "If that happens, and if even one of my men are killed because they have advance information, then you'll be tried for murder, you will be found guilty, and you will hang."

"You've got no right to talk to me like that," Simpson said.

"On the contrary, Mr. Simpson. I have every right That is the nature of martial law. The administrator that's me, has absolute authority. The citizens, that's you have no rights except the rights I let you have."

* * *

Sheriff Monte Carson sat in the outer chamber of the governor's office at the capital building in Denver. He had been waiting for some time, and as he held his hat in his hand, he fiddled with the hatband. Finally, the governor's personal secretary came over to him.

"Sheriff, Governor Cooper will see you now."

"Thanks," Monte said, rising from his chair.

Governor Cooper was a large man with puffy cheeks and a well-groomed handlebar mustache. A lawyer, he had moved to Colorado from Illinois several years ago and had become wealthy, not only in the law business, but also in insurance, mining, and cattle. With a politician's smile and an extended hand, he came halfway to the door to greet Monte.

"Sheriff Carson, it's good to see you again," the governor said. "How are things down in Las Animas County?"

"Not good, Governor," Monte answered.

"Oh? I heard about the Indian uprising, but it was my belief that Colonel Covington had things well under control."

"Perhaps too much control," Monte suggested.

"What do you mean?"

"Governor, Sam Covington has established martial law. And under the auspices of that declaration, he has suspended all civil rights. No telegrams can be sent or received, the newspaper is under his direct censorship, I have been relieved of my duties, the mayor and city council have been relieved of their duties, he has established a ten o'clock curfew, and abolished the right of peaceful assembly. And he has done all of that under your authority."

"What?" Governor Cooper replied, barking the word out. "Has the man lost his mind? I granted him no such sweeping power as you describe!"

Monte smiled. "I'm glad to hear you say that, sir. In fact,

I was sure you would say that. That's why I came up here to see you."

The governor returned to his desk, then took out a piece of paper and began writing. "I am hereby revoking this martial law. In fact, I am revoking his commission. Sheriff, I am charging you with the responsibility to reestablish civil law. Do you want a document to that effect?"

"Thank you, Governor, but with Covington out of the way, I don't need any further documents. As the duly elected sheriff, I already have the mandate to reestablish and uphold civil law. And that I intend to do."

"I'm glad you came to see me," the governor said. "And please keep me informed of what happens down there."

"I will, sir," Monte said.

22

Covington's Cavalry had been on the trail for half the morning the next day, when Dingo came across Indian sign indicating scores of horses, plus the tracks of a dozen or more travois. He pointed it out to Covington, who immediately halted the march, then ordered his officers and noncommissioned officers to a conference.

As the officers and NCOs arrived, Covington was sitting casually in his saddle with one leg hooked across the pommel. He was distractedly tapping that leg with his riding quirt and he smiled broadly at his officers.

"Well, gentlemen, it would appear this is our day," he said. "Do you see this?" He pointed to the ground behind him where the Indian trail could be easily seen, from the hoofprints and travois tracks to the horse droppings. "The hostiles have made it easy for us. They have practically sent us an open invitation."

"Colonel, doesn't that worry you a little?" Captain Roach asked.

"Worry me? No. Why in heavens name should it worry me?"

"I mean, think about it for a moment," Roach said. "These are people who can make their trail disappear. Now, all of a sudden, it's almost as if they are putting up signposts saying, 'This way.' And that's not bothering you?"

"What are you suggesting, Captain Roach?"

"I'm just saying that we aren't exactly sneaking up on them. From the looks of things, they're moving their entire camp, including women, children, and dogs. It just doesn't seem right they would make it so easy for us to track them."

"Well, Captain, have you considered the fact that they may have no choice?" Covington asked.

"I'm not following you, sir."

"I mean, even Indian horses have to eat," Covington said, as if explaining something to a child. "And what goes in at the front of the horse, inevitably comes out at the rear." Covington pointed again to the trail. "Unless they have their squaws following behind picking up horse turds, they are going to be easy to follow."

Several of the others laughed at the mental image of a group of Indian women walking along behind the horses, picking up the horses' droppings. Captain Roach, without laughing, took his hat off and examined it for a moment.

"That's what I'm talking about, Colonel. You see, I've seen squaws do just that."

"You've fought Indians before, have you, Roach?"

"I have."

"Why is it you haven't mentioned it before now?"

"I was with the Seventh during the little fracas we had up in Montana a few years ago. Custer rode into a trap, and you see what happened to him."

"You were with Custer?"

"That's right. In Reno's Battalion. The reason I haven't mentioned it before is because it isn't something I'm very proud of. Fact is, I joined with you to sort of even up the score."

"And now you're getting nervous that something like that might happen to us?"

"I'm saying that we could be riding into a trap, yes, sir."

"Nonsense. What happened to Custer was the result of pure numbers. There were a lot more Indians than there were soldiers. Well, plainly, we don't have that situation here. We outnumber the Indians. And as far as riding into a trap?" Covington laughed, a scoffing laugh. "Believe me, I know Indians, and I know that they aren't smart enough to conceive such a thing."

"I hope you are right."

"I am right," Covington insisted. "Now, here is my plan. I'm going to form four squadrons. Captain Roach, you will take one squadron, go south for one mile, then ride west, parallel with our line of march. Lieutenant Conklin, you will take one squadron to the north of our line of march, then proceed west in parallel with our course. That will leave two squadrons, which I will lead, right up the middle of the trail until we encounter the savages. And then, gentlemen, we will attack, leaving the squadrons on each wing in position to cut off any possible retreat."

"Colonel, you are going to divide the command?" Roach asked.

"Do you have a problem with that?"

"If we divide our command, no single element will outnumber the Indians. And I would remind you, Colonel, that Custer divided his command."

"Stop comparing me with that fool Custer," Covington said.

"Very well, sir. Shall we agree upon some signal for assistance?" Roach asked.

Covington chuckled. "I scarcely think that will be the problem," he said. "No, sir, the problem will be in keeping them from running away. All right, gentlemen, let us proceed."

Roach and Conklin pulled their squadrons away in accordance with Covington's instructions, while Covington continued right up the path of broken and chewed grass and brown and green horse apples.

"Well, First Sergeant Dingo, it's clear to see that Roach doesn't agree with me. What do you think of my plan of battle?" Covington asked.

"You're the commander, Colonel, and it's your plan It don't matter what Roach thinks."

"My sentiments exactly," Covington said. It didn't dawn on him that Dingo's reply was rather nonspecifi without offering an endorsement.

Covington stopped the advance while he stared through a pair of field glasses. "Damn," he said aloud "How the hell did they get over there?"

"Beg your pardon?" Dingo asked.

Covington pointed toward a cloud of dust in the distance, south of the direction they were traveling.

"It would seem that the Indians have left us a broad highway to travel while they positioned themselves for an attack at my flank. Captain Roach is about to be engaged. Dingo, I want you to overtake Captain Roach Tell him that I will send Conklin around to cut off an possible retreat, and instruct him to strike at the enem at once. Do you have that? He is to attack at once."

"Yes, sir," Dingo said.

The ground over which Dingo rode ascended in a long, gradual slope that made riding relatively easy, and a short time later he pulled up at the head of Roach' column.

"Has Covington seen them?" Roach asked, indicating the Indians in front of him. Here, the trail had opened into a high meadow.

"Yes, sir. He says you should strike against them from the front as soon as you can engage them."

"A frontal assault?" Roach asked.

"That's what he said. He's moving Conklin's squadron in position to block the Indians' retreat, while he come to your support."

"He is coming to support?"

"That's what he said, Captain."

Roach sat his saddle for a moment, then sighed. "All right," he said. "Will you be joining me, Sergeant Dingo?

"Yes, sir."

"I'm glad. It'll be good to have another man with

experience. You take the left side, I'll take the right." Roach stood in his stirrups and addressed his command.

"Men, I think you should understand that this won't be like the attack on the village. There, we killed women, children, and old men. They were unarmed and they were asleep." He pointed toward the Indians. "These are warriors, armed, deadly, and ready for us."

What had started out as a lark suddenly changed, and the men experienced fear for the first time. The horses as well seemed to sense the impending danger, perhaps from the men atop them, and they grew a bit skittish. A couple of the horses began nervously prancing around, moving in and out of the line. A couple of the riders had to turn their mounts in a full circle to get them back into position.

"Forward at a trot!" Roach shouted, and the squadron started out across the meadow.

"They are coming," Teykano said.

Although the total number of soldiers was greater than the total number of Comanche, Quinntanna had outmaneuvered Covington. In addition, Covington had split his forces so that, as the two bodies of men came together, the Comanche would be the superior force on the field.

"Good. We are ready for them," Quinntanna replied.

The soldiers' advance surged forward at top speed, and soon the sound of galloping horses' hooves was like rolling thunder. Above all the noise, though, the soldiers could clearly hear the Indians as they whooped and shouted in anticipation of battle. They hurtled toward one another. There were two armies: one uniformed, the other in buckskin—both determined.

As the two groups closed on each other, both sides opened fire. In the opening fusillade, both Indians and soldiers went down with bleeding bullet wounds. Then the enemies came together in closer, more brutal combat, saber against war club. In that battle the Indians had the clear advantage, for they had used war clubs their entir lives for everything from games to hunting, whereas th soldiers were, for the most part, unfamiliar with and ur trained in the use of the saber.

Dingo was one of the first to go down, his head bashe in by a blow from a war club. Seeing Dingo killed, man of the men panicked and started running. Roach trie to rally them, but he was killed as well. When the other realized that they no longer had anyone in comman they quit fighting and turned to gallop away, leavin three-fourths of their original number dead on the fiel behind them. Some of the Indians started after the fe remaining survivors, but Quinntanna called them bac

"Let them go!" he shouted. "More soldiers are comin We must be ready for them!"

When Lieutenant Conklin brought his squadron u he thought he would be providing support for Roach. I stead, he arrived at the spot where the battle had take place, marked by the bodies lying on the field. An among the dead, there were many, many more wearin uniforms than there were wearing buckskins.

"Lieutenant! There's Captain Roach!" one of the me said, pointing to Roach's bloodied body.

"And Dingo!" another said.

Suddenly, and from all around them, Indians spran up, screaming hideous war yells. It was as if they had ju materialized, so good had been their concealment. Th Indians opened fire, shooting as fast as they could coc and fire their rifles. Bullets whistled through Conklin command, slamming into men and horses. There wer shouts of panic and screams of pain as the Indian pressed their attack, firing almost methodically into th demoralized soldiers. Very few soldiers even had th presence of mind to return fire.

"Retreat! Retreat!" Conklin shouted. He would hav given the order a third time, but he was hit in the templ with a bullet. As if shooting cows in a pen, the Indians continued to work the levers on their rifles, firing at the soldiers until every last one was dead. Then, and only then, did the shooting stop.

"Aiyee!" one of the Indians yelled, realizing that their victory was complete. The others began yelling and shouting as well.

"Collect the guns and bullets!" Quinntanna said. "Hurry! We must go now! We must return to our people and get them through the pass to safety."

Colonel Covington, who had started toward Roach to support him, was surprised to see just over half-a-dozen men in uniform galloping toward him. They were shouting long before they were close enough to be heard or understood. Finally, the gallopers reached Covington's two squadrons.

"Hold it!" Covington shouted. "Hold up here! What's going on?"

"Dead!" one of the men said. "They're all dead!"

"Who is all dead?"

"All of them! All the rest of Roach's squadron. And Conklin's squadron as well."

Covington shook his head. "No, that's impossible," he said. "They can't all be dead."

"Colonel, you want to go look for yourself?" one of the six soldiers said. All had panic-stricken faces, and all were breathing hard from the exertion of their wild flight.

"Give me those glasses," Covington said, reaching his hand out toward a nearby sergeant. The sergeant handed the binoculars to Covington, who raised them to his eyes to study the meadow. He swept his vision back and forth across the field in front of him.

"I don't see anyth . . . holy shit!" Covington said in mid-sentence. He trained the glasses on one spot.

"What do you see, Colonel?" asked the sergeant.

"Bodies," Covington replied. "Lots of bodies." Sweeping

the field beyond the bodies, Covington saw several Indians leaving the field.

"Do you see any Indians?" someone asked fearfully.

Covington continued to study the retreating Indians. By rights, he should be going after them. Sighing, he lowered the glasses.

"What are they doing?" his sergeant asked.

"What is who doing?" Covington replied.

"The Indians. What are they doing?"

Covington sighed. "There are no Indians," he said. "They seem to have left the field. Come on, let's take care of our dead, then go back home. We are going to have to reorganize before we can continue this campaign. By God, maybe people will listen to me now. We have a full-blown Indian war on our hands, as big and dangerous as any uprising in the past."

"For many years, our people will sing around the campfire of our great victory on this day," Teykano said excitedly as they rode back to the place where they had left their people.

"I think not," Quinntanna answered.

"What? How can you think that? In all the stories of our people, there has never been a war chief like you. And there has never been a victory like the one we had today."

"Perhaps this is so," Quinntanna agreed. "But I think our village will be no more. Too many were killed. There are no young women for our young men. There are no children to grow up to be warriors and wives, no squaws to have new children. I think soon our young men must go to other villages and other places to find women, and when they do, they will not come back."

"You are right," Teykano said. "The village of Stone Eagle is no more." He was silent for a moment, then he smiled. "But those who came in the night to murder our people are no more as well."

"Yes," Quinntanna agreed, joining Teykano's smile

with his own. "At least those who came to murder our people are now dead."

"What about the place of Howling Winds?" Teykano asked. "Shall we go there now to buy bullets?"

"There is no need to buy bullets now. The white man's army has provided us with many bullets, and we did not have to spend one thousand more dollars."

23

Much higher in the mountains, almost all the way to the top of the pass, Tatum relieved himself, then turned back toward Blue Horses and Swift Bear. "You are certain they said they would meet us in the place of the Howling Winds?"

"Yes," Swift Bear replied.

"And you are sure this is the place of the Howling Winds?" Pigiron asked.

"I think it must be," Sanchez said. "Can you not hear the winds howling like the cry of El Diablo?"

"This is the place," Tatum said. "I've been here before."

"Maybe the Injuns ain't goin' to show up," Pigiron suggested.

"They'll show up. They want the bullets," Tatum insisted.

"How long are we going to wait for them?"

"As long as it takes."

"For a lousy thousand bucks, we are going to stay here for as long as it takes?"

"More than a thousand bucks," Tatum said.

"What do you mean, more than a thousand bucks?" Pigiron asked. "Ain't that what we said we'd sell the rest of the ammunition for?"

"Well, for one thing, there ain't no more bullets to sell. We didn't get any more. So what difference does it make how much we told Quinntanna we would sell the bullets to him for? And for another thing, if Quinntanna has a thousand dollars, then you can believe he has much more than that on him. So I figure that when we meet up with him, we'll just take all of it."

"Yeah, well, I don't like being this far up in the mountains at this time of the year," Pigiron said. "What if the snow comes in and traps us? What then?"

"You afraid of a little snow?" Tatum asked.

"Damn right I'm afraid. Ain't you ever heard of the Donner Party?"

"Donner Party?" Tatum replied. He shook his head. "No, I ain't never heard of nothin' called a Donner Party."

"They was a group of people tryin' to go West by wagon train," Pigiron explained. "Only, they got started too late, and they wind up getting theirselves caught up in the mountains at a place called Donner Pass. Thing is, Donner Pass was filled up with snow, and they couldn't go through it, and they couldn't go back, so they had to just stay there. But pretty soon, just staying there where they was, they run out of food."

"You tellin' me a whole wagon train of people starved to death?" Tatum asked.

"Not all of 'em starved. Some of 'em made it through by eatin' the dead."

"They done what?" Tatum gasped.

"They got so hungry they et the ones that had already died."

"They did no such thing!" Tatum said.

"Yes, they did. I can't believe you ain't never heard that story. It was in all the newspapers and everything."

"Yeah, well, it ain't goin' to happen to us," Tatum said. "Now, ever'body pick 'em out a position and stay there 'till the Injuns come. Once they're here, open up on 'em. We'll kill 'em all, ever last one of 'em. Then we'll take whatever money we can find on 'em." Suddenly, and inexplicably, Tatum smiled broadly. "Not only will we get the money, we'll get the credit for killin' off the Injuns that's been raisin' hell around here. Why, we'll be heroes."

It was very cold, and as Quinntanna moved his village higher into the mountains, vapor clouds formed around the noses and mouths of the horses and people. The tops of the mountains were shrouded by a low-lying bank of clouds, and here and there Quinntanna could see patches of snow, lying brilliantly white in the sunshine and dark azure in the shadows. To spare the horses for the climb, Quinntanna made all but the very lame dismount, or leave the travois, and walk, so as not to overtax the animals. Teykanno came up to walk beside him.

"I do not know if our people will get through," he said.

"We must," Quinntanna replied. "For only after we are on the other side will we be safe."

Teykano pointed to the cloud-covered spine at the mountain's top. "It is as if the Great Spirit himself is guarding the pass."

For the next hour they continued up the trail, step by laborious step. What little sun there had been earlier was gone now, and it turned into a dark, dreary day—so heavily overcast that the exact position of the sun couldn't be made out, even by the faintest glow. Individual clouds couldn't be seen either, for a thick blanket shrouded the towering mountains so effectively that the peaks disappeared into the slate gray sky itself. Finally, as they reached a high plateau, Teykano came to Quinntanna and asked him to call a halt.

"We can't stop now," Quinntanna said. "We are not even halfway up the mountain."

"Night is coming," Teykano said. "If we continue, some of our people might get lost in the darkness. Is it not better to keep everyone together?"

With every fiber of his being, Quinntanna felt that it was best to keep going, but as he looked into the faces of he people he was trying to lead to safety, he gave in. 'Very well," he said with a surrendering sigh. "We will tay here tonight."

They camped where they stopped. Later, when they hrew their blankets and skins out on top of the snow, Teykano came over to Quinntanna.

"Quinntanna, I am sorry if you think I betrayed you."

Quinntanna looked at Teykano in surprise. "Betrayed ne? How do you think you have betrayed me?"

"I know you wanted to go on."

"Yes, but I think you are right. I do not believe our people could have gone any farther."

A flash of golden light suddenly illuminated the area. Along with the light came a wave of heat. Quinntanna ooked toward the source of heat and illumination, and aw that someone had set fire to some mossy scrub brush.

"Uhm, that is good," Quinntanna said. He and Teykano moved their blankets and skins closer to the burning bush, joining with the others who were also inding positions around the fire. They sat there for a ong moment, as if mesmerized by the flames. The burnng shrub popped and snapped as it was consumed. And because they were exhausted by their labors, they fell asleep easily, warmed by the fire.

They were oblivious to the cold, oblivious to the precariousness of their position, and oblivious to the large lakes of snow that, just after midnight, began tumbling lown through the blackness.

The snow fell silently, moving in unnoticed by the sleeping Indians.

When Smoke Jensen woke up in the morning, he was immediately aware of the change that had taken place since the night before. Last night, he had gone o sleep on top of the snow. This morning, he awoke under it. A pristine blanket of snow covered everyhing in sight. The trail that he had been following was no longer visible. Neither was the trail behind them. There were no footprints, no signs of the encampment that he, Pearlie, and Tom had made. Everything was completely covered in a mantel of white. It was as if man had never been here before, and yet he knew that the ones who had attacked Miller's Switch, the people he suspected had attacked Tom Burke's ranch, were ahead of them.

The scenery was spectacular this morning, not only because of the new-fallen snow, but also because the air had been washed clean. Whereas low-hanging clouds had shrouded the mountains yesterday, today the clouds were all gone, and even the most distant mountains were clearly visible.

"Pearlie, Tom, wake up," he said.

Tom and Pearlie woke up, then tossed their snow-covered blankets aside to look around.

"Holy shit, look at this," Tom said.

"So, what do we do now?" Pearlie asked. "Do we back-track, or do we go ahead?"

"If Tatum and his bunch got over the pass, it won't do us any good to go ahead," Tom said. "There's no way anyone can get through that pass now."

"On the other hand, if they didn't get through the pass before this snow, there is no way they can get through either. That means that we may have them trapped, and they can't get away without coming back through us," Smoke said. "I think we should press on."

"Damn! If this ain't the shits!" Pigiron said, looking up toward the pass. He turned toward Tatum. "I told you last night, we didn't have no business staying here. Now what?"

"We go back down, that's what," Tatum said.

"Even goin' back down ain't goin' to be all that easy," Pigiron insisted. "I mean, look at those folks in the Donner Party."

"Will you shut up about the Donner Party?" Tatum said

"I don't believe there was such a thing anyway. Everyone up. Get saddled, but we'd better lead the horses down."

There was a good deal of grumbling as the men started breaking camp.

"You know what I think?" Wheeler said. "I think we ought to divide up the money and go out on our own."

"That's what you think, is it?"

"Yeah. I mean, we've got enough money to have near three hundred dollars apiece if we was to divide it now. That's pretty good money."

"You'd have it spent on liquor, women, and cards in one night," Tatum said.

"Yeah, but at least I'd have me a good time that one night," Wheeler said.

"How would you know?" Pigiron asked. "You'd get drunk first thing; then you wouldn't remember any of it."

The others laughed.

Swift Bear had been leading the way back down the trail. Now he came back up the trail quickly.

"Men come," he said.

"Men? What men? Injuns?" Tatum asked.

"White men."

"Who the hell could that be?" Pigiron asked.

"I don't know," Tatum said. "But whoever they are, it ain't good."

"What are we going to do?"

"We're goin' to kill 'em," Tatum said. "Everyone, get in position. Soon as you figure you got yourself a pretty good shot, take it."

"What about the horses?" Pigiron asked.

"Leave 'em, they ain't goin' nowhwere," Tatum said. "They can't move any better'n we can."

Tatum, Pigiron, Wheeler, Sanchez, Arino, Swift Bear, Blue Horses, and Jim moved on down the trail for a short distance, then found places of cover and concealment while they waited for whoever was coming up the trail. Jim, because he had the buffalo gun, and also because he tended to keep himself separated from the others anyway, moved a little farther down the trail.

Smoke, Pearlie, and Tom trudged through the deep snow as they climbed the trail. They had left their horses behind them for the simple reason that they couldn't ride them anyway, and there was no need to wear them out. The man in the lead had the most difficult task of the three, since he had to break through the snow, whereas the two following could move through the trail he cut. Because of that, they traded off the lead position about every fifteen minutes. They had just traded positions, and now Tom Burke was in the lead.

"You think we'll find them on this side of the pass?" Pearlie asked.

"I hope we find them," Tom said. "I hope we find them half froze to death."

Pearlie laughed. "Just half froze to death?"

"Damn right. I want the pleasure of finishin' them off my—"

Tom's sentence was interrupted by the angry buzz of a bullet. It creased his cheek, bringing blood, then ricocheted off a snow-covered rock. The sound of the rifle shot rolled down the mountainside.

"Down!" Smoke shouted, diving for cover behind a nearby rock. The other two did the same.

"What the hell was that?" Pearlie asked.

"From the sound of it, I would say that was a .52-caliber buffalo gun," Smoke said. "Isn't that what you would say, Tom?"

"Sounded like it to me," Tom replied.

"You all right?"

"Yeah, just a nick in the cheek. You see anything?" Tom asked.

Even as Tom was asking the question, Smoke was looking up the trail. He saw a flash of light and a puff of smoke, followed by the angry whine of a bullet. An instant later, he heard the sound of the gunshot.

"Tom, do you see that cone-shaped rock off to your left about five hundred yards up the trail?"

"No," Tom said.

"See the three rocks together there?"

"Yes."

"Look just to the left of them. What do you see?"

"Nothing," Tom said.

"Damn, you aren't in position."

Another bullet whined by.

"Toss your buffalo gun to me," Smoke said.

Tom raised up to his knees, then tossed the rifle to Smoke. Smoke caught it, then got back down in position. He rested the rifle on the log in front of him while he drew a bead on the cone-shaped rock about five hundred yards up the trail. He waited until he saw a shoulder, then half a head, then an entire head move into position. It was Jim, getting ready to take another shot.

"Damn," he said. "It's a black man."

"The driver said there was a black man with the ones who hit Miller's Switch," Tom said.

Smoke put the front bead right on the black shooter's forehead, then squeezed the trigger. The rifle boomed, and rocked back against his shoulder. A second later, his target fell out from behind the rock, facedown, arms spread in the snow. His rifle slid down several feet in front of him.

"You got 'im!" Pearlie said.

"Tatum, they got Jim!" Pigiron called.

"I saw it. You think I'm blind?" Tatum replied.

"Who is it? Who's down there?" Pigiron said.

Suddenly Tatum got a glimpse of two of the men. One was Jensen, the other was Tom Burke.

"Son of a bitch. It's Jensen!" Tatum said.

24

"Tom!" Smoke called. "See if you can work your way over here to where I am!"

Tom nodded, then drawing a deep breath, made a run from his position behind a tree over to the log where Smoke had taken cover. As he dashed across the open area, Tatum and all of his men shot at him, and their bullets whined passed him, but he wasn't hit. When he closed to within five yards of the log, he dived headfirst, and slid through the snow for the last couple of feet. He lay behind the log for a moment, panting for breath.

"You all right?" Smoke asked.

Still drawing air in in deep, cold gasps, Tom nodded his head in the affirmative.

"Good," Smoke said. He handed Tom's rifle back to him. "Here's your rifle."

Tom's eyes grew wide. "You called me over here to give me my rifle?"

"Hell, yes," Smoke said, laughing. "You didn't think I was going to run across that open area to give it to you, did you?"

Tom blinked, not certain if Smoke was teasing or not.

"I called you over here because you've got a better view from here," Smoke said. "I want you to use that long gun to cover us while Pearlie and I move up the hill toward them."

"Whoa!" Pearlie said from his position about ten feet away. "You and me are going to charge up that hill after them? We didn't vote on that, did we? Because I don't remember casting my vote."

"I voted for you," Smoke said.

"Oh, well, that's different then," Pearlie replied. "I mean, as long as I got a chance to vote."

Tom took a handful of shells from his pocket, then wiped the snow away to have a place to put them. He opened the breech, flipped out the empty shell casing from the shot Smoke had taken, then slid a new shell in. Closing the breech, he laid the weapon across the log and pointed it in the general direction of Tatum's men.

"All right," he said. "I'm ready. If I see anyone drawing a bead on either of you, I'll pick him off."

"Good man. Pearlie, you ready?"

"I guess I have to be, seein' as I've already voted on it," Pearlie replied.

Smoke pointed to the left. "Looks like there are several rocks, trees, and logs over there," he said. "You work your way up on that side. I'll go up the right."

"Give me the word," Pearlie said. Gone was the joking. He was all business now.

Smoke and Pearlie started up the trail toward Tatum. They were violating every dictum in the book of military strategy, a book that says that those on the attack need many more men than those in defense in order to balance the scales. And if the attack is made against higher ground, then the number needs to be even greater.

Smoke and Pearlie were only two men, and they were attacking seven men, seven men who had good positions of cover on higher ground. As Smoke and Pearlie worked their way up the hill, they heard Tom's rifle bark from behind them, and at almost the same time, they saw one of Tatum's men pitch forward in the snow.

Now there were only six.

"Sanchez!" Tatum shouted. "Damn you, Jensen, you just killed Sanchez. He was my friend!"

"Who are you trying to fool, Tatum?" Smoke replied. "People like you don't have friends."

"I'm going to kill you, you son of a bitch!" Tatum shouted.

Smoke saw one of Tatum's men rise up slightly to have a look around. That little bit of exposure was all Smoke needed and he fired, then saw his target fall back.

"Tatum, he got Paco," someone yelled.

"Shut up, Pigiron! No need lettin' him know about it!" Tatum replied.

Now there were five.

Another of Tatum's men tried to get into position to take a shot, and when he did so, he exposed himself to Tom's buffalo rifle. A loud boom, and he went down. Almost immediately after that, Pearlie got one. In less than a minute, Tatum's numerical advantage had disappeared. There were now only three of the outlaws left.

"I'm gettin' the hell out of here!" Pigiron shouted.

"Me too!" Wheeler said.

"Don't you leave me here, you cowardly bastards!" Tatum shouted.

The two men stood then, and firing wildly back down the hill, tried to run. Pearlie and Smoke took them out with one shot each.

"White men!" Teykano said, hurrying back down the trail to join Quinntanna.

"Soldiers?"

"No."

"Then who?" one of the other Indians asked.

"I think I know who," Quinntanna said.

"Who?" Teykano asked.

"Those who burned the stagecoach house. I believe also they are the ones who attack the white man's ranch.

"Then they are the ones who brought trouble to us," Teykano said.

"Yes. They are the reason our families are no more," another said.

"Let us make war on them, Quinntanna," Teykano said. "Let us make war on them. Then our revenge will be complete."

Quinntanna looked at the little band of people he was leading. He did not want to leave them unprotected. But neither did he want the opportunity for revenge against those who brought so much sorrow to his village to pass him by. He looked into the eager faces of the warriors around him.

"Very well," he said. "We will make war."

Quickly, Quinntanna moved his people into shelter. The shelter played the dual role of keeping them out of the elements as well as safe from discovery. Once they were safely in place, Quinntanna moved up the trail a few yards, then examined the area thoroughly. Not until he was satisfied that the encampment was totally secure did he give orders to the others.

"We go now," he said.

One of the Indians let out a war whoop, but he was quickly shushed by the others, who realized the importance of silence for this particular war party.

One mile up the trail from where the Comanche were making their encampment, Smoke, Pearlie, and Tom were waiting. It had been several minutes since Pigiron and Wheeler were killed, and Smoke was certain that only one man remained. That one man was Jack Tatum, but so far, Tatum had stayed under cover.

"Smoke," Pearlie called. "Smoke, you think he's still here?"

"He's there."

"How come he don't say nothin'?"

"Tatum!" Smoke called. "Tatum, you're all alone now."

There was no answer, but Smoke didn't really expect one.

"Tatum?"

Still no answer.

"Hey, Smoke, maybe we got 'em all," Pearlie suggested.

"I don't think so. At least, he's not one of the bodies I can see."

"He could've been hit and just died up there where he was," Pearlie said.

"No, I think it's more likely that he's just hiding up there," Smoke said. "Tom!" he called.

"Yeah?"

"Come on up here, then you and Pearlie keep your eyes open. I'm going the rest of the way up to see if I can root him out."

"All right," Tom called back.

Smoke waited until Tom worked his way up the trail to a place that was even with Smoke and Pearlie. Then, getting in position to provide cover, Tom nodded at Smoke.

"Anytime you're ready," Tom said.

Smoke nodded back, then started toward the area where Tatum had set up his defense. He passed by Jim's body first. The black shooter was already stiffening in the cold, his rifle lying on the snow beside him.

Damn nice rifle, Smoke thought.

A few more feet farther up, he saw the two Mexicans then the two Indians. Finally, he passed by the bodies o Pigiron and Wheeler.

But he still saw no sign of Tatum.

Suddenly, he heard a sound behind him and turning saw Tatum leaping at him, knife in hand. Tatum mad a slash with his knife, and the blade sliced into Smoke' gun hand, causing him to drop his pistol into the snow Smoke made a quick grab for the pistol, but another slic ing motion of Tatum's knife forced Smoke away. Smok started backing away from Tatum.

"Where you goin', you son of a bitch?" Tatum asked

He shook his head. "Ain't nowhere you can go now that'll get you away from old Jack Tatum."

Tatum continued to advance toward him, an evil smile on his face. He was holding his knife in front of him, the point facing Smoke, weaving back and forth slightly, like the head of a coiled snake.

"I'm goin' to cut you good," Tatum said with a snarl. "I'm goin' to open up your belly and let your guts spill out onto the snow."

All the time Smoke was backing away from Tatum, he was reaching for his own knife. Because he was wearing a heavy coat, his knife wasn't that easy to get to, but finally he found it. His fingers wrapped around the knife handle. Then he pulled it from its scabbard and brought it around to the front.

When Tatum saw that Smoke also had a knife, the smile, as well as some of the smug confidence, left his face. He stared at the knife clutched in Smoke's bloody hand.

"You didn't expect this, did you?" Smoke said.

Trying to regenerate his own sense of self-confidence, Tatum turned his left hand, palm up, and began making a curling motion with his fingers, as if beckoning Smoke to him.

"Come on," Tatum said. "Come on and get some of this."

"Now then, you were saying something about opening up my stomach, I believe?" Smoke challenged.

Tatum's attempt at bravado fell short, and he began licking his lips nervously. For a moment it looked as if he might take flight. Then, from somewhere deep inside, he summoned up one last bit of courage. With a defiant yell he leaped forward, making a wide, slashing motion with his knife.

Had Smoke not been wearing his sheepskin jacket, had this been a fight in the summertime, Tatum's attack would have been devastatingly effective. As it was, Tatum succeeded only in cutting a long, deep slash in Smoke's jacket. Uninjured, Smoke then made a counterthrust under Tatum's extended arm. Smoke drove his knife, point-first, into Tatum's abdomen. Smoke's knife was turned flat, allowing it to penetrate between the third and fourth ribs. The point of the knife punched into Tatum's heart, and dark, red blood spilled out around the wound.

Smoke withdrew his blade, then stepped back. Tatum put both hands over the wound, then looked down, as if surprised to see the blood spilling through his fingers. He staggered a few steps away from Smoke, then fell on his back in the snow. His arms flopped out to either side of him as his eyes, still open, stared into the sky. The white snow around his body turned crimson from his flowing blood.

By then both Pearlie and Tom had joined Smoke, and the three men stood there, looking down at Tatum's body. At Tatum's throat, something flashed in the sunlight. It was a shining gold chain from which was suspended a brilliant diamond pendant.

"Isn't that what you gave Jo Ellen for her anniversary?" Pearlie asked.

"Yes," Tom replied in a choked voice. Then, he shouted at Tatum's body. "You son of a bitch!" Tom raised his boot and kicked Tatum so hard in the head that some of his teeth popped out. "Bastard! I wish you were still alive so you could feel this!" Tom kicked him several more times, until Tatum's face was all but unrecognizable. Then he dropped to his knees and removed the chain. When he stood up again, there were tears in his eyes.

Smoke put his hand on Tom's shoulder. "I'm sorry, Tom," he said. "I'm very sorry."

"Yeah," Tom replied. He sighed, then wiped his eyes. "Well, at least I have the satisfaction of knowing for sure that we got the right ones. Now, I won't have to go through the rest of my life wondering who did it."

"Let's go home," Smoke said.

"What about them?" Pearlie asked, pointing to the bodies that were lying around.

"What about them?" Tom replied.

"Shouldn't we bury them or something?"

"To hell with them," Tom said.

"To tell the truth, I don't think the bastards deserve to be buried either," Smoke said. "But if we just leave them here, it's going to be awfully ripe-smelling around these parts come next spring's thaw."

"All right, but one hole for all of them," Tom said.

Smoke chuckled. "Oh, I agree. I didn't say I was in favor of giving them a funeral."

The first thing they did was to go through everyone's pockets. They were surprised to find twenty-five hundred dollars in cash on Tatum. Then they looked around for a place to bury the outlaws, and finding a narrow ravine, pushed them into it. After that, they collapsed the ravine's sides down onto the bodies, then piled several rocks on top. The result was a grave that would be secure against predators, as well as keep the bodies from deteriorating on the open trail.

"Good enough," Smoke said. He handed the packet of money to Tom. "By rights, this should be yours."

"Mine? Why?"

"He took more from you than he did anyone else," Smoke said. "I know this can't compensate you for your family, but it might help build your barn and granary back."

"Thanks," Tom said, taking the money.

"And if nobody has any objections, I'm going to take this rifle," Smoke said, picking up the rifle Jim had used against them. "It looks to me like it's a pretty good weapon."

"It is a good rifle," Tom agreed, looking at it.

"What are you going to use it for?" Pearlie asked, laughing. "There's no buffalo to hunt anymore."

"Well, you never know when a good rifle like this might come in handy," Smoke replied.

At that very moment a bullet whizzed by so close they could all hear its angry buzz. Then, looking ahead, they saw several Indians coming up the hill toward them.

"Like now, for instance!" Smoke shouted. "Get down!"

And once more, the three men found themselves scrambling to get behind cover as they were being attacked, this time by a band of wild, screaming Indians.

25

Smoke got behind a rock, then raised up to look at the Indians who were working their way up the snowy trail. He shoved a heavy round into the buffalo gun he had picked up from beside Jim's body, took aim, and fired. As it so happened, Tom had picked out his own target and fired at the same time.

Two of the attacking Indians went down, one with a bullet in the heart, the other with a bullet in the head. The Indians had thought themselves well out of range at this distance, and when they saw two of their number go down, they stopped their advance and looked around in surprise. They stopped, but they failed to seek cover. As a result, two more shots dropped two more of the Indians.

"They are devils with guns!" one of the Indians said. He and the remaining Indians scattered, running to both sides of the trail to find places of cover and concealment.

Quinntanna looked back toward the four Indians who were lying in the snow. Three were dead, the fourth was wounded. The wounded Indian was Teykano.

"Teykano!" Quinntanna called. "Teykano, are you still alive?"

"Yes," Teykano answered, his voice strained with pain.

"I will come get you," Quinntanna said.

"No. If you come, the devils with guns will shoot you too."

"I will come get you," Quinntanna said again. Laying aside his rifle, Quinntanna got down on his stomach and started moving through the snow, slithering on his belly.

Smoke saw the Indian slithering across the snow. To his left, he saw Tom raising the rifle to his shoulder.

"No!" Smoke called to Tom. "Don't kill him."

Nodding, Tom lowered his rifle. Smoke raised his rifle, and fired, not aiming directly at the crawling Indian, but aiming at the snow in front of him. His bullet hit just in front of the Indian, sent up a spray of snow, then whined on down the mountainside.

The Indian quit crawling, but only for a moment. Then he started crawling again.

"That fella's not going to give up," Smoke said, shooting a second time, again just in front of the Indian.

The Indian stopped a second time, waited a moment, then resumed his crawling. This time, just before he resumed crawling, however, he glanced up the hill toward Smoke's position . . . almost as if challenging him to shoot again. That was when Smoke got a good look at him.

"Damn!" Smoke said. "That's Quinntanna!"

"Quinntanna? I thought you and Quinntanna was old friends," Tom replied. "Sharing that elk and all, like you done."

Smoke cupped his hands around his mouth.

"Quinntanna!" he called.

Surprised to hear himself addressed by name, Quinntanna looked up the hill again.

"Quinntanna, it's me, Smoke Jensen? Let's parley!" Smoke tied a white handkerchief to the end of his rifle, then held it above the rock and waved it back and forth.

Quinntanna raised to his knees, then turned toward Smoke. In so doing he was making himself an obvious target, a way of showing his own trust.

"What now?" Pearlie asked.

"I'm going to go talk to him," Smoke said. "I want to know why he started shooting at us."

Smoke stepped out from behind the rock, held the rifle up, then tossed it to one side. It was a symbolic disarmament only, for he still had his pistol strapped around his waist, though it was covered by the heavy coat he was wearing. Holding his arms out to his side in a nonthreatening manner, he started down the sloping path toward Quinntanna.

For his part, Quinntanna stood up and started up the path toward Smoke. The two men walked toward each other for a moment, meeting approximately halfway between their respective starting points. At this position, both Quinntanna and Smoke made easy targets for those who had stayed back.

"Smoke Jensen," Quinntanna said. "It is good to see you."

Smoke chuckled. "Good to see me? You tried to kill us."

"I didn't know who you were," Quinntanna said. "I thought you were here to kill us."

"Why would we want to kill you?"

"Because the whites think Comanche people burned the white man's ranch, and burned the buildings where people-wagon stops."

"People-wagon? You mean the stagecoach? Are you talking about Miller's Switch?"

"Yes," Quinntanna said. "We saw that place. It was burned, and there was much death there."

Smoke shook his head. "We know you didn't do that," he said.

"How do you know that?"

"The driver wasn't killed. He told us who did it. It was Comancheros."

"It does not matter. They think we burned the ranch and. . . ."

Smoke held out his hand to stop Quinntanna in mid-sentence. "No," he said. "We know you didn't do that either. The Comancheros who burned the stage depot also burned Tom Burke's ranch, killed his wife, children, and all his hands."

"If this is known, why have the soldiers attacked us?"

"Nobody knew until now," Smoke said. "But when we get back, we will tell what we have learned."

"And the soldiers will go after the Comancheros?"

Smoke shook his head. "It's too late for that," he said. "My friends and I have already killed them all."

Quinntanna was quiet for a moment. Then he sighed and nodded his head. "Then there can be peace between us," he said. "I will let you go. But I think there can be no peace between the Comanche and the whites. We have killed too many of their soldiers."

"If the Indians will make no more war, I will see to it that the whites will make peace," Smoke promised.

Quinntanna looked back down the hill and saw that Teykano was now sitting up, holding his hand to his shoulder. His fingers were red from the blood that had flowed from his wound.

"You are a mighty warrior, Smoke Jensen. I believe you when you say there will be peace. From this day, I will fight no more war forever."

Smoke and Quinntanna put their hands on each other's shoulders as a sign of friendship. Then each turned and started back toward their own. After a few steps, Smoke turned back toward Quinntanna. "One of the men with me, Tom Burke, is pretty good at doctoring people," he said. "If you would like, he can take a look at your friend."

"Yes," Quinntanna said. "White man shoot, white man make well. That would be good."

* * *

Tom Burke didn't go all the way back to Big Rock with Smoke and Pearlie, but left them when they reached the road that turned off to his ranch. Pearlie headed on to Sugarloaf to tell Sally that they were back and in one piece.

In town, Smoke went straight to the sheriff's office.

"Well, look what the winter winds have blown in," Monte said, getting up from his desk and crossing over to extend his hand in greeting.

"That coffee sure smells good," Smoke said, nodding toward the pot that simmered on top of the stove.

"Have a cup, sit down, tell me what's been going on," Monte invited.

Smoke poured his own coffee, then sat in a chair across the desk from Monte. He took a swallow of his coffee, slurping it between extended lips to cool it. Then he looked up at Monte and smiled.

"We got them, Monte," he said.

"Got them? Got who?"

"We got the people who raided Tom's ranch."

"Indians?"

Smoke shook his head. "Comancheros. Mixed pack of outlaws—whites, Indians, Mexicans, and a black man. Tatum was the leader."

"I'll be damned," Monte said. "You're sure they are the ones who did it?"

"There's no doubt. You remember that diamond on a chain that Tom bought for Jo Ellen? Well, he pulled it off Tatum's neck after we killed him."

"So the son of a bitch is dead then?"

"Yes. All of them are."

"Probably just as good. Save us a trial."

"Colonel Covington won't like it. Won't get a chance to show off in the courtroom anymore."

"Oh, he isn't a colonel anymore," Monte said.

"He's not? What happened?"

Monte told about going to see the governor to get martial law lifted, and Covington's commission revoked.

"Bet he didn't take that too well."

"No, he's been pouting around here for a few days now. Ever since he got back from his last expedition against the Indians. He got about forty of his men killed in that little fracas."

"If you ask me, just getting his commission taken away isn't enough," Smoke said. "I'd put the son of a bitch in jail, if not for murder for killing a lot of innocent Indians, then for manslaughter for getting his own people killed."

"Funny you should say that," Monte said. He picked up a yellow envelope that was lying on his desk. "This telegram just came from the governor. It's a warrant to be served against Covington. The governor wants him arrested for exceeding the scope of his authority. But now that you mention it, I may just add manslaughter to the charge."

"When you going to serve it?"

"I was getting ready to just before you came in," Monte said. "Would you like to come with me?"

"No, I'll let you worry about that," Smoke said. "If it's all the same to you, I'll just finish my coffee, then get on out to the ranch. It's been a while since I was home, and I'm anxious to get back to Sally."

Although Smoke didn't realize it, Sally had been coming in town to do some shopping anyway, and when she met Pearlie on the road and learned that Smoke was back, she slapped the reins against the animals' backs, hurrying them into a trot. She was every bit as anxious to see Smoke as he was to see her.

At the opposite end of the street from the sheriff's office, Fred Dunn, the telegrapher, was standing in Covington's office. Earlier, Fred had been incensed by Covington's insistence that he share every telegram with him, in violation of Western Union rules. What he was doing now was a violation of those same rules, but he had no compunctions about sharing this one. In fact, he was going to take particular pleasure in looking into Covington's face as he read the telegram.

"What is this?" Covington asked as Fred handed a copy of the telegram to him.

"Why don't you just read it and find out, Mr. High and Mighty, Call Me Colonel Covington," Fred said with a sneer. "I guess you won't be coming in my office anymore, demanding to see all the telegrams. According to this, you're all through."

"I don't know what you're talking about," Covington said.

"I'm talking about that telegram. I gave a copy to the sheriff. It's from the governor, telling Sheriff Carson to arrest you. And as far as I'm concerned, it's good riddance."

Covington read the telegram with increased irritation, reacting exactly as Fred had wanted him to react.

"This will never stick," Covington said in a blustering voice. "I was well within the scope of my authority with everything I did."

"Yeah? Well, there are a few widows and family folk around town who don't think so. They think you got their men killed."

"Preposterous," Covington said. "We'll just see about this."

Brushing by Fred, Covington went outside. Just as he stepped into the street, he saw the sheriff striding purposefully up the street toward him. All of a sudden he lost his resolve to have it out with him. At the same time, he saw Sally Jensen climbing down from a buckboard, not ten feet away from him.

"Covington! Hold it right where you are!" Monte shouted. "You're under arrest!"

Sally was at a disadvantage. She was halfway down from the buckboard, and her pistol was still on the seat, under the buffalo robe she had wrapped around her to keep warm for the drive into town. Had she not been at that disadvantage, Covington would never have been able to do what he did next.

Stepping over to her quickly, he put his left arm around her neck. With his right hand, he pointed his pistol at Sally's head.

"Stay back, Sheriff!" he shouted. "Stay back, or I'll kill her!"

Monte stopped. "Don't be a fool, Covington," he said. "Let her go."

Covington started dragging Sally across the street, in the direction of the livery.

"I'll be waiting in the livery," he shouted to the sheriff. "You go down to the bank and clear out my account. Bring it and a saddled horse to me."

"Covington, you know I can't do that," Monte replied.

"Oh, you can do it, all right. You can and you will, because if you don't, I'll kill this woman."

Hearing the shouting from the street, Smoke stepped out of the sheriff's office to see what was going on. When he saw that Covington had Sally, and was holding a pistol to her head, he started running up the street toward them.

"Covington!" he shouted. "Let her go, you son of a bitch!"

Covington fired at Smoke. The bullet hit the dirt just in front of Smoke, then ricocheted up between his legs, and he got an uneasy, tingling sensation in his groin when he realized how close the bullet had come to it.

Smoke pulled his pistol to shoot back, but realized that he couldn't do it without fear of hitting Sally. Laughing out loud, Covington pulled Sally into the shadows of the livery.

"Covington!" Smoke called again, cautiously moving closer to the livery.

"That's far enough, Jensen," Covington called from

inside. "If you come any closer, I'm going to kill your woman."

"You don't want to do that, Covington. There's no charge of murder against you. Why don't you give yourself up?"

"There's no charge of murder against me," Covington replied, "but I'm sure there are charges of manslaughter forthcoming. I could get ten years in prison for manslaughter. I don't intend to serve one day in prison."

"Sally. Sally, are you all right?" Smoke called.

"Yes, I'm fine," Sally said. "Smoke, if you get the chance, kill him."

"Shut up, bitch!" Covington snarled. Even from outside, Smoke could hear the sound of him hitting her. Sally cried out in pain.

"If you hit her again, you'd better turn that gun on yourself," Smoke shouted angrily. "Because I'll be coming after you."

"You're going to war with me, are you, Jensen?" Covington asked in a taunting voice.

"I'll give you a war you won't believe," Smoke said menacingly.

Covington took another shot at Smoke, who heard the pop loudly as it snapped by just inches away from his ear.

Covington laughed. "My advice to you, Mr. Jensen, is to go find out what's keeping the sheriff. I'm getting a little antsy in here. If I don't see the sheriff with my money and a saddled horse here in two more minutes, I'm going to start shooting."

Smoke realized that he was an easy target in the street, so he moved over to stand behind the barbershop pole. There, he was out of Covington's immediate line of fire, and he also had a view of the front of the livery.

"Covington, give it up," Smoke shouted. "You know you aren't going to get away with this."

By now several people had been drawn to the area. They stood as close to the action as they could, without exposing themselves to Covington's fire.

One of the people who had gathered in the street was Abner Norton, the prosecuting attorney.

"Sam," Norton called. "Sam, this is Abner Norton. I urge you to give yourself up. I promise you a fair trial."

"A fair trial?" Covington replied. "Who would I get to defend me, sir? I am the best defense attorney in the state of Colorado, of that there is no doubt. But I'm quite sure you are aware of the old chestnut, 'The lawyer who defends himself has a fool for a client.'"

"Don't throw away everything you've worked for all these years," Norton said.

"Don't you understand? I've already thrown it away," Covington replied. Another shot rang out, and those people who had gathered dangerously close to the livery stable hurried to get out of the line of fire.

"If the sheriff doesn't get here soon, I'll kill this girl. Someone had better find him and explain that to him."

While Covington was engaged with Norton and the other people out front, Smoke managed to slip around the corner of the barbershop, then run to the drainage ditch that ran along the back. He ducked down into the ditch, then ran to the back of the livery barn. Once behind the barn, he ran from the ditch to the barn, then climbed up into the hayloft. Moving quickly but silently from the back of the hayloft to the front, he found himself in position to look down on Covington. He was in a good position to take a shot, but it would have to be a perfect shot, because Smoke was holding Sally close to him. Smoke raised up to take aim.

Two pigeons had taken roost in the hayloft very near where Smoke was standing, and when he stood up they were frightened into flight. The rapid beating of their wings caused Covington to look up, and when he did, he saw Smoke. He pulled the hammer back on the pistol he was holding against Sally's head.

"Drop your gun, Jensen!" Covington called. "I mean it! Drop your gun, or I will kill her!"

For an instant, Smoke started to shoot him anyway. He

had an opening, though it was very tiny. Then, almost as if sensing that the opening was there, Covington shifted his position slightly so that it was too risky for Smoke to take a chance. Slowly, Smoke lowered his gun hand.

"I said drop it!" Covington called up to him.

Smoke dropped his pistol, but he dropped it only to the floor of the hayloft, not to the ground below.

"Very smart," Covington said sarcastically. "Now, kick it off onto the ground."

Smoke moved the gun with his foot, advancing with it slowly, until he was standing at the very edge of the hayloft.

"Kick it off," Covington said, and as he spoke, he took his gun away from Sally's head and used it to point.

Sally had been waiting for that very moment. Suddenly she rammed her elbow into Covington's gut, then spinning out of his grasp, turned and kicked him in the groin.

Smoke didn't hesitate for a second. He leaped from the hayloft the instant he saw Sally make her move. Right on the heels of Sally's kick to the groin, Smoke's leap terminated on top of Covington, sending Covington to the ground. Covington managed to squeeze off one shot. Although Smoke was singed by the flash, the bullet thudded harmlessly into the roof of the barn.

Smoke was on top of Covington now, and with his left hand he jerked the gun out of Covington's grasp. He tossed it a full thirty feet away. With his right hand, Smoke backhanded Covington, driving the man's head down against the dirt. Then, still with his right hand, he caught Covington with a wicked cross, driving his head into the dirt again. He repeated the maneuver time and time again, until Covington was just lying there, inert against his blows.

"Smoke! Smoke!" Norton shouted. "You're going to kill him!"

Smoke put his left hand to Covington's collar and twisting it, raised Covington's chin for another punch. He drew back his right hand and held it for a moment.

Then, with a sigh, he let his hand drop. He got up and stared down at Covington's unconscious form.

"I wanted to kill the son of a bitch," Smoke admitted.

"Killing him is too good for him," Norton said. "Let him spend ten or twenty years in prison. Believe me, he would welcome death over that."

"All right, I guess we'd better get him down to the jail," Smoke said.

"I'll get a couple of men to carry him."

"No need for that," Smoke said. Looking over toward one of the livery stalls, he saw that a horse was already saddled. Taking a rope from the saddle, he looped one end of the rope around Covington's feet, then tied the other end to the saddle pommel. He clicked at the horse, then led the horse down the street toward the jail. He guided the horse so that it dragged Covington through every pile of manure along the way.

Covington sputtered awake after a few feet.

"Hey! Hey, what are you doing?" he shouted.

"I'm taking you to jail," Smoke said.

"You're dragging me through shit!" Covington shouted. "I'm all covered with shit!"

Smoke stopped and looked back at him.

"Now how the hell can you tell?" he asked. The question was met with uproarious laughter from those who had gathered to see the show.

It was two weeks later when Tom Burke showed up unexpectedly at Sugarloaf Ranch.

"Tom," Smoke said. "Good to see you. Come on in. Sally will have lunch on the table soon. Eat with us."

Tom smiled. "I promise you, I didn't time my visit just to get an invite," he said. "On the other hand, I'd be a fool to turn it down. Especially since I've been having to eat my own cooking lately."

"You're more than welcome here anytime," Sally said

"Thank you, Sally. I appreciate that." Then to Smoke: "Did you see the paper? Covington got ten years."

"I saw it," Smoke said. "When you consider all the Indians he murdered, it should've been twenty years."

The two men engaged in small talk for a few minutes more, until Sally had the meal on the table and called them to dinner. After they sat down, Tom asked if he could say grace, and Smoke and Sally agreed.

It was a quick grace. Then when the others looked up, they saw that Tom was holding something in his hand. "Sally," he said. "It would pleasure me more than I can say if you would accept this."

"What is it?"

"It belonged to Jo Ellen."

Tom opened his fingers and there, in his hand, was the gold chain and diamond pendant he had given Jo Ellen less than two months earlier.

"Oh, Tom! I can't take that!" Sally said. "That was Jo Ellen's!"

"Please take it," Tom said. He looked at Smoke. "That is, if you take no offense, Smoke."

"No, I take no offense," Smoke said.

"I know it was Jo Ellen's, and she was proud of it. But I know in my heart she would dearly love to look down from heaven and see that pretty thing hanging around the neck of her best friend. Would you do that for me, Sally?"

Sally took the chain and pendant in her hand and stared at it for a moment.

"If you put it that way, of course I'll wear it. I'd be happy to. No, I would be proud to," she said. "Would you put it around my neck?"

"Smoke?" Tom asked, looking at him for permission to personally hang the necklace around Sally's neck.

"Yes, of course you can," Smoke said.

Sally tilted her head forward slightly as Tom slipped the chain and pendant around her neck.

"Beautiful," he said.

"It's the most beautiful thing I've ever seen," Smoke agreed.

Sally looked up at them. The diamond at her throat was glistening brightly, but no brighter than the tears that were glistening in her eyes.